amazing [treehouse with his friend] Terry and together they make funny books, just like the one you're holding in your hands right now. Andy writes the words and Terry draws the pictures. If you'd like to know more, read the Treehouse series (or visit www.andygriffiths.com.au).

 Terry Denton lives in an amazing treehouse with his friend Andy and together they make funny books, just like the one you're holding in your hands right now. Terry draws the pictures and Andy writes the words. If you'd like to know more, read the Treehouse series (or visit www.terrydenton.com).

 Jill Griffiths lives near Andy and Terry in a house full of animals. She has two dogs, one goat, three horses, four goldfish, one cow, two guinea pigs, one camel, one donkey, one cat and so many rabbits she has lost count. If you'd like to know more, read the Treehouse series.

Books by Andy Griffiths
Illustrated by Terry Denton

The 13-Storey Treehouse
The 26-Storey Treehouse
The 39-Storey Treehouse
The 52-Storey Treehouse
The 65-Storey Treehouse
The 78-Storey Treehouse
The 91-Storey Treehouse
The 104-Storey Treehouse
The 117-Storey Treehouse

The Treehouse Fun Book
The Treehouse Fun Book 2

THE TREEHOUSE FUN BOOK

JiLL GRiFFiTHS
ANDY GRiFFiTHS
and TERRY DENTON

MACMILLAN CHILDREN'S BOOKS

First published 2016 in Pan by Pan Macmillan Australia Pty Ltd
First published 2017 by Macmillan Children's Books

This edition published in the UK 2018 by Macmillan Children's Books
an imprint of Pan Macmillan
The Smithson, 6 Briset Street, London, EC1M 5NR
Associated companies throughout the world
www.panmacmillan.com

ISBN 978-1-5098-6044-9

5 7 9 8 6

A CIP catalogue record for this book is available from the British Library.

Typeset in 11/11.5 Drawzing by Seymour Designs
Printed in Poland

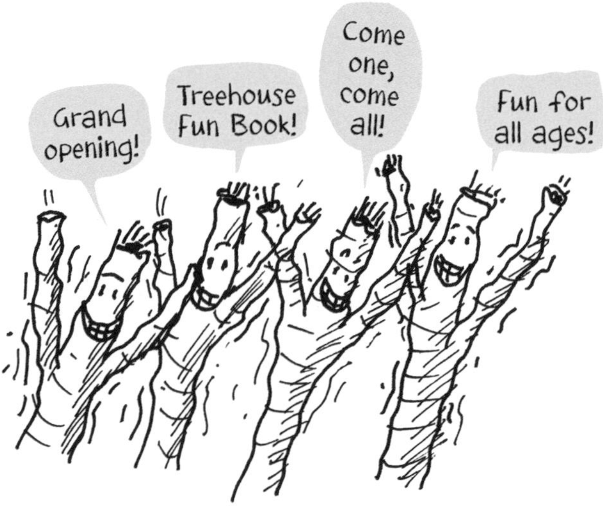
Grand opening!
Treehouse Fun Book!
Come one, come all!
Fun for all ages!

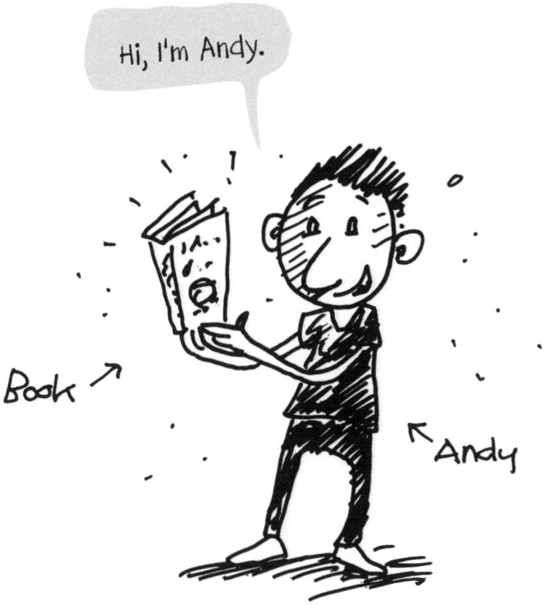
Hi, I'm Andy.
Book
Andy

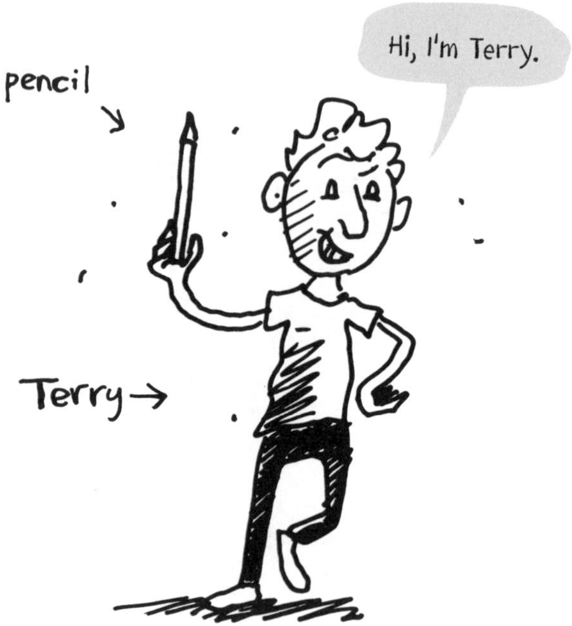
Hi, I'm Terry.
pencil
Terry

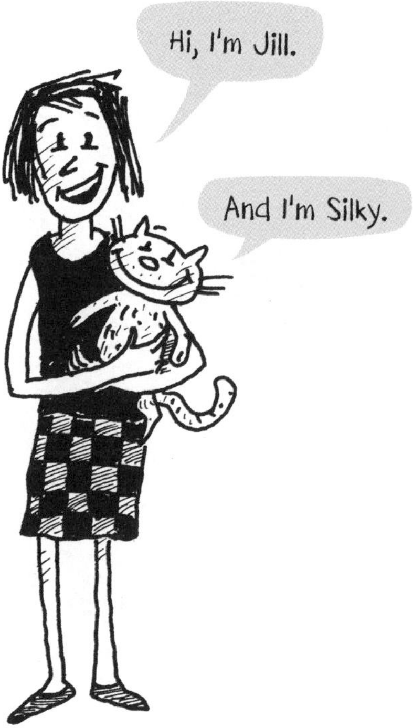
Hi, I'm Jill.
And I'm Silky.

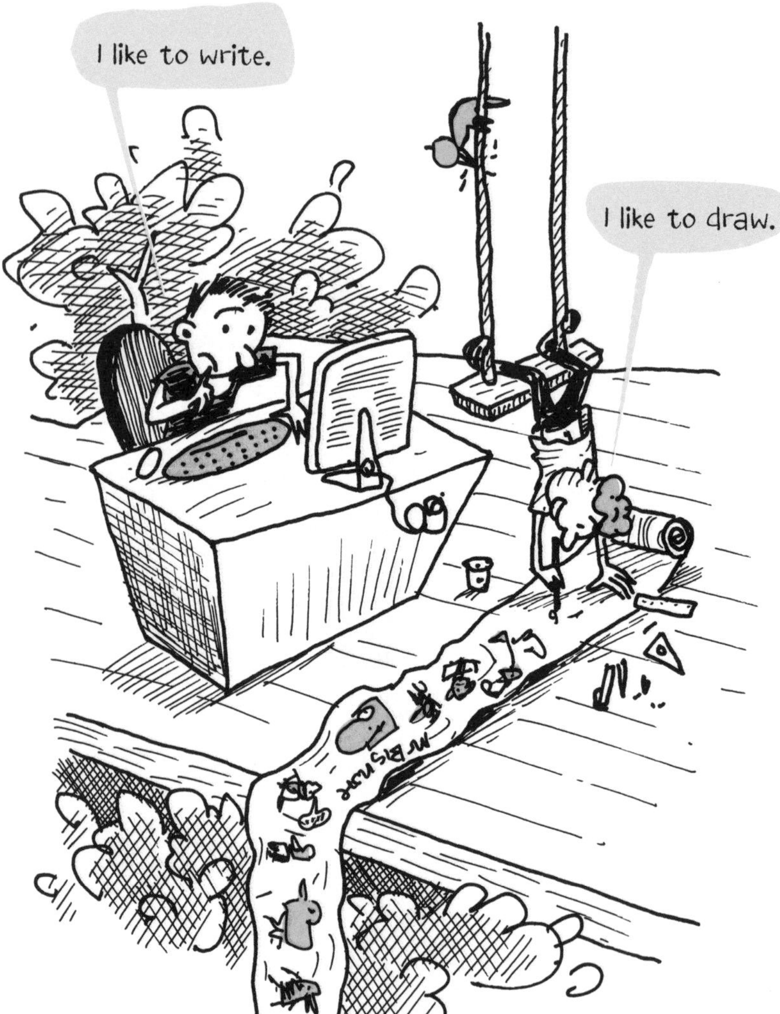
I like to write.
I like to draw.

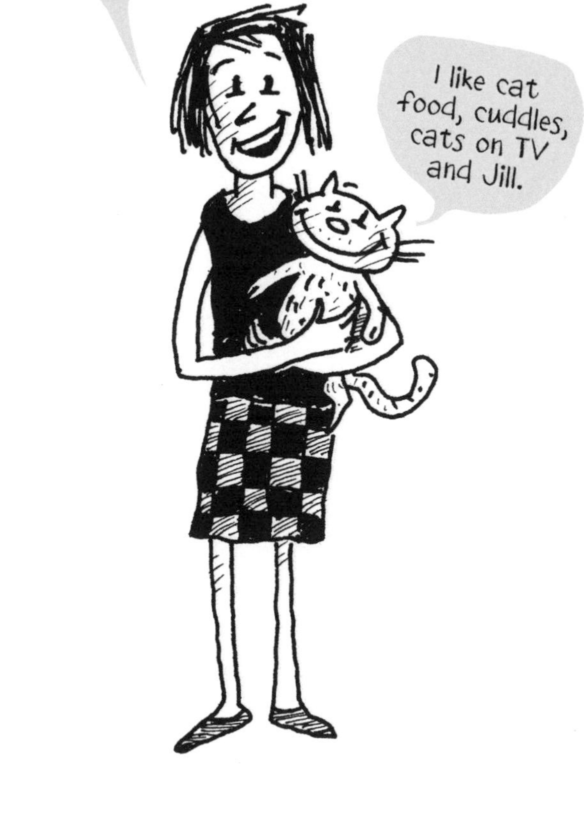
I like animals. I also like solving problems and doing puzzles.
I like cat food, cuddles, cats on TV and Jill.

DRAW YOURSELF

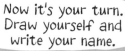

Now it's your turn. Draw yourself and write your name.

Hi, I'm Freddie

Draw your pet, too, if you have one. If you don't, you could draw one you would like to have.

DRAW SOMETHING YOU LIKE

Draw something you like or something you like to do.

I like ice cream

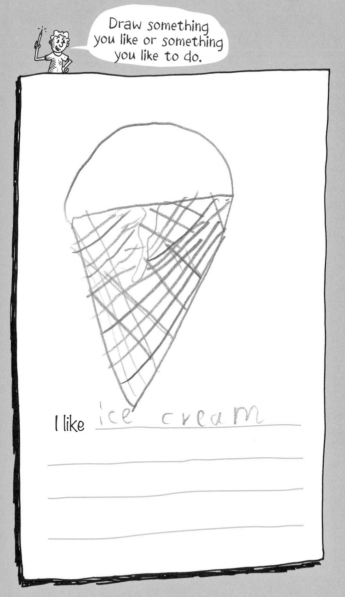

DRAW SOMETHING YOU DON'T LIKE

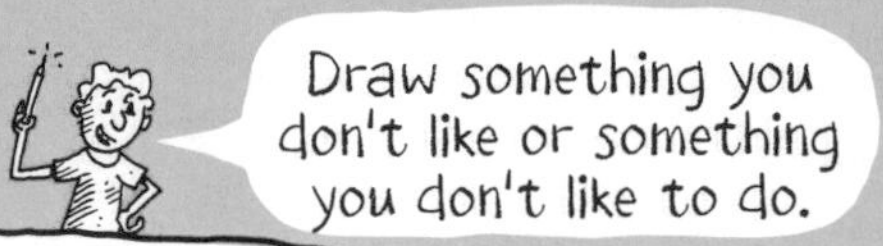
Draw something you don't like or something you don't like to do.

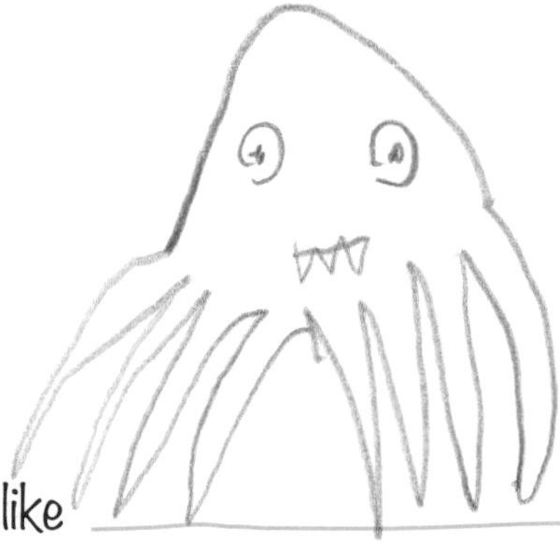

I don't like spiders

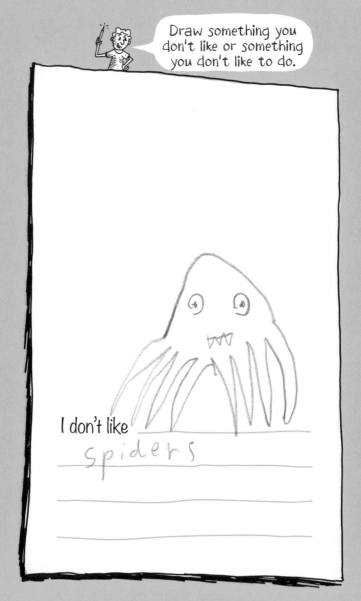

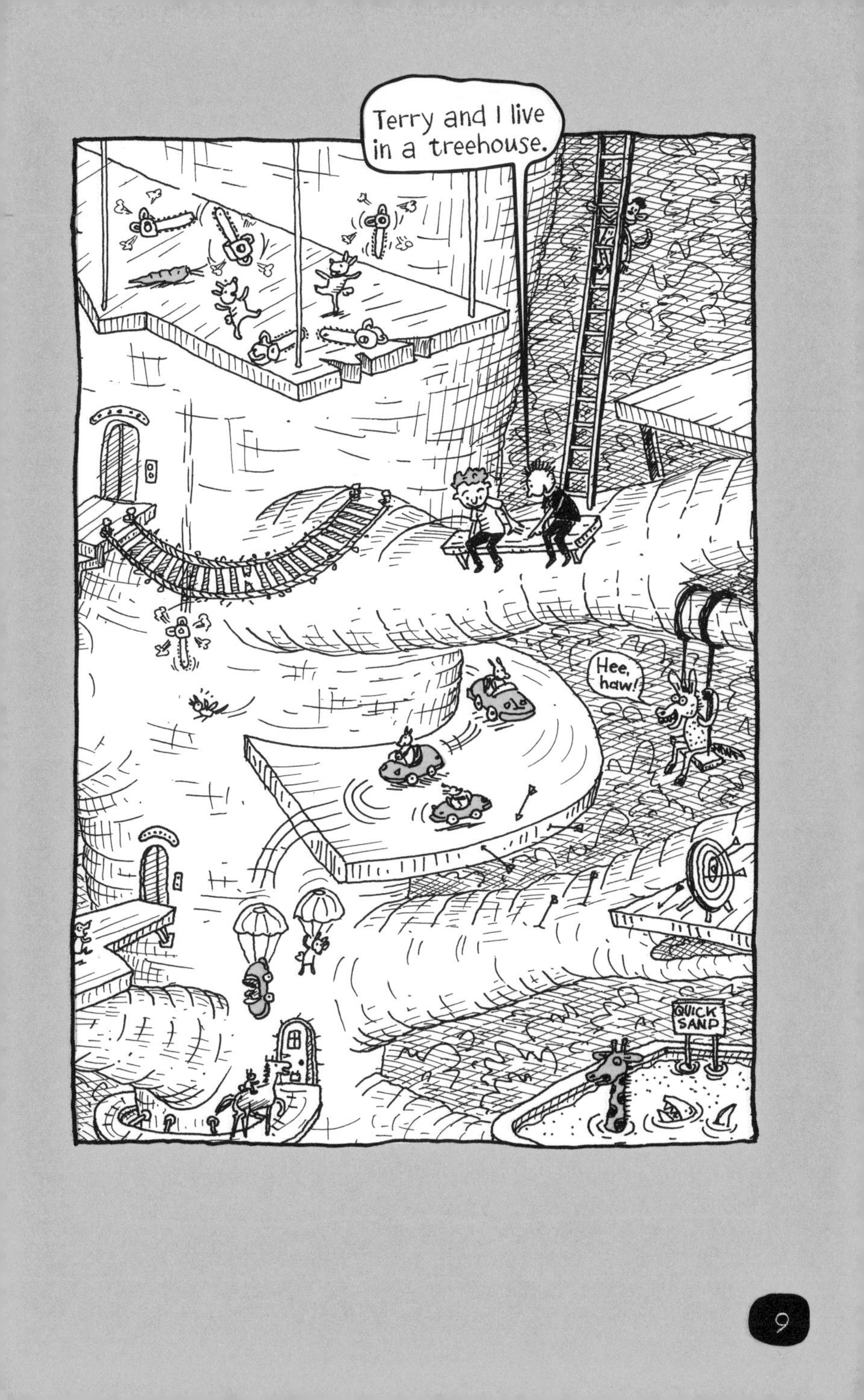
Terry and I live in a treehouse.
Hee, haw!
QUICK SAND

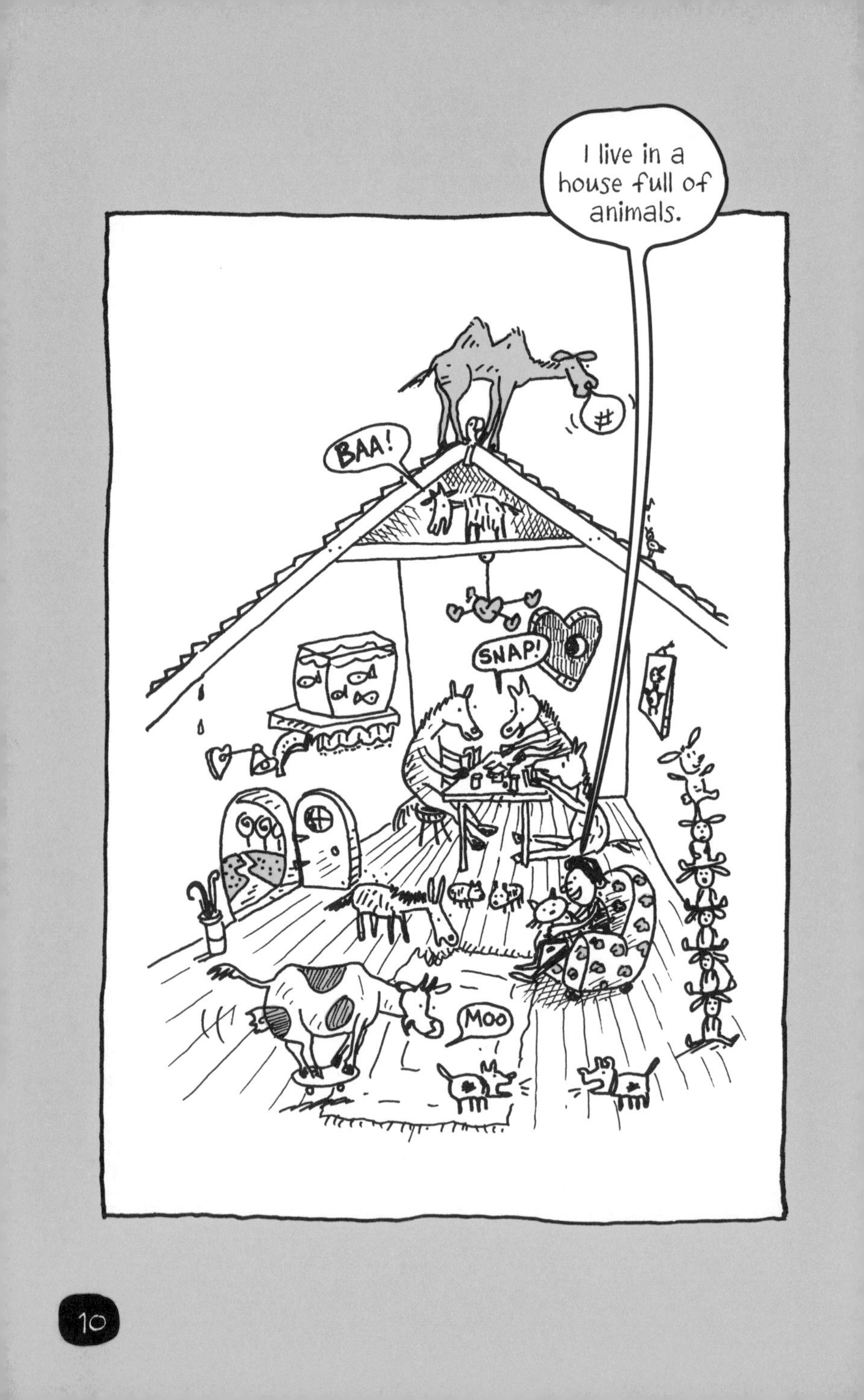
I live in a house full of animals.
BAA!
SNAP!
MOO

DRAW WHERE YOU LIVE

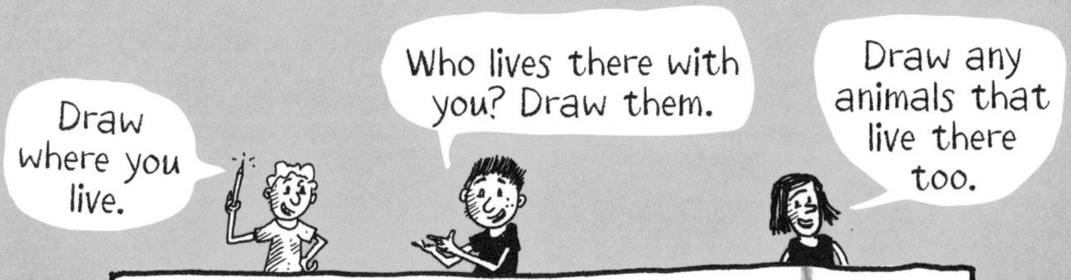
Draw where you live.
Who lives there with you? Draw them.
Draw any animals that live there too.

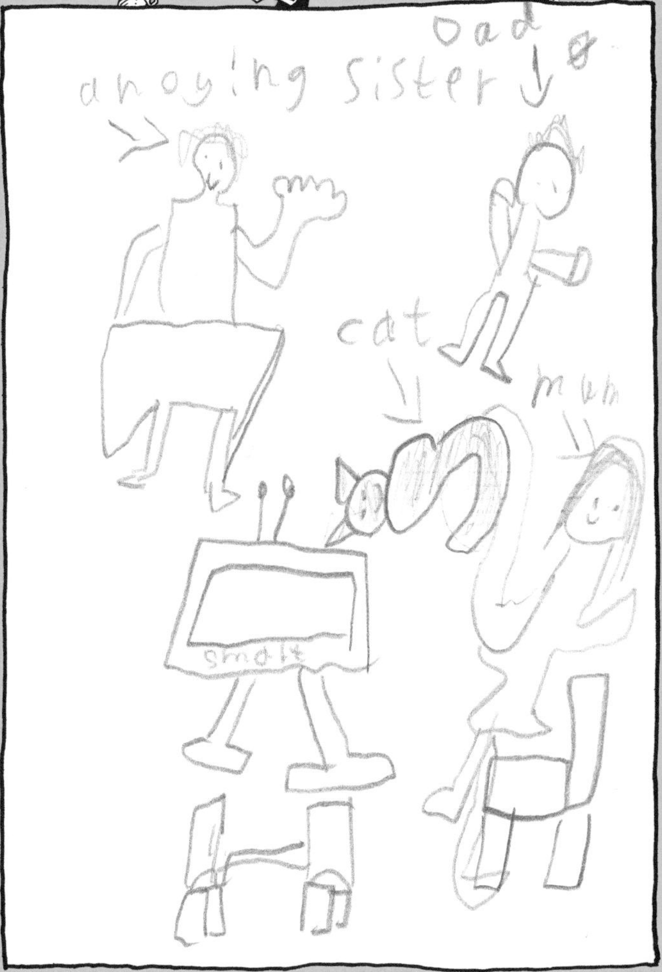
Dad
anoying Sister
cat

LIST NEW TREEHOUSE LEVELS

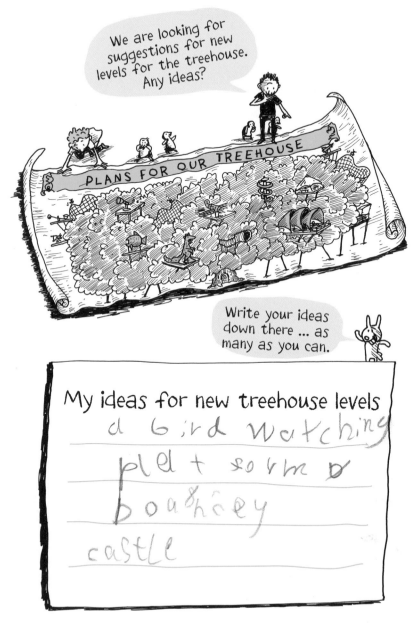

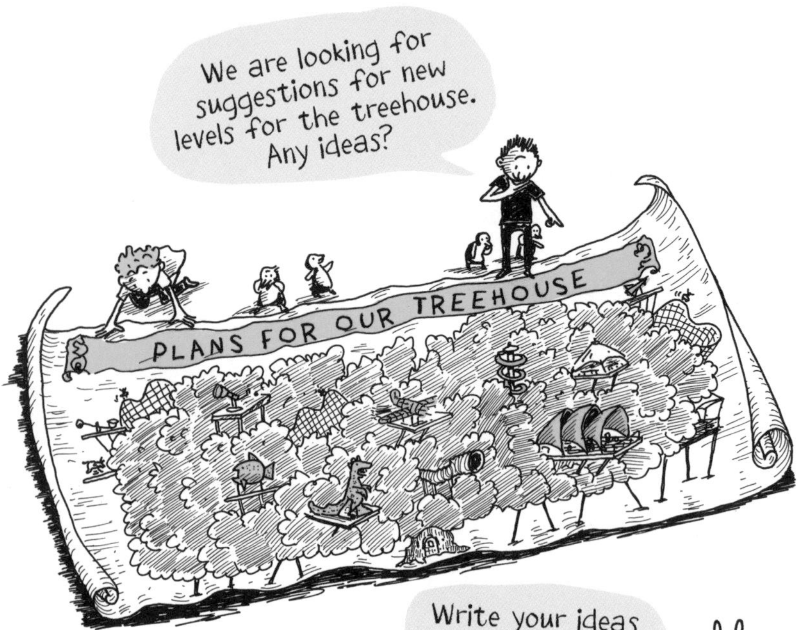
We are looking for suggestions for new levels for the treehouse. Any ideas?
PLANS FOR OUR TREEHOUSE

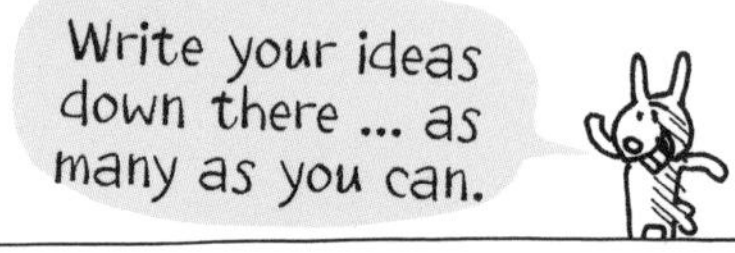
Write your ideas down there ... as many as you can.

My ideas for new treehouse levels

a bird watching

plat form

boathoey

castle

Write your ideas up there.

DRAW NEW TREEHOUSE LEVELS

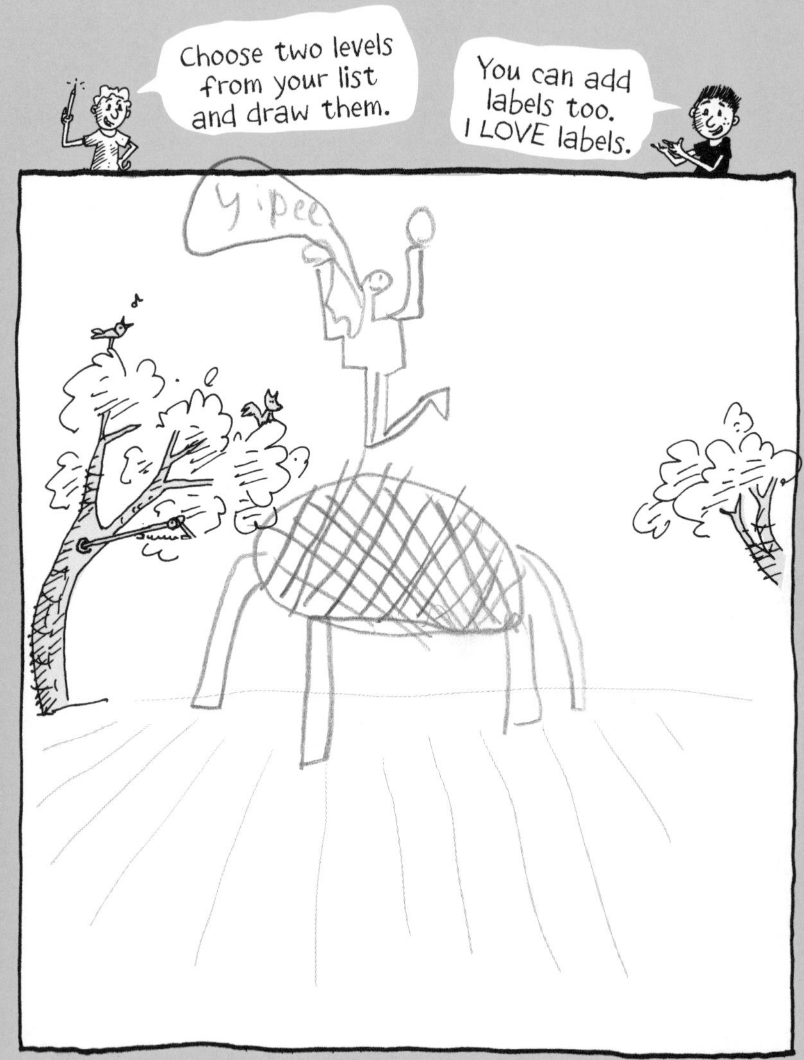
Choose two levels from your list and draw them.
You can add labels too. I LOVE labels.
Yipee

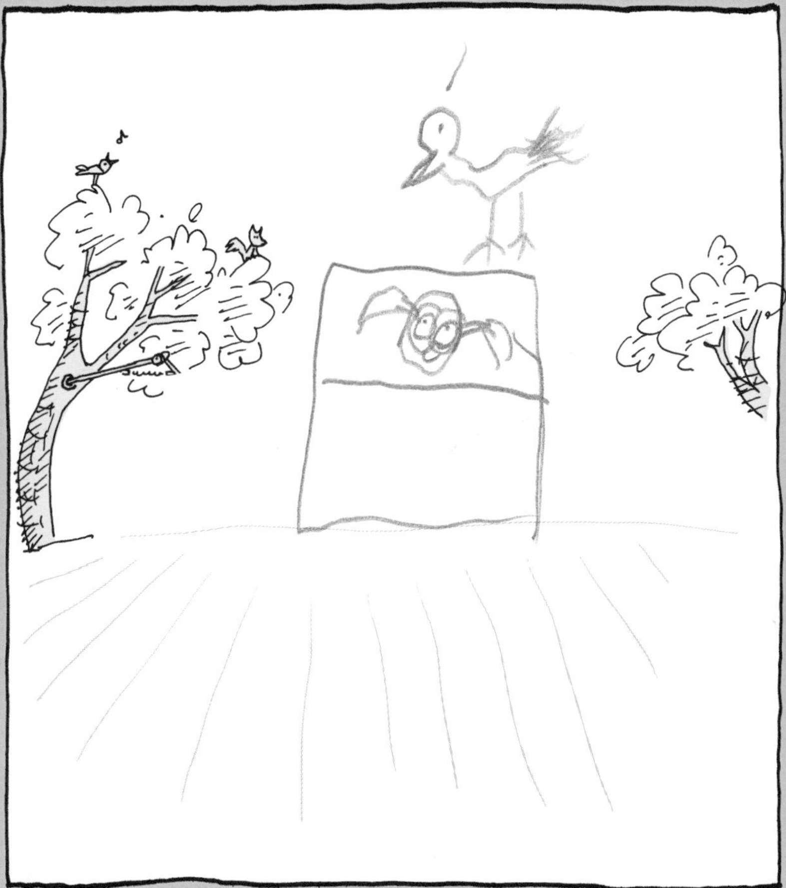

PLAN YOUR TREEHOUSE VISIT

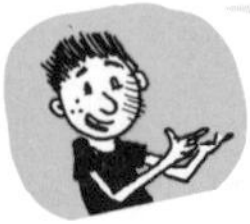

There is a lot of fun stuff to do in our treehouse. Here are 13 things you can do. What order—from 1 to 13—would you do them in?

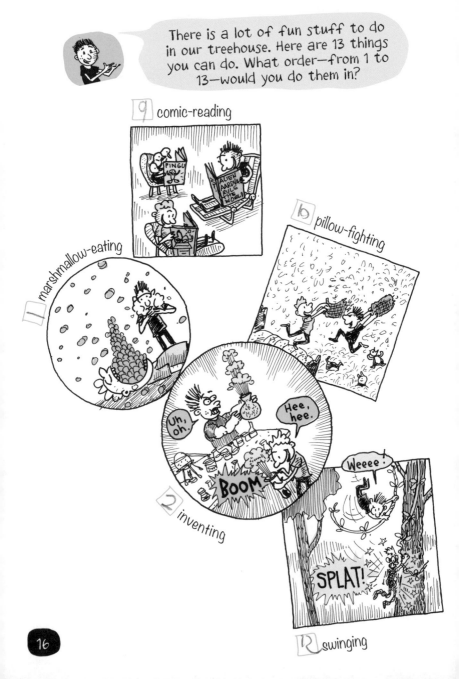

☐ comic-reading

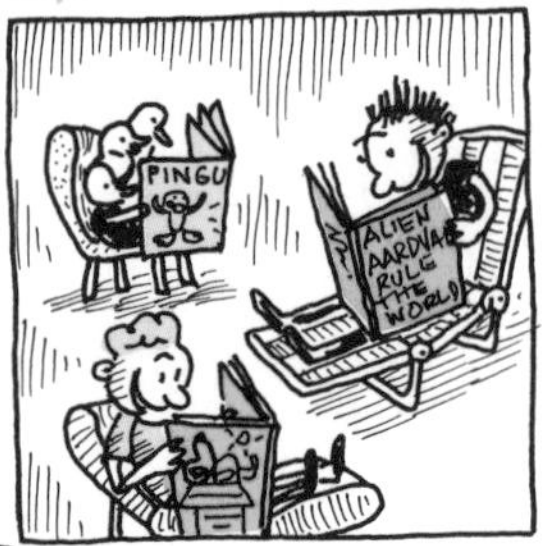
PINGU
ALIEN
RULE
THE
WORLD

☐ pillow-fighting

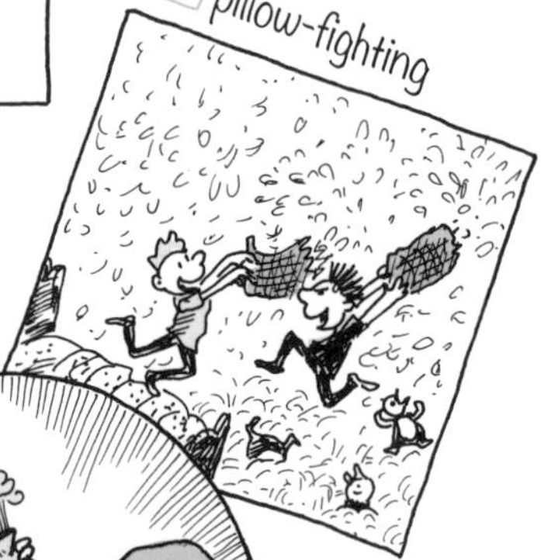

☐ marshmallow-eating

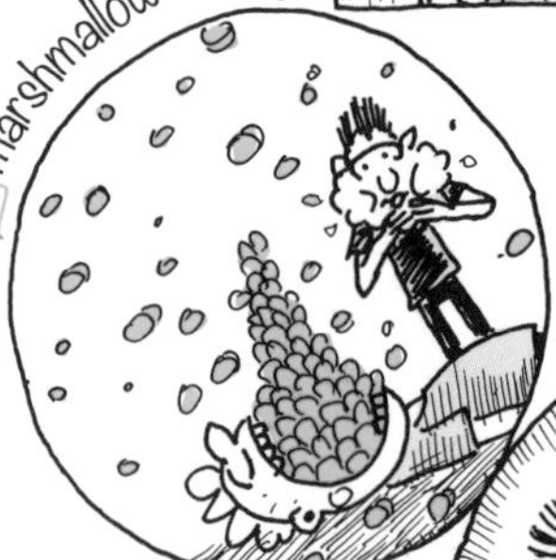

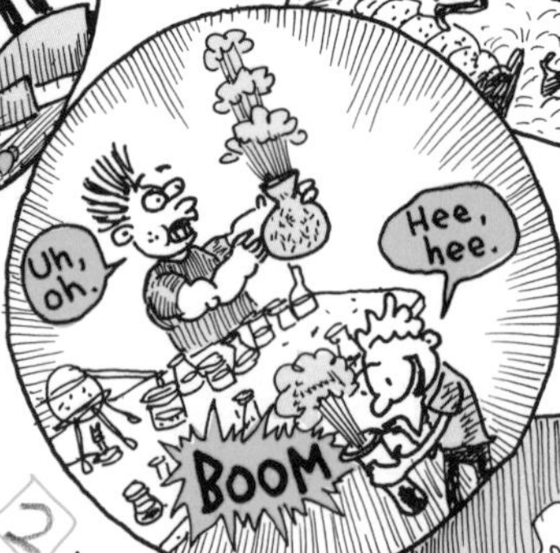
Uh, oh.
Hee, hee.
BOOM

☐ inventing

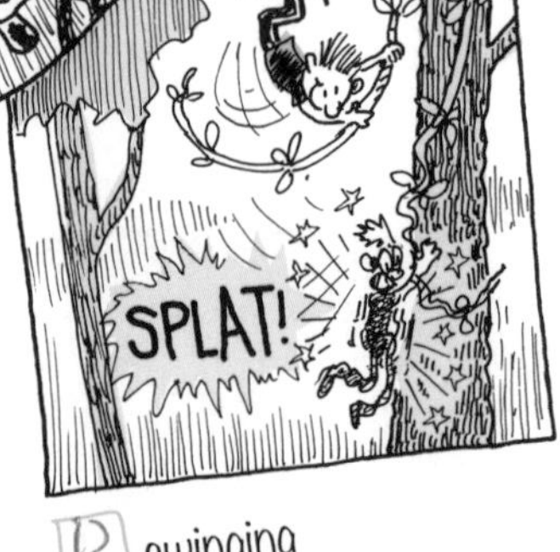
Weeee!
SPLAT!

☐ swinging

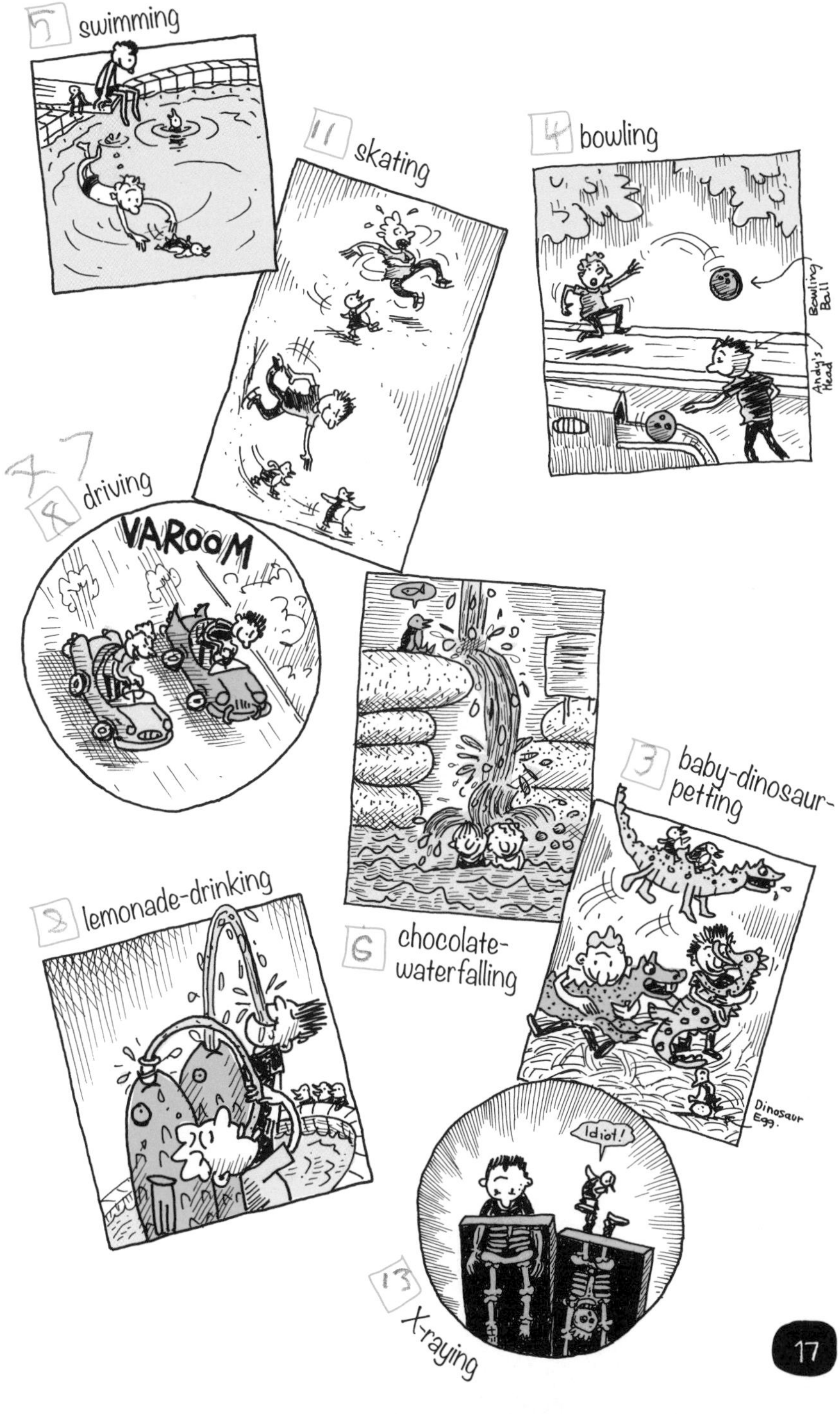
5 swimming
11 skating
4 bowling
Bowling Ball
Andy's Head
7 7
8 driving
VAROOM
chocolate-waterfalling
6
3 baby-dinosaur-petting
Dinosaur Egg.
2 lemonade-drinking
Idiot!
13 X-raying

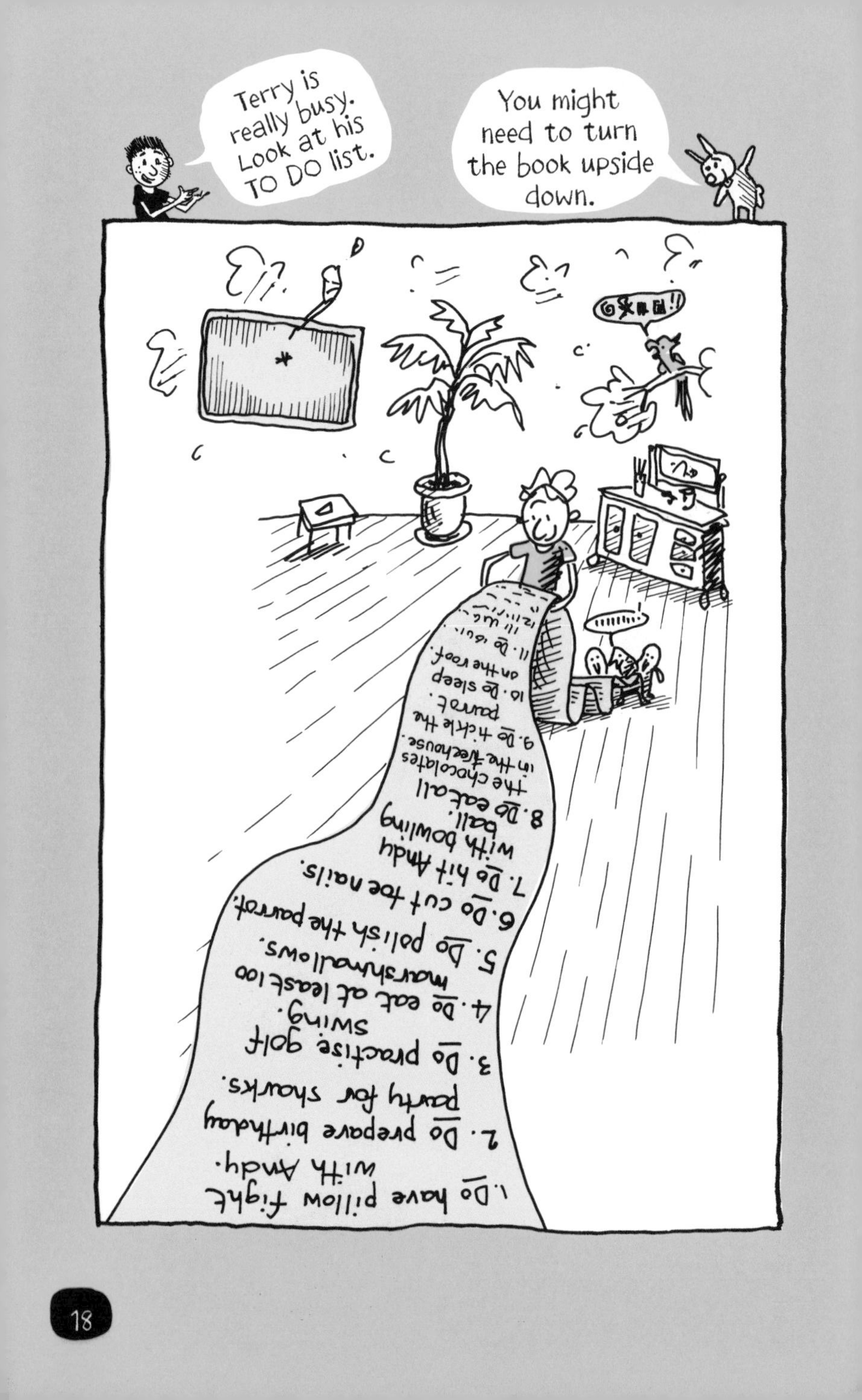
Terry is really busy. Look at his TO DO list.
You might need to turn the book upside down.
1. Do have pillow fight with Andy.
2. Do prepare birthday party for sharks.
3. Do practise golf swing.
4. Do eat at least 100 marshmallows.
5. Do polish the parrot.
6. Do cut toe nails.
7. Do hit Andy with bowling ball.
8. Do eat all the chocolates in the treehouse.
9. Do tickle the parrot.
10. Do sleep on the roof.

WRITE YOUR TO DO LIST

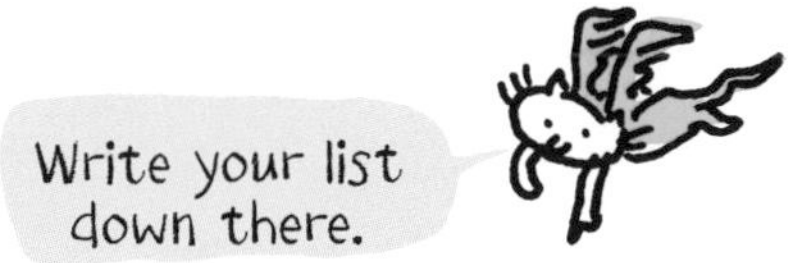
Write your list down there.

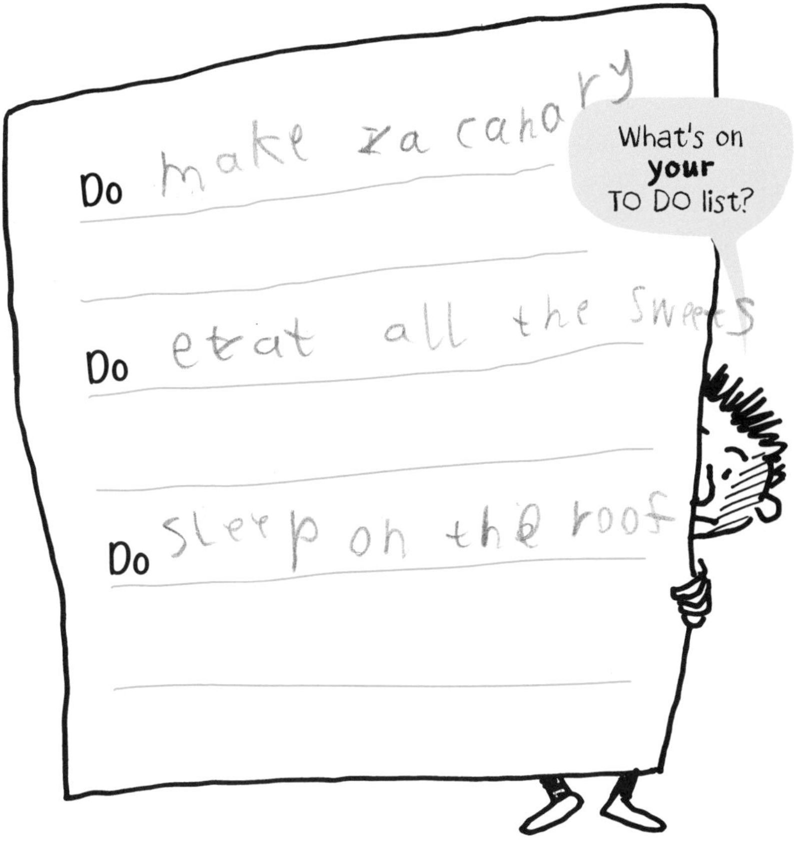
What's on **your** TO DO list?
Do make a canary
Do eat all the sweets
Do sleep on the roof

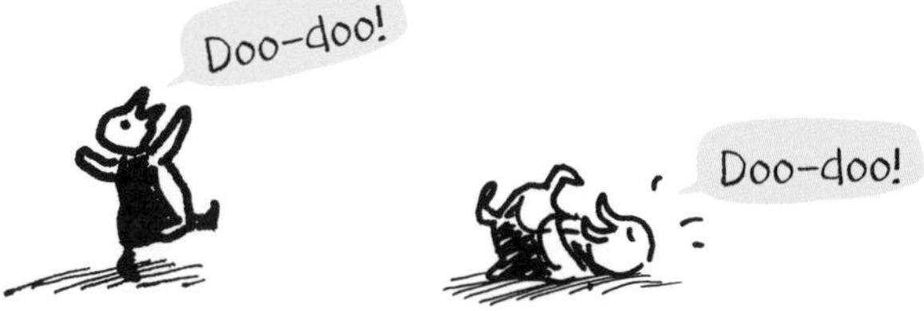
Doo-doo!
Doo-doo!

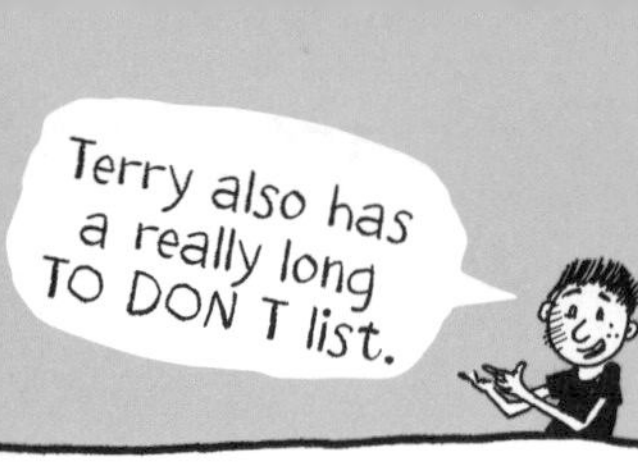
Terry also has a really long TO DON T list.

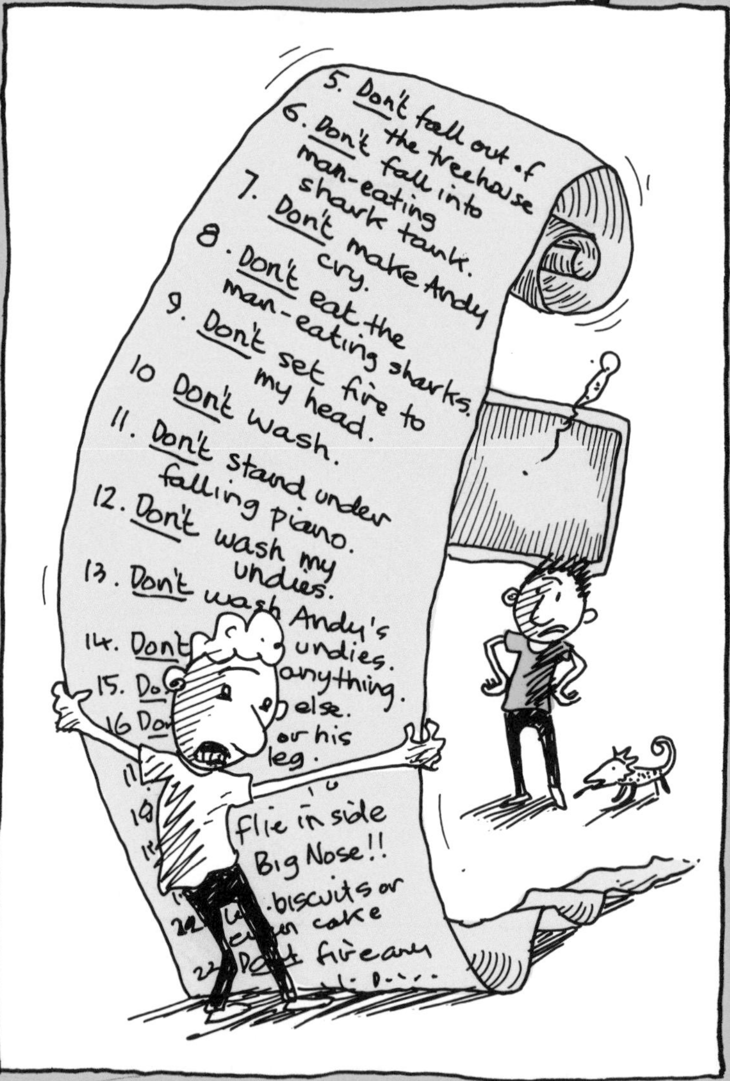
5. Don't fall out of the treehouse
6. Don't fall into man-eating shark tank.
7. Don't make Andy cry.
8. Don't eat the man-eating sharks.
9. Don't set fire to my head.
10 Don't wash.
11. Don't stand under falling piano.
12. Don't wash my undies.
13. Don't wash Andy's
14. Dont undies.
anything
else.
or his
leg.
flie in side
Big Nose!!
biscuits or
cake

WRITE YOUR TO DON'T LIST

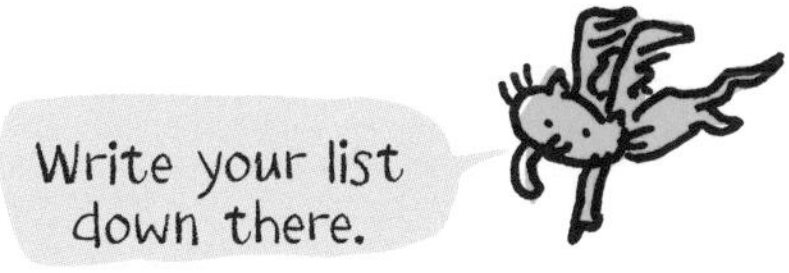
Write your list down there.

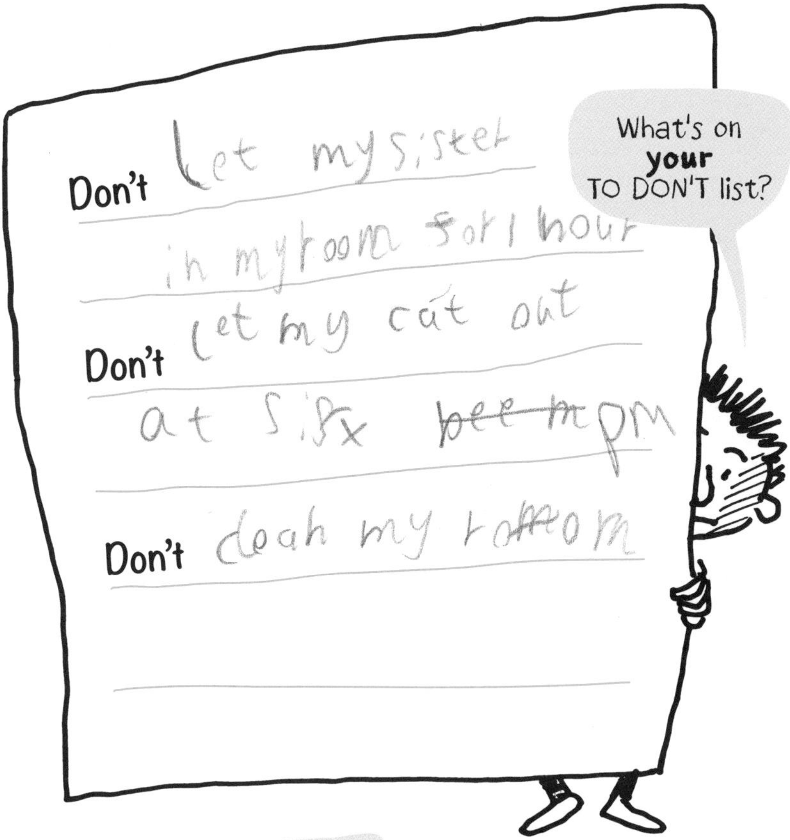
Don't let mysister
in myroom for 1 hour
Don't let my cat out
at sisx ~~bee m~~ pm
Don't cleah my r~~om~~om
What's on **your** TO DON'T list?

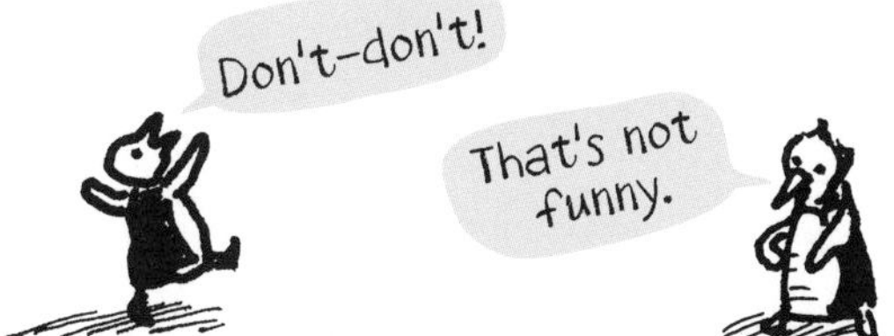
Don't-don't!
That's not funny.

ICE-CREAM TIME

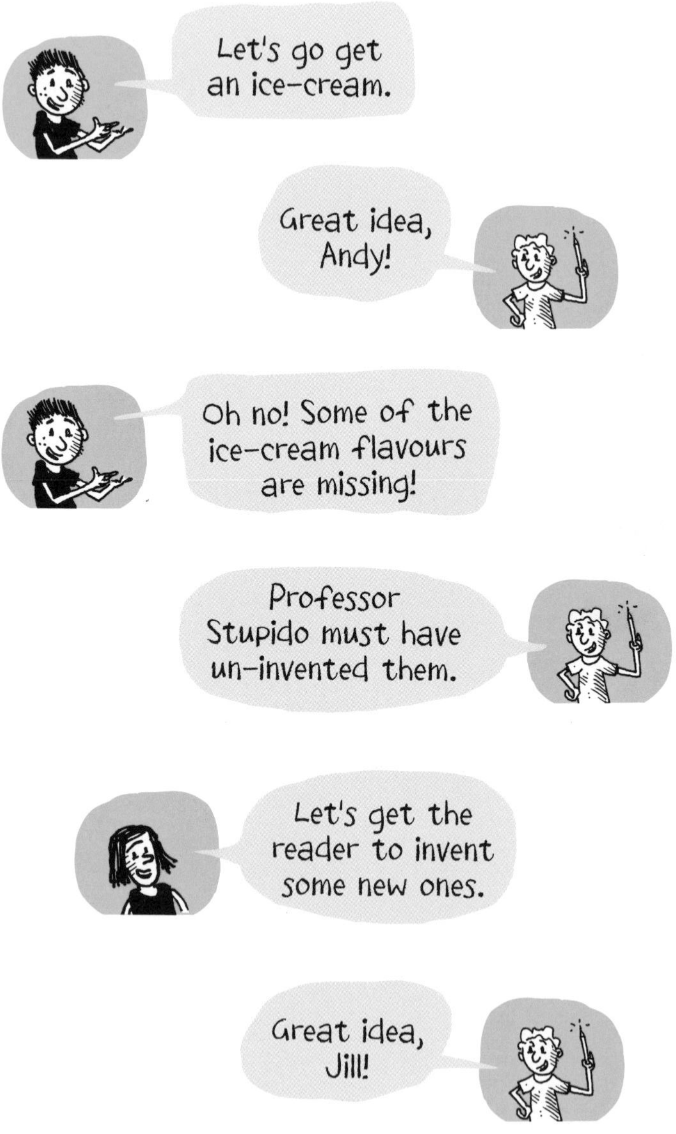
Let's go get an ice-cream.
Great idea, Andy!
Oh no! Some of the ice-cream flavours are missing!
Professor Stupido must have un-invented them.
Let's get the reader to invent some new ones.
Great idea, Jill!

DRAW NEW ICE-CREAM FLAVOURS

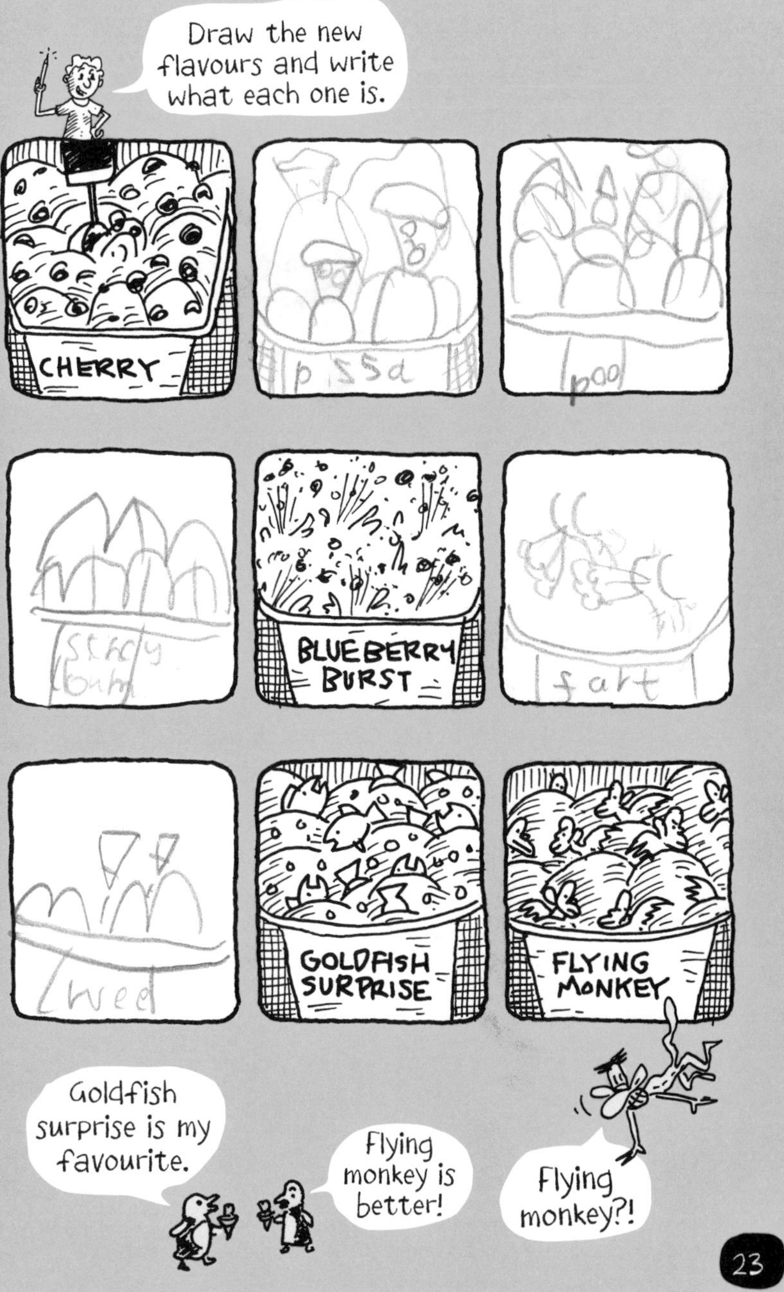
Draw the new flavours and write what each one is.
CHERRY
BLUEBERRY BURST
GOLDFISH SURPRISE
FLYING MONKEY
Goldfish surprise is my favourite.
Flying monkey is better!
Flying monkey?!

FLYING TIME

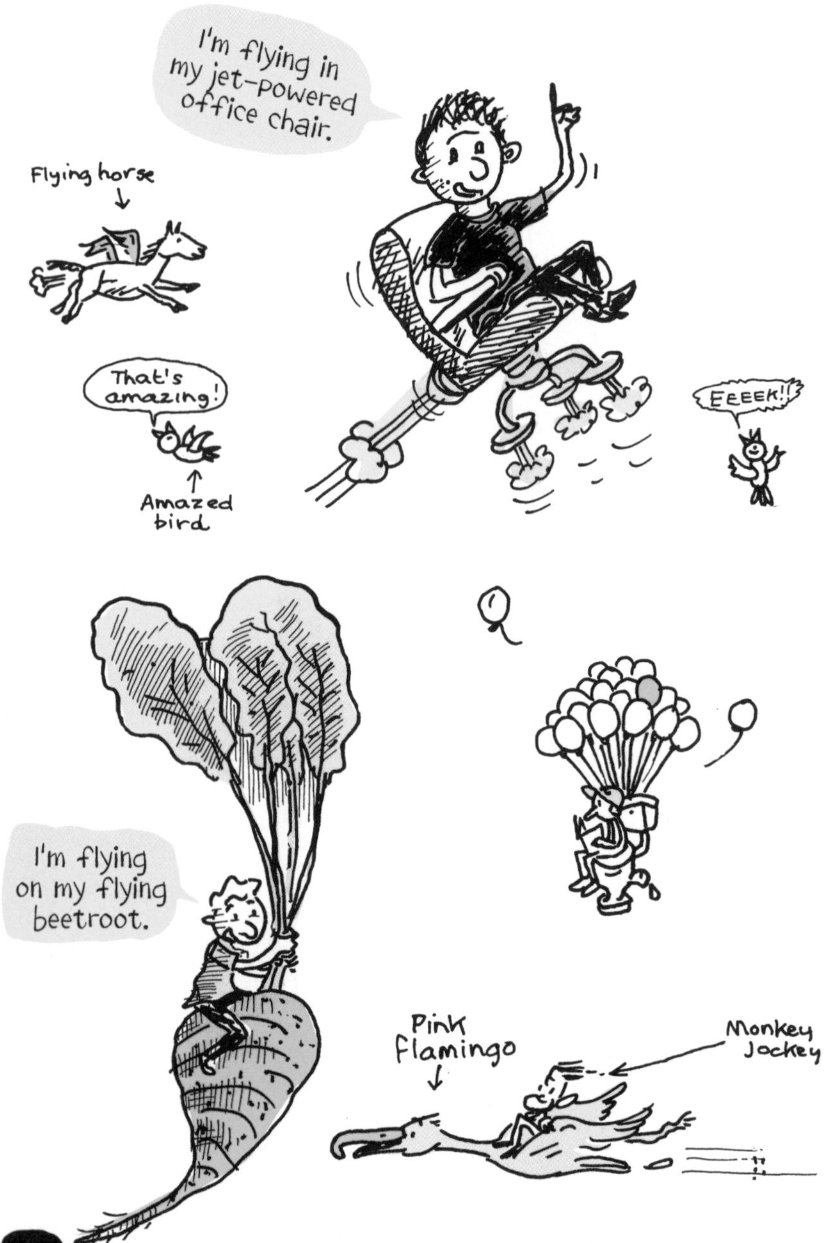

I'm flying in my jet-powered office chair.
Flying horse
That's amazing!
Amazed bird
EEEEK!!
I'm flying on my flying beetroot.
Pink Flamingo
Monkey Jockey

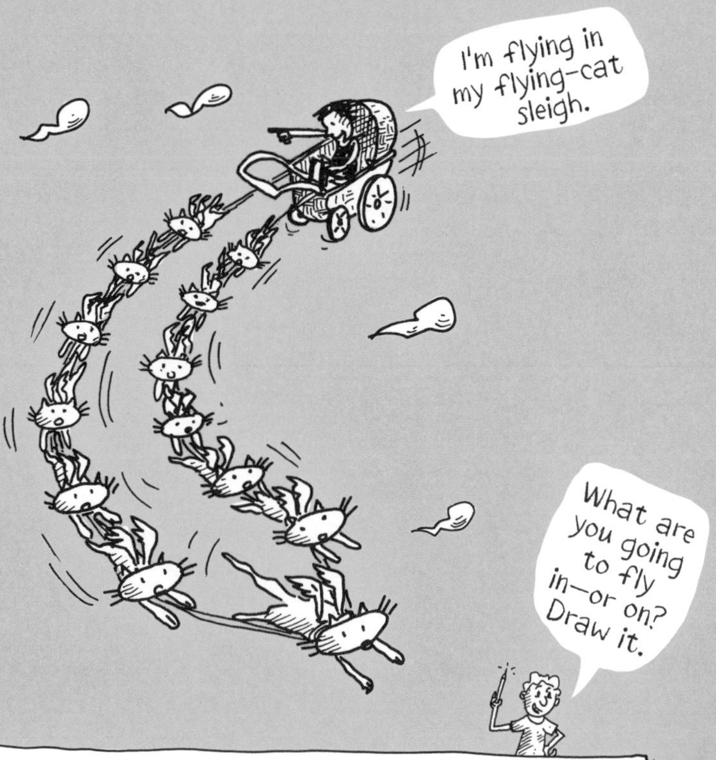
I'm flying in my flying-cat sleigh.
What are you going to fly in—or on? Draw it.

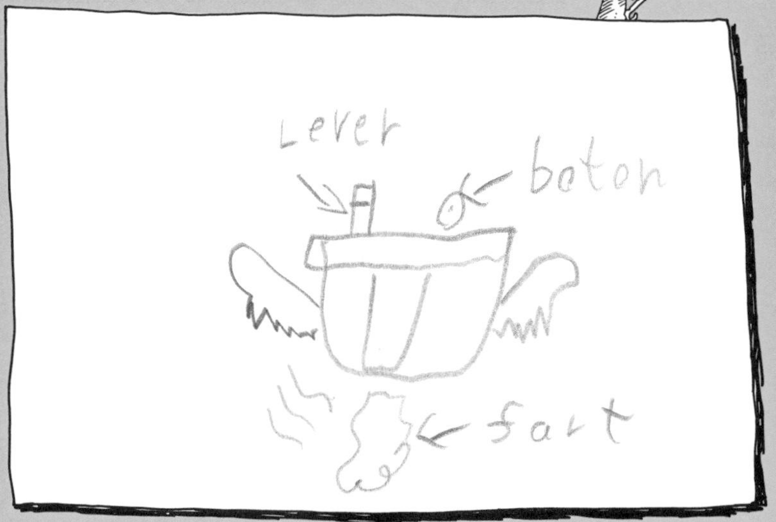
Lever
boton
fart

DOT-TO-DOT FUN

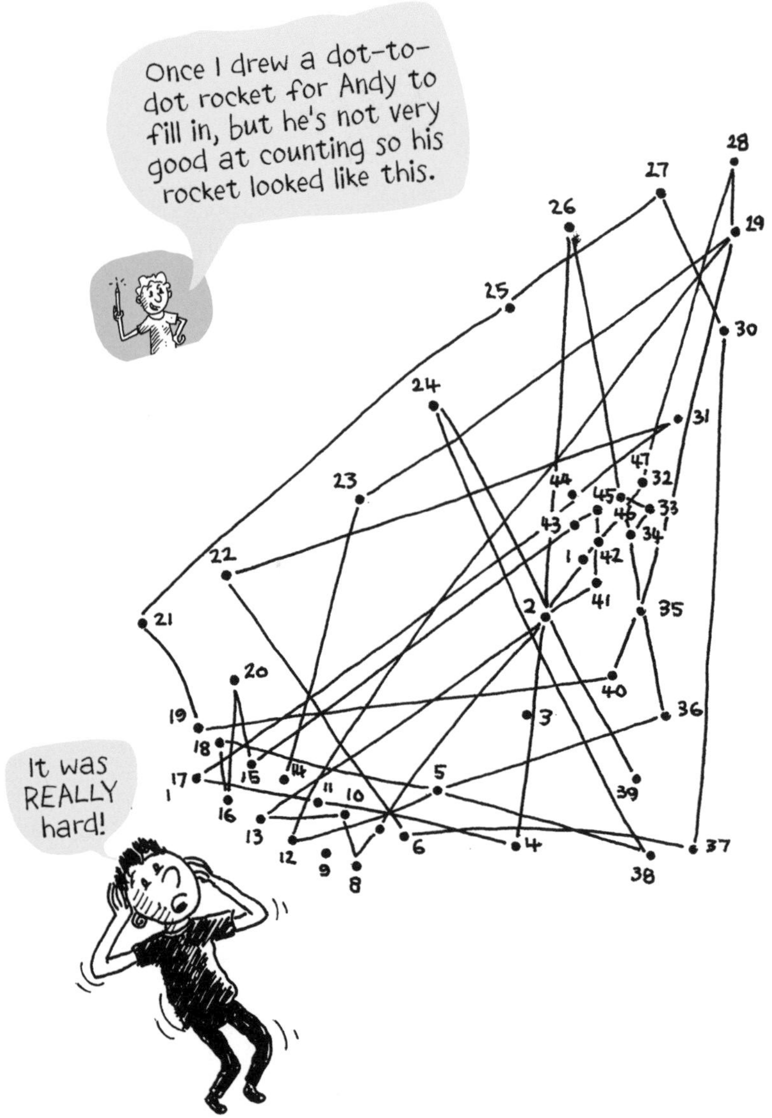
Once I drew a dot-to-dot rocket for Andy to fill in, but he's not very good at counting so his rocket looked like this.
It was REALLY hard!

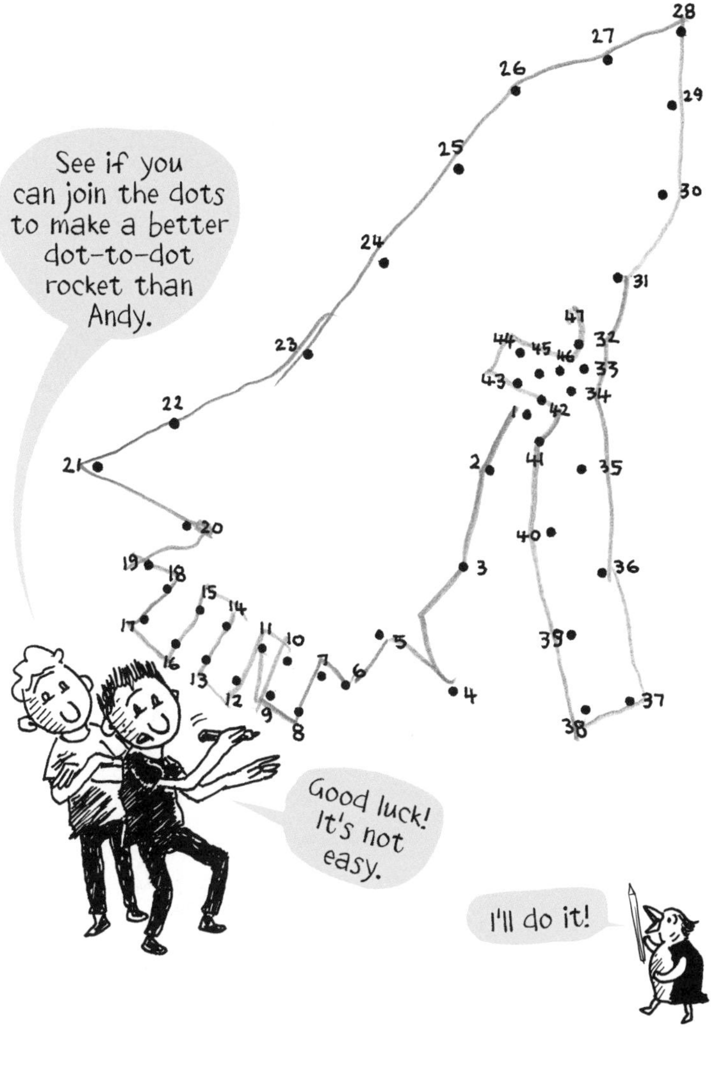

See if you can join the dots to make a better dot-to-dot rocket than Andy.
Good luck! It's not easy.
I'll do it!

COUNT US DOWN

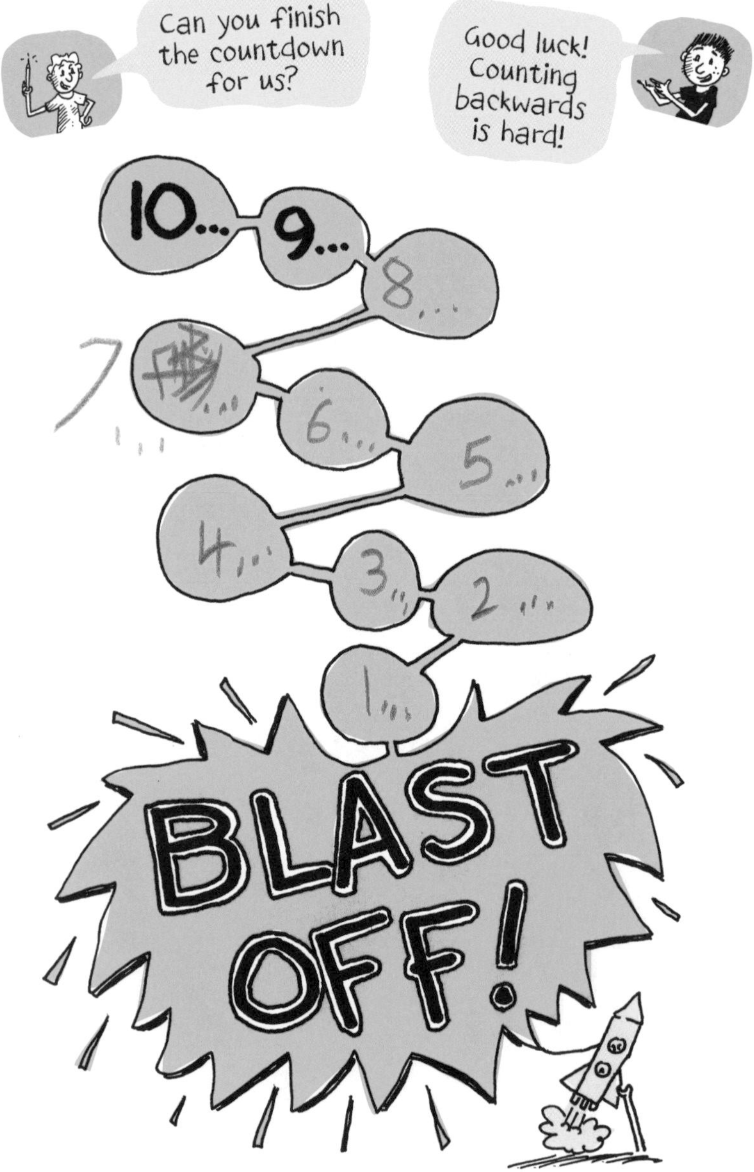

Can you finish the countdown for us?
Good luck! Counting backwards is hard!
10...
9...
BLAST OFF!

Our journey to the moon and back looked like this.
THE DAY OUR ROCKET WENT COMPLETELY OUT OF CONTROL ALL OVER THE UNIVERSE AND THEN CRASH-LANDED ON THE MOON
ICED DONUT
VERY BIG PLANET
TINY PLANET
SQUARE PLANET
PLANET TERRY
CRAB NEBULA
BILL & PHIL
EARTH
PLANET BOWLING BALL
SATURN
SPACE SHIP
IDIOTS!
DARK SIDE OF THE MOON
PLANET ANDY
WEIRD THING
SEA URCHIN
ORANGE
THE DAY OUR ROCKET WENT COMPLETELY OUT OF CONTROL AND FLEW ALL OVER THE UNIVERSE AND CRASH-LANDED ON EARTH
LARGE VANILLA SLICE
PLANET UGLY
HORSE HEAD NEBULA
BLACK HOLE
DARK SIDE OF THE MOON
WHITE HOLE
PLANET HANDSOME
SPACE BILL
RUNAWAY TOASTER
ANDY'S LONG-LOST SKATEBOARD
EARTH

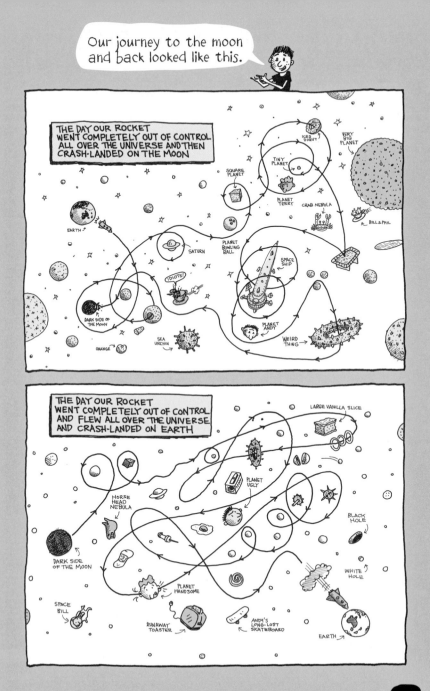

DRAW YOUR SPACE JOURNEY

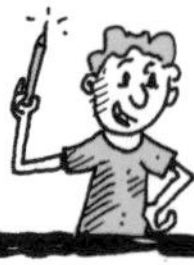

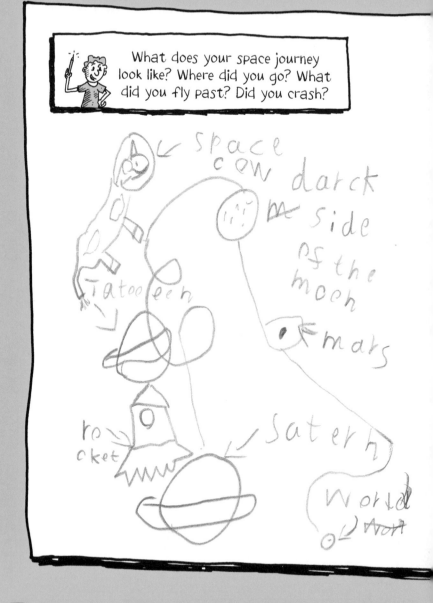

What does your space journey look like? Where did you go? What did you fly past? Did you crash?

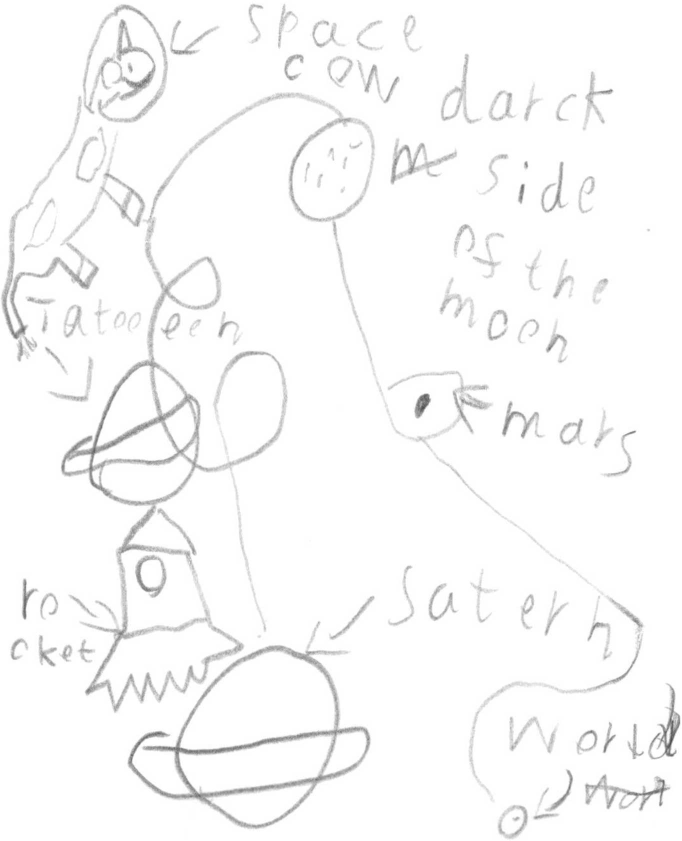
space cow
darck side of the moon
Tatooeen
mars
saterh
ro cket
World

apel
jues

scying
noodl

SPOT THE DIFFERENCE

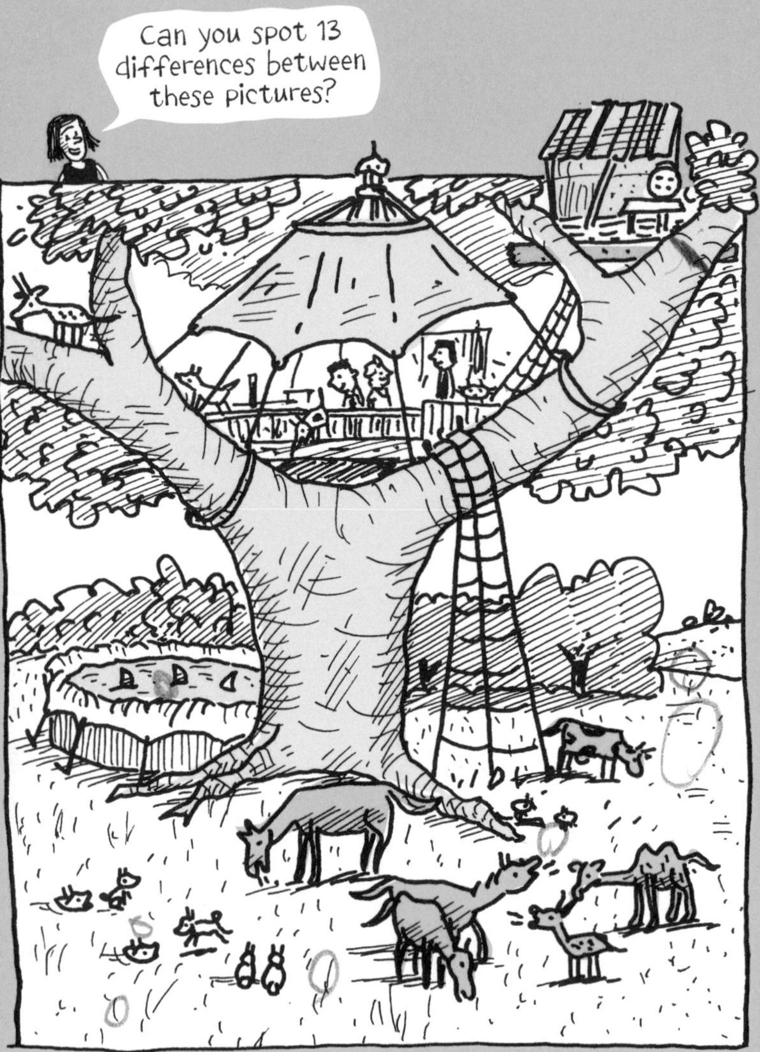
Can you spot 13 differences between these pictures?

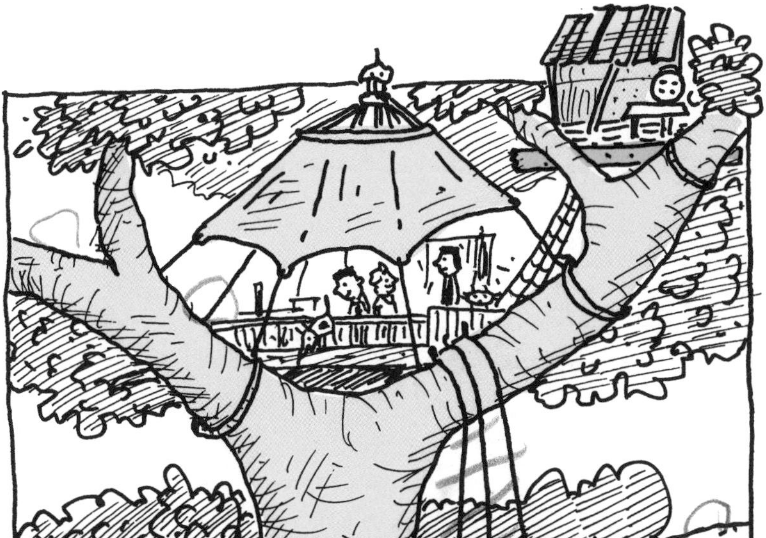

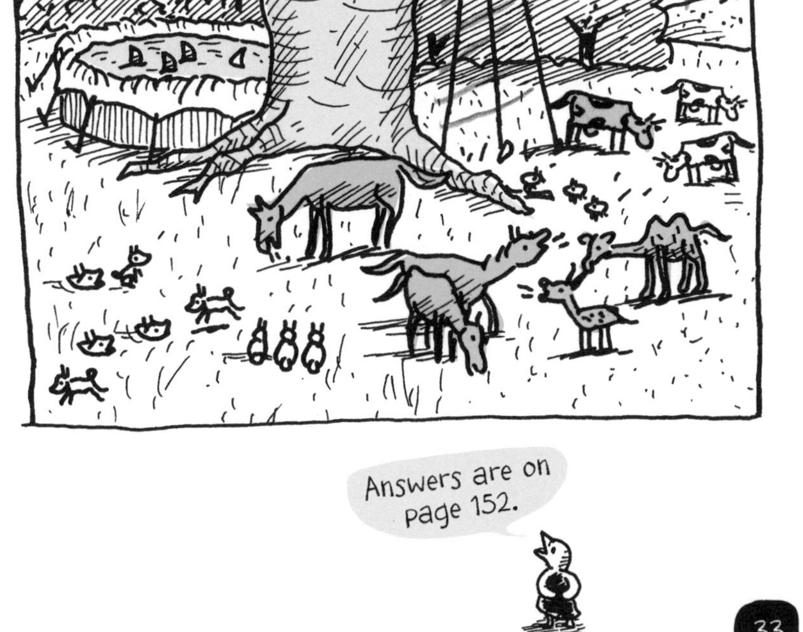
Answers are on page 152.

DRAW OUR SHARKS

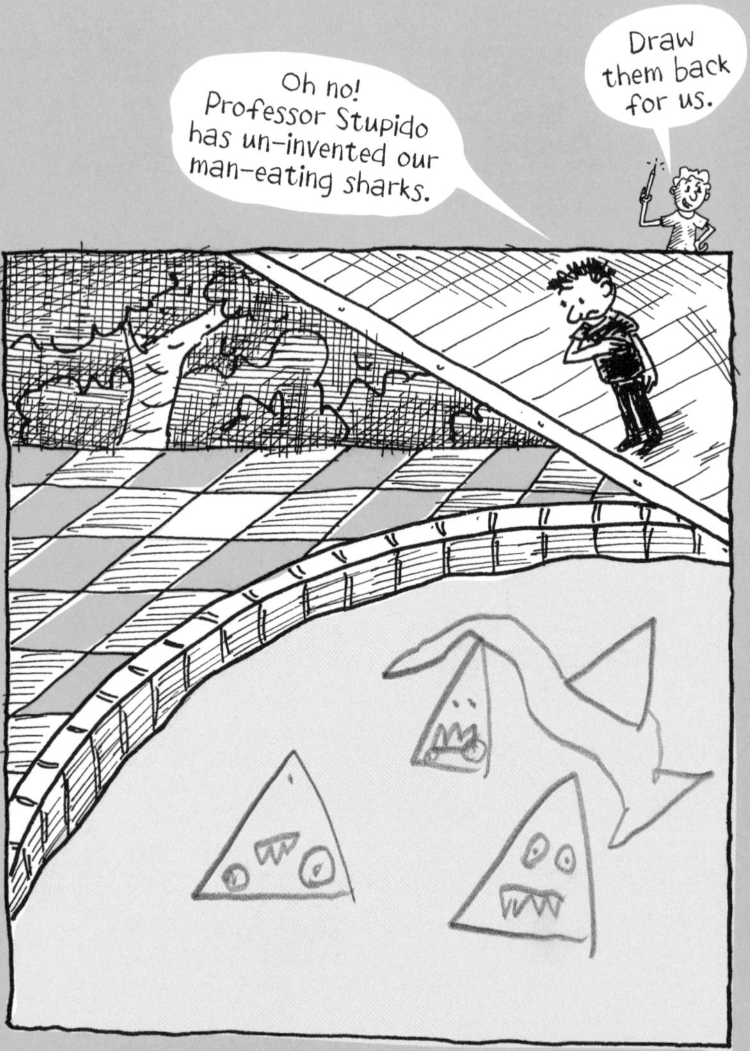
Draw them back for us.
Oh no! Professor Stupido has un-invented our man-eating sharks.

UN-INVENT SOMETHING

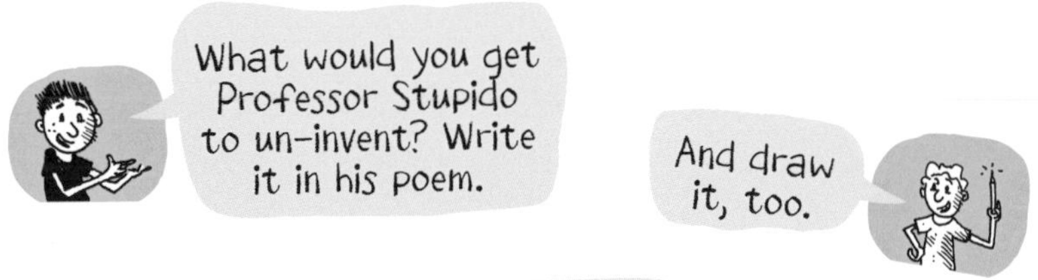
What would you get Professor Stupido to un-invent? Write it in his poem.
And draw it, too.

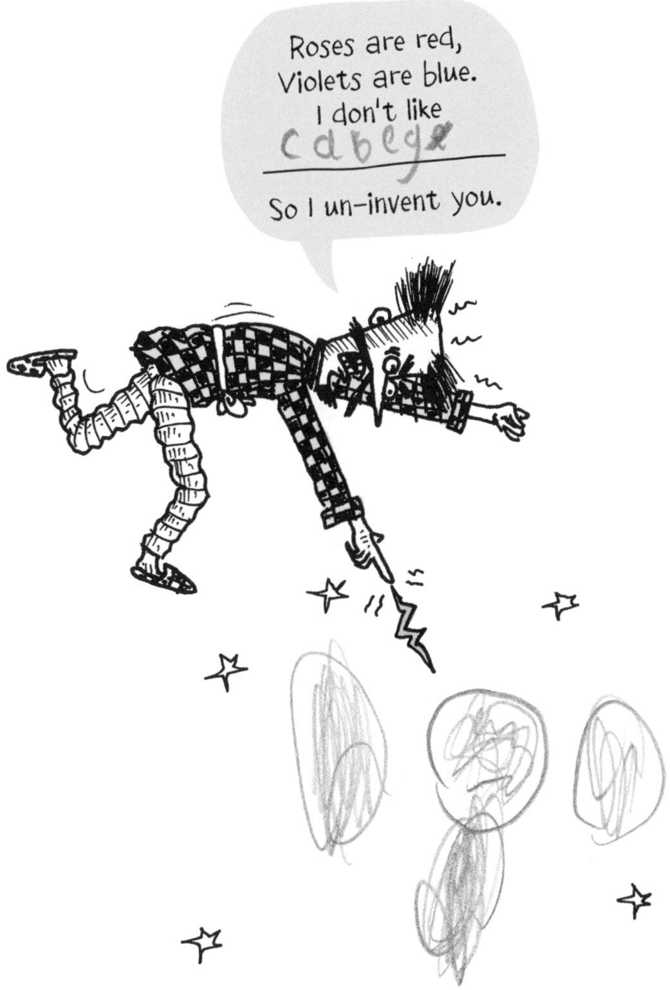
Roses are red,
Violets are blue.
I don't like
So I un-invent you.

BARKY TIME

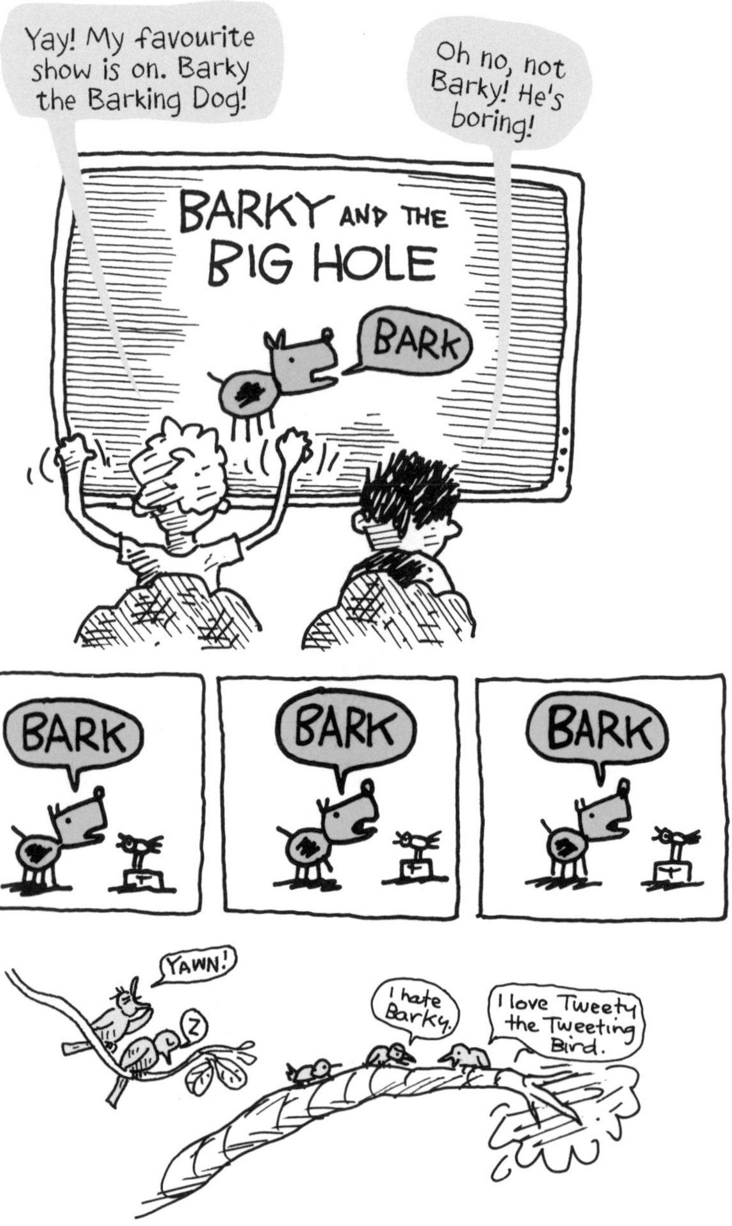

Yay! My favourite show is on. Barky the Barking Dog!
Oh no, not Barky! He's boring!
BARKY AND THE BIG HOLE
BARK
BARK
BARK
BARK
YAWN!
Z
I hate Barky.
I love Tweety the Tweeting Bird.

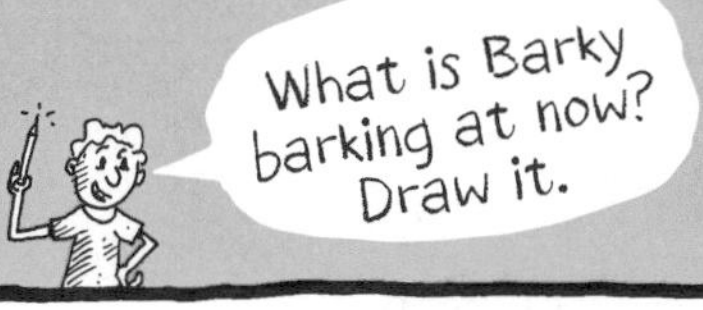
What is Barky barking at now? Draw it.

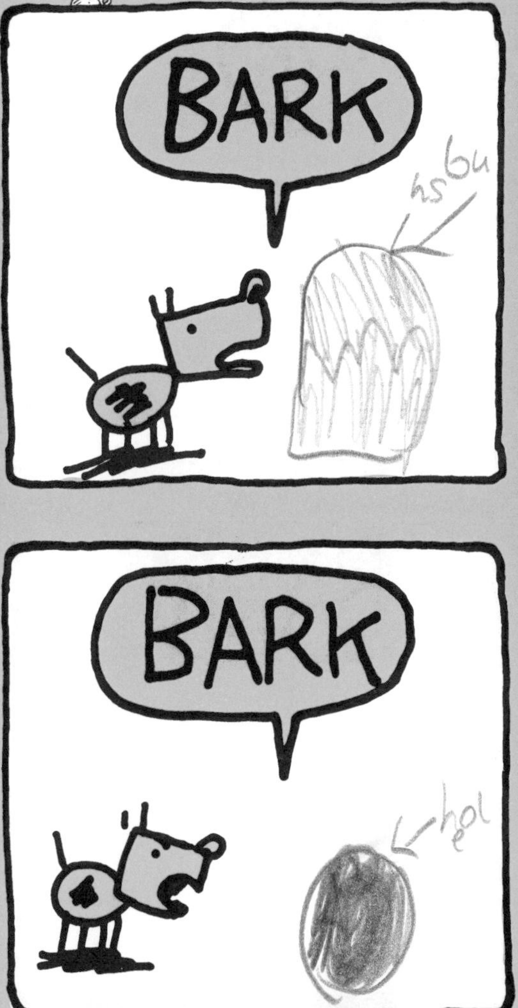
BARK
BARK

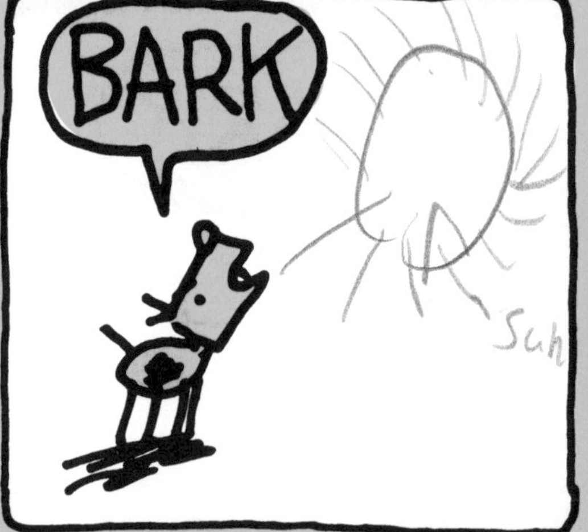
BARK
Sun

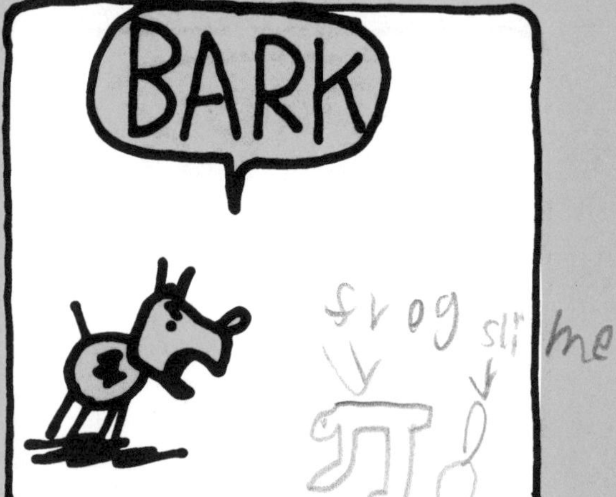
BARK
frog
slime

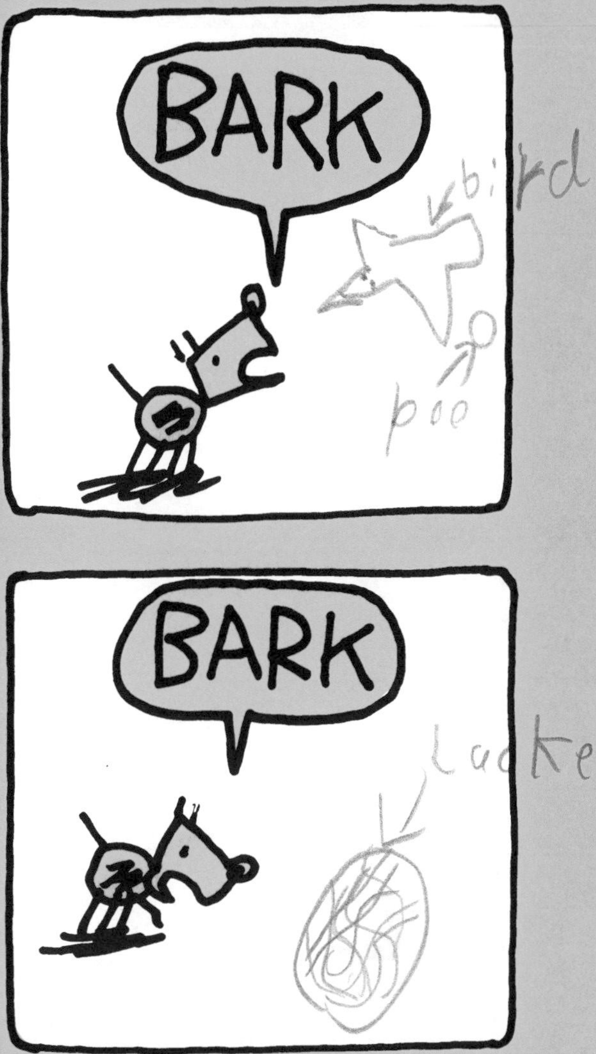
BARK
BARK

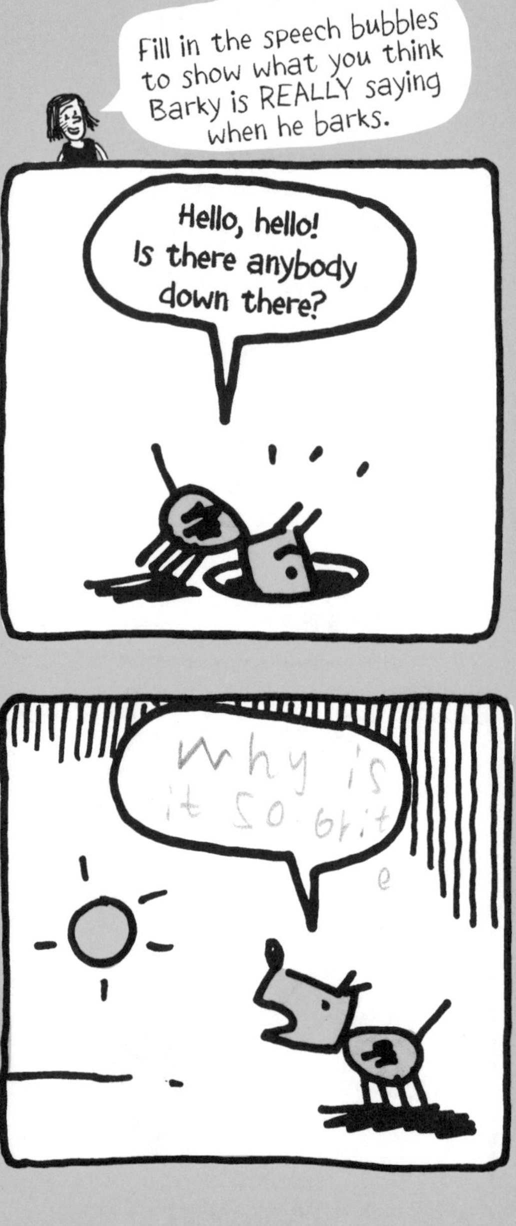
Fill in the speech bubbles to show what you think Barky is REALLY saying when he barks.
Hello, hello! Is there anybody down there?
why is

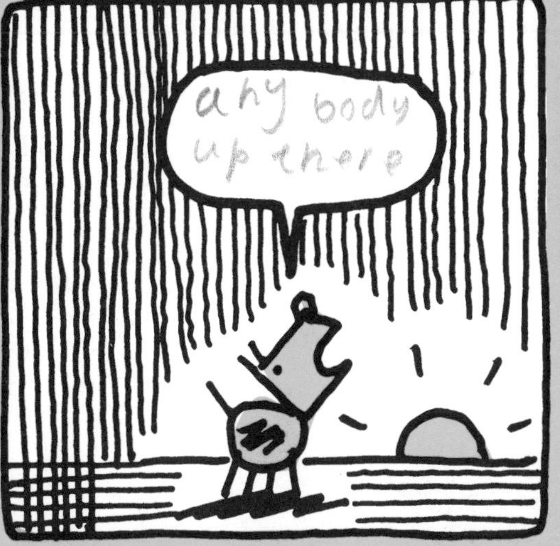
any body up there

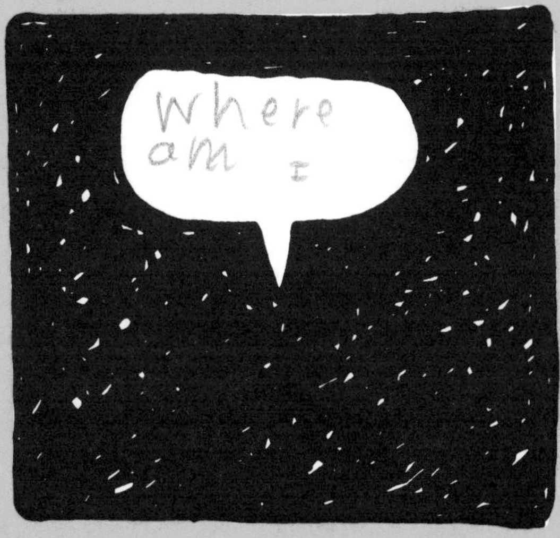
where am I

SPOT THE DIFFERENCE

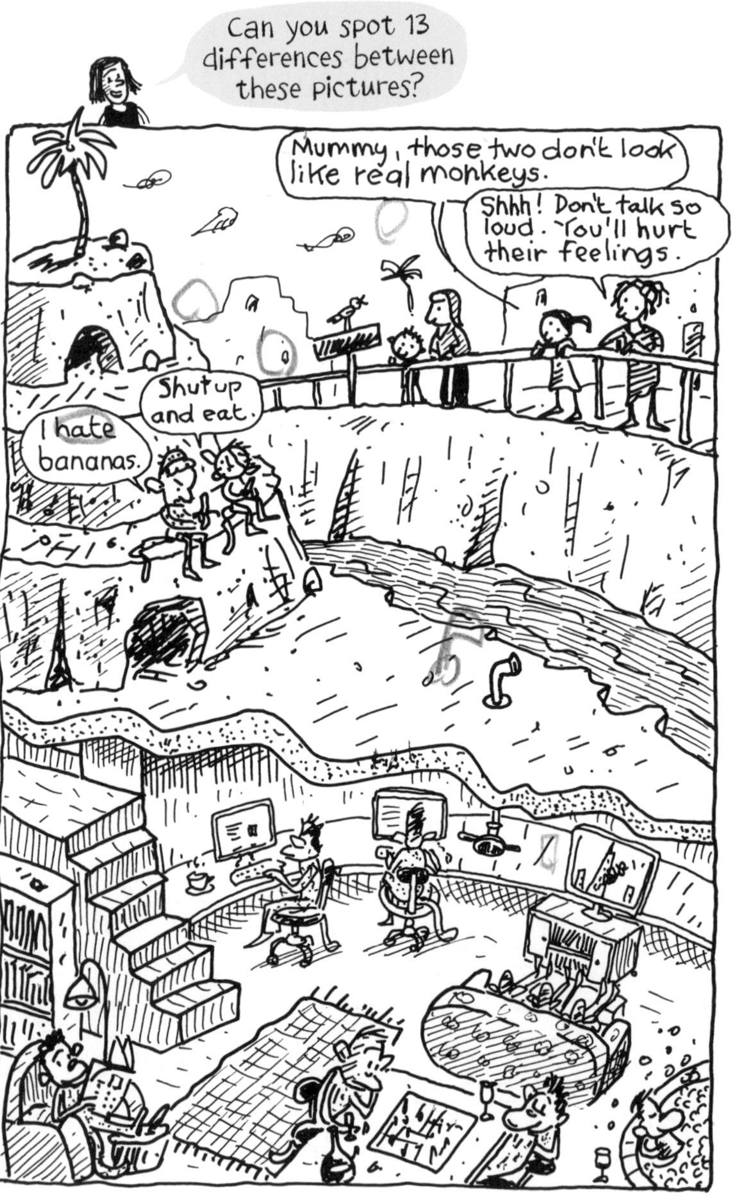
Can you spot 13 differences between these pictures?
Mummy, those two don't look like real monkeys.
Shhh! Don't talk so loud. You'll hurt their feelings.
Shut up and eat.
I hate bananas.

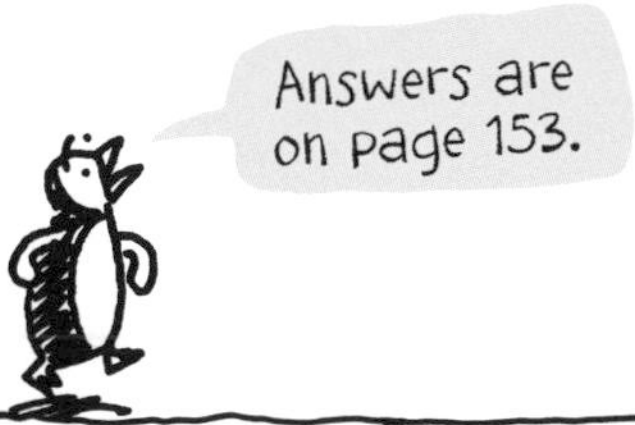
Answers are on page 153.

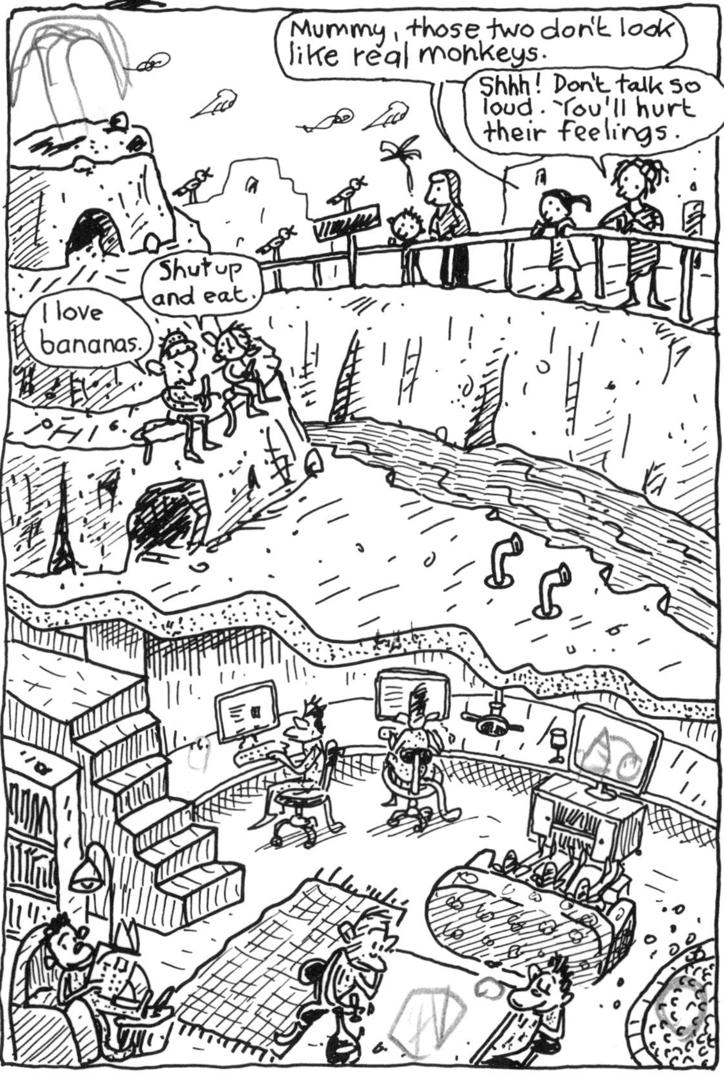
Mummy, those two don't look like real monkeys.
Shhh! Don't talk so loud. You'll hurt their feelings.
I love bananas.
Shut up and eat.

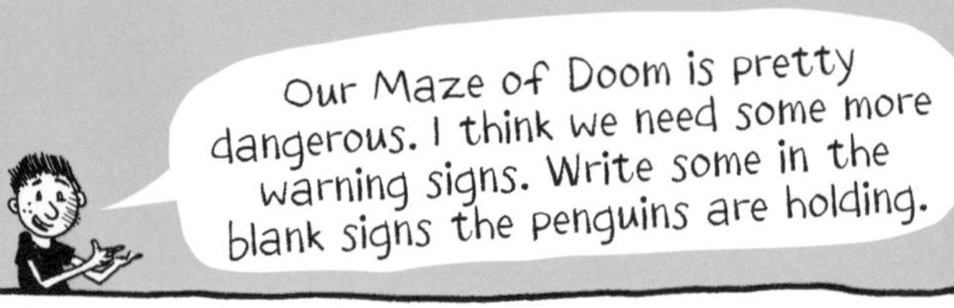
Our Maze of Doom is pretty dangerous. I think we need some more warning signs. Write some in the blank signs the penguins are holding.

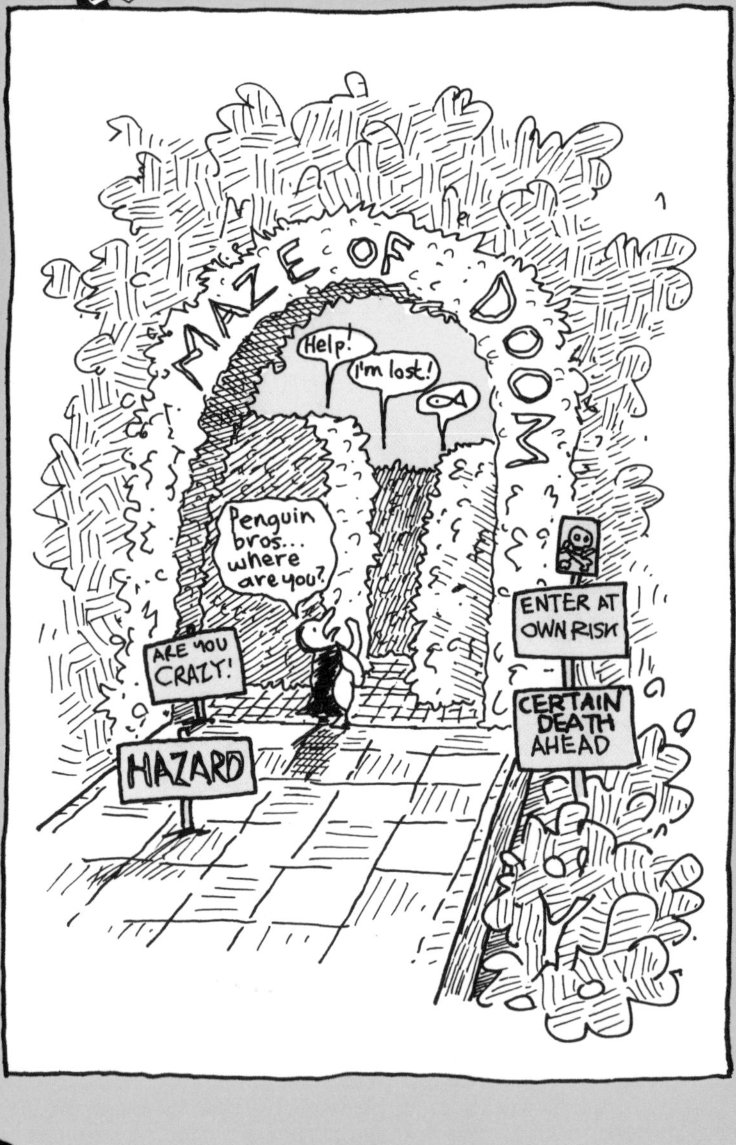
MAZE OF DOOM
Help!
I'm lost!
Penguin bros... where are you?
ENTER AT OWN RISK
ARE YOU CRAZY!
CERTAIN DEATH AHEAD
HAZARD

WRITE SOME WARNING SIGNS

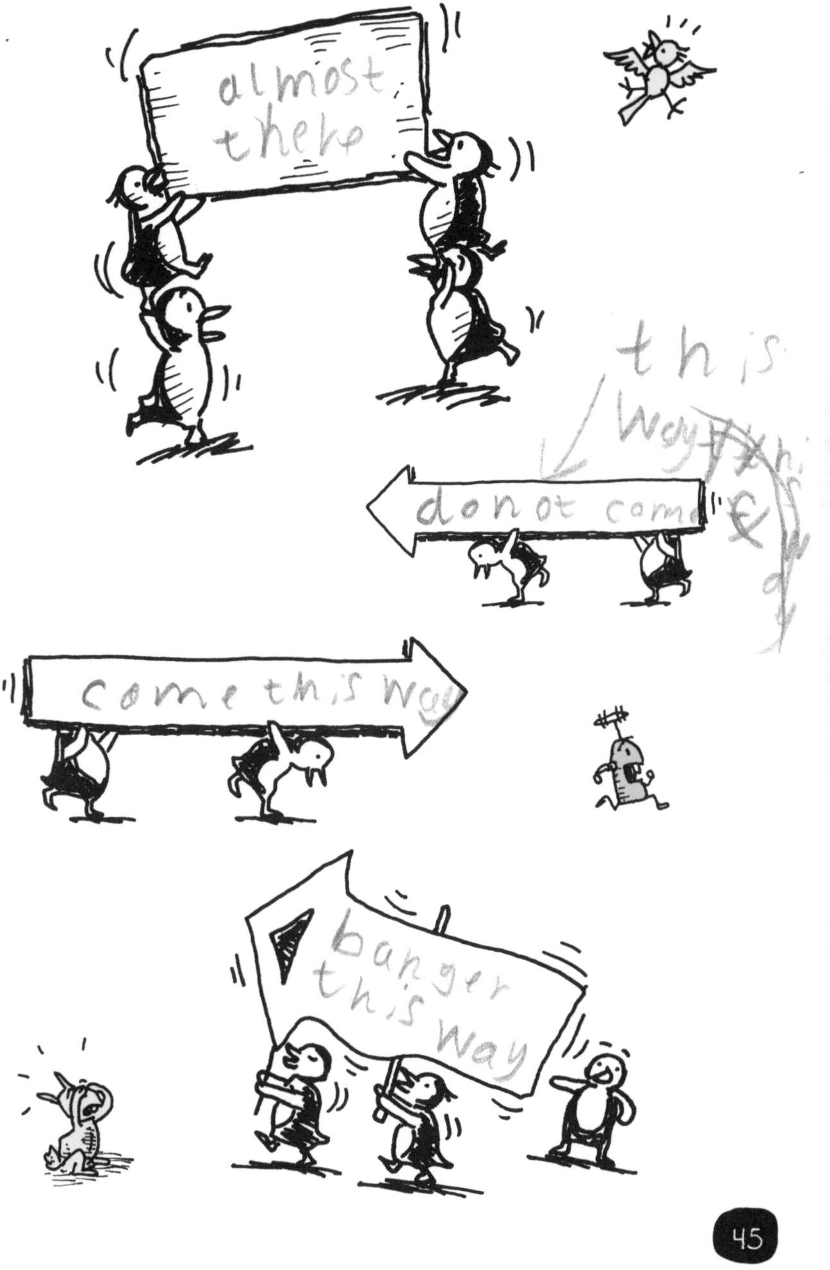
almost there
this way
donot come
come this way
banger this way

ESCAPE THE MAZE OF DOOM

(IF YOU CAN!)

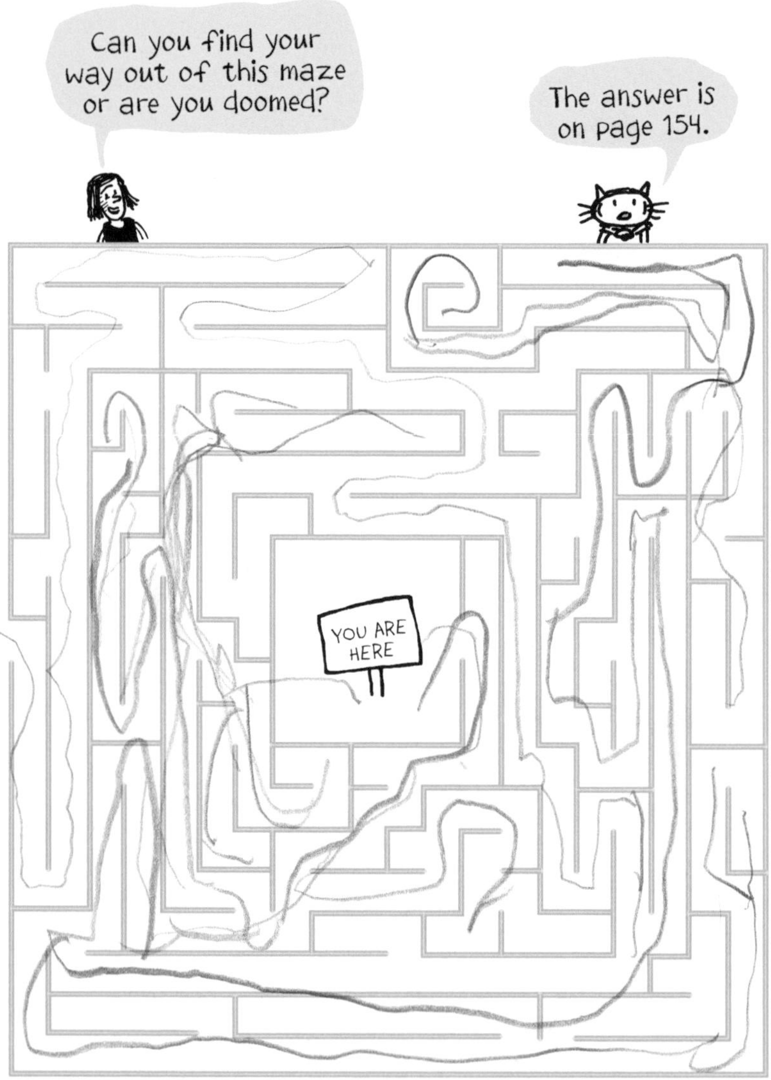

ENLARGING TIME

Would you like something enlarged? Draw it under my enlarging ray.

Draw it up there.

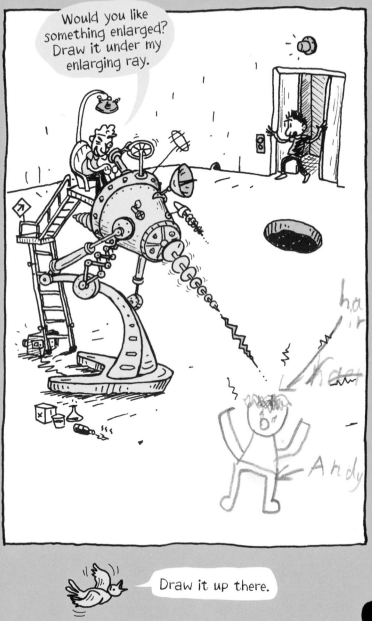

13-STOREY TREEHOUSE WORD SEARCH

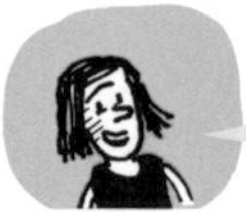

When you have finished there should be 13 letters left over that spell out something to do with the story.

Answers are on page 155.

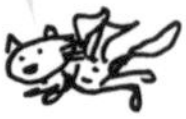

WORD LIST

BANANA
BATHROOM
BOWLING
CATAPULT
CHAOS
EGGS
KITCHEN
LABORATORY
MONKEY
NOISE
PAWS
SEAMONKEYS
SWINGING
VINES

S	E	A	M	O	N	K	E	Y	S
C	G	A	N	A	N	A	B	R	W
A	N	S	M	O	O	B	N	O	I
T	I	N	G	K	I	A	V	T	N
A	L	E	S	G	S	T	I	A	G
P	W	H	W	E	E	H	N	R	I
U	O	C	A	Y	M	R	E	O	N
L	B	T	P	A	D	O	S	B	G
T	N	I	C	H	A	O	S	A	E
Y	E	K	N	O	M	M	S	L	S

SOLUTION: _ _ _ _ _ _ _   _ _ _ _ _ _ _ _

COLOUR IN JILL'S HOUSE

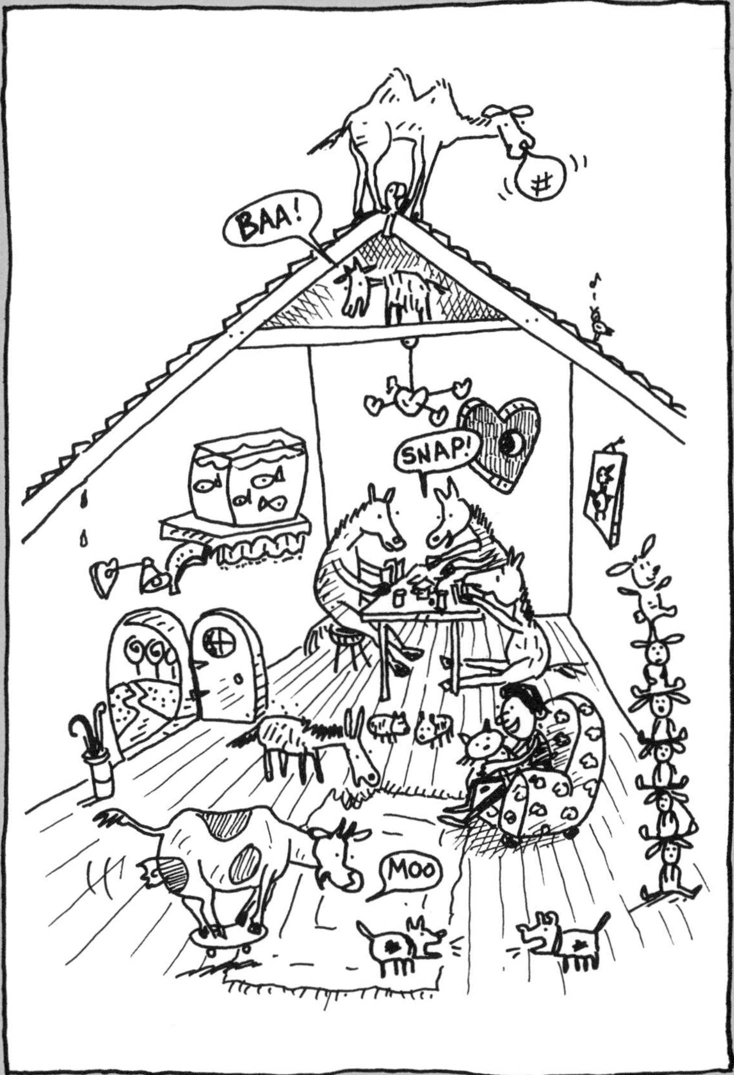
BAA!
SNAP!
MOO

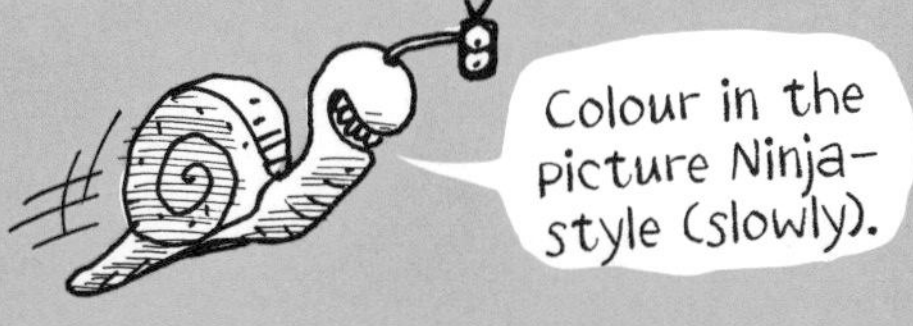
Colour in the picture Ninja-style (slowly).

PIZZA TIME

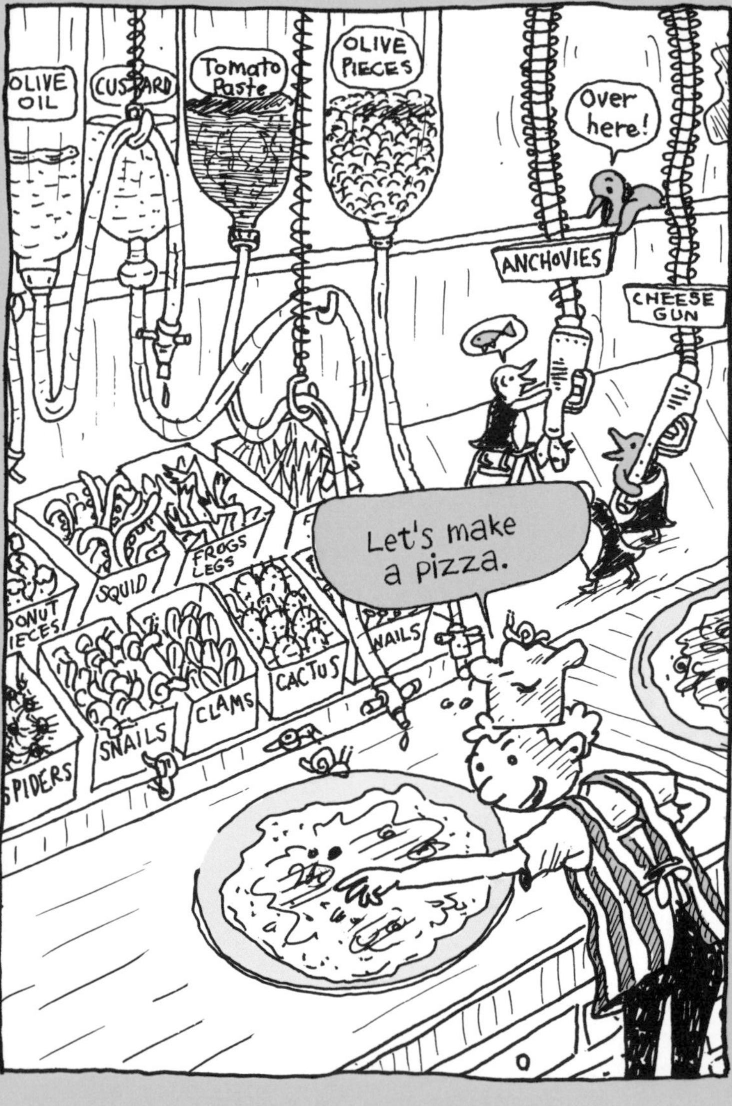
OLIVE OIL
CUSTARD
Tomato Paste
OLIVE PIECES
Over here!
ANCHOVIES
CHEESE GUN
SQUID
FROGS LEGS
CACTUS
CLAMS
SNAILS
SPIDERS
Let's make a pizza.

DRAW YOUR OWN PIZZA

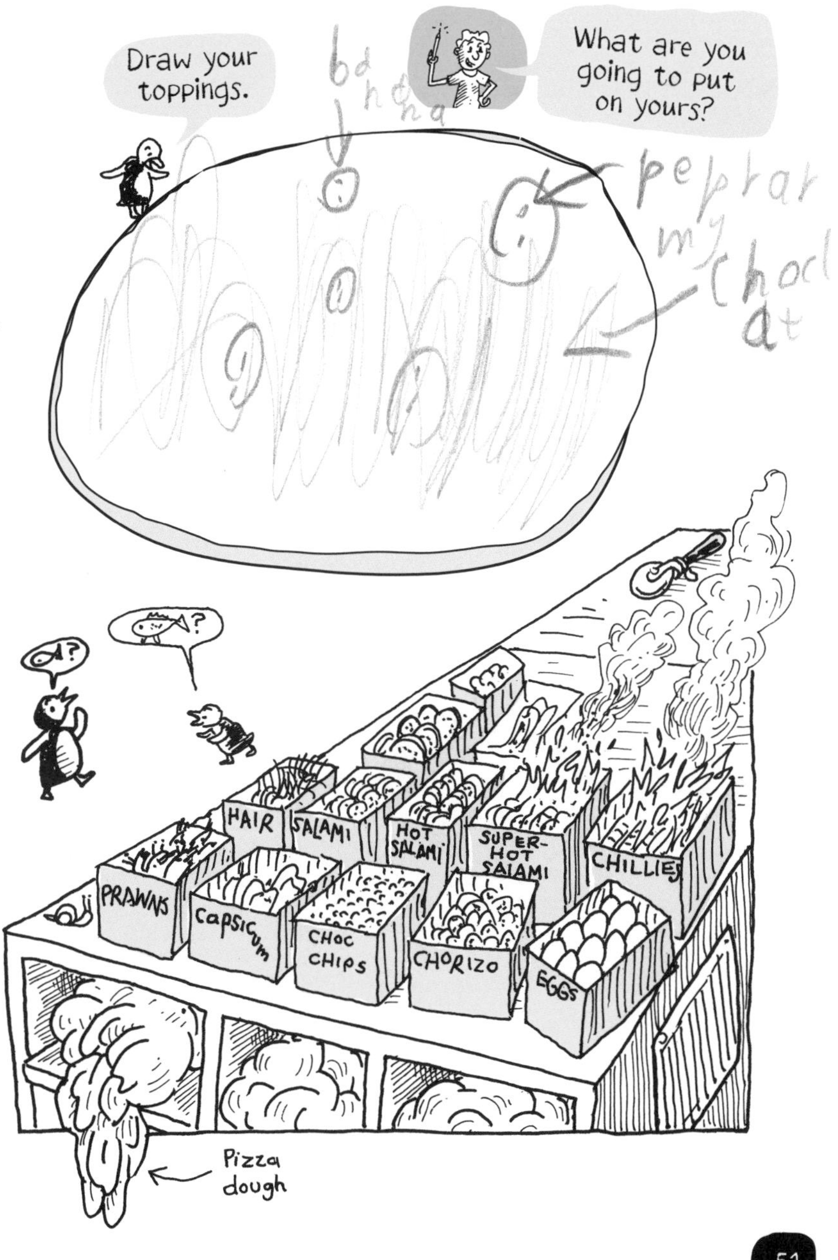
Draw your toppings.
What are you going to put on yours?
HAIR
SALAMI
HOT SALAMI
SUPER-HOT SALAMI
CHILLIES
PRAWNS
Capsicum
CHOC CHIPS
CHORIZO
EGGS
Pizza dough

ANIMAL PIZZAS

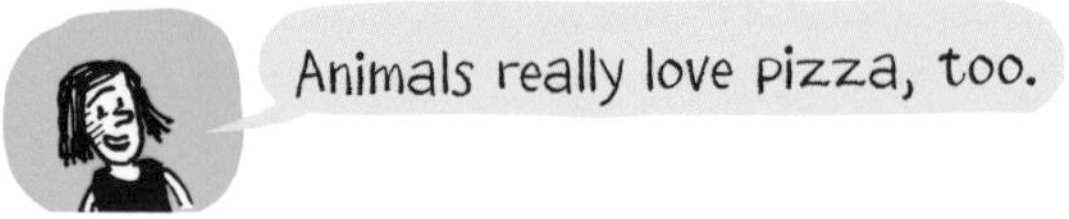
Animals really love pizza, too.

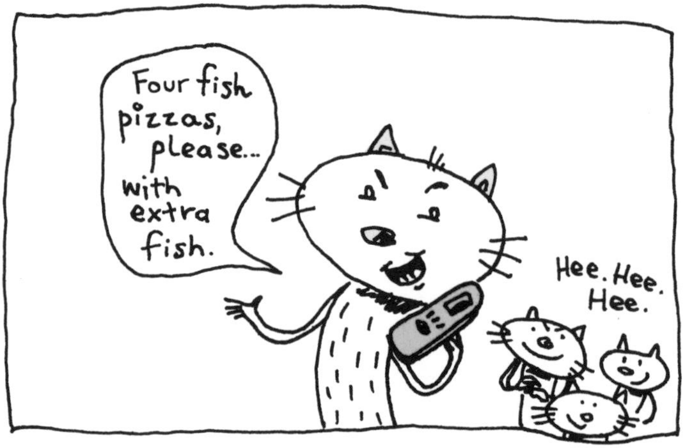
Four fish pizzas, please... with extra fish.
Hee. Hee. Hee.

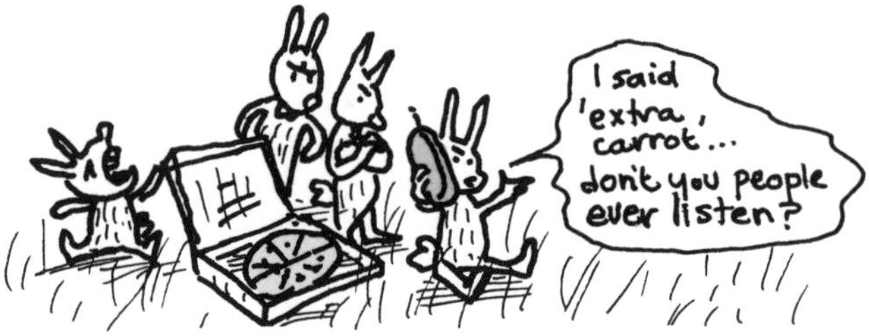
I said 'extra carrot'... don't you people ever listen?

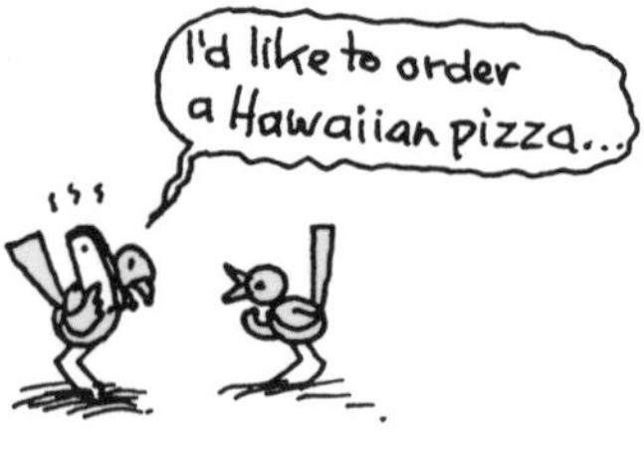
I'd like to order a Hawaiian pizza...

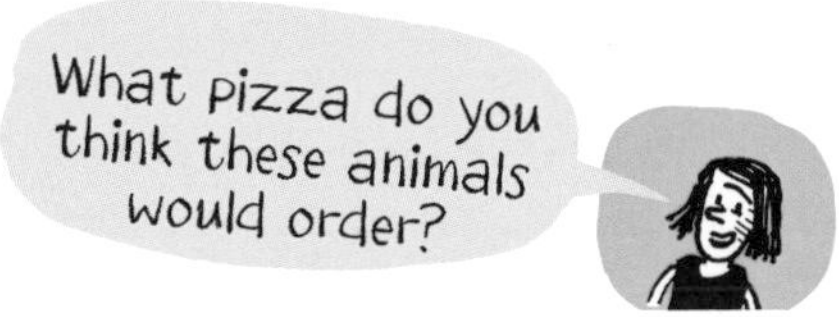
What pizza do you think these animals would order?

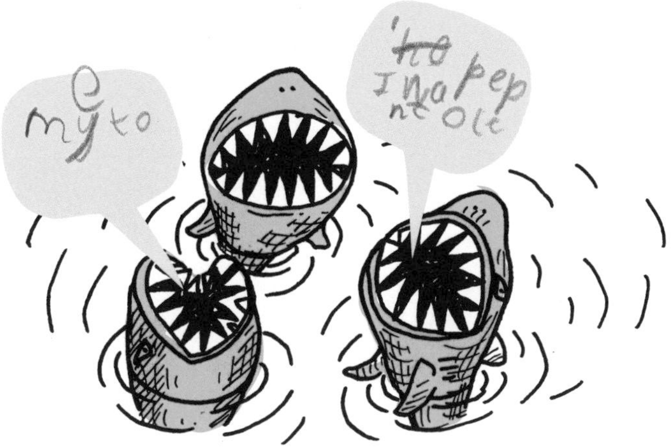
myto

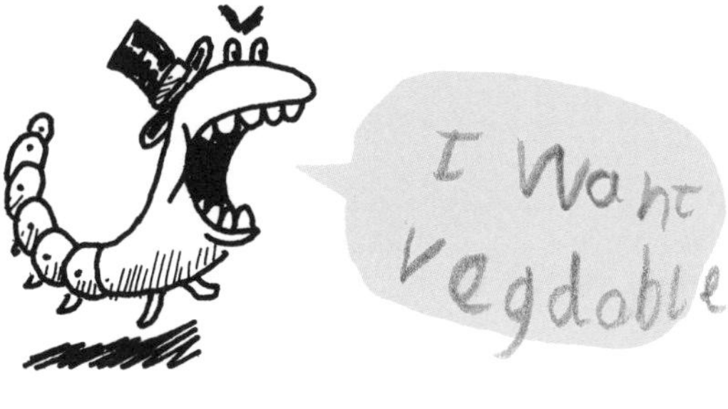
I Want vegdable

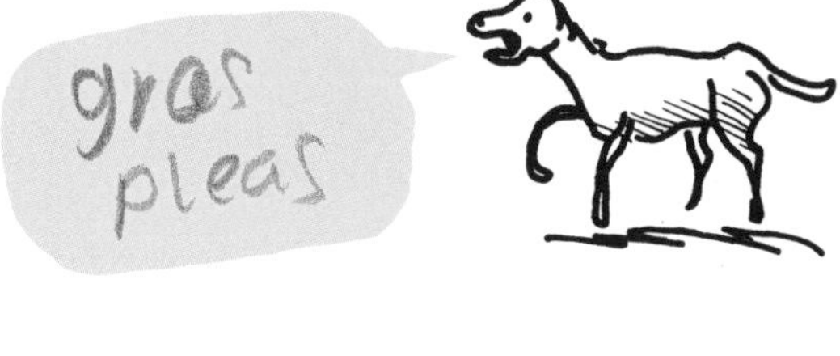
gras pleas

26-STOREY TREEHOUSE WORD SEARCH

W	O	O	D	E	N	H	E	A	D
I	T	O	I	D	U	T	S	L	U
C	A	L	O	O	P	C	N	O	M
E	T	S	L	L	U	A	R	Z	U
C	T	E	S	U	C	P	H	N	D
R	O	T	K	E	B	T	Y	O	F
E	O	A	A	Z	K	U	M	G	I
A	Y	R	T	A	P	R	E	R	G
M	I	I	E	M	R	E	A	O	H
T	S	P	L	A	T	D	E	G	T

WORD LIST

BULL
CAPTURED
GORGONZOLA
ICECREAM
MAZE
MUDFIGHT
PIRATES
POOL
SKATE
SPLAT
STUDIO
TATTOO
RHYME
WOODENHEAD

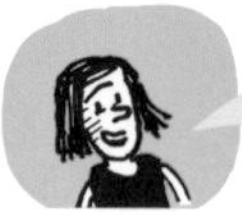

When you have finished there should be 13 letters left over that spell out something to do with the story.

Answers are on page 156.

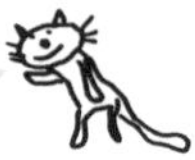

SOLUTION: _ _ _ _ _ _ _ _   _ _ _ _ _ _ _

COLOUR IN THE SHARK TANK

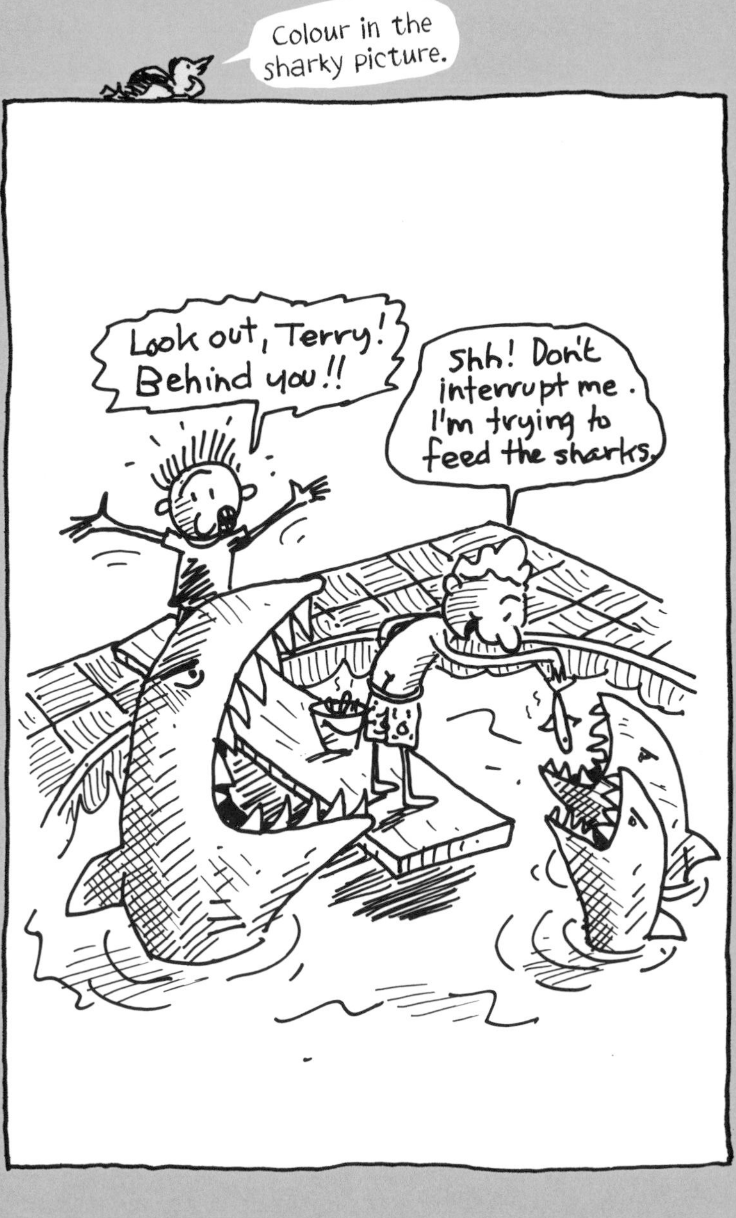
Colour in the sharky picture.
Look out, Terry! Behind you!!
Shh! Don't interrupt me. I'm trying to feed the sharks.

DRAWING TIME

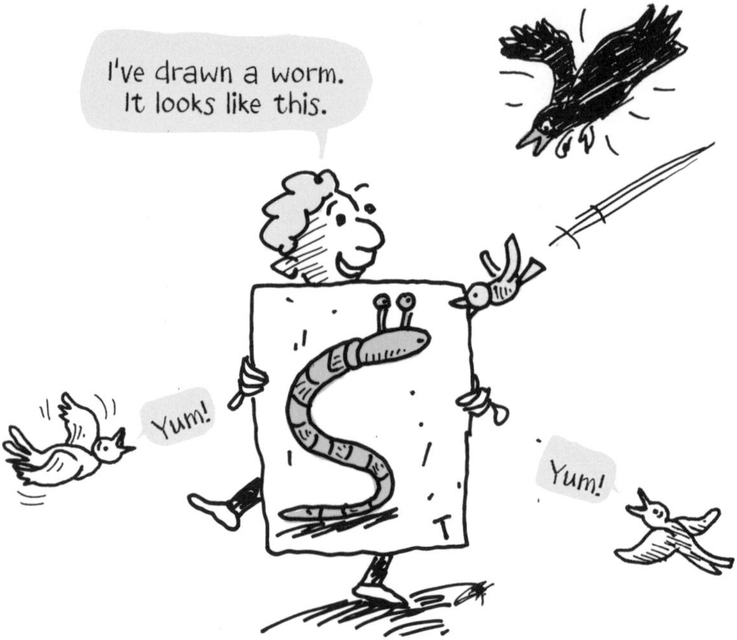
I've drawn a worm.
It looks like this.
Yum!
Yum!
T

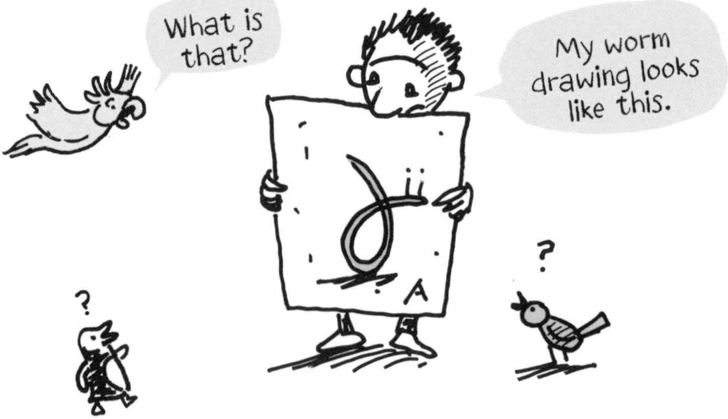
What is that?
My worm drawing looks like this.
A
?
?

DRAW A WORM

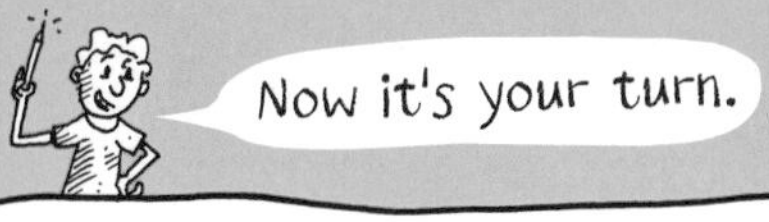
Now it's your turn.

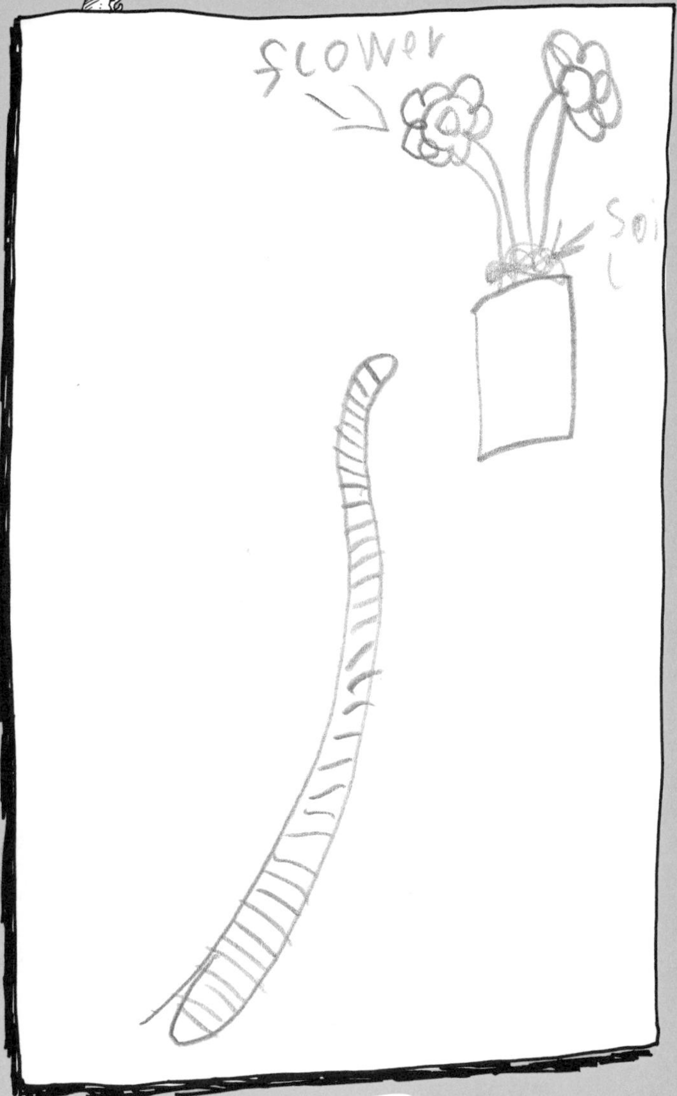
flower
Soil

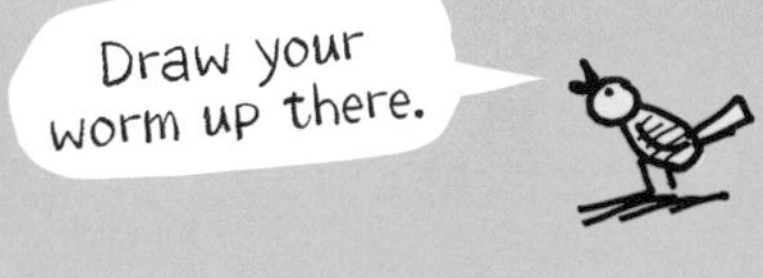
Draw your worm up there.

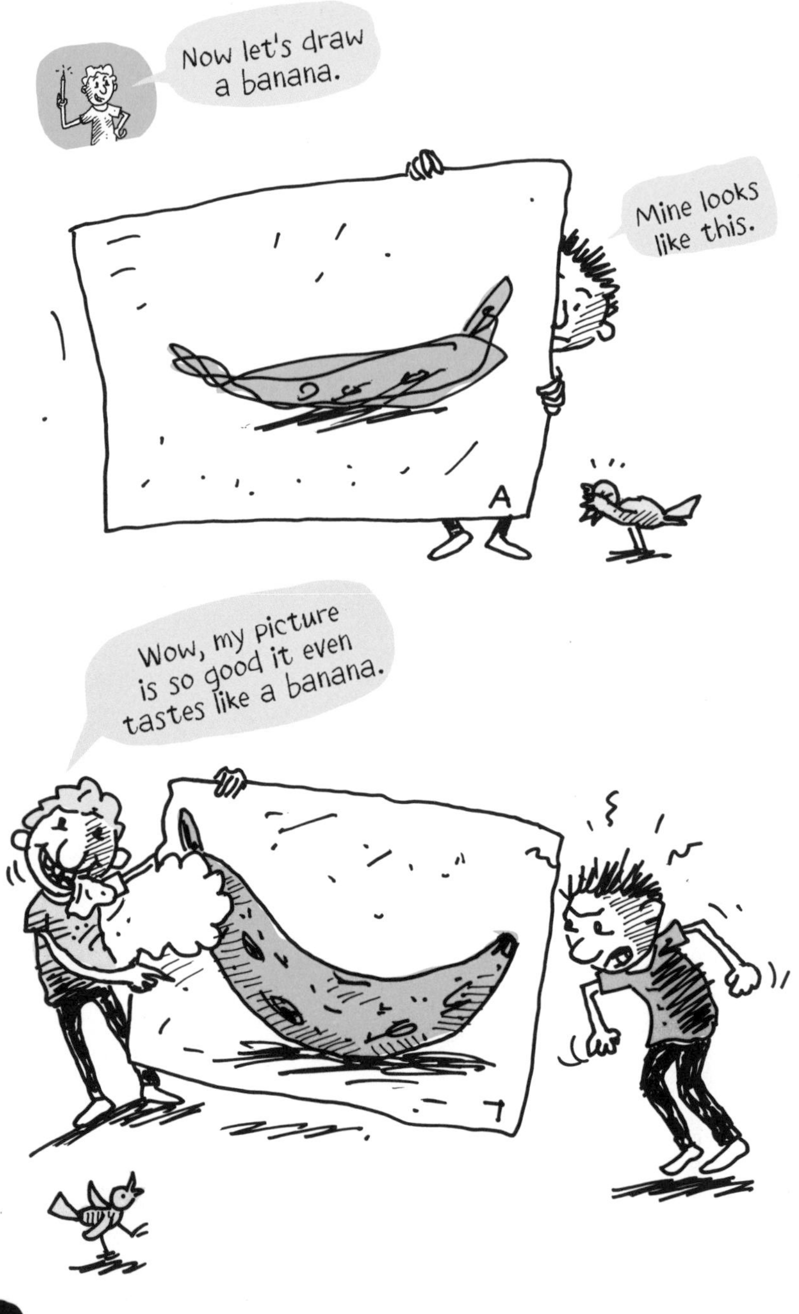
Now let's draw a banana.
Mine looks like this.
A
Wow, my picture is so good it even tastes like a banana.

DRAW A BANANA

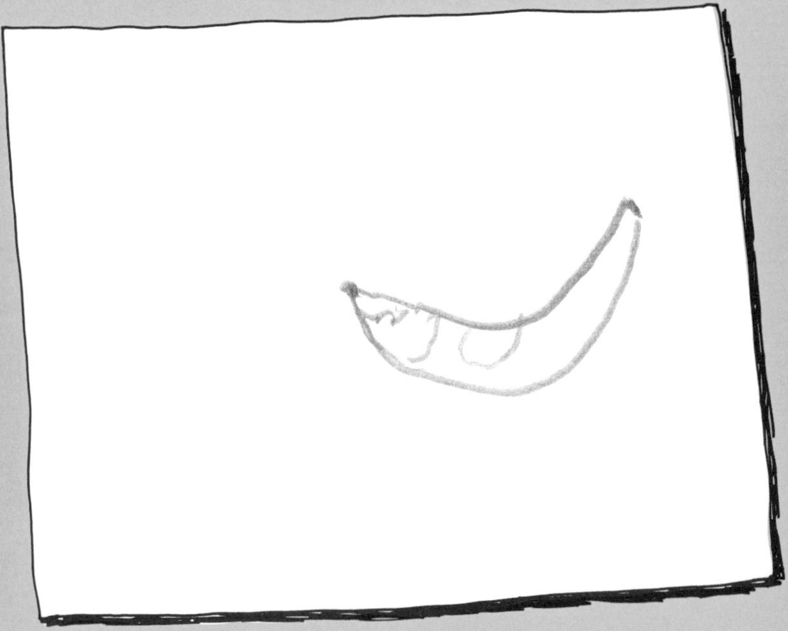

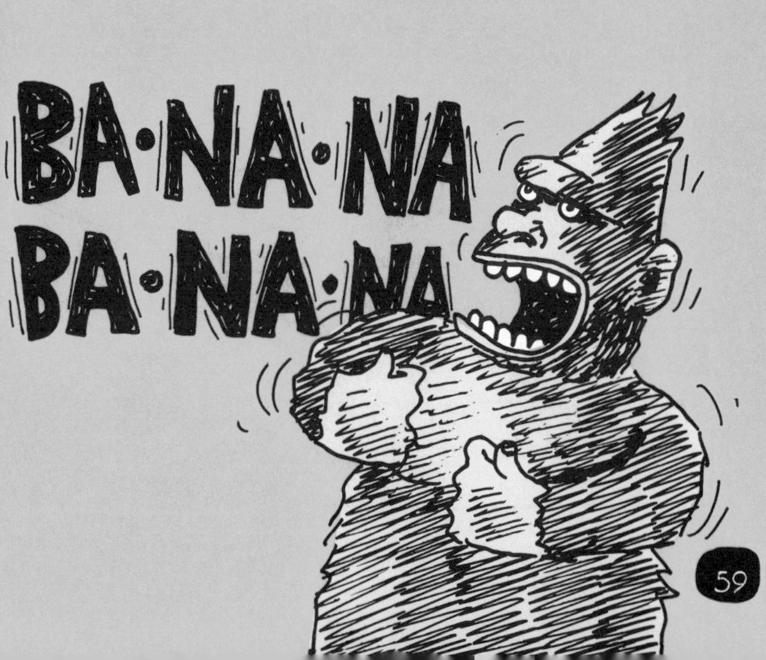
BA·NA·NA
BA·NA·NA

COLOUR IN CHEESELAND

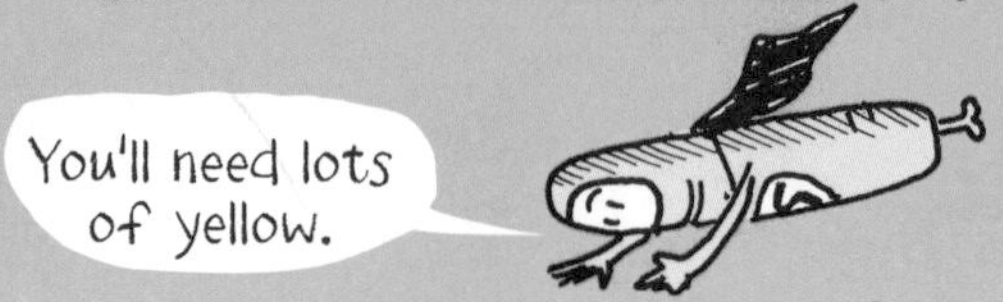
You'll need lots of yellow.

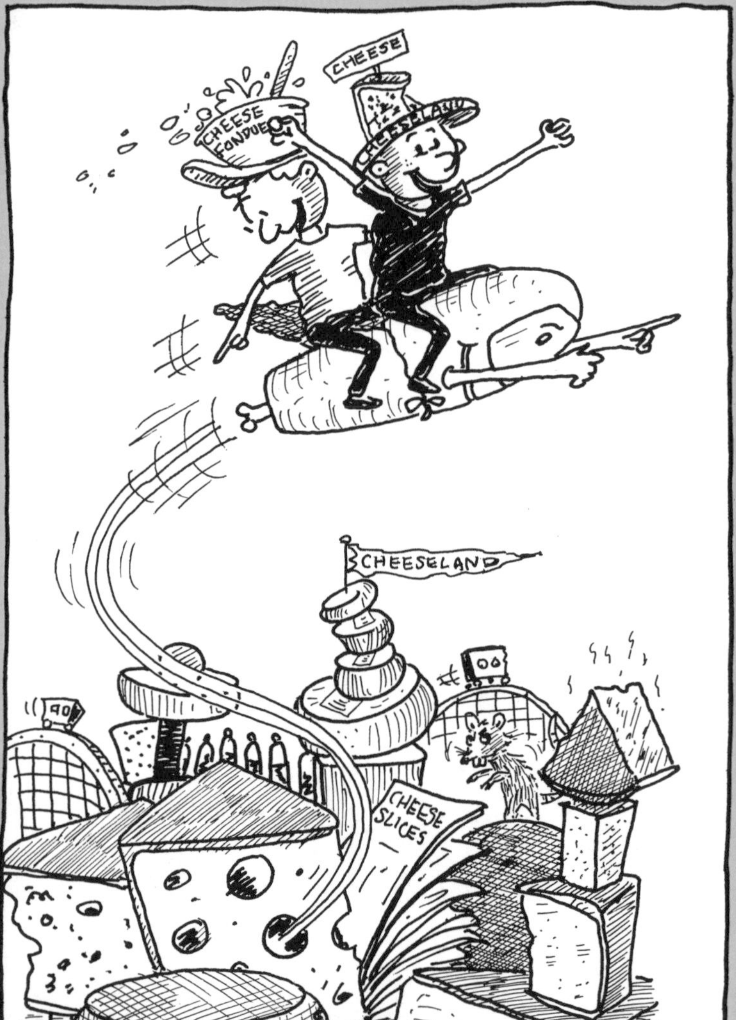
CHEESE
CHEESE FONDUE
CHEESELAND
CHEESELAND
CHEESE SLICES

39-STOREY TREEHOUSE WORD SEARCH

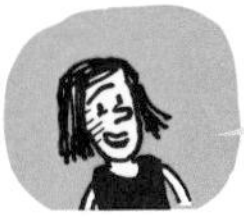

When you have finished there should be 12 letters left over that spell out something to do with the story.

WORD LIST

ANDY
BEETROOT
CHOCOLATE
MOON
ROCKET
SILKY
SPOONCIL
STUPIDO
TERRY
TRAMPOLINE
UNINVENT
VOLCANO
WATERFALL

Answers are on page 157.

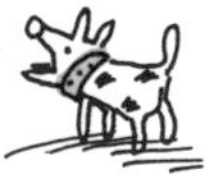

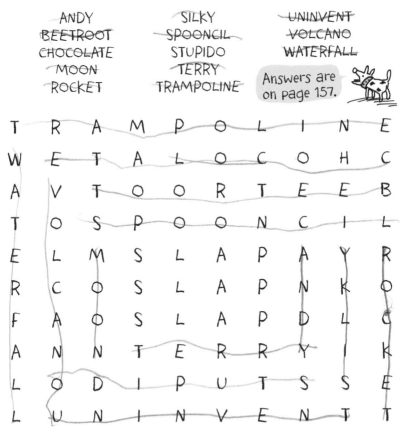

T	R	A	M	P	O	L	I	N	E
W	E	T	A	L	O	C	O	H	C
A	V	T	O	O	R	T	E	E	B
T	O	S	P	O	O	N	C	I	L
E	L	M	S	L	A	P	A	Y	R
R	C	O	S	L	A	P	N	K	O
F	A	O	S	L	A	P	D	L	C
A	N	N	T	E	R	R	Y	I	K
L	O	D	I	P	U	T	S	S	E
L	U	N	I	N	V	E	N	T	T

SOLUTION: _ _ _ _   _ _ _ _ _   _ _ _ _ _

TATTOO TIME

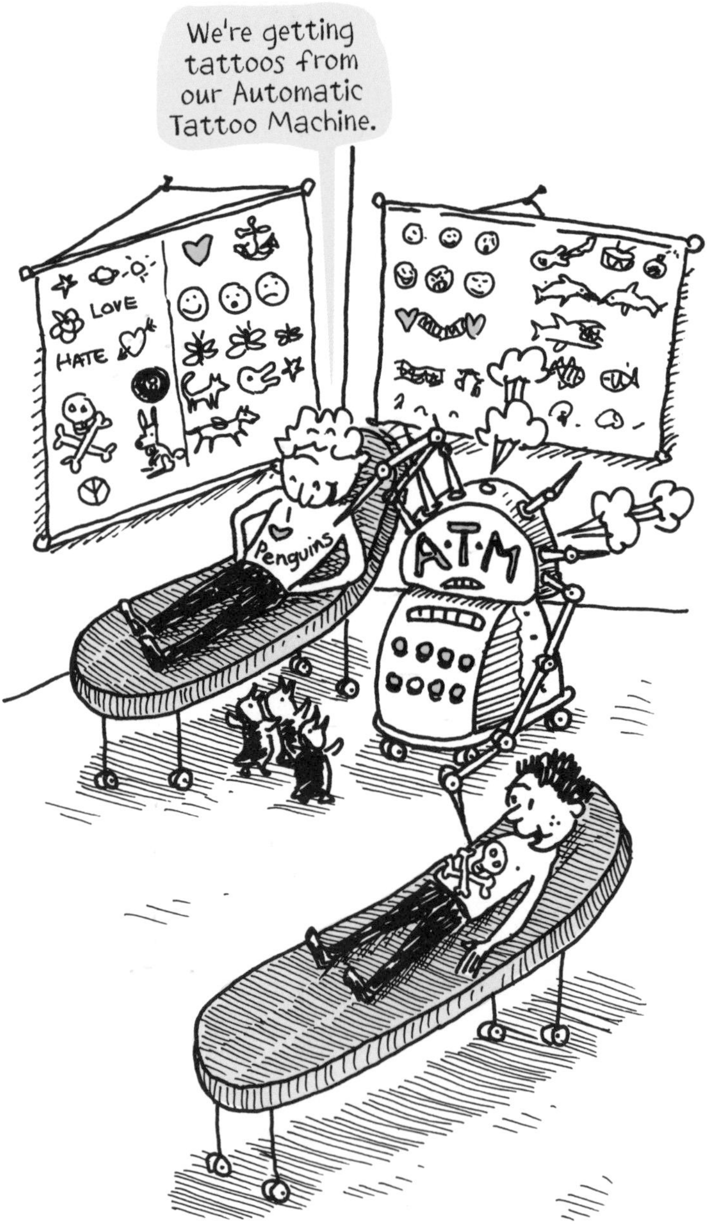
We're getting tattoos from our Automatic Tattoo Machine.
LOVE
HATE
Penguins
A·T·M

DESIGN YOUR OWN TATTOO

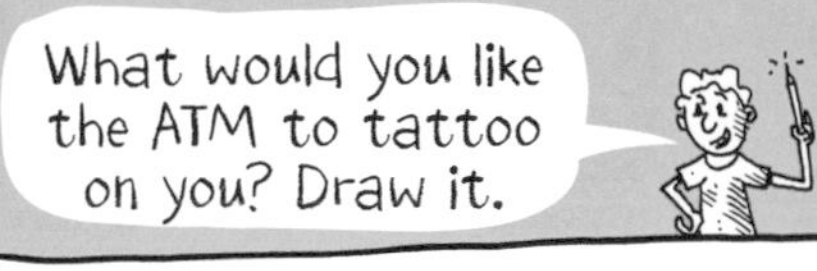
What would you like the ATM to tattoo on you? Draw it.

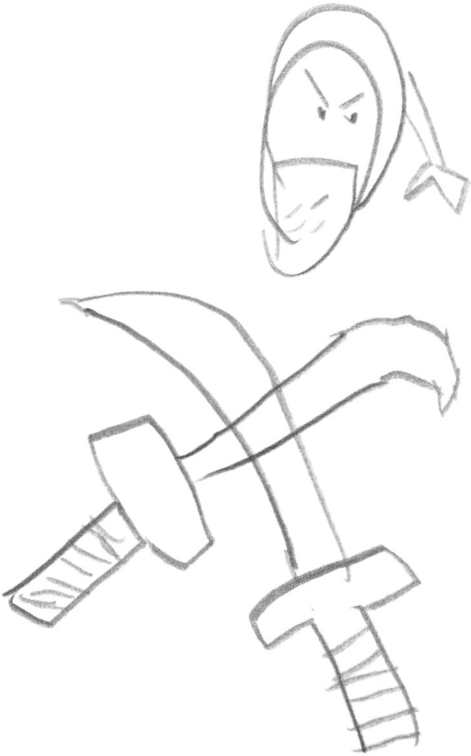

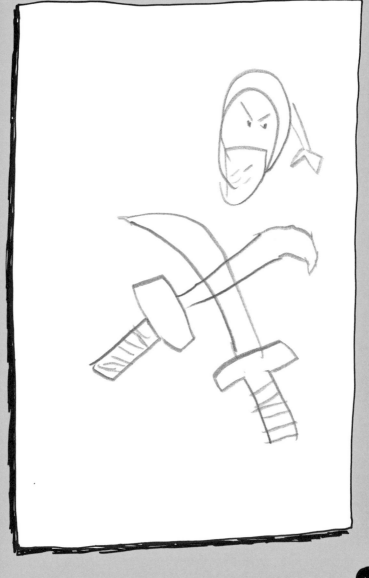

SPOT THE DIFFERENCE

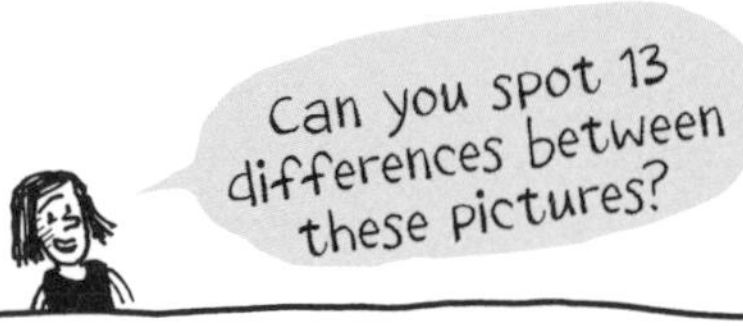
Can you spot 13 differences between these pictures?

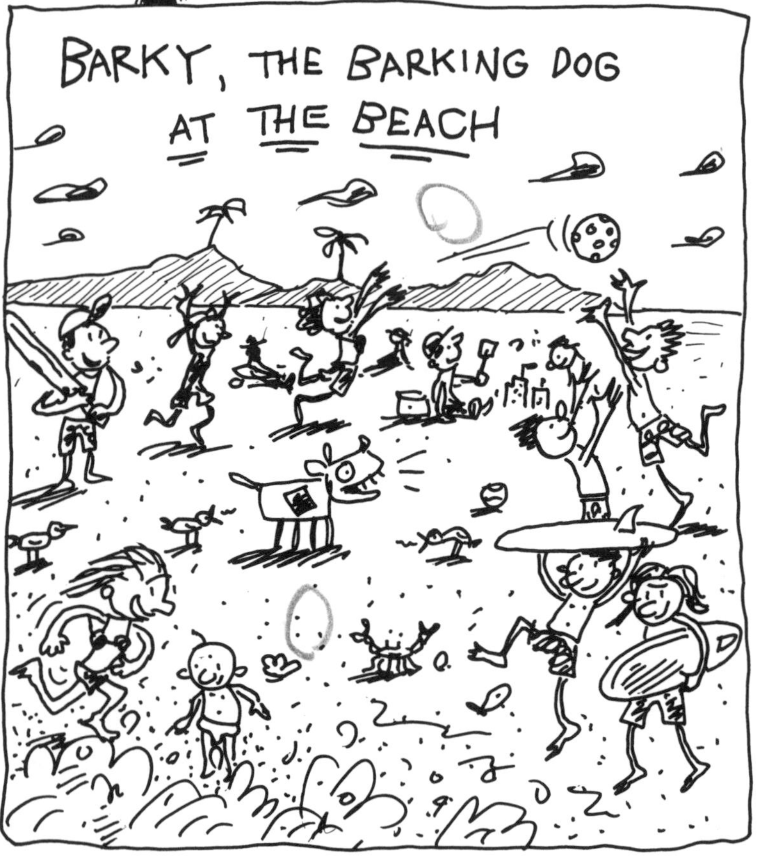
BARKY, THE BARKING DOG
AT THE BEACH

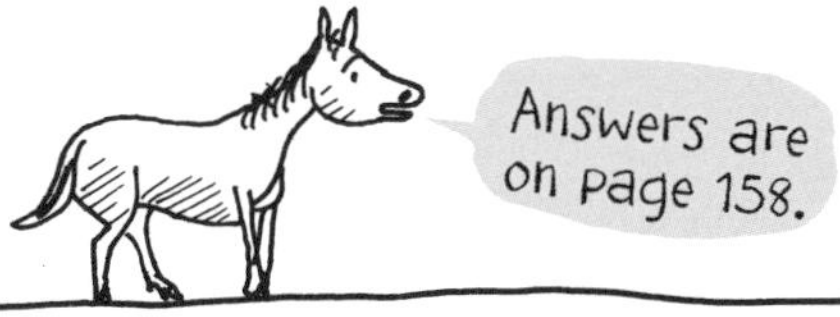
Answers are on page 158.

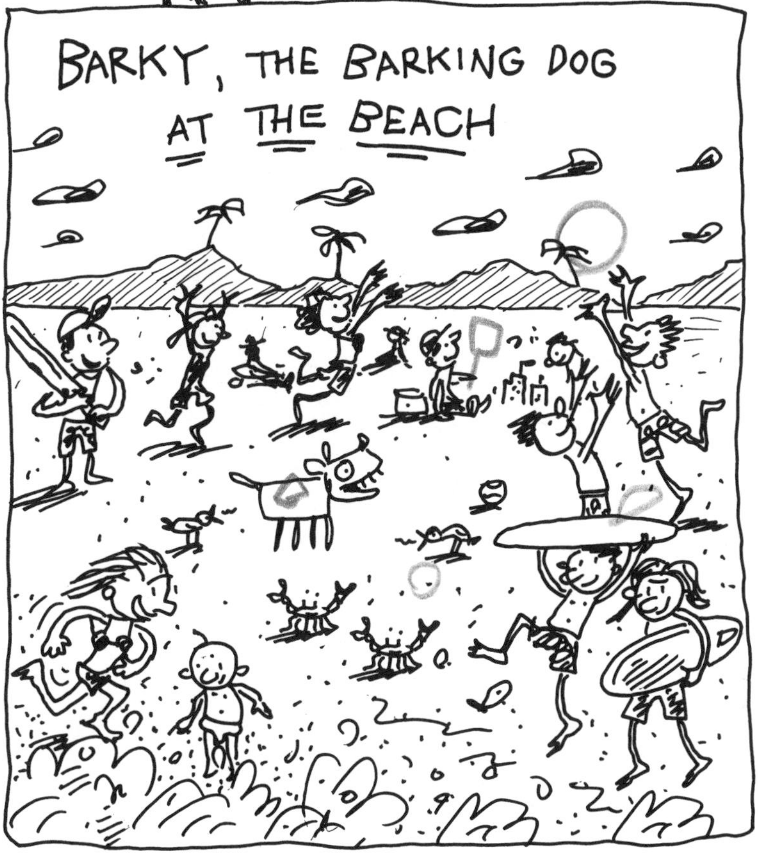
BARKY, THE BARKING DOG
AT THE BEACH

SUPERFINGER TIME

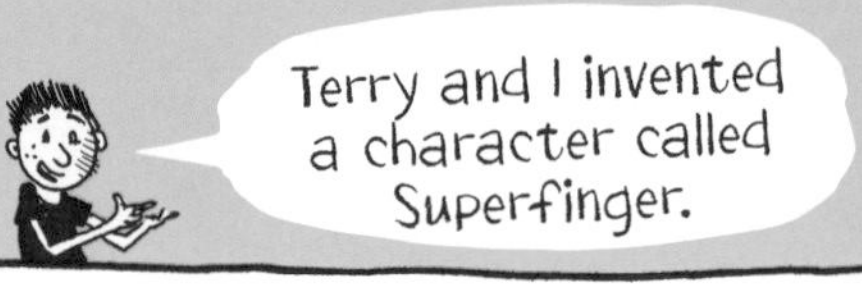
Terry and I invented a character called Superfinger.

Once upon a time there was a finger. But it was no ordinary finger ... it was a Superfinger!

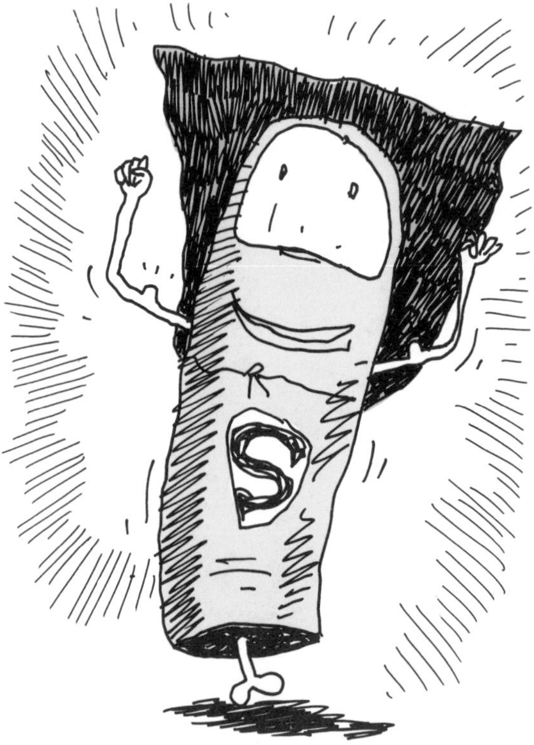

Superfinger solves problems that need finger-based solutions—he can help you tie a bow, point you in the right direction and help you clear a blocked nose. Any time you need an extra finger, Superfinger is there!

CREATE A SUPERHERO

Draw your own Superhero.

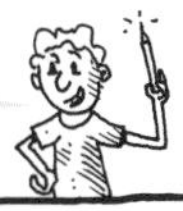

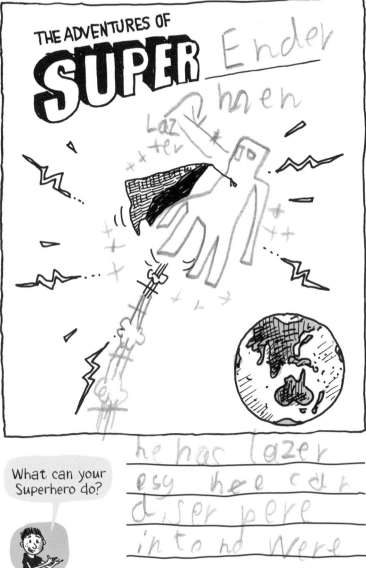

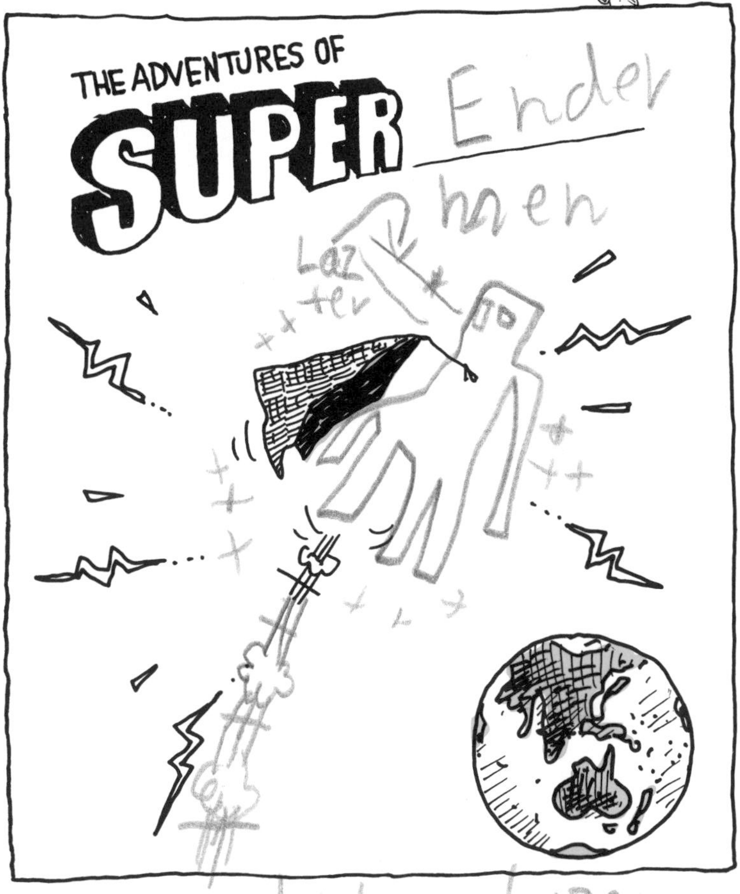
THE ADVENTURES OF
SUPER Ender

What can your Superhero do?

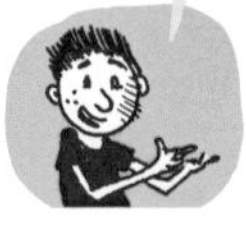

he has lazer
esy hee can
diser pere
into no were

REMEMBERING TIME

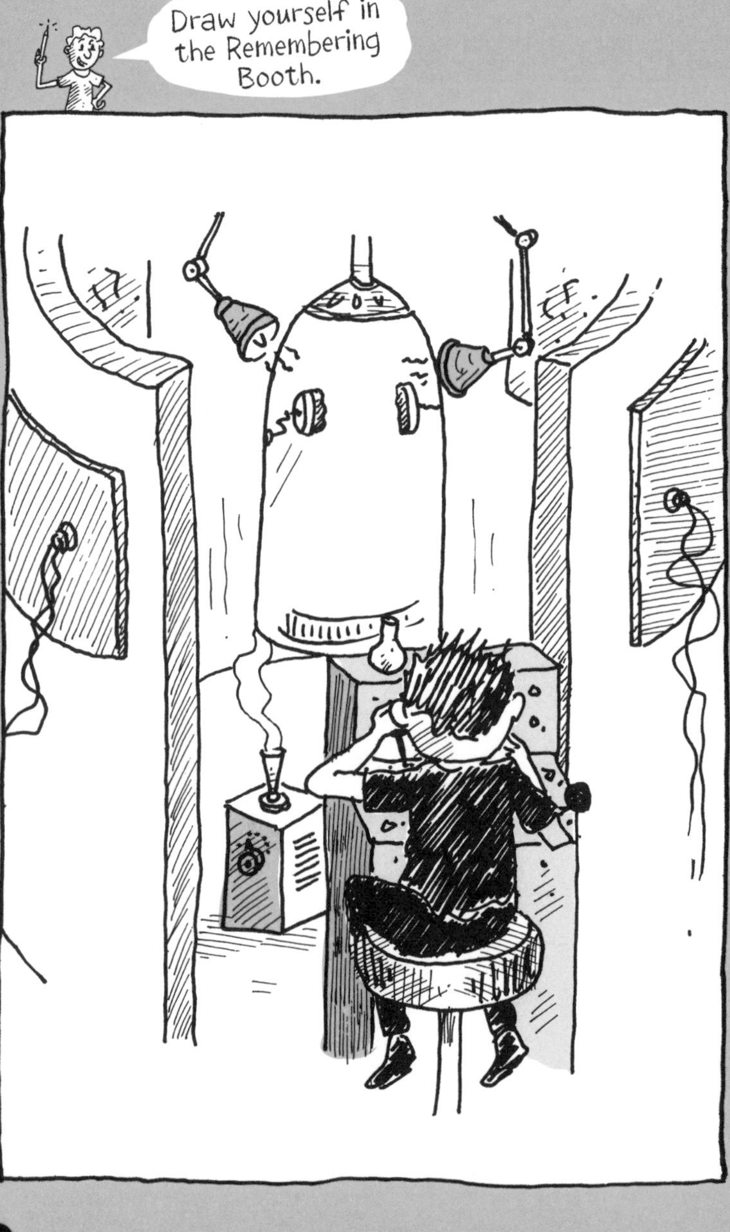
Draw yourself in the Remembering Booth.

I REMEMBER ...

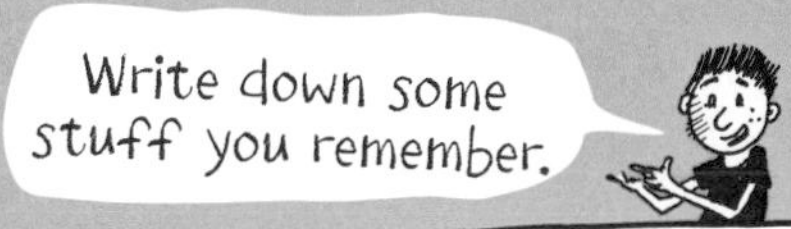
Write down some stuff you remember.

A fun holiday I had was gowingto italy

A time I was embarrassed was

A funny thing that happened to me was

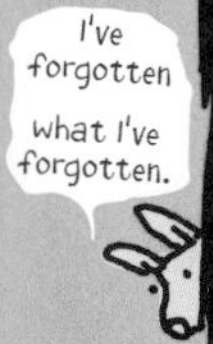
I've forgotten what I've forgotten.

A time I was really scared was

TREEHOUSE TRIVIA

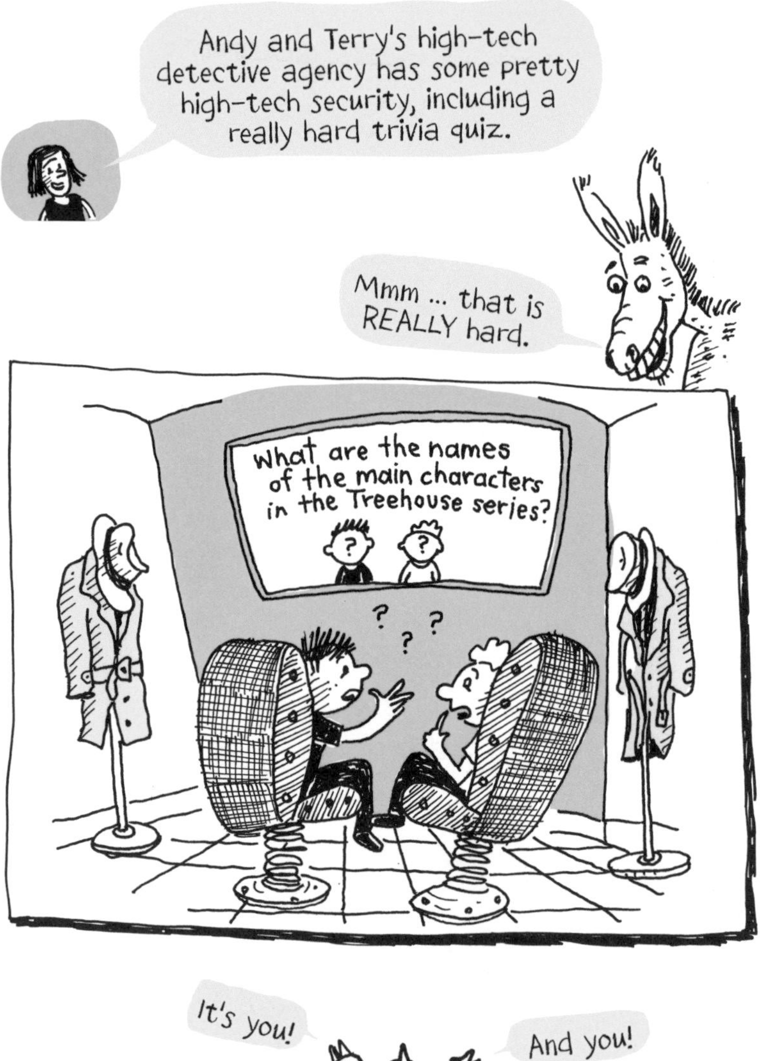
Andy and Terry's high-tech detective agency has some pretty high-tech security, including a really hard trivia quiz.
Mmm ... that is REALLY hard.
What are the names of the main characters in the Treehouse series?

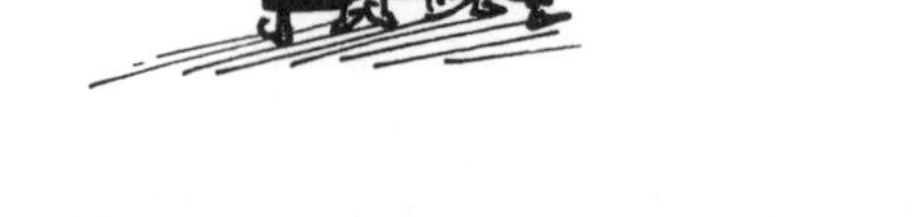
It's you!
And you!

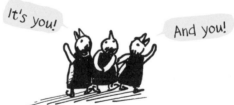

How many of these trivia questions can you answer?

1. What is the name of the sea monster Terry fell in love with?

   ~~man~~ er maidai

2. What is the worst job Andy and Terry ever had?

   Si ~~baby siting~~ ~~ying~~
   for monkey s at the soo

3. What is Terry's favourite TV show?

   barky

4. What colour did Terry paint Silky?

   gelew

5. What is the name of Andy and Terry's publisher?

   mr bignose

6. What is the name of the pirate who captured Andy, Terry and me?

   capten wooden head

7. How many flavours of ice-cream are there in Edward Scooperhands' ice-cream parlour?

   ~~1000~~ 78

Answers are on page 159.

MISSING PET POSTER

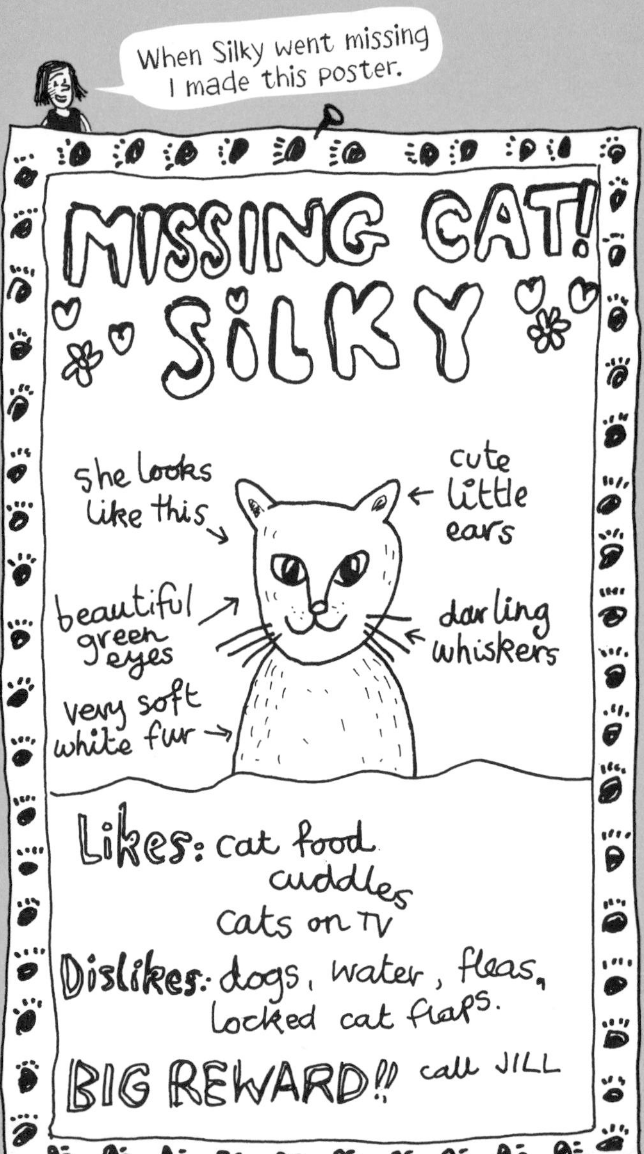
When Silky went missing I made this poster.
MISSING CAT!
SILKY
she looks like this
cute little ears
beautiful green eyes
darling whiskers
very soft white fur
Likes: cat food
cuddles
cats on TV
Dislikes: dogs, water, fleas, locked cat flaps.
BIG REWARD!! call JILL

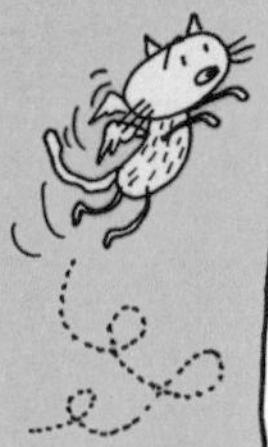

Make your own missing pet poster. It could be for a pet you have or a made-up one.

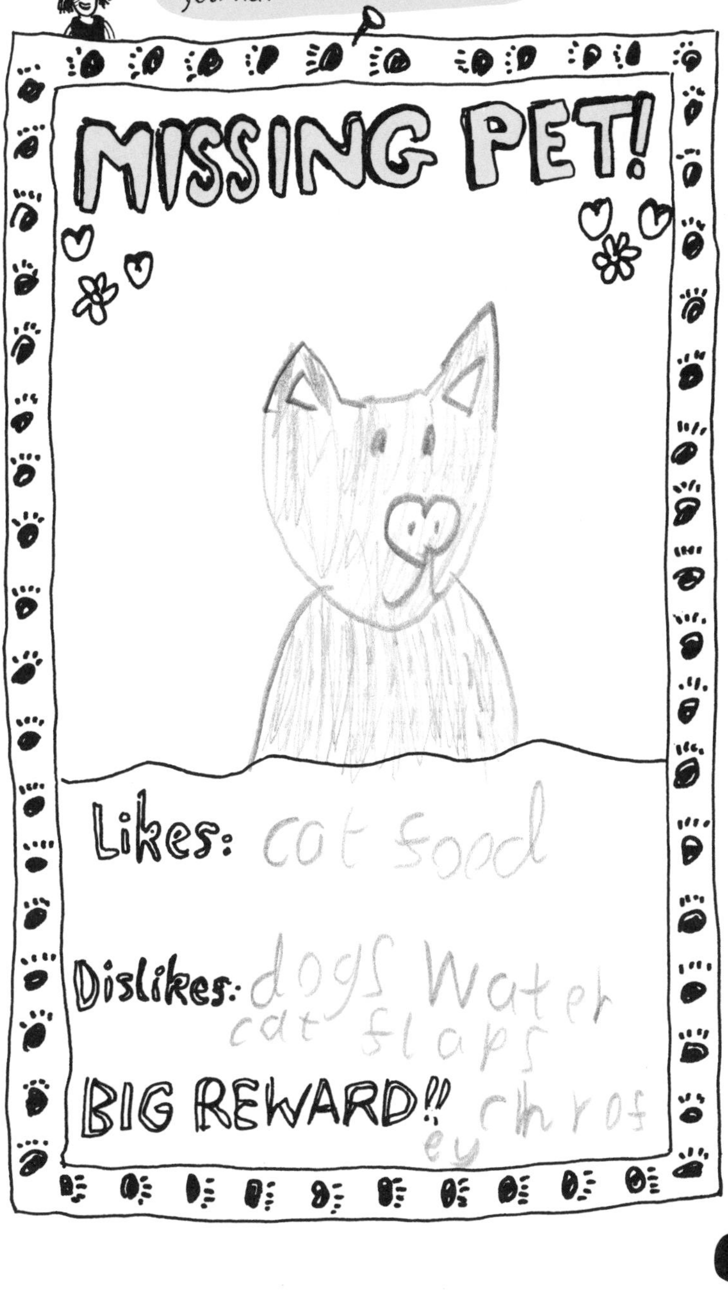

MISSING PET!
Likes: cat food
Dislikes: dogs water cat flaps
BIG REWARD!!

SPOT THE DIFFERENCE

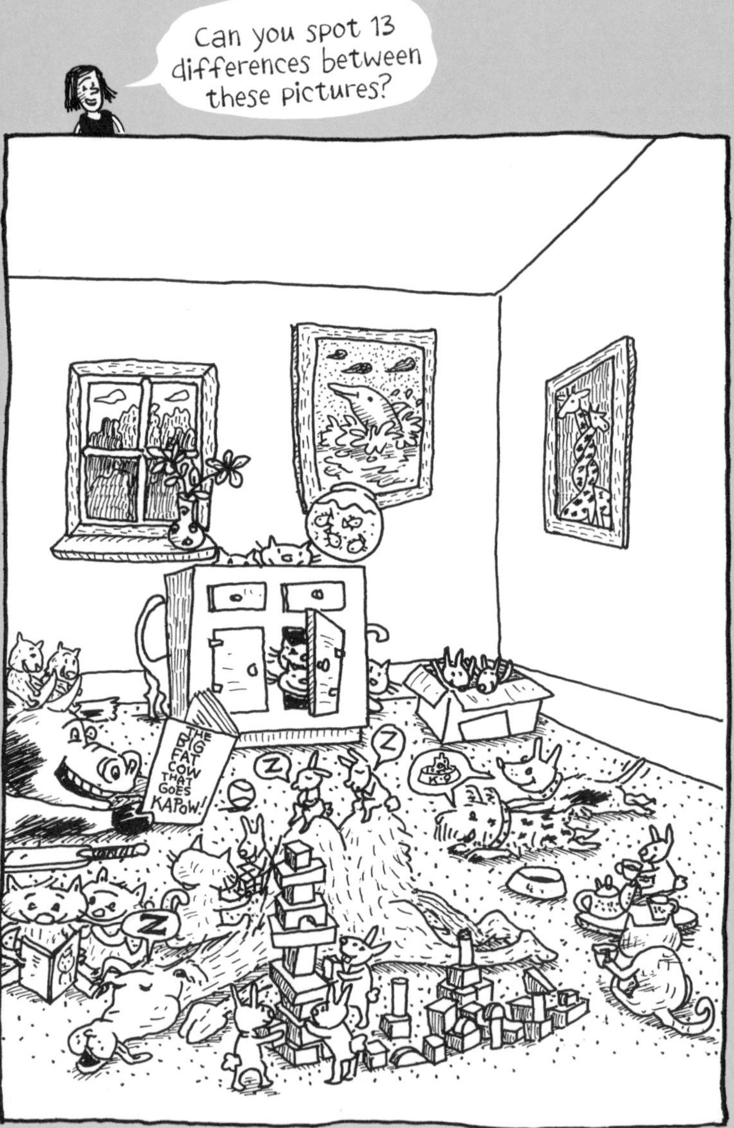

Can you spot 13 differences between these pictures?
THE BIG FAT COW THAT GOES KAPOW!
Z
Z
Z

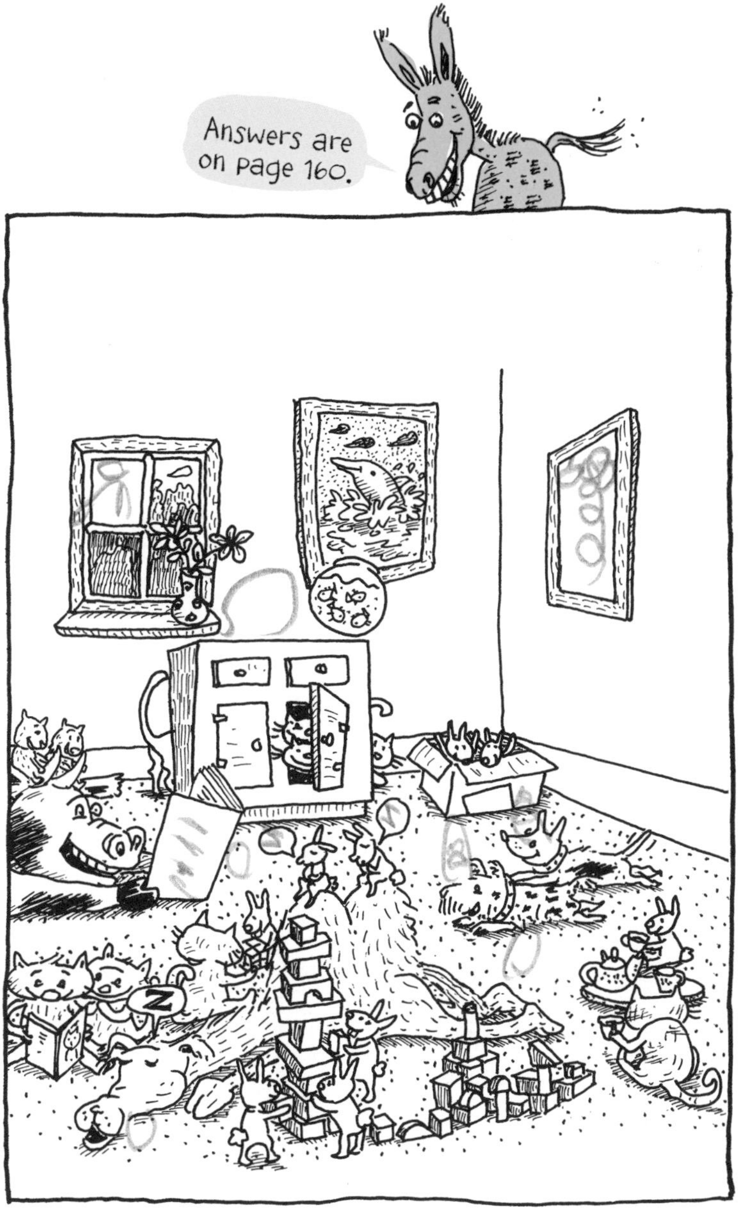
Answers are on page 160.

52-STOREY TREEHOUSE WORD SEARCH

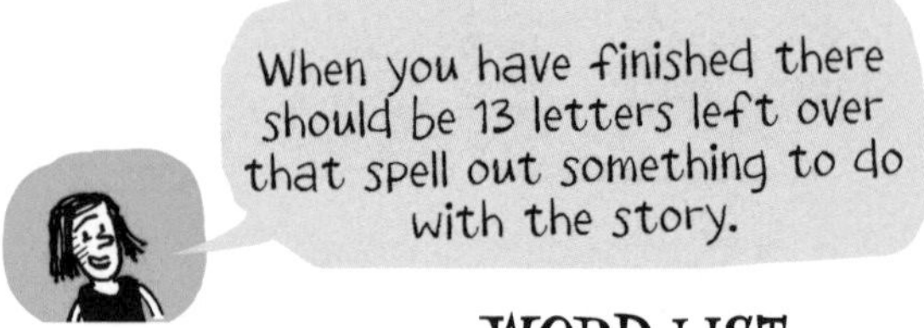
When you have finished there should be 13 letters left over that spell out something to do with the story.

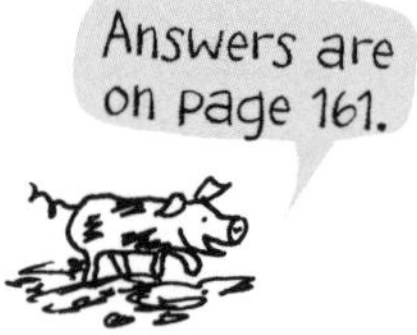
Answers are on page 161.

WORD LIST

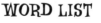

ANDY
BIG
BUTTERFLY
DETECTIVES
DISGUISE
EGGPLANT
NINJA
NOSE
PATTY
POTATO
PRINCE
REMEMBER
SNAILS
TERRY

D	E	T	E	C	T	I	V	E	S
E	P	E	C	N	I	R	P	Y	E
G	O	N	B	I	G	D	A	L	R
G	T	S	O	T	V	I	P	F	E
P	A	N	N	S	E	S	A	R	M
L	T	A	I	Y	E	G	T	E	E
A	O	I	N	D	G	U	T	T	M
N	E	L	J	N	T	I	Y	T	B
T	A	S	A	A	B	S	L	U	E
E	T	E	R	R	Y	E	S	B	R

SOLUTION: _ _ _   _ _ _ _ _ _ _ _ _ _

VEGETABLE COLOURING TIME

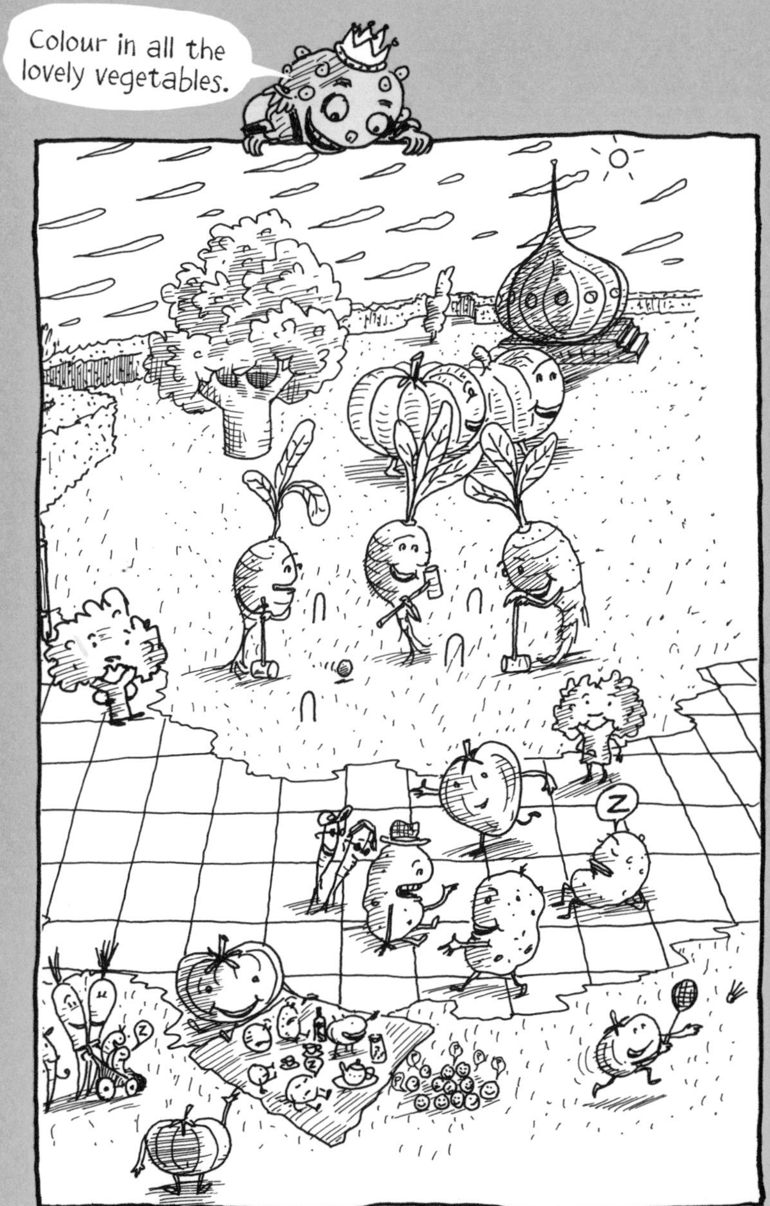
Colour in all the lovely vegetables.

MIXED-UP ANIMALS

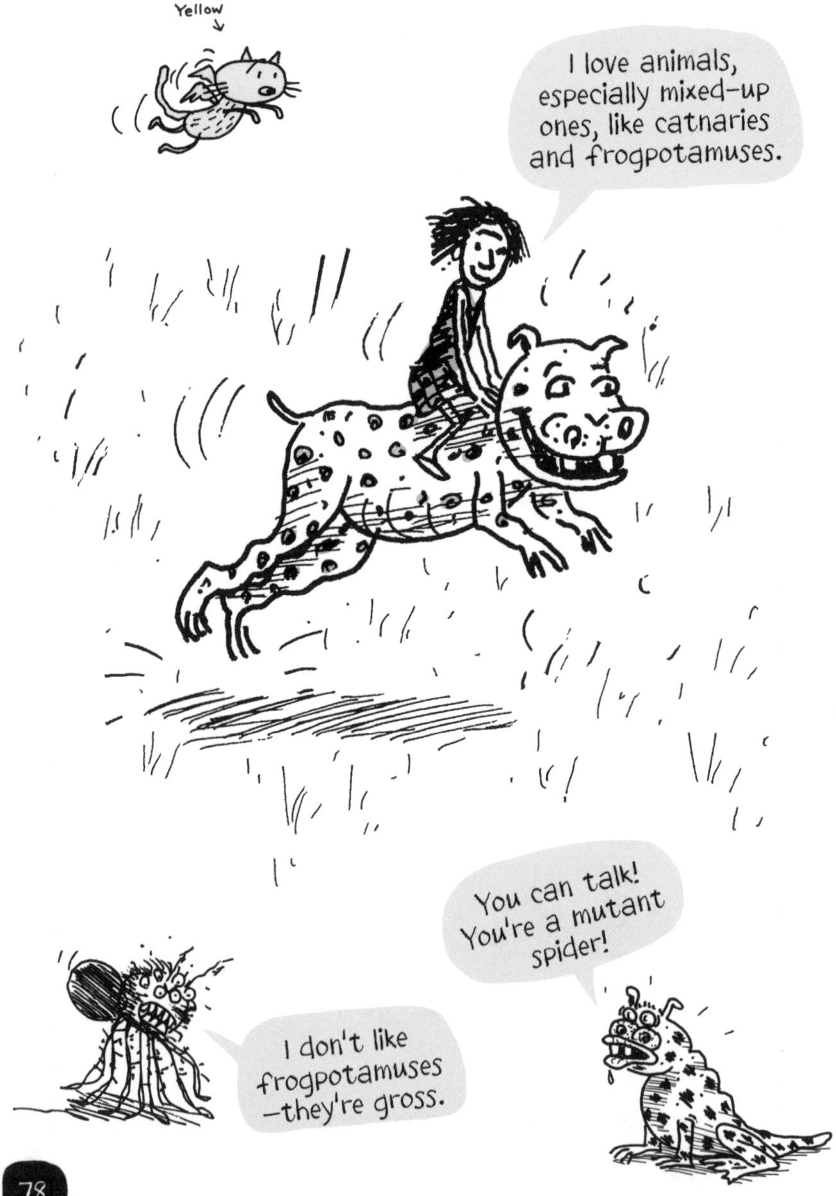
Yellow
I love animals, especially mixed-up ones, like catnaries and frogpotamuses.
You can talk! You're a mutant spider!
I don't like frogpotamuses –they're gross.

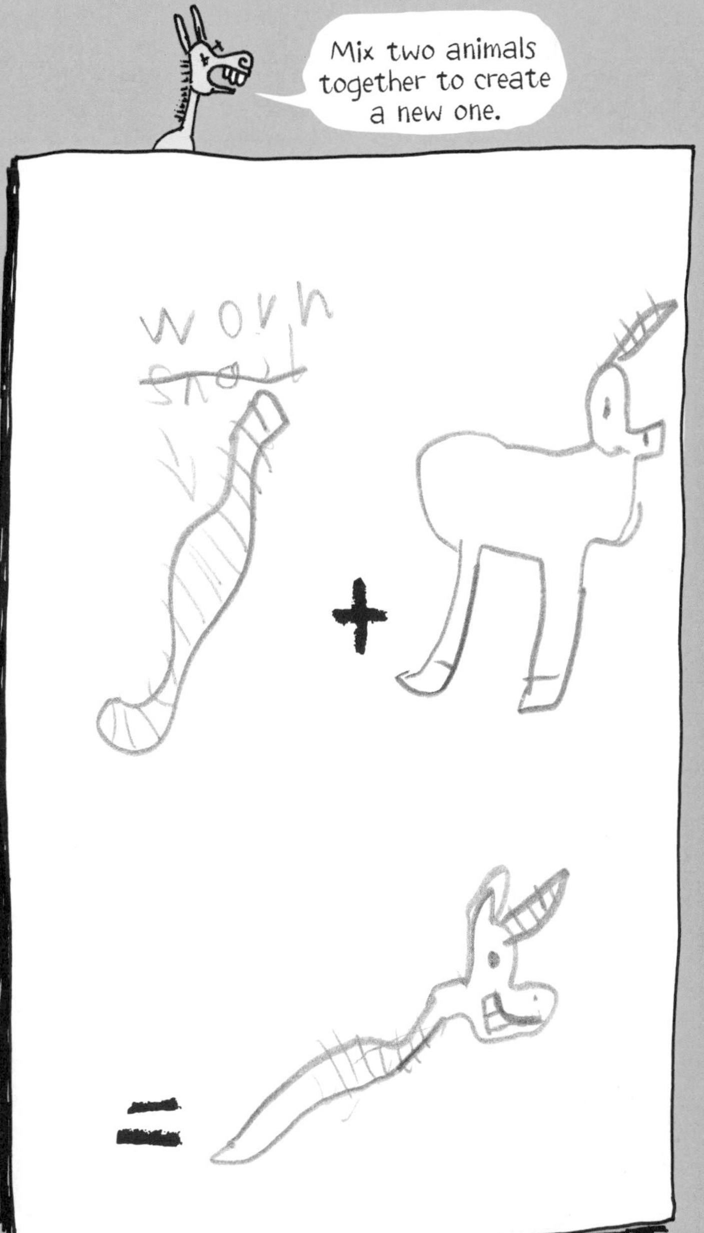
Mix two animals together to create a new one.
worn
~~snail~~
+
=

PET MAKE-OVER TIME

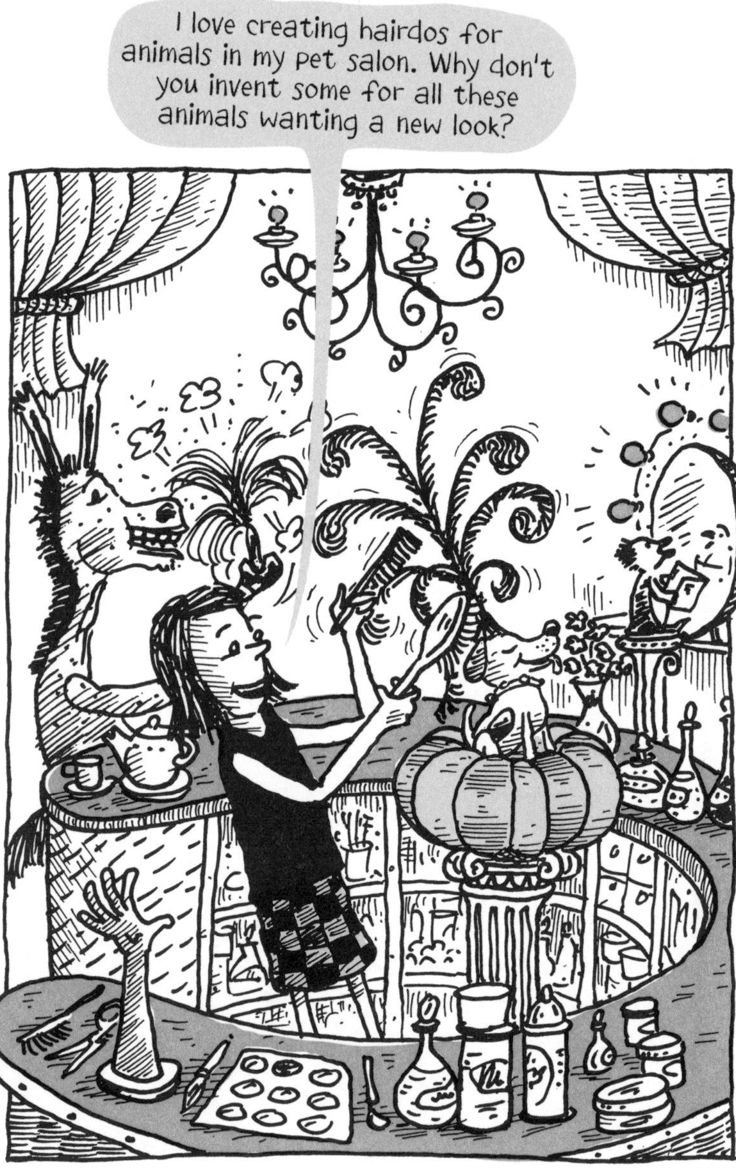
I love creating hairdos for animals in my pet salon. Why don't you invent some for all these animals wanting a new look?

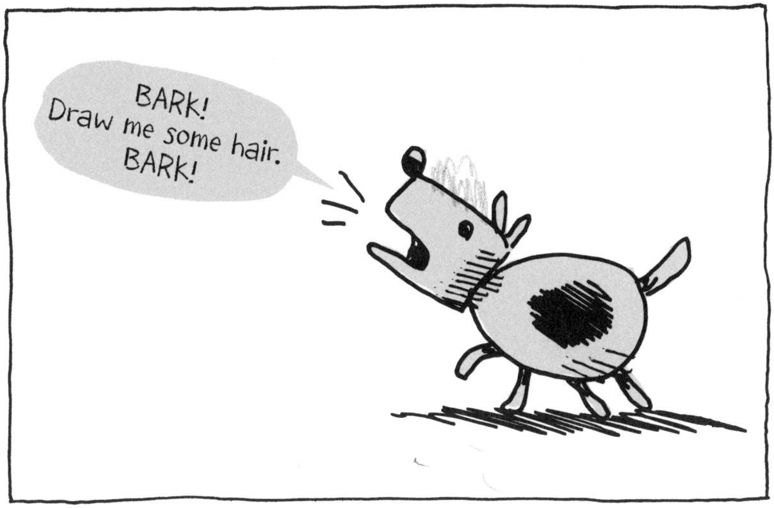
BARK! Draw me some hair. BARK!

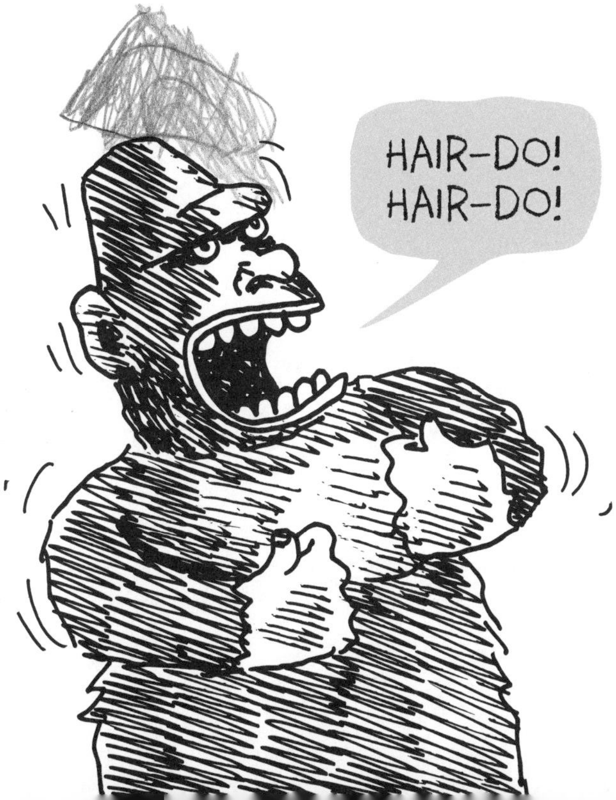
HAIR-DO! HAIR-DO!

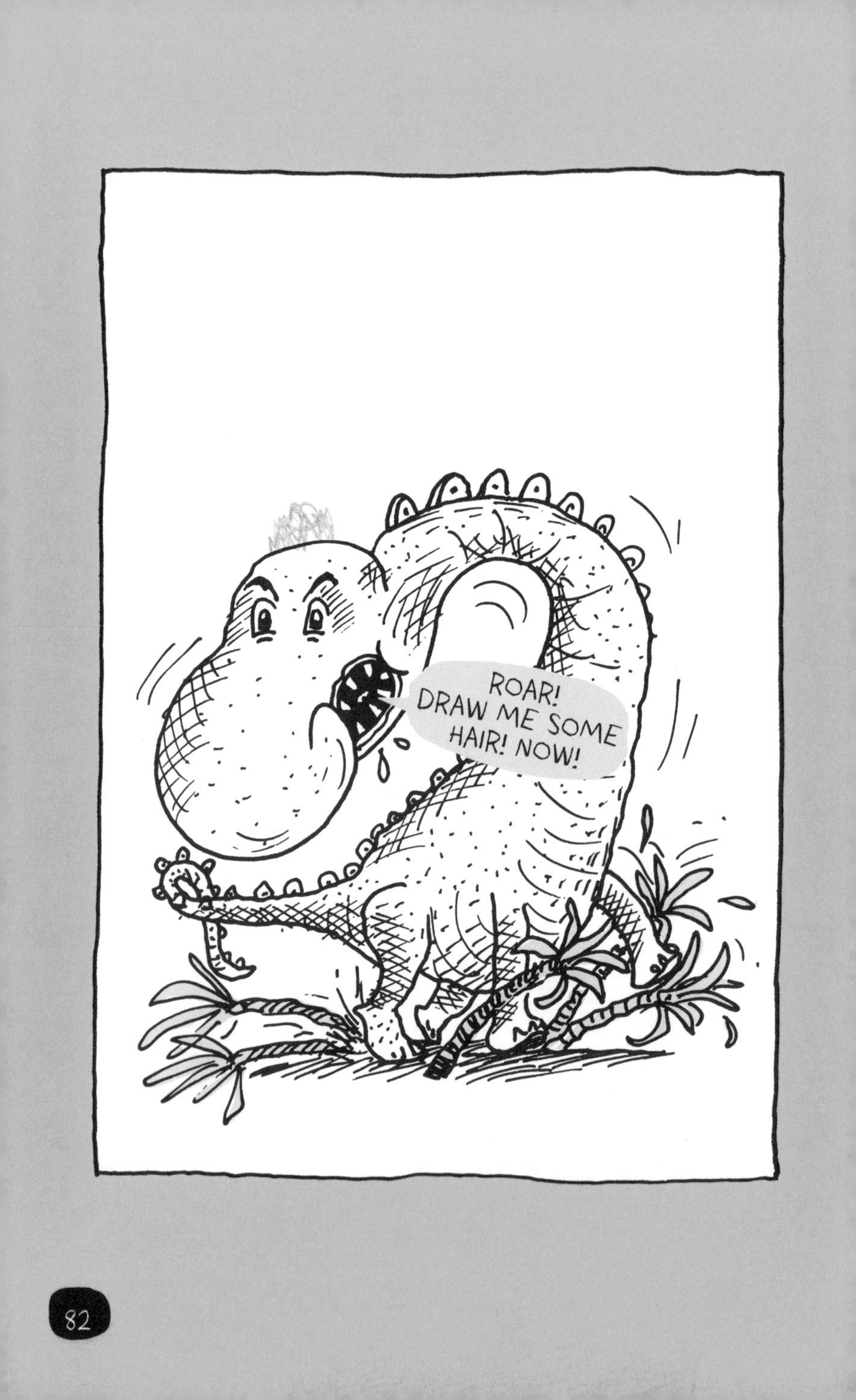
ROAR! DRAW ME SOME HAIR! NOW!

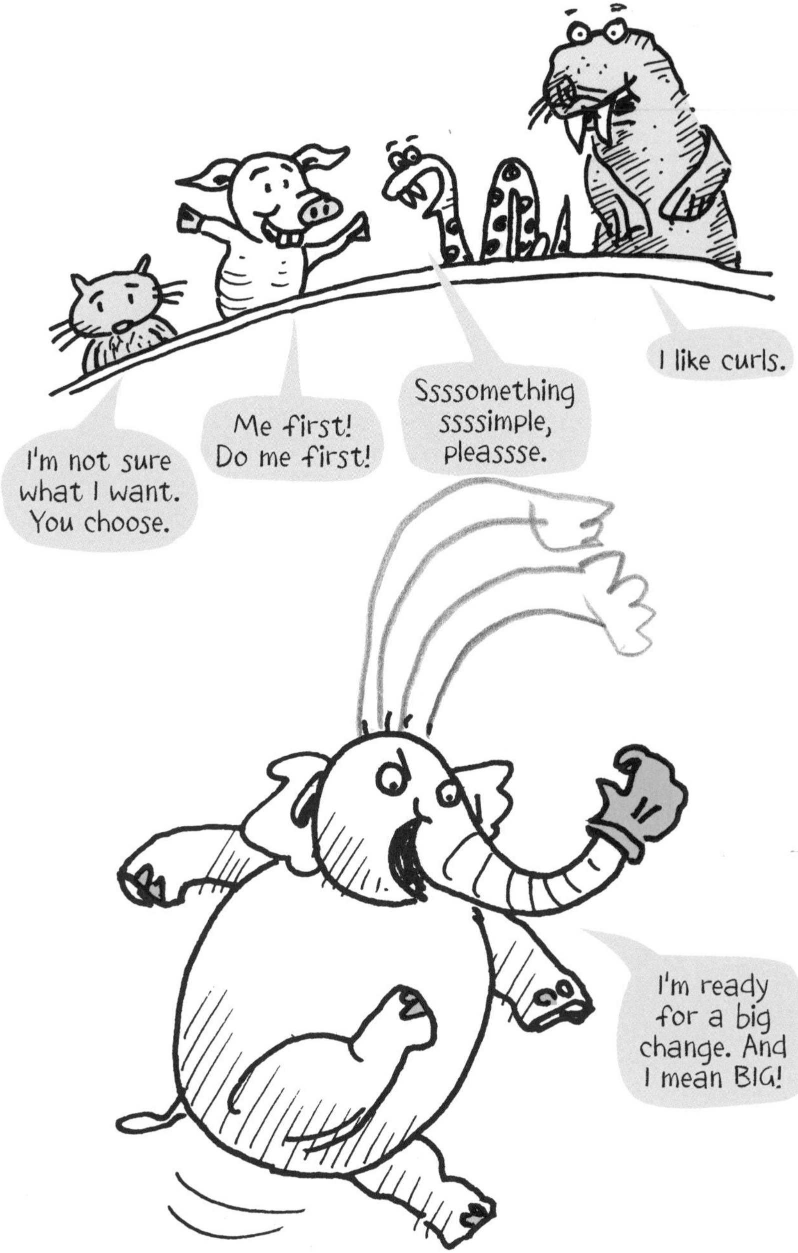
I'm not sure what I want. You choose.
Me first! Do me first!
Ssssomething sssssimple, pleassse.
I like curls.
I'm ready for a big change. And I mean BIG!

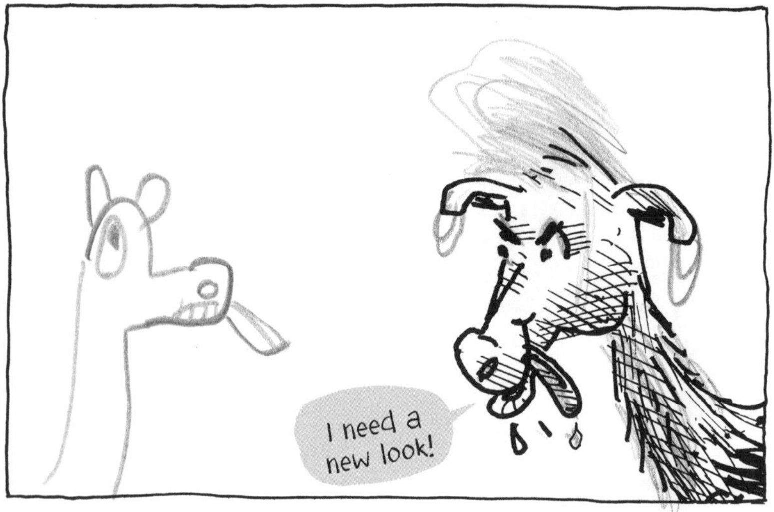
I need a new look!

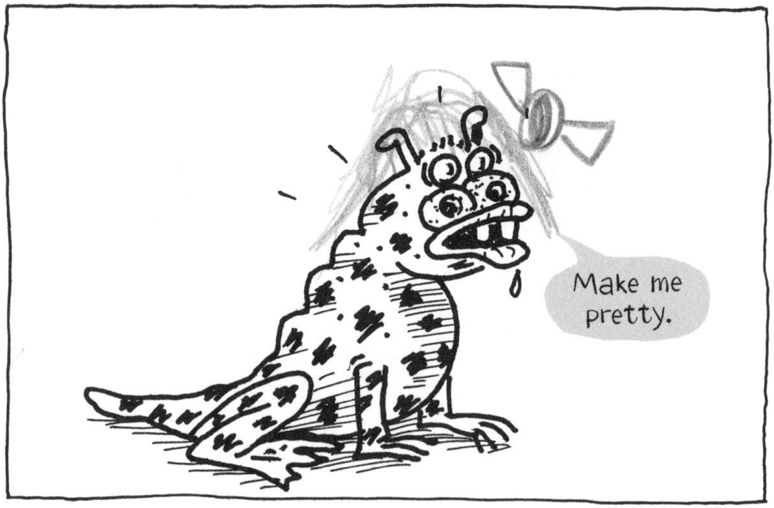
Make me pretty.

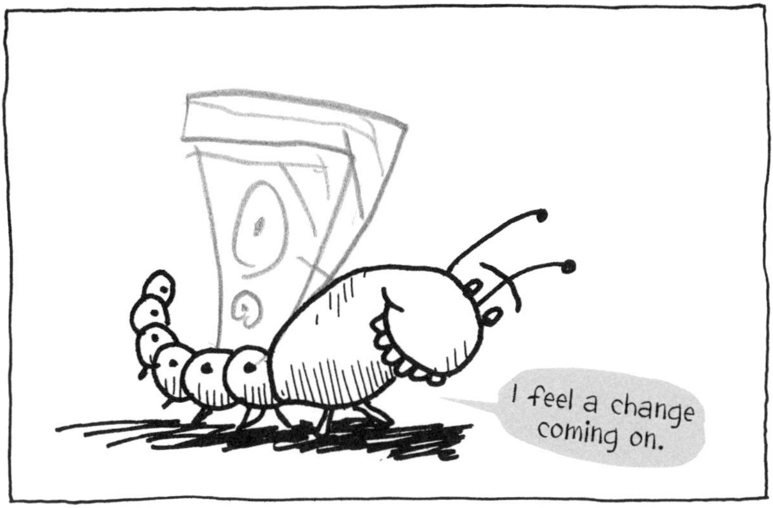
I feel a change coming on.

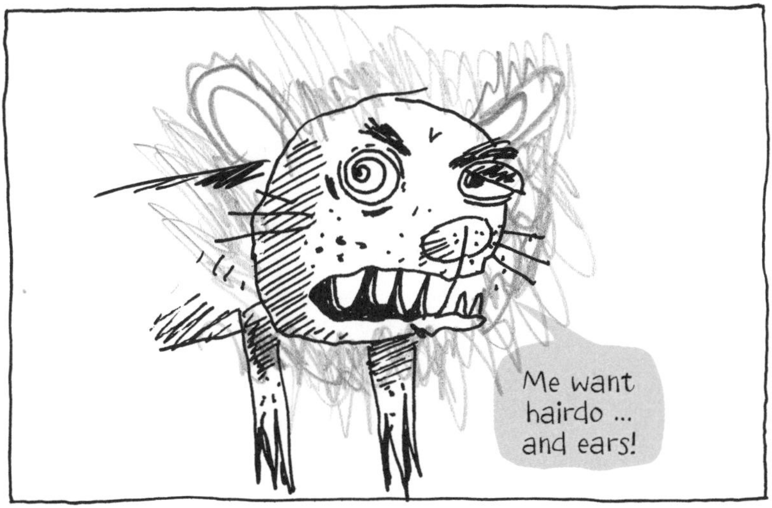
Me want hairdo ... and ears!

SPOT THE DIFFERENCE

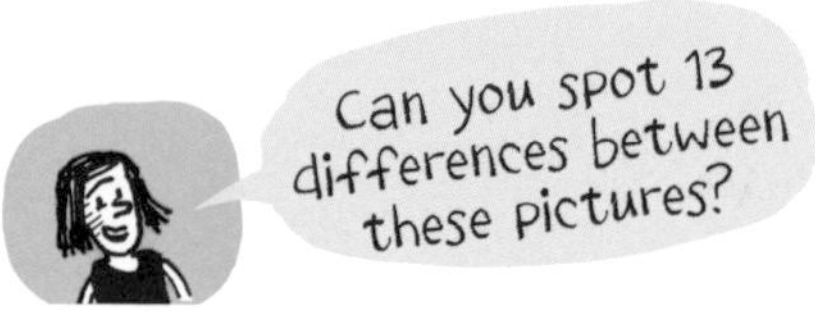
Can you spot 13 differences between these pictures?

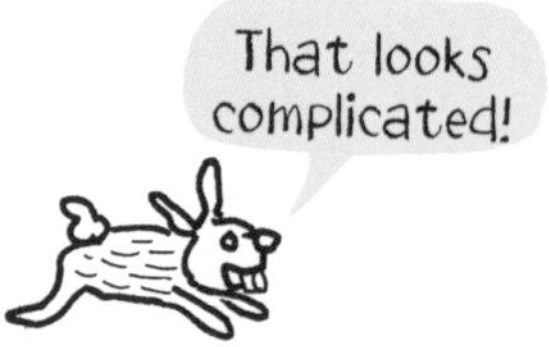
That looks complicated!

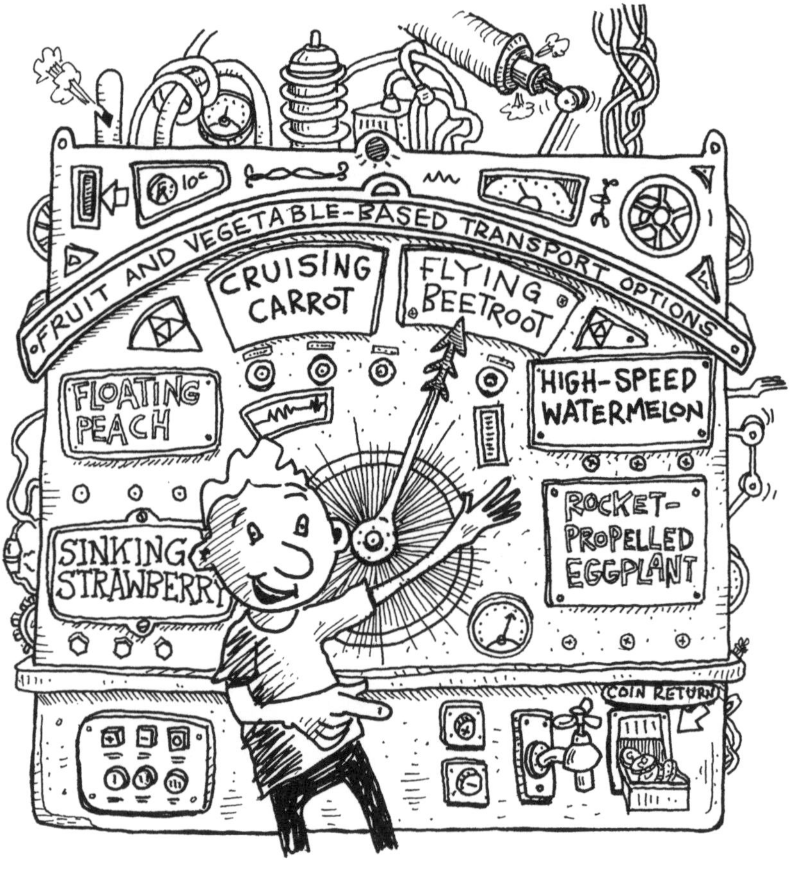
FRUIT AND VEGETABLE-BASED TRANSPORT OPTIONS
CRUISING CARROT
FLYING BEETROOT
FLOATING PEACH
HIGH-SPEED WATERMELON
SINKING STRAWBERRY
ROCKET-PROPELLED EGGPLANT
COIN RETURN
10c

EXPLODING TIME

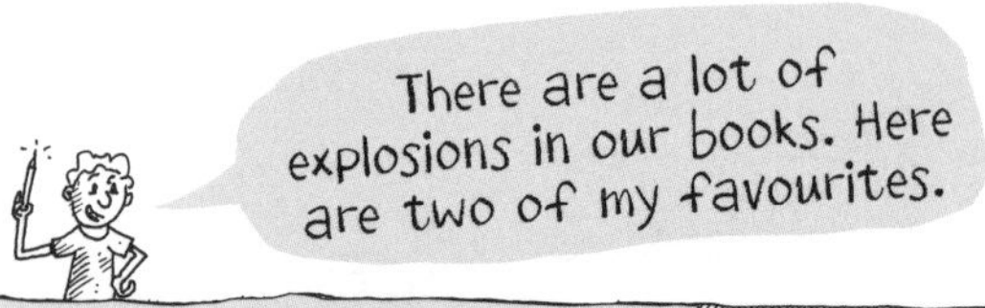
There are a lot of explosions in our books. Here are two of my favourites.

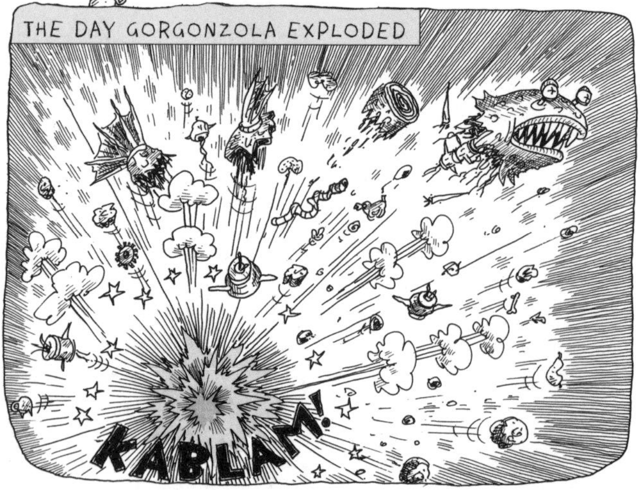
THE DAY GORGONZOLA EXPLODED
KABLAM!

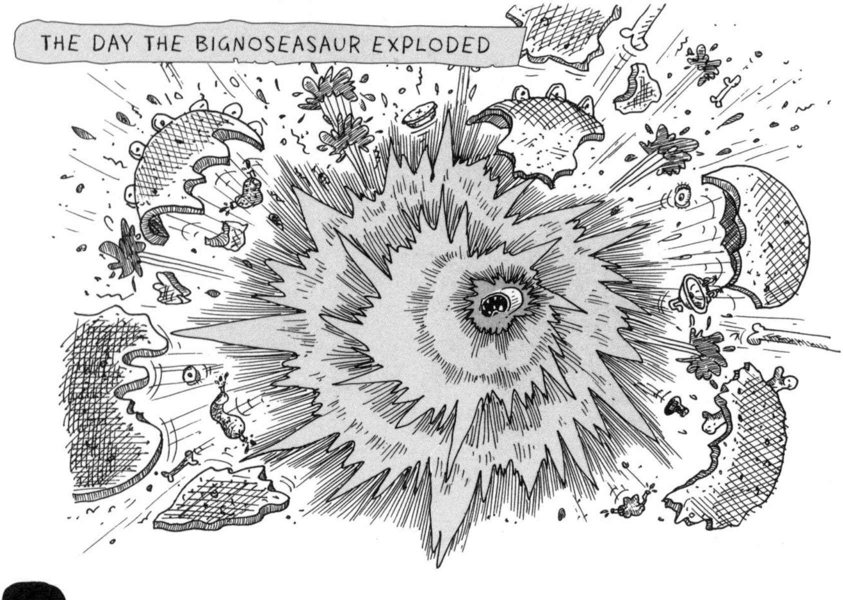
THE DAY THE BIGNOSEASAUR EXPLODED

DRAW AN EXPLOSION

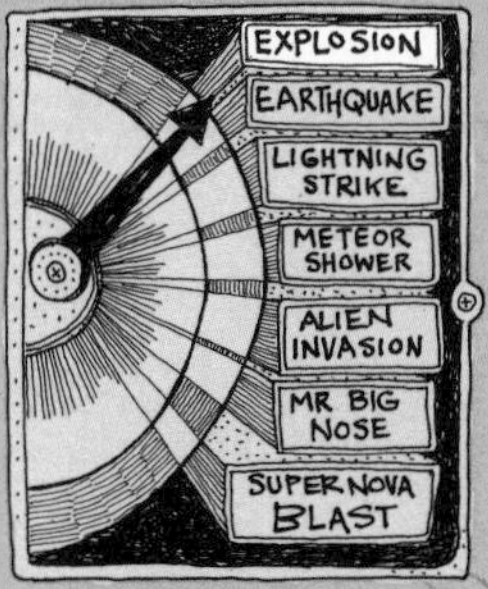
EXPLOSION
EARTHQUAKE
LIGHTNING STRIKE
METEOR SHOWER
ALIEN INVASION
MR BIG NOSE
SUPERNOVA BLAST

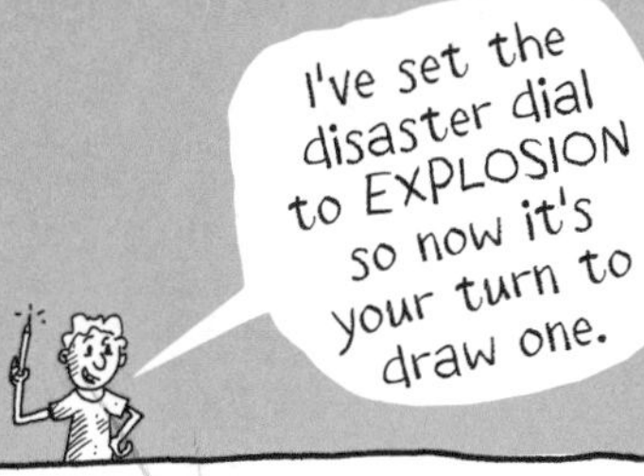
I've set the disaster dial to EXPLOSION so now it's your turn to draw one.

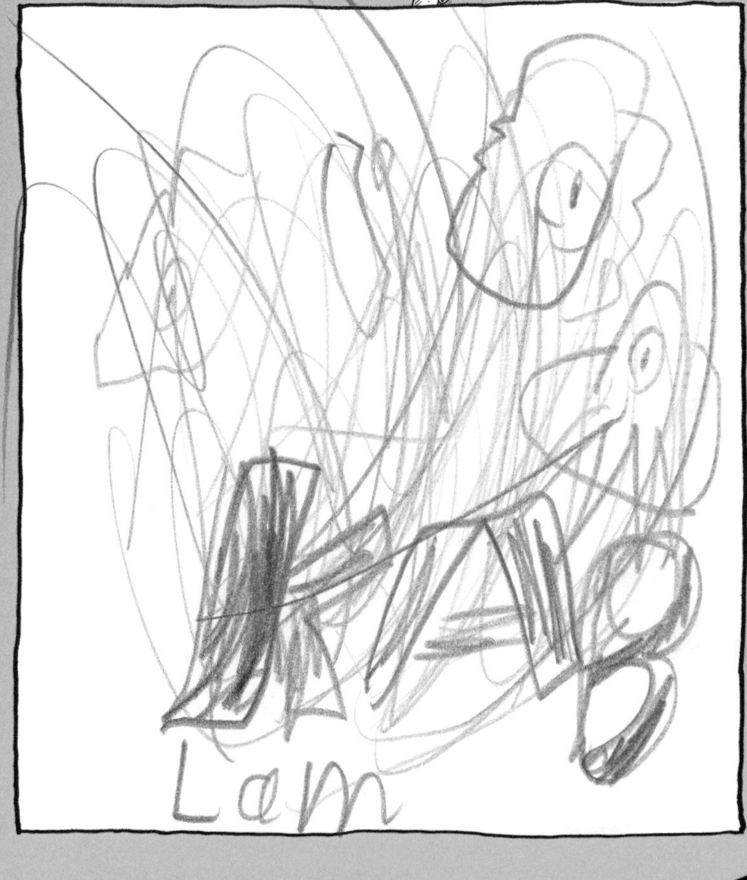
Lam

ANIMAL SCRAMBLES

My animals' names are all mixed up. Can you fix them?

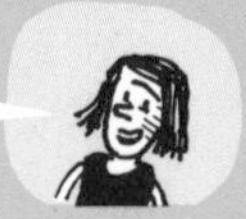

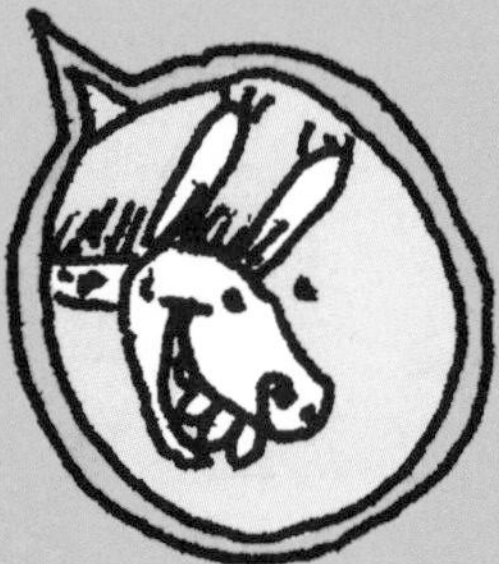

RM EEH WAH

mr WAHeeH

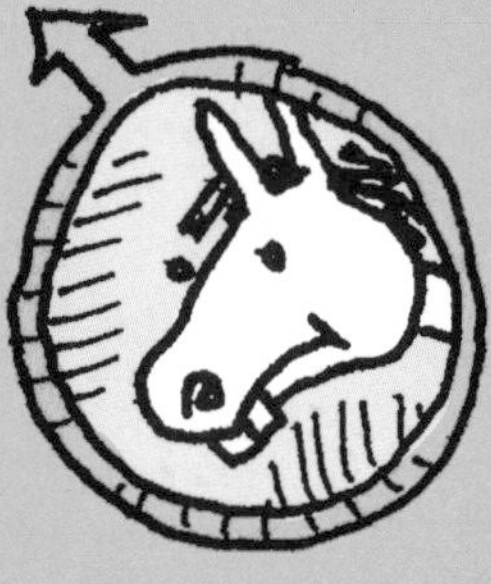

EMO

Moe

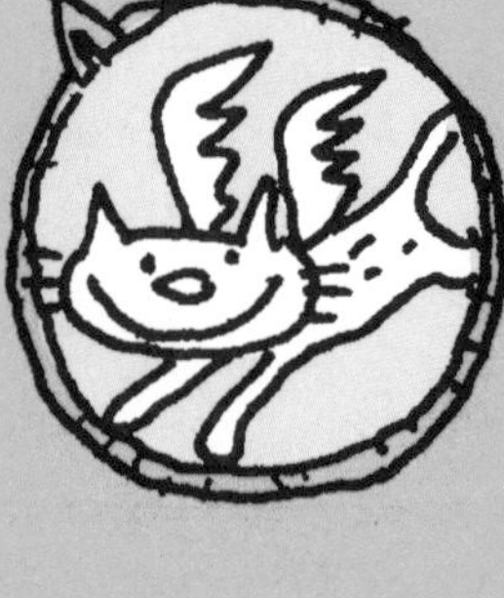

SLIYK

Silky

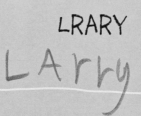

Answers are on page 163.

LRARY

LArry

BLLI & PILH

Bill and phil

TAP

pAT

SCREECHY COLOUR IN

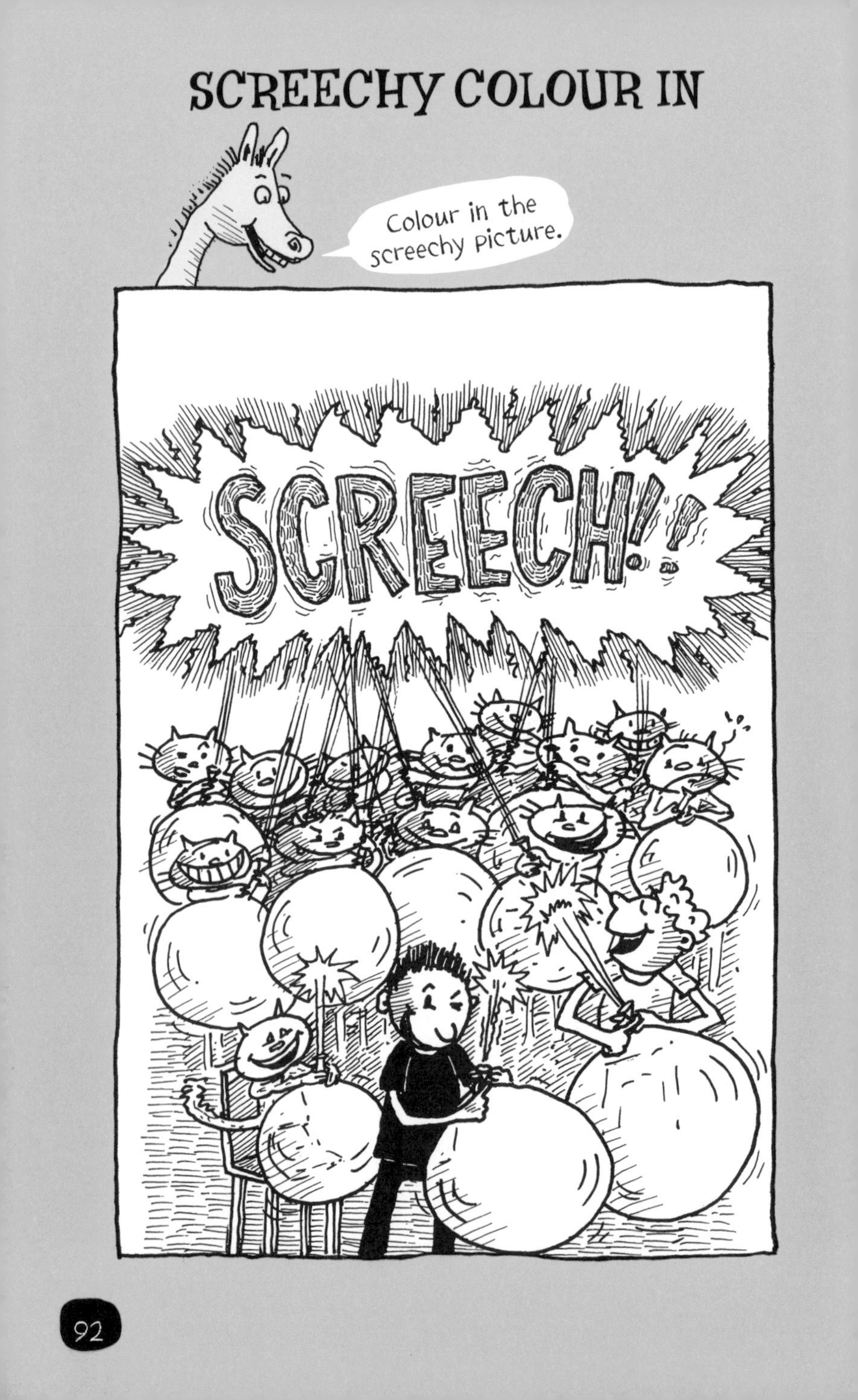
Colour in the screechy picture.
SCREECH!!

65-STOREY TREEHOUSE WORD SEARCH

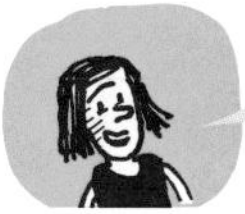

When you have finished there should be eight letters left over that spell out something to do with the story.

Answers are on page 164.

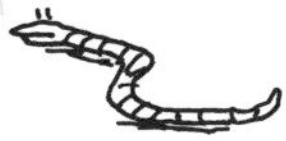

WORD LIST

ANTS
ASPS
BIN
BUBBLEWRAP
CLONING
CRAB
EGYPT
FIRE
INSPECTOR
OWLS
PERMIT
PONDSCUM
RAMPS
SELFIE
SUPER BW
TIME TRAVEL
TREE NN

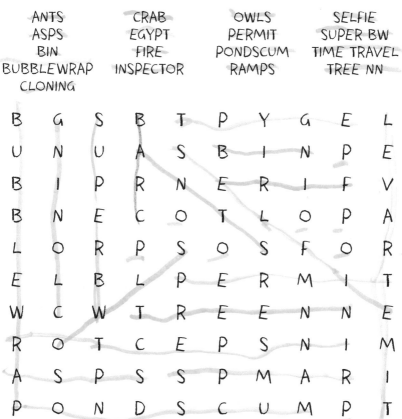

B	G	S	B	T	P	Y	G	E	L
U	N	U	A	S	B	I	N	P	E
B	I	P	R	N	E	R	I	F	V
B	N	E	C	O	T	L	O	P	A
L	O	R	P	S	O	S	F	O	R
E	L	B	L	P	E	R	M	I	T
W	C	W	T	R	E	E	N	N	E
R	O	T	C	E	P	S	N	I	M
A	S	P	S	S	P	M	A	R	I
P	O	N	D	S	C	U	M	P	T

SOLUTION: _ _ _ _   _ _ _ _

FIND THE ODD ONE OUT

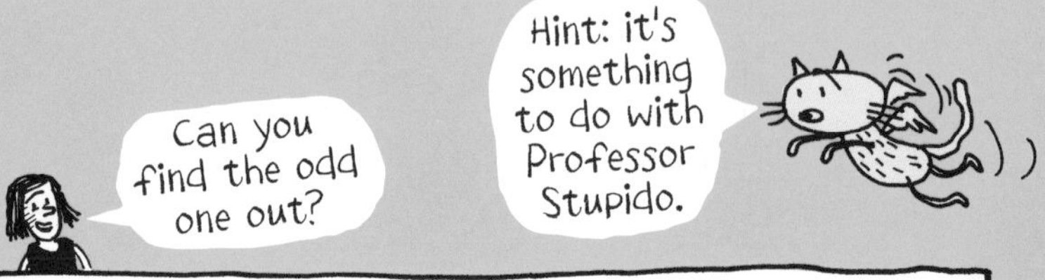
Can you find the odd one out?
Hint: it's something to do with Professor Stupido.

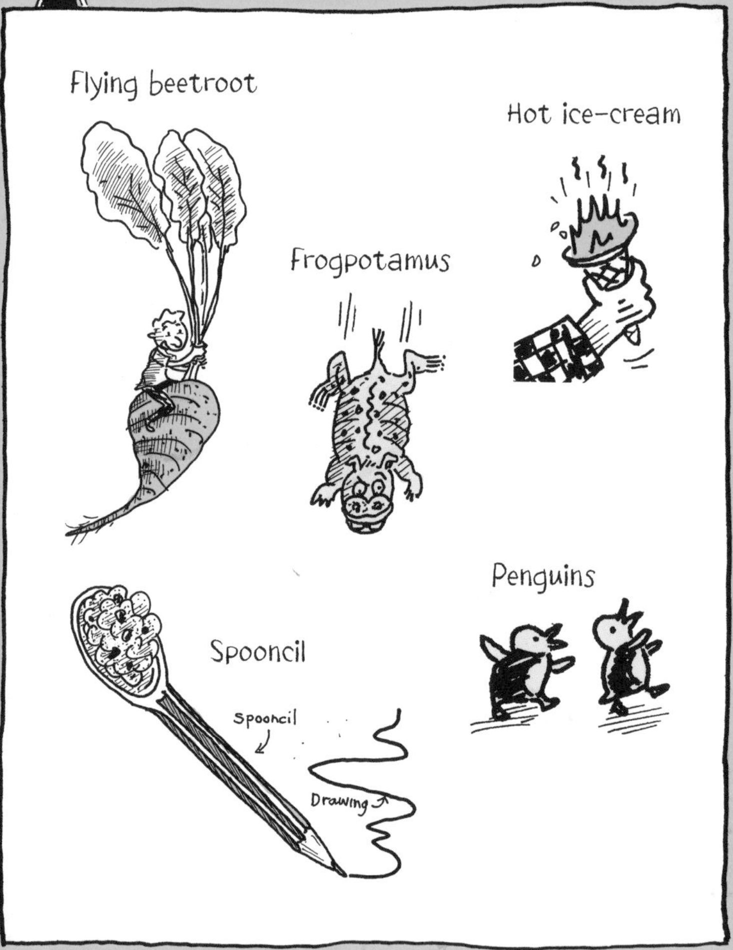
Flying beetroot
Hot ice-cream
Frogpotamus
Penguins
Spooncil
Spooncil
Drawing

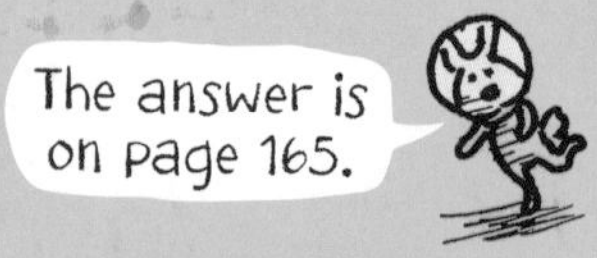
The answer is on page 165.

SOUND EFFECTS FUN

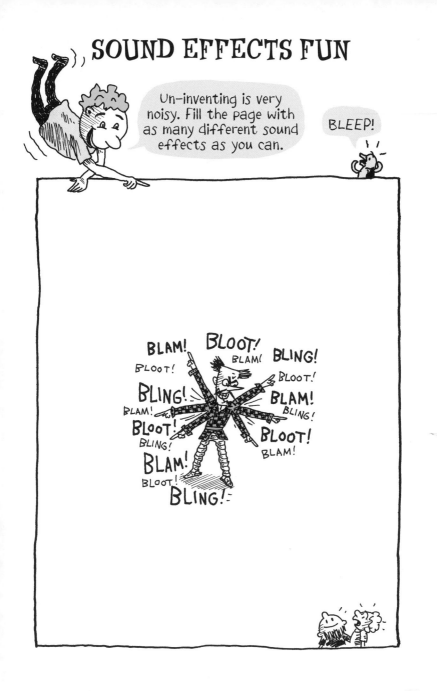

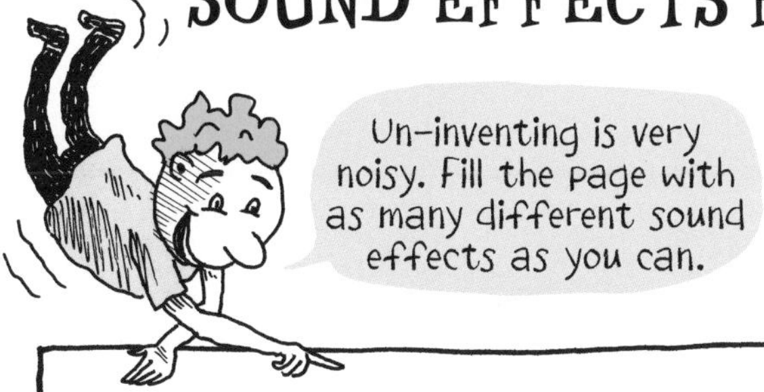
Un-inventing is very noisy. Fill the page with as many different sound effects as you can.

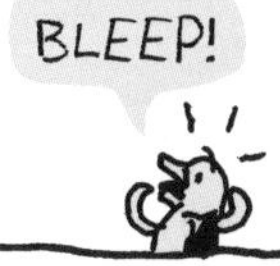
BLEEP!

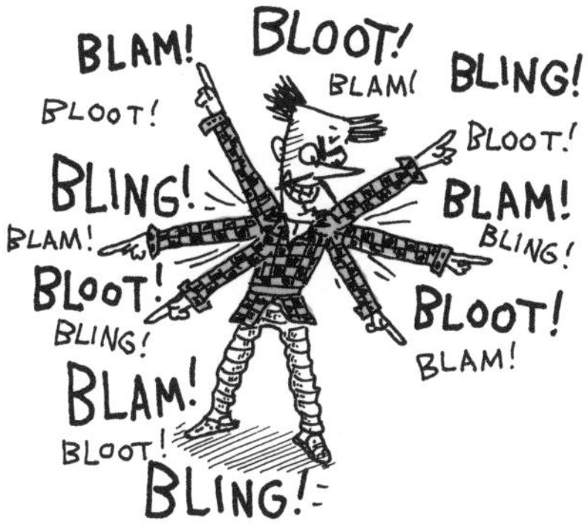
BLAM!
BLOOT!
BLAM!
BLING!
BLOOT!
BLOOT!
BLING!
BLAM!
BLAM!
BLING!
BLOOT!
BLOOT!
BLING!
BLAM!
BLAM!
BLOOT!
BLING!

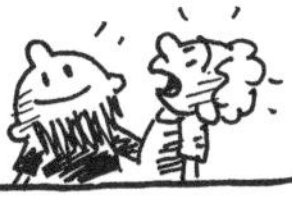

VEGETABLE DISGUISE TIME

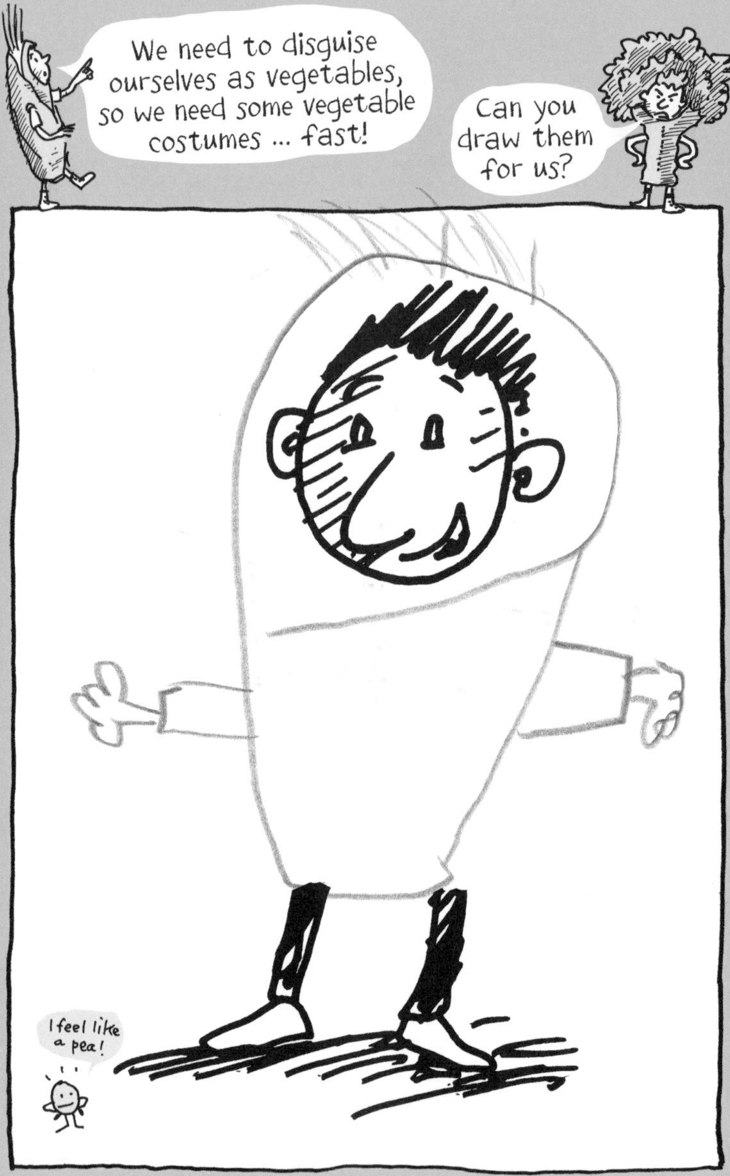
We need to disguise ourselves as vegetables, so we need some vegetable costumes ... fast!
Can you draw them for us?
I feel like a pea!

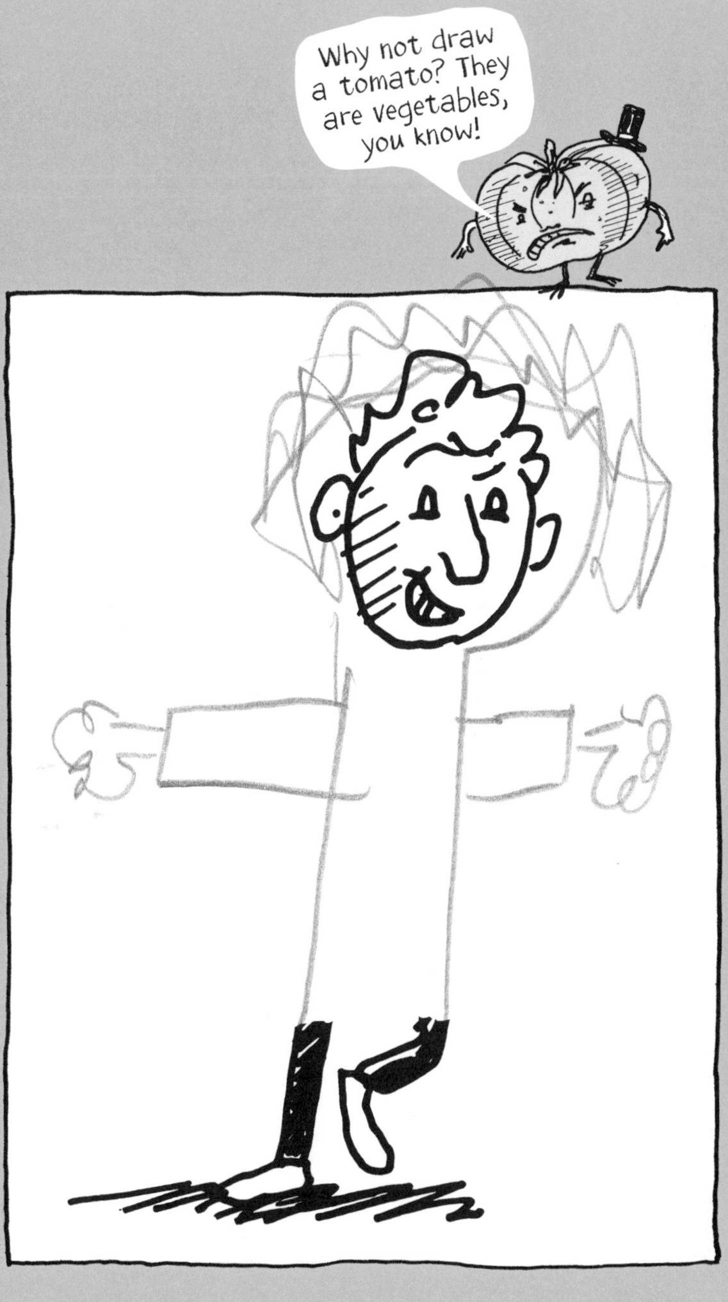
Why not draw a tomato? They are vegetables, you know!

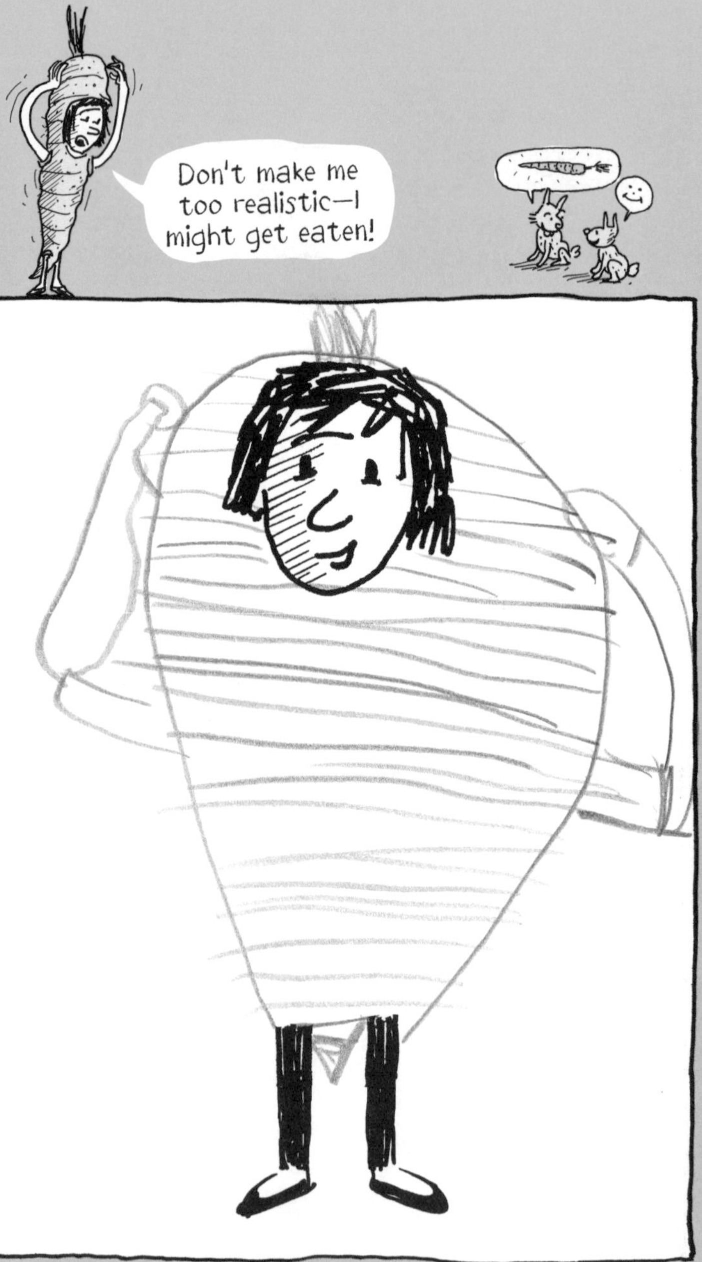
Don't make me too realistic—I might get eaten!

COLOUR THIS IN ... OR ELSE!

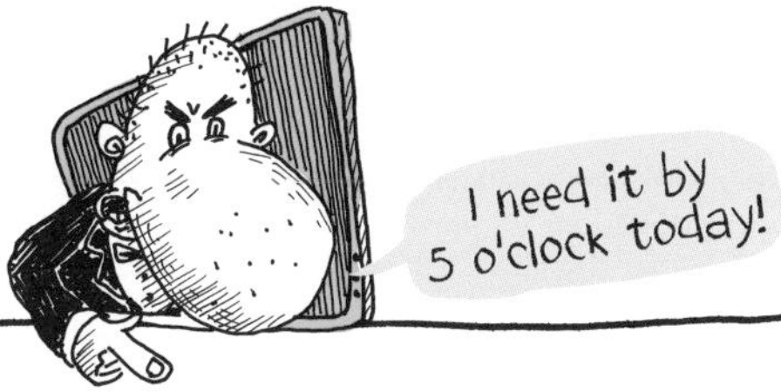
I need it by
5 o'clock today!

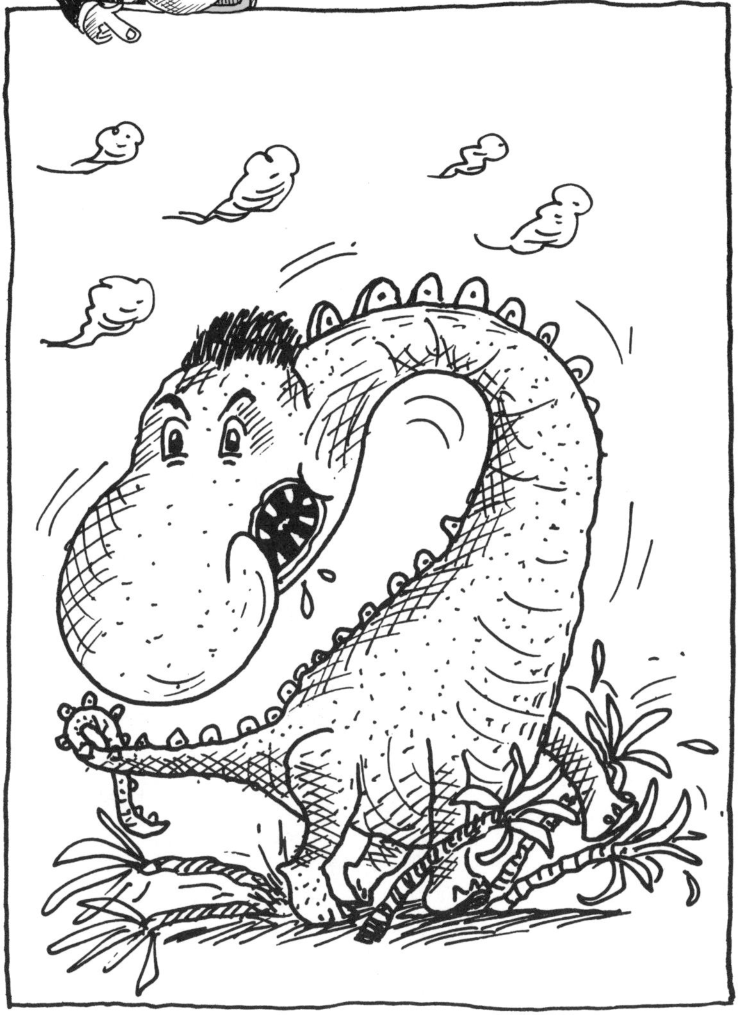

ADVERTISEMENT TIME

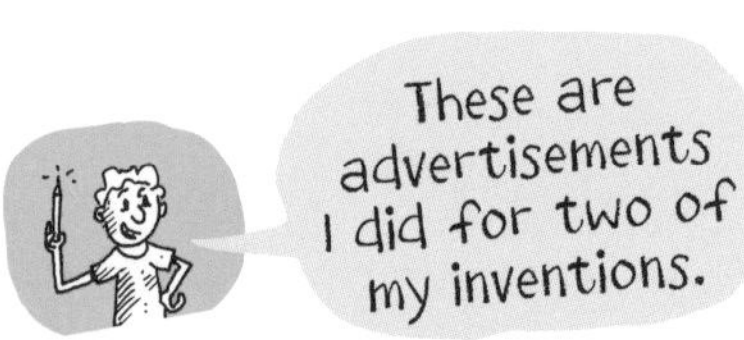
These are advertisements I did for two of my inventions.

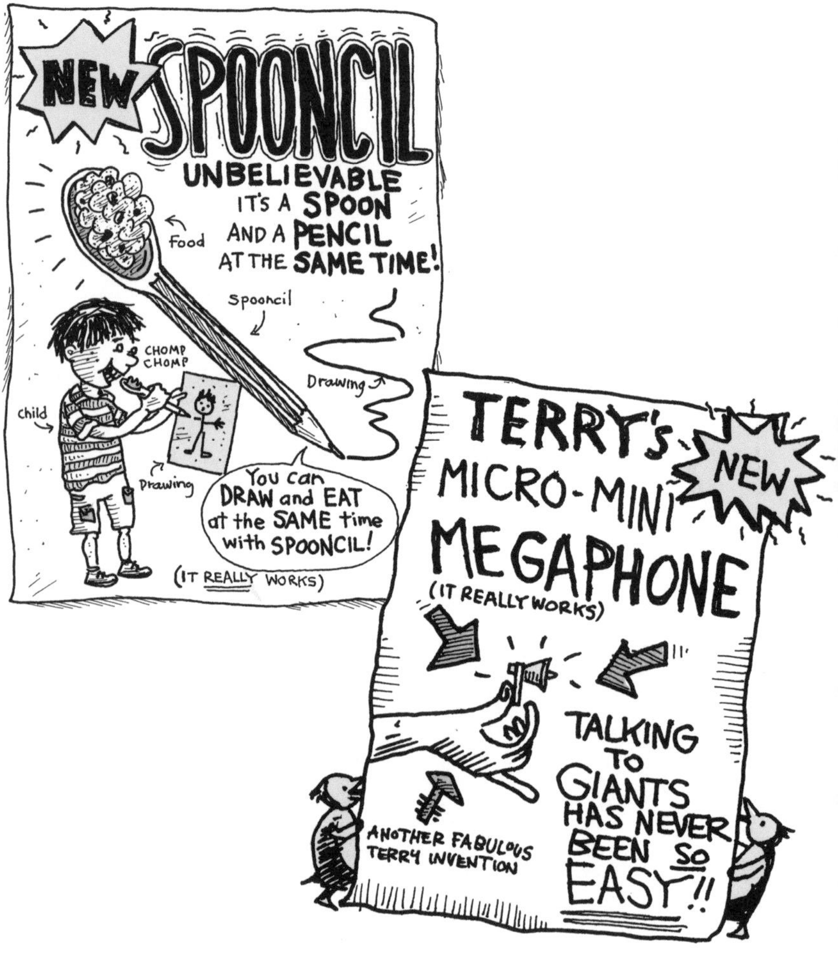
NEW
SPOONCIL
UNBELIEVABLE IT'S A SPOON AND A PENCIL AT THE SAME TIME!
Food
Spooncil
CHOMP CHOMP
Drawing
child
Drawing
You can DRAW and EAT at the SAME time with SPOONCIL!
(IT REALLY WORKS)
TERRY'S
NEW
MICRO-MINI MEGAPHONE
(IT REALLY WORKS)
TALKING TO GIANTS HAS NEVER BEEN SO EASY!!
ANOTHER FABULOUS TERRY INVENTION

Create your own advertisement for a product you'd like to invent.

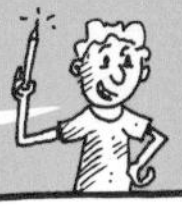

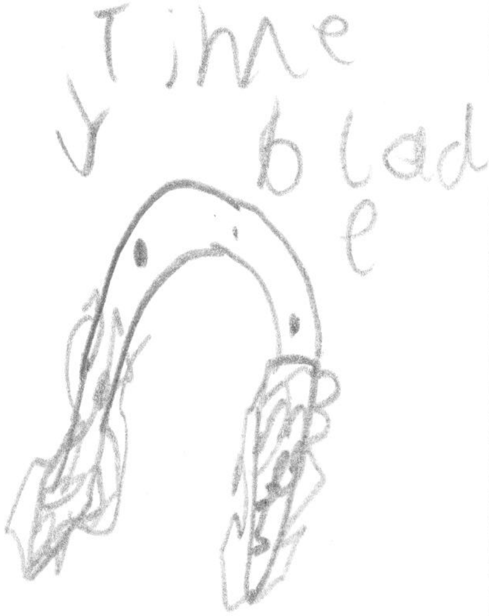
Time
blad
e

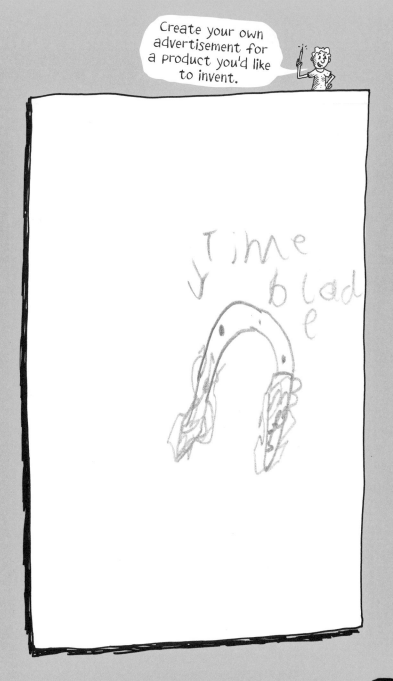

VAPORISING VEGETABLES TIME

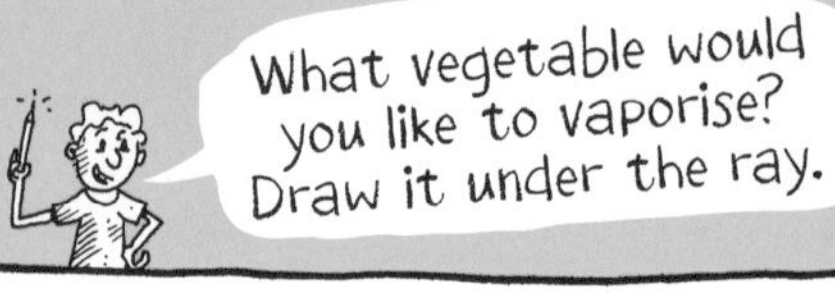
What vegetable would you like to vaporise? Draw it under the ray.

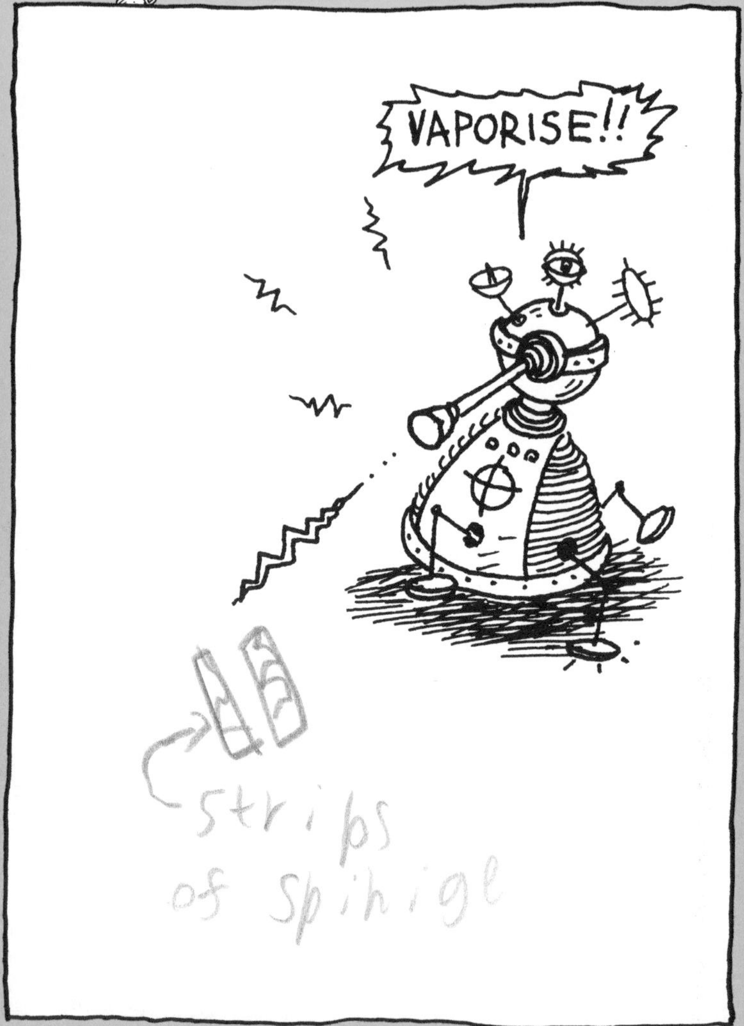
VAPORISE!!

FEEDING TIME

Terry and I have a marshmallow machine that automatically shoots marshmallows into our mouths whenever we're hungry.

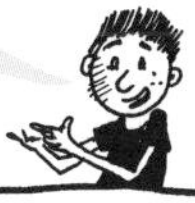

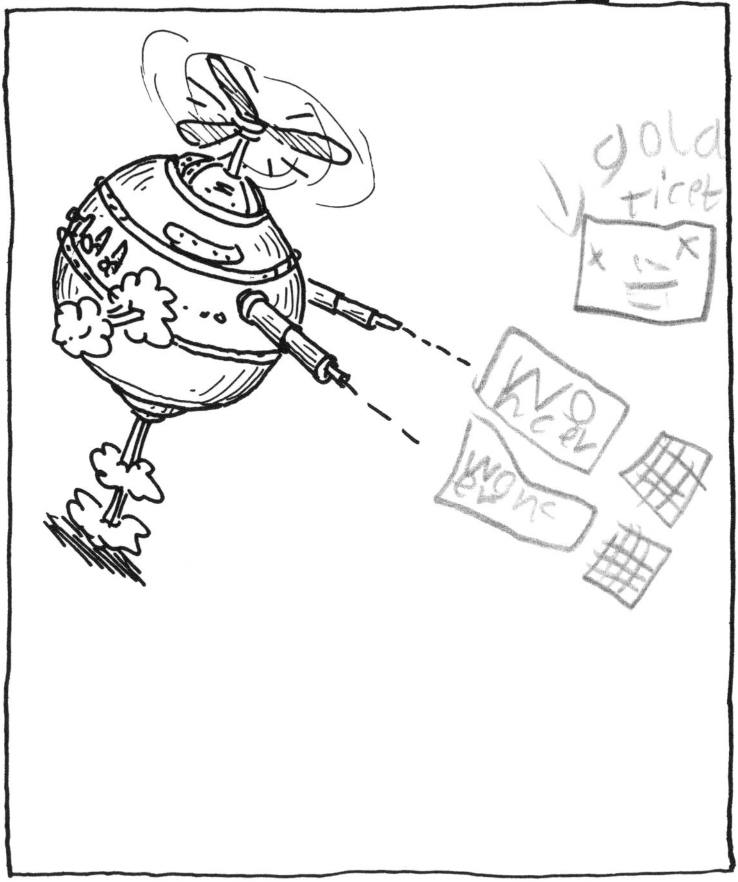
gold
ticet

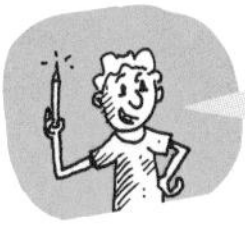

If you had a machine like this what food would you like it to feed you? Draw it.

SAFETY TIME

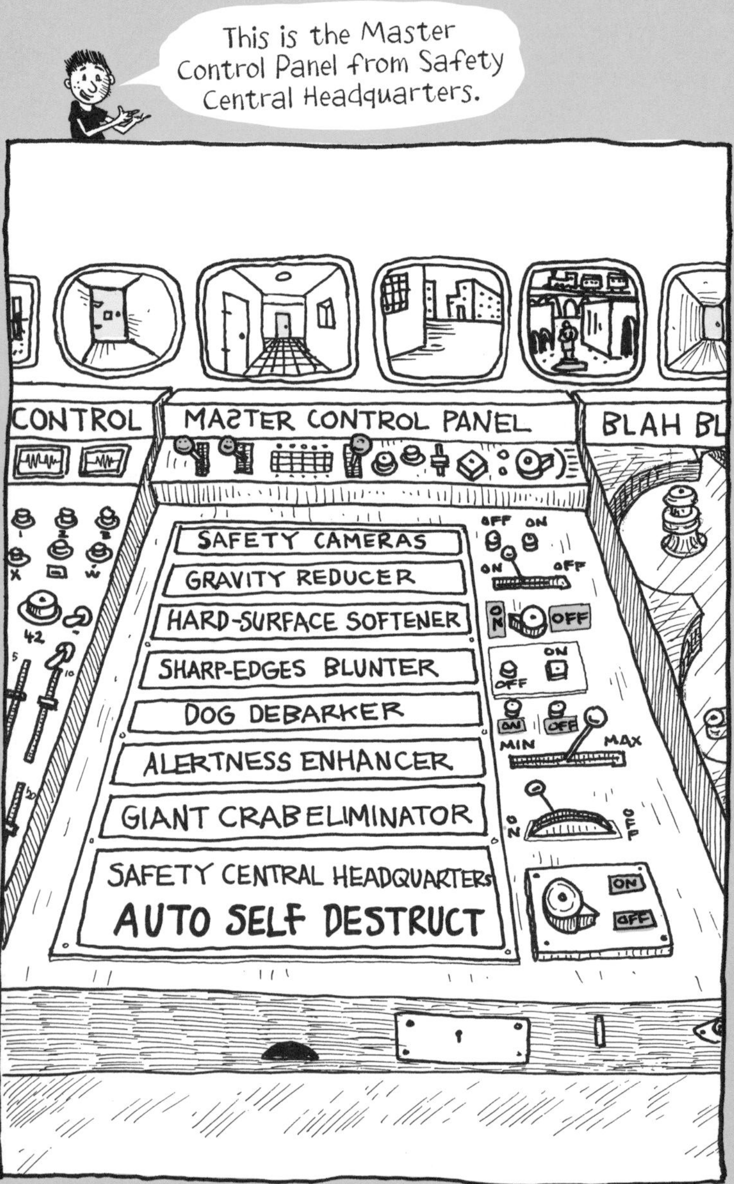
This is the Master Control Panel from Safety Central Headquarters.
CONTROL
MASTER CONTROL PANEL
BLAH BL
SAFETY CAMERAS
GRAVITY REDUCER
HARD-SURFACE SOFTENER
SHARP-EDGES BLUNTER
DOG DEBARKER
ALERTNESS ENHANCER
GIANT CRAB ELIMINATOR
SAFETY CENTRAL HEADQUARTERS
AUTO SELF DESTRUCT
OFF ON
ON OFF
ON OFF
ON OFF
ON OFF
MIN MAX
ON OFF
ON OFF
42

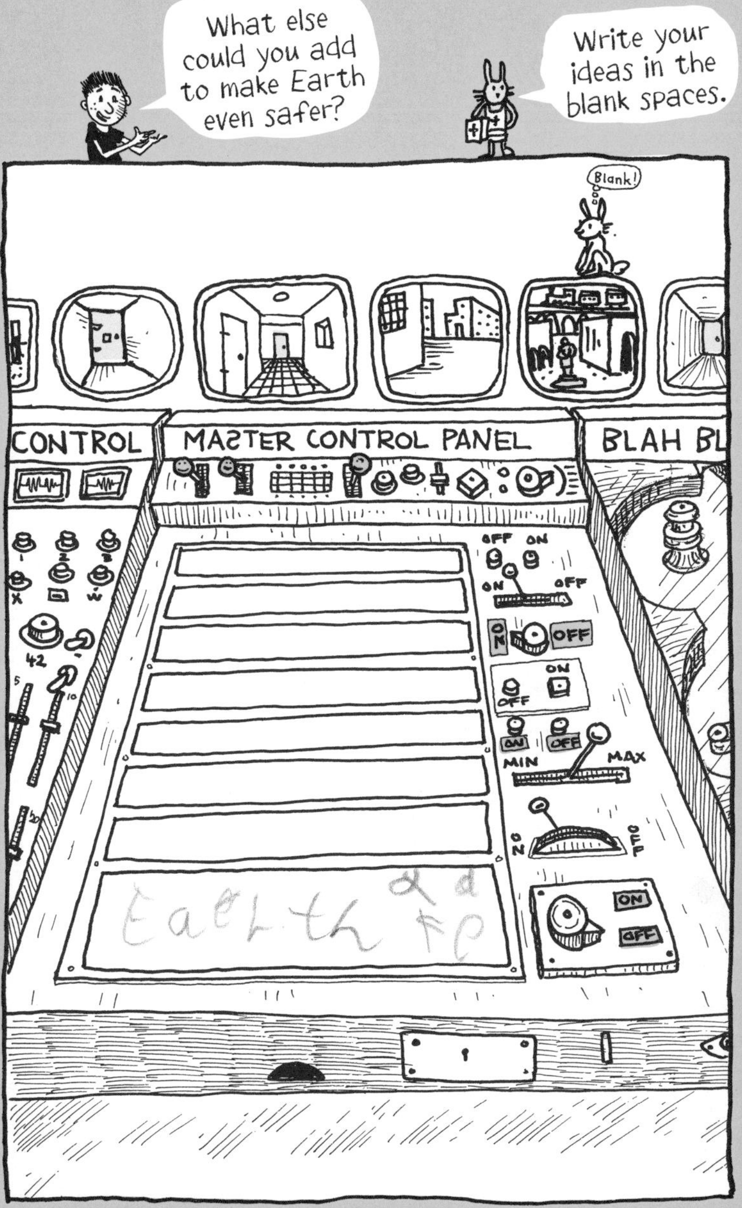
What else could you add to make Earth even safer?
Write your ideas in the blank spaces.
Blank!
CONTROL
MASTER CONTROL PANEL
BLAH BL
OFF ON
ON OFF
ON OFF
ON
OFF
ON OFF
MIN MAX
ON OFF
ON
OFF
42

WHAT'S CHASING ANDY?

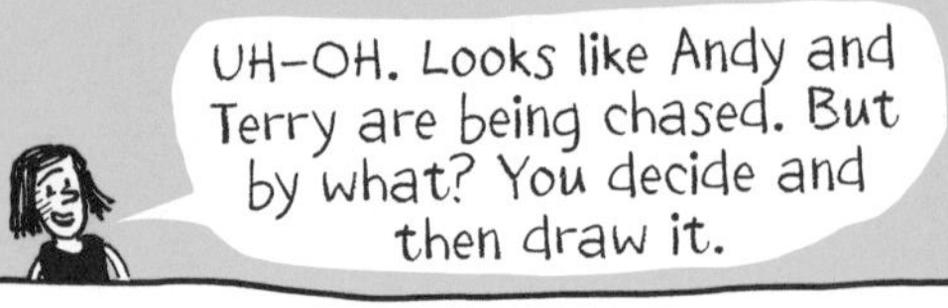
UH-OH. Looks like Andy and Terry are being chased. But by what? You decide and then draw it.

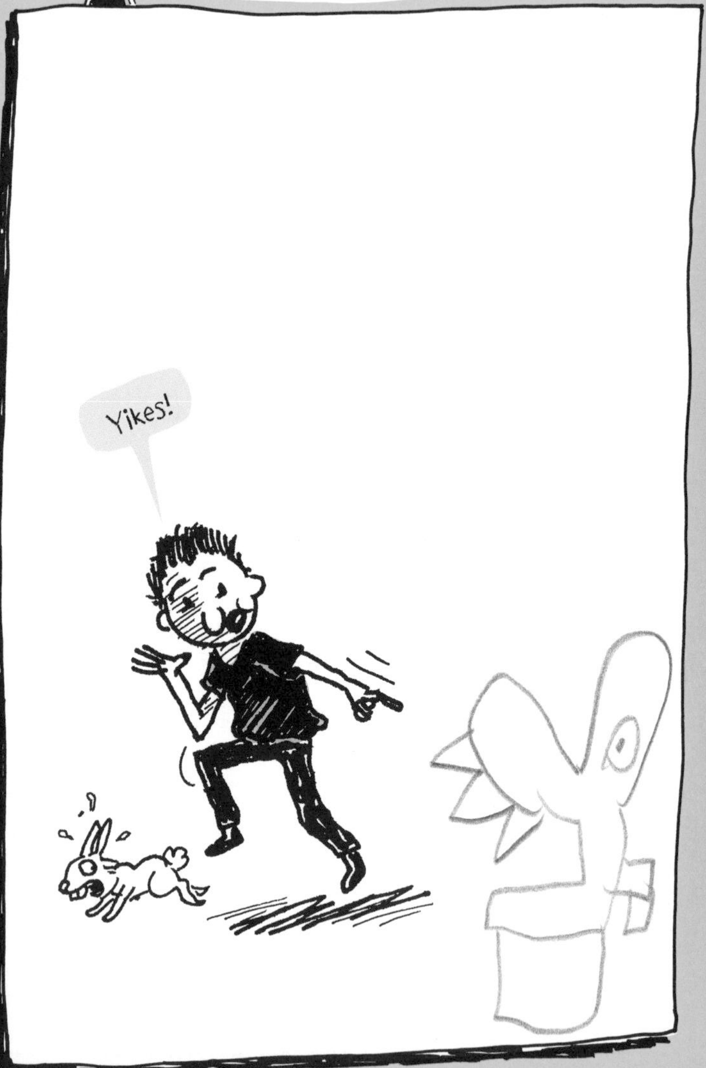
Yikes!

WHAT'S CHASING TERRY?

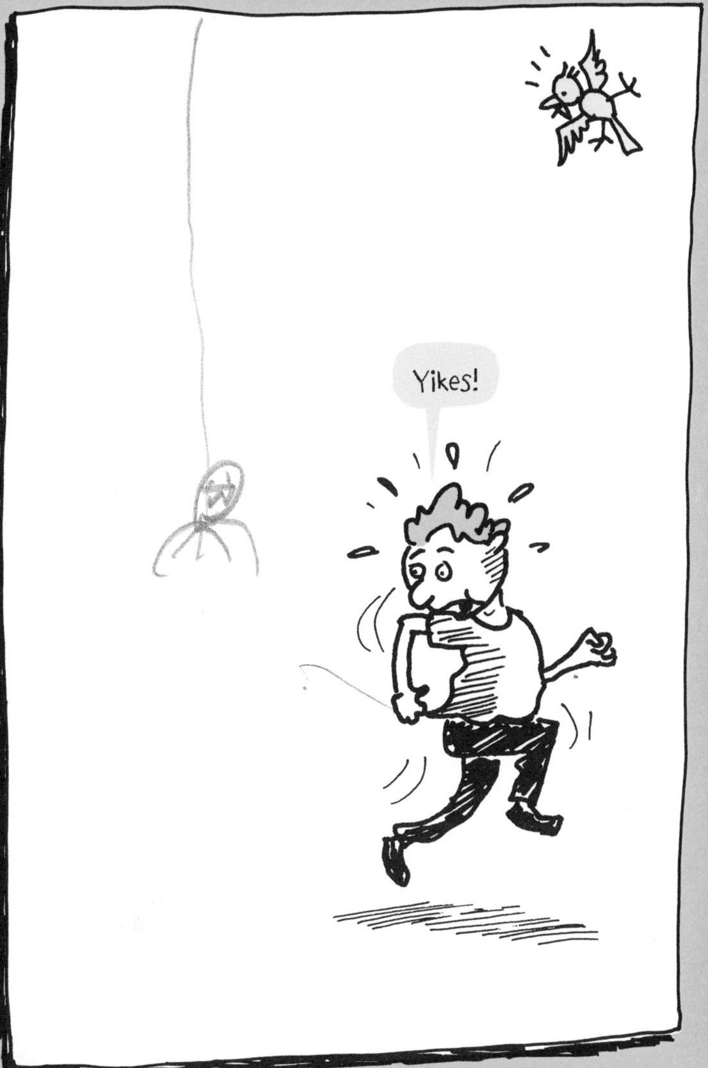
Yikes!

FUN FOOD LEVEL

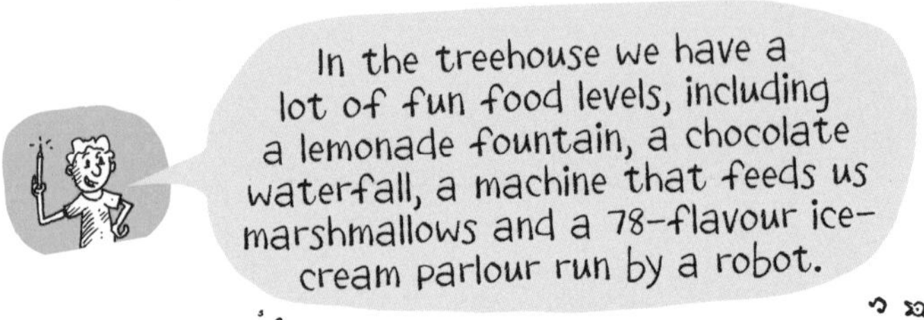
In the treehouse we have a lot of fun food levels, including a lemonade fountain, a chocolate waterfall, a machine that feeds us marshmallows and a 78-flavour ice-cream parlour run by a robot.

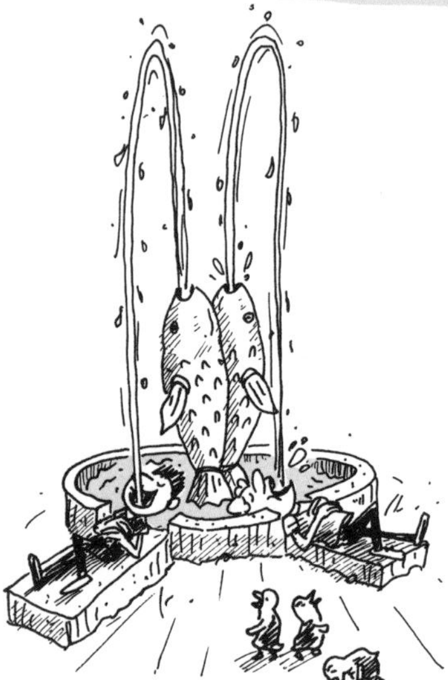

LEMONADE FOUNTAIN

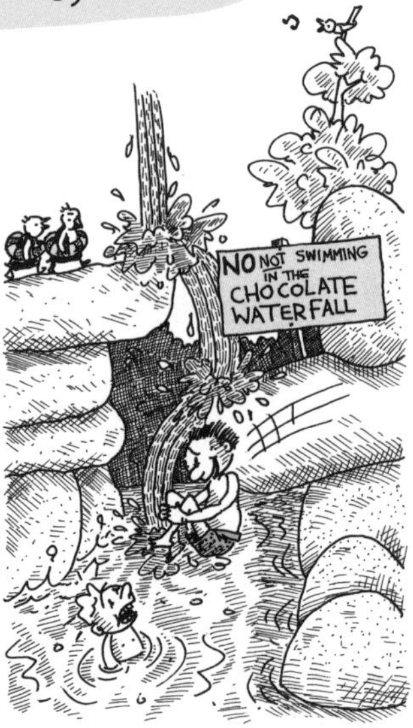
NO NOT SWIMMING IN THE CHOCOLATE WATERFALL

CHOCOLATE WATERFALL

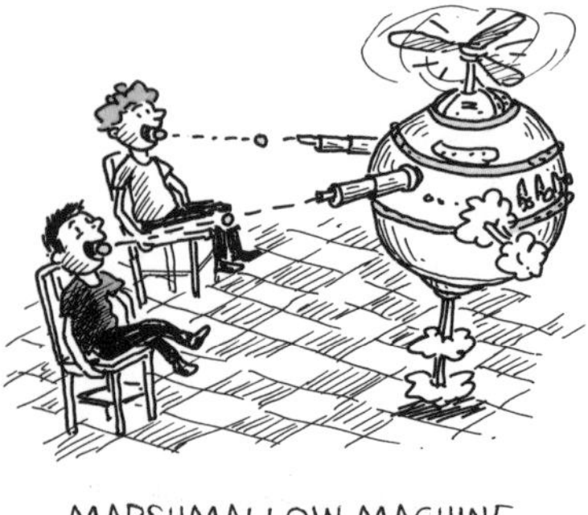

MARSHMALLOW MACHINE

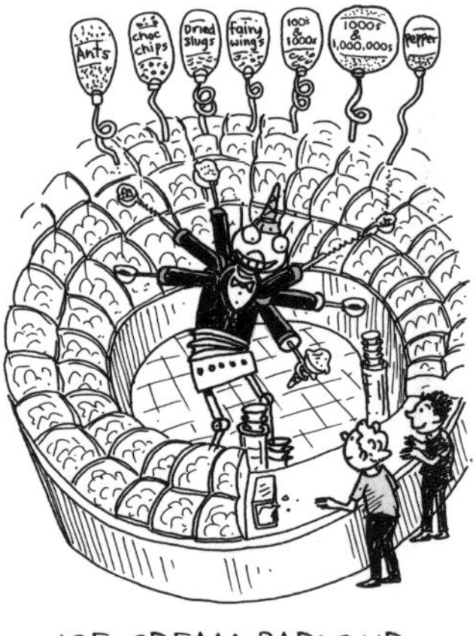
Ants
choc chips
Dried slugs
fairy wings
100s & 1000s
1000s & 1,000,000s
Pepper

ICE-CREAM PARLOUR

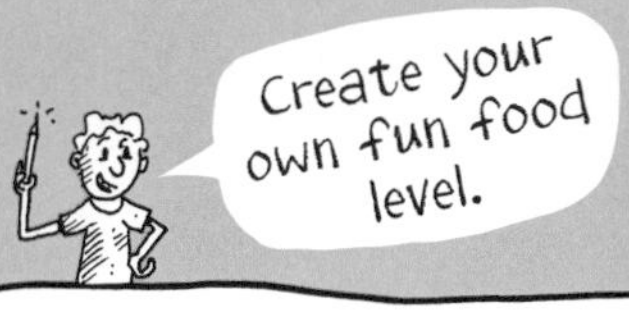
Create your own fun food level.

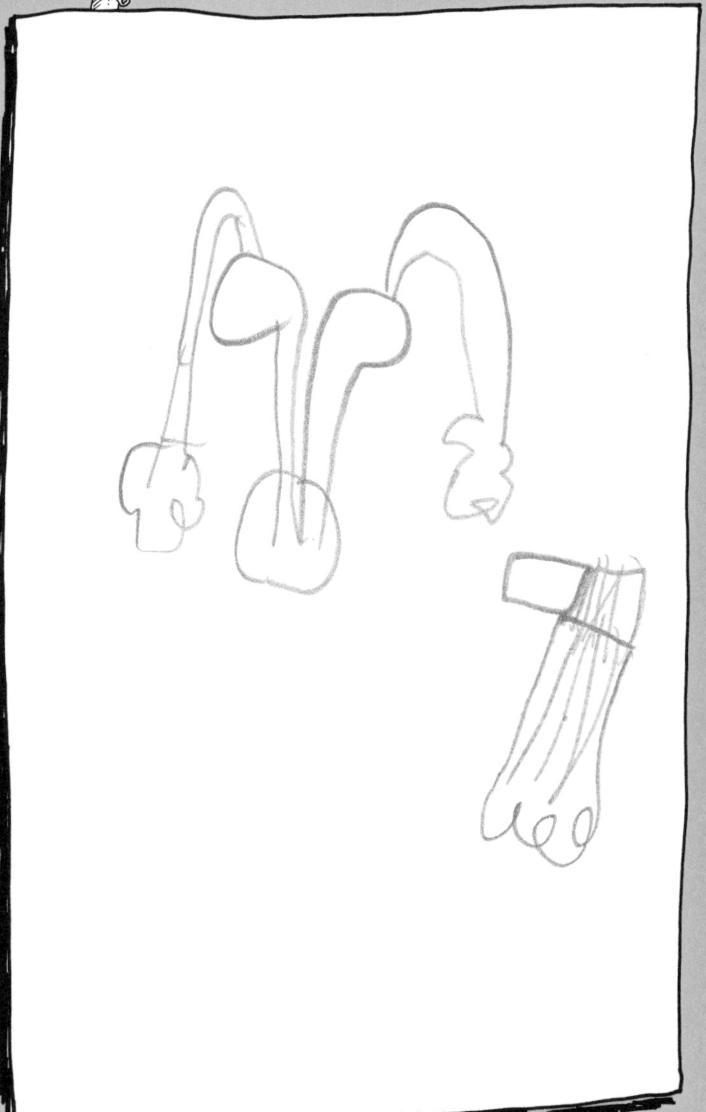

STORY TIME

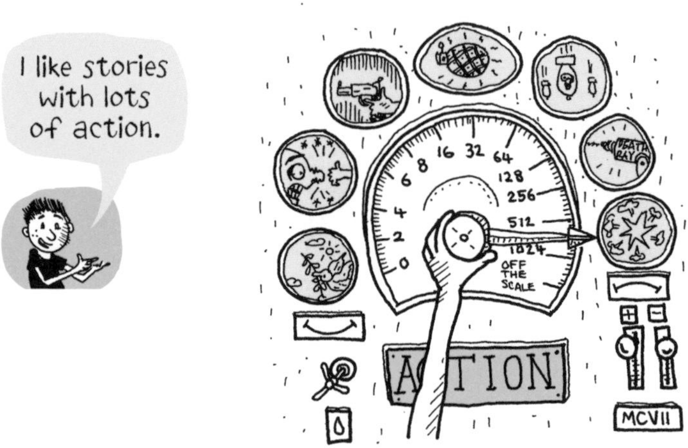
I like stories with lots of action.
0
2
4
6
8
16
32
64
128
256
512
1024
OFF THE SCALE
DEATH RAY
ACTION
MCVII

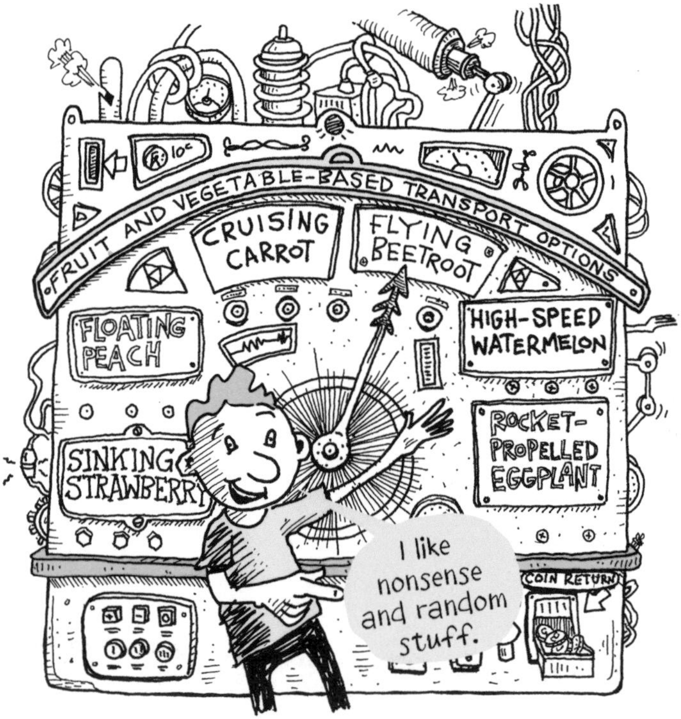
FRUIT AND VEGETABLE-BASED TRANSPORT OPTIONS
CRUISING CARROT
FLYING BEETROOT
FLOATING PEACH
HIGH-SPEED WATERMELON
ROCKET-PROPELLED EGGPLANT
SINKING STRAWBERRY
COIN RETURN
I like nonsense and random stuff.

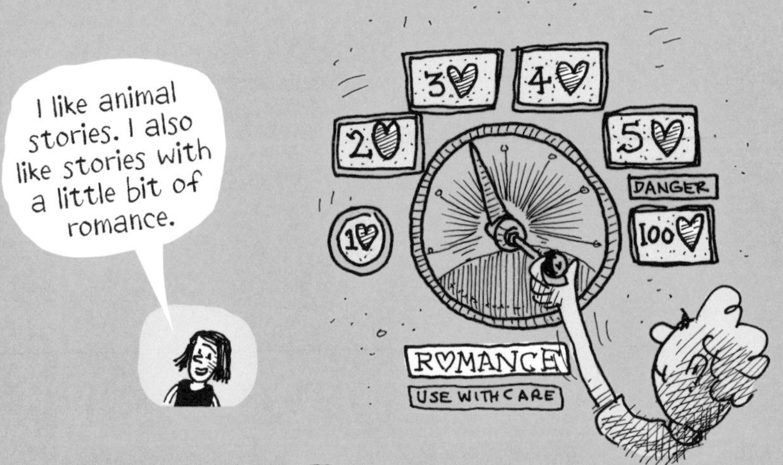
I like animal stories. I also like stories with a little bit of romance.
1
2
3
4
5
DANGER
100
ROMANCE
USE WITH CARE

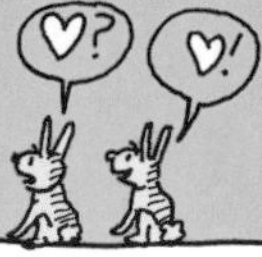

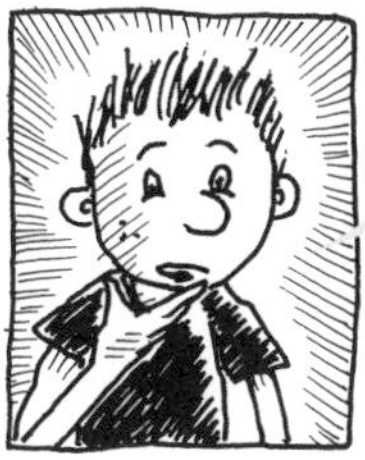

What sort of stories do you like?

I like stories with fiting

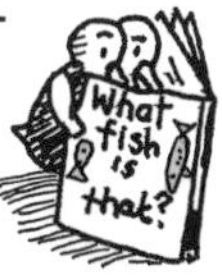
What fish is that?

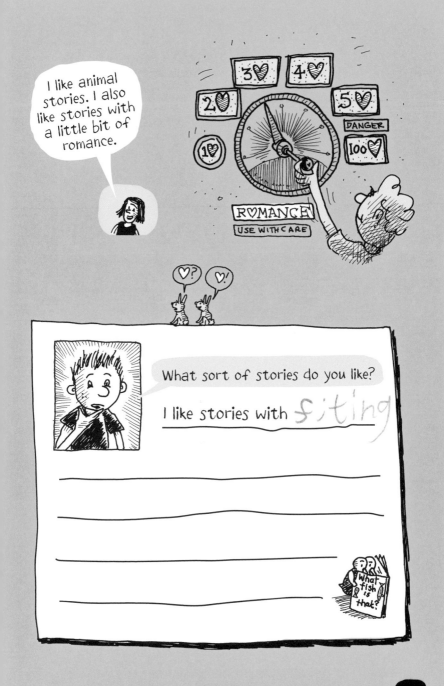

COLOUR IN THE CRASH

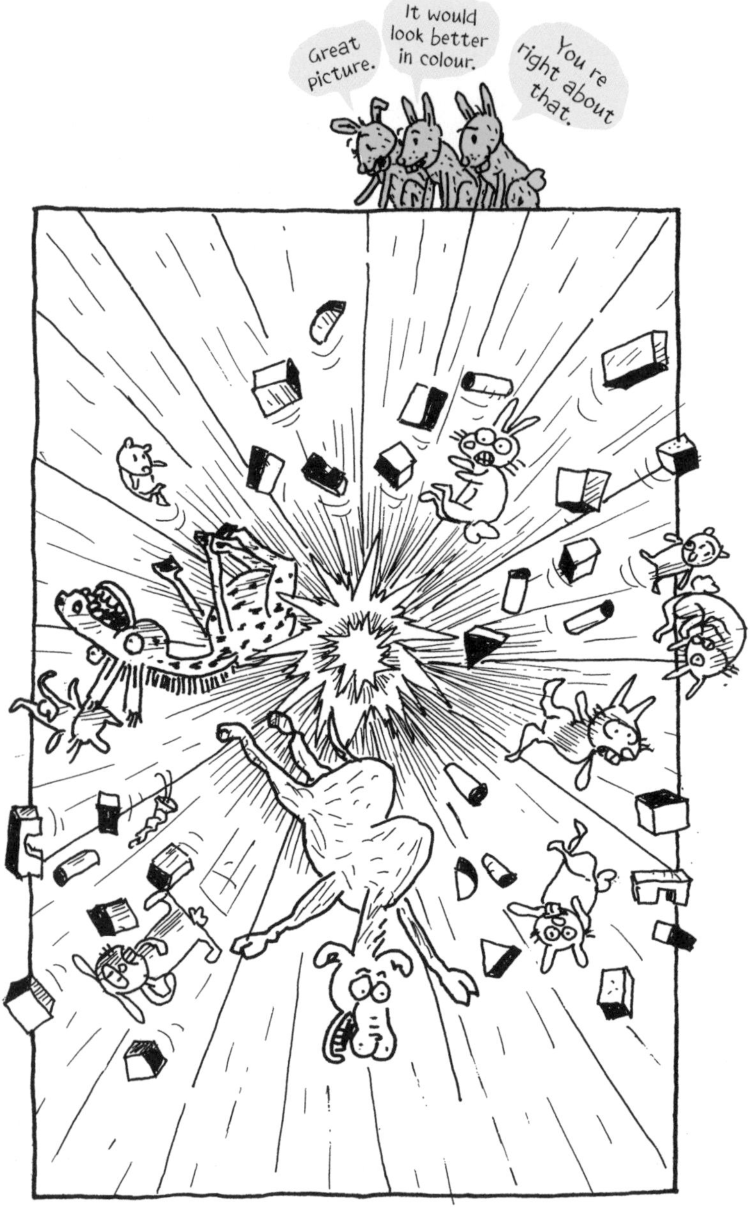

Great picture.
It would look better in colour.
You re right about that.

COLOUR IN THE COVER

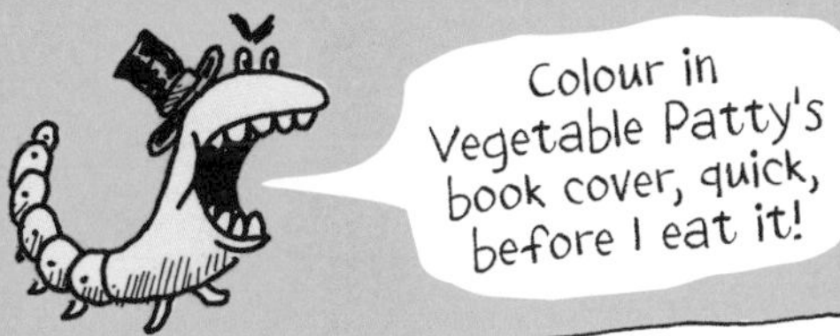
Colour in Vegetable Patty's book cover, quick, before I eat it!

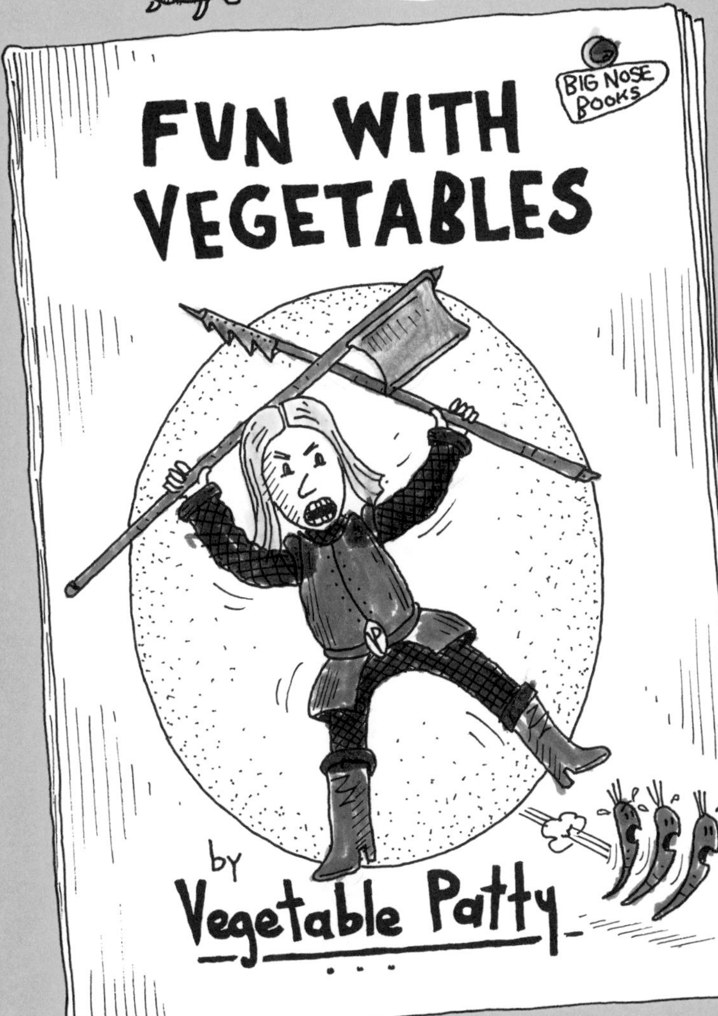
BIG NOSE BOOKS
FUN WITH VEGETABLES
by
Vegetable Patty

TREEHOUSE CODE TIME

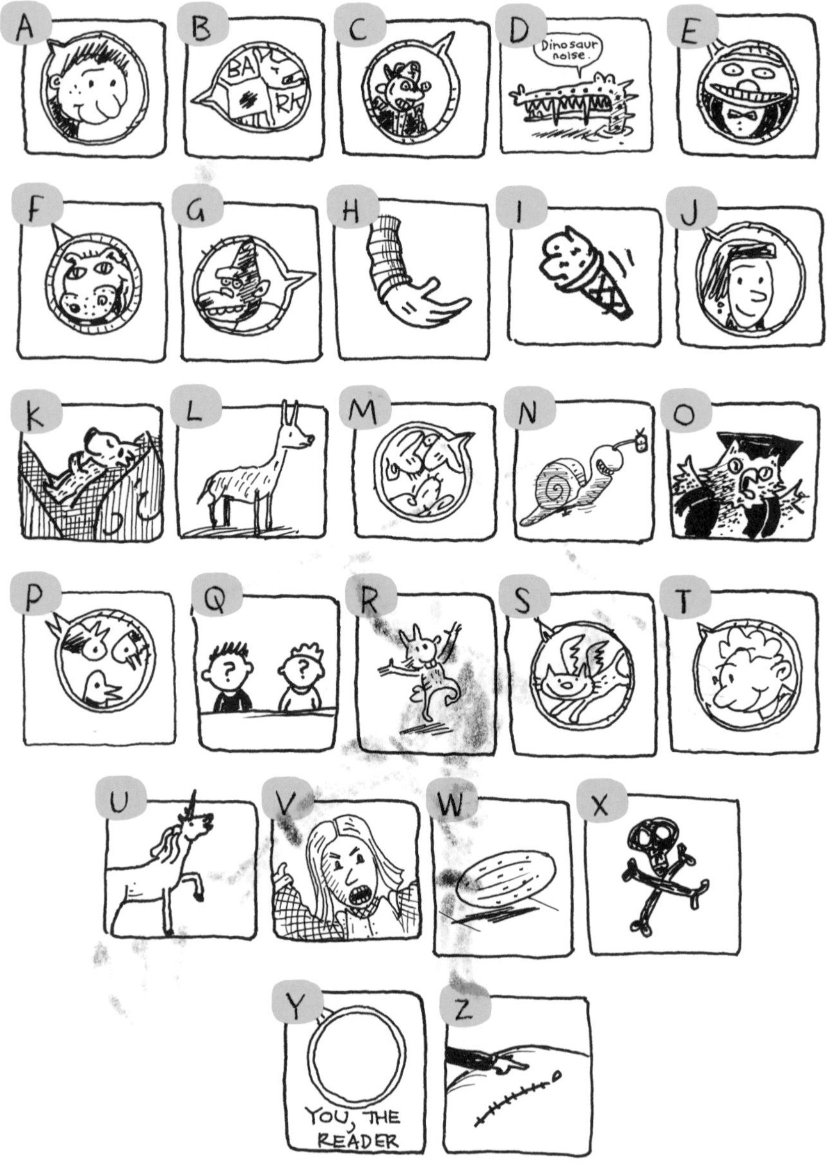
A
B
BA
RK
C
D
Dinosaur noise.
E
F
G
H
I
J
K
L
M
N
O
P
Q
R
S
T
U
V
W
X
Y
YOU, THE READER
Z

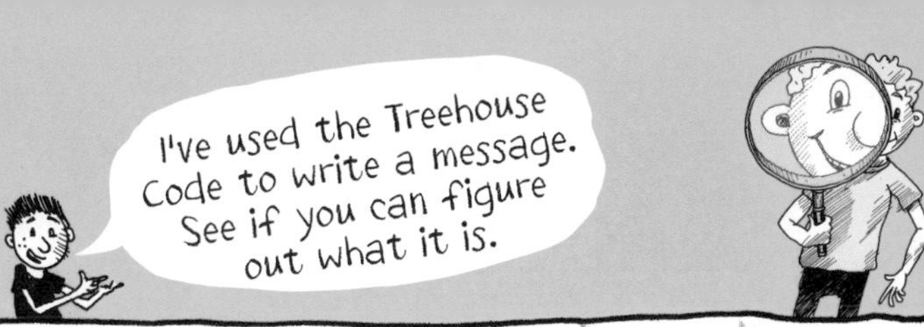
I've used the Treehouse Code to write a message. See if you can figure out what it is.

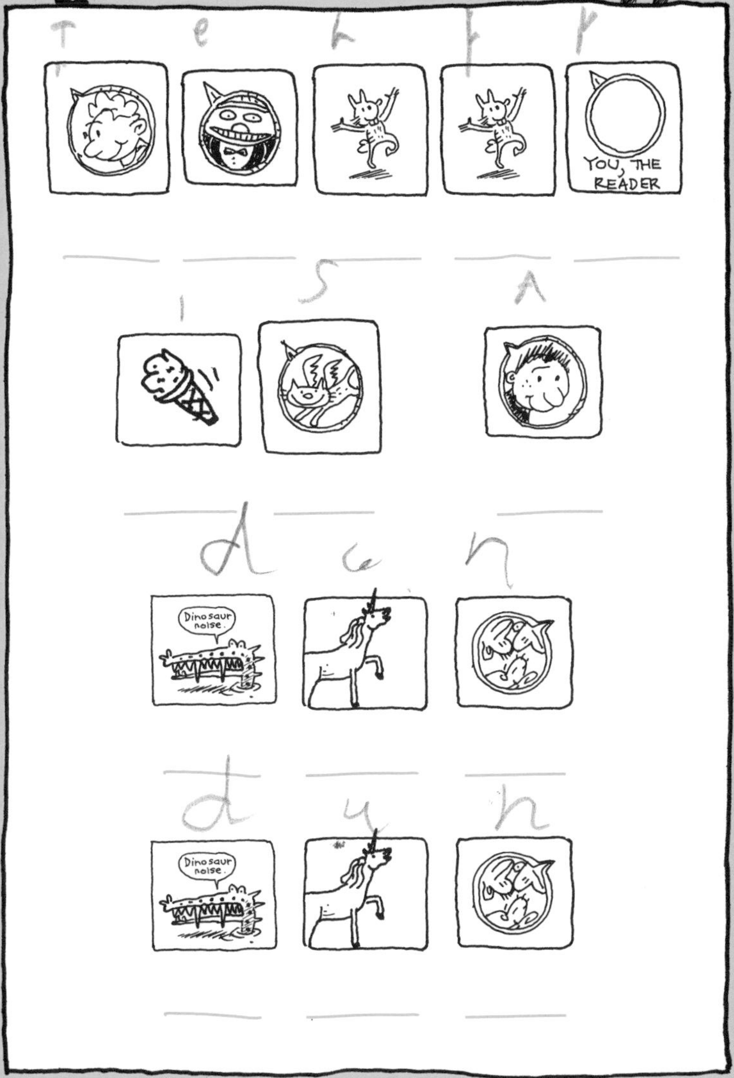
YOU, THE READER
Dinosaur noise.
Dinosaur noise.

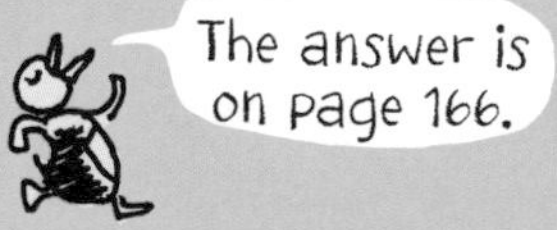
The answer is on page 166.

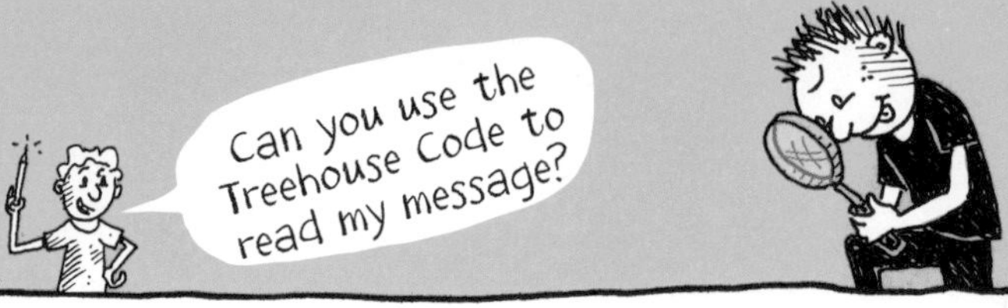
Can you use the Treehouse Code to read my message?

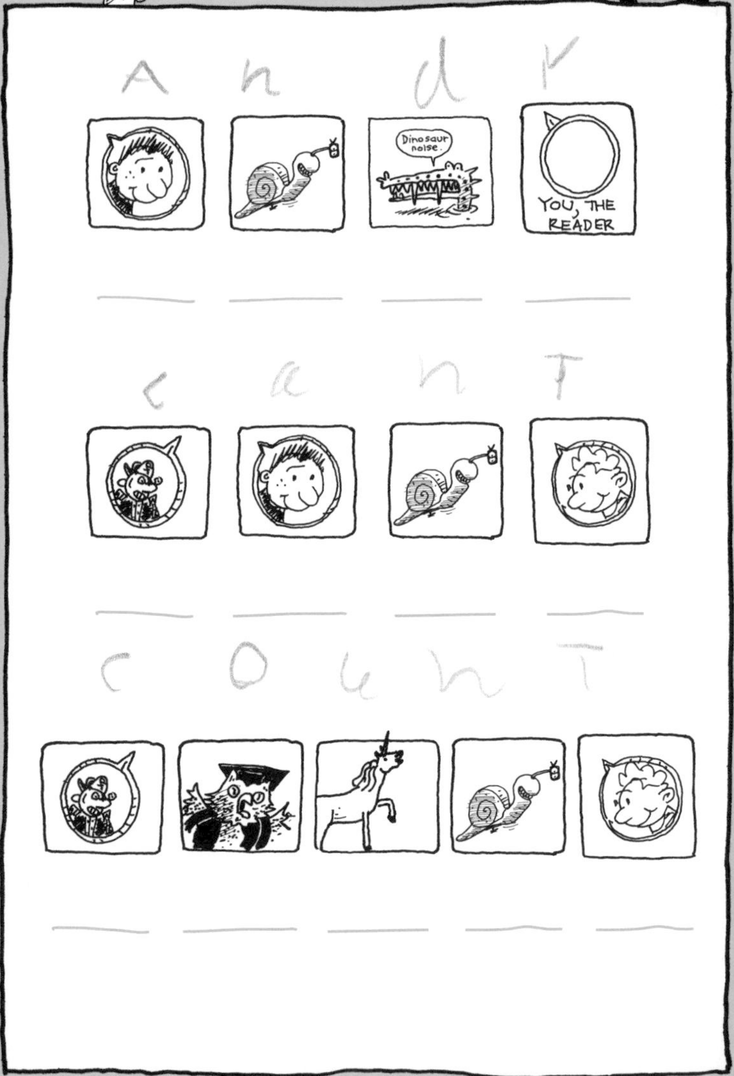
Dinosaur noise.
YOU, THE READER

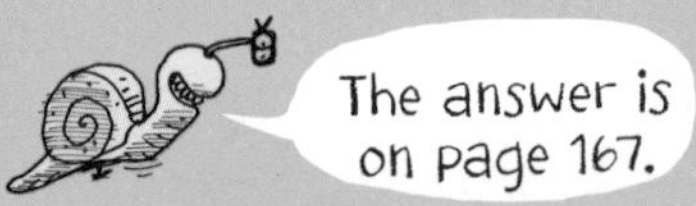
The answer is on page 167.

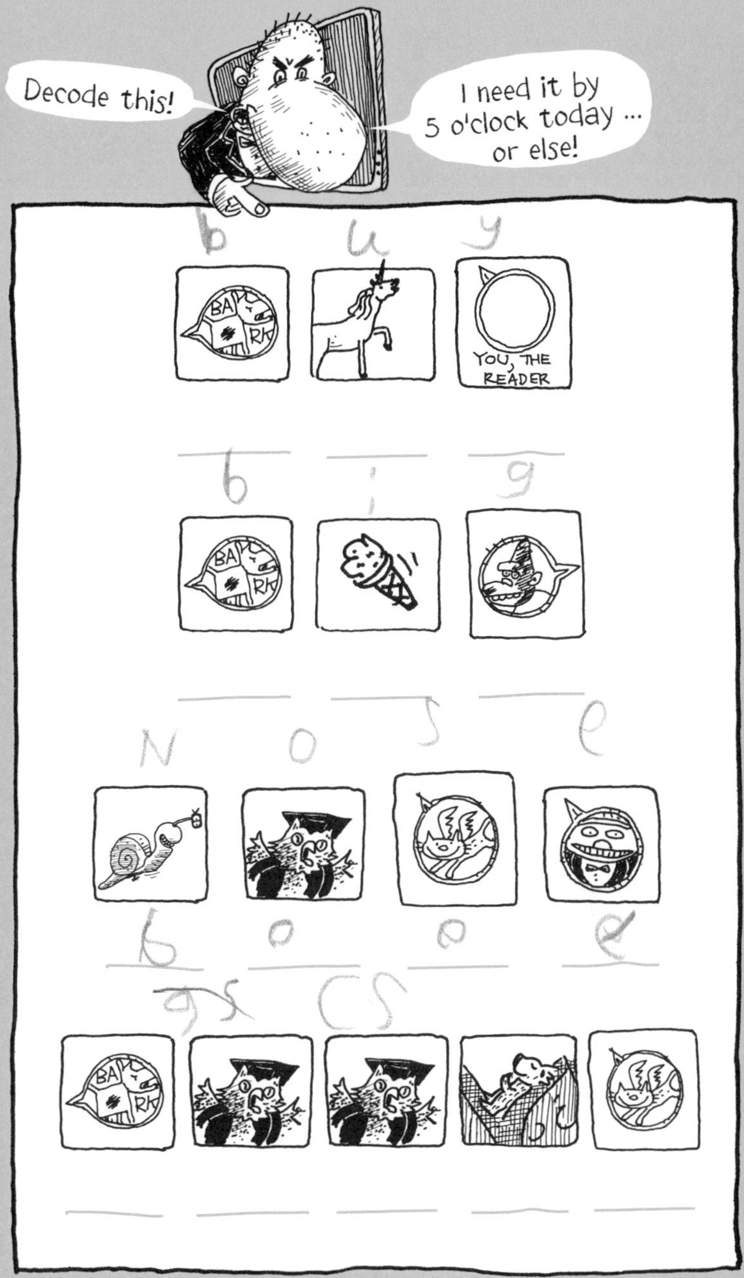
Decode this!
I need it by 5 o'clock today ... or else!
YOU, THE READER

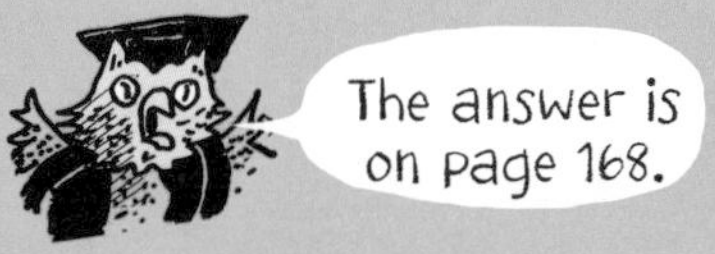
The answer is on page 168.

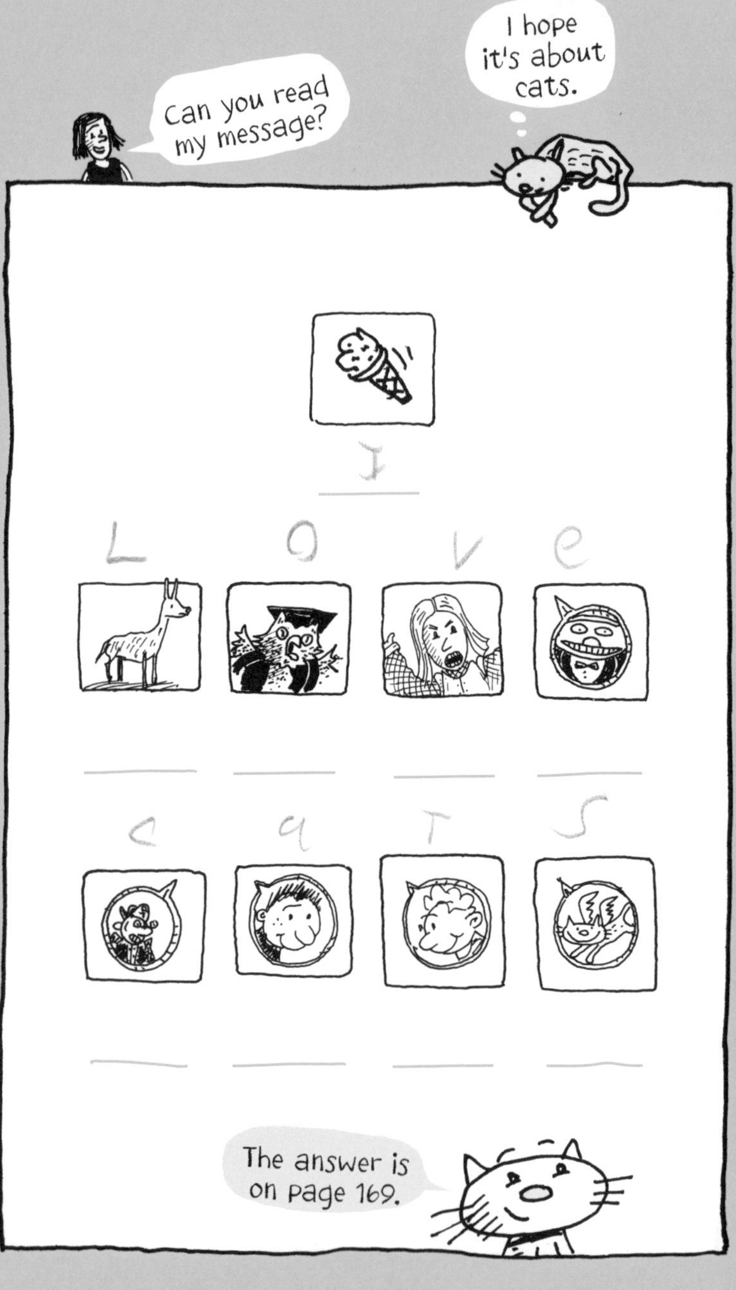
Can you read my message?
I hope it's about cats.
I
L o v e
c a T S
The answer is on page 169.

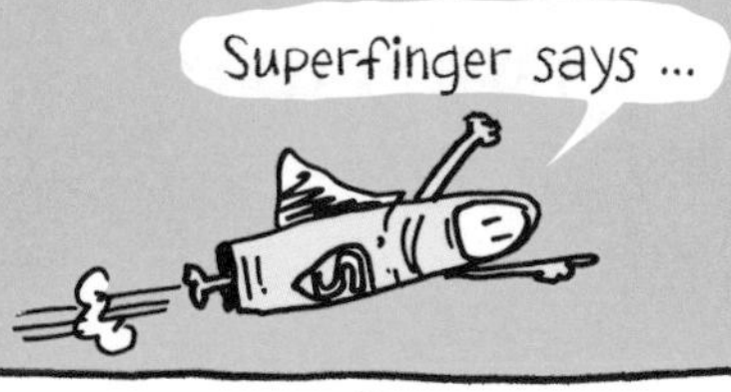
Superfinger says ...

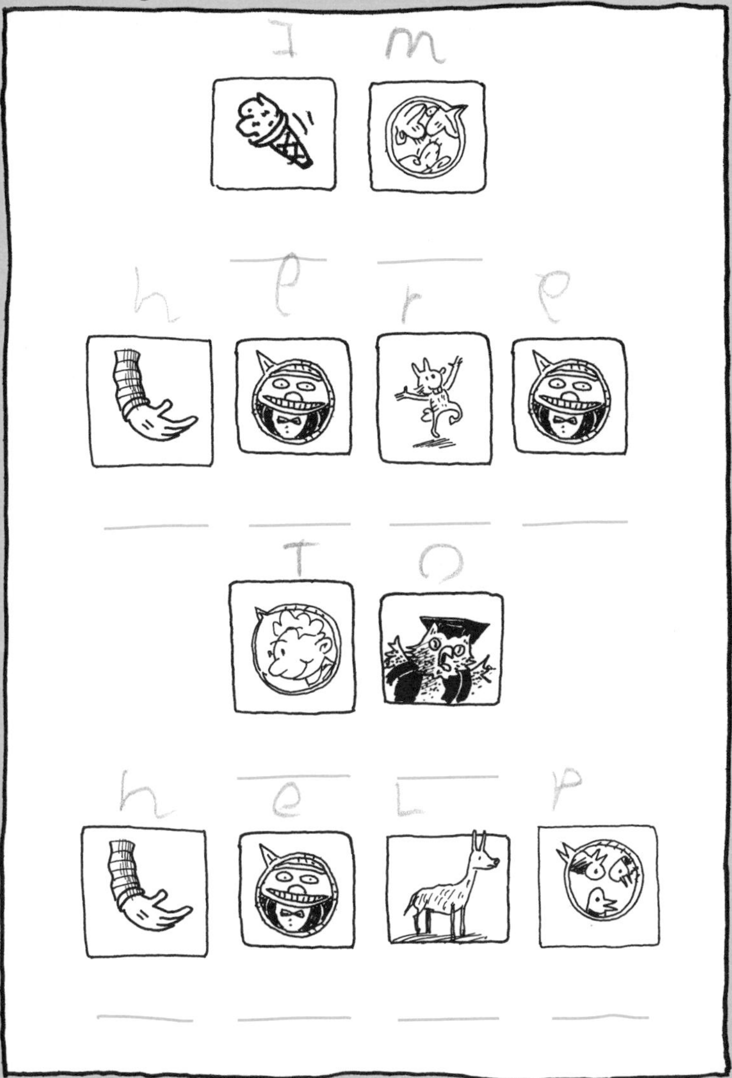

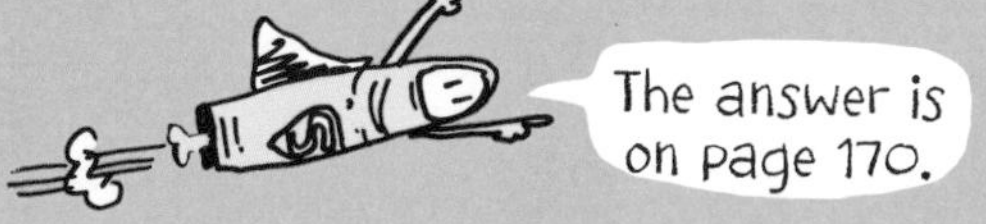
The answer is on page 170.

FIND-THE-UNICORN FUN

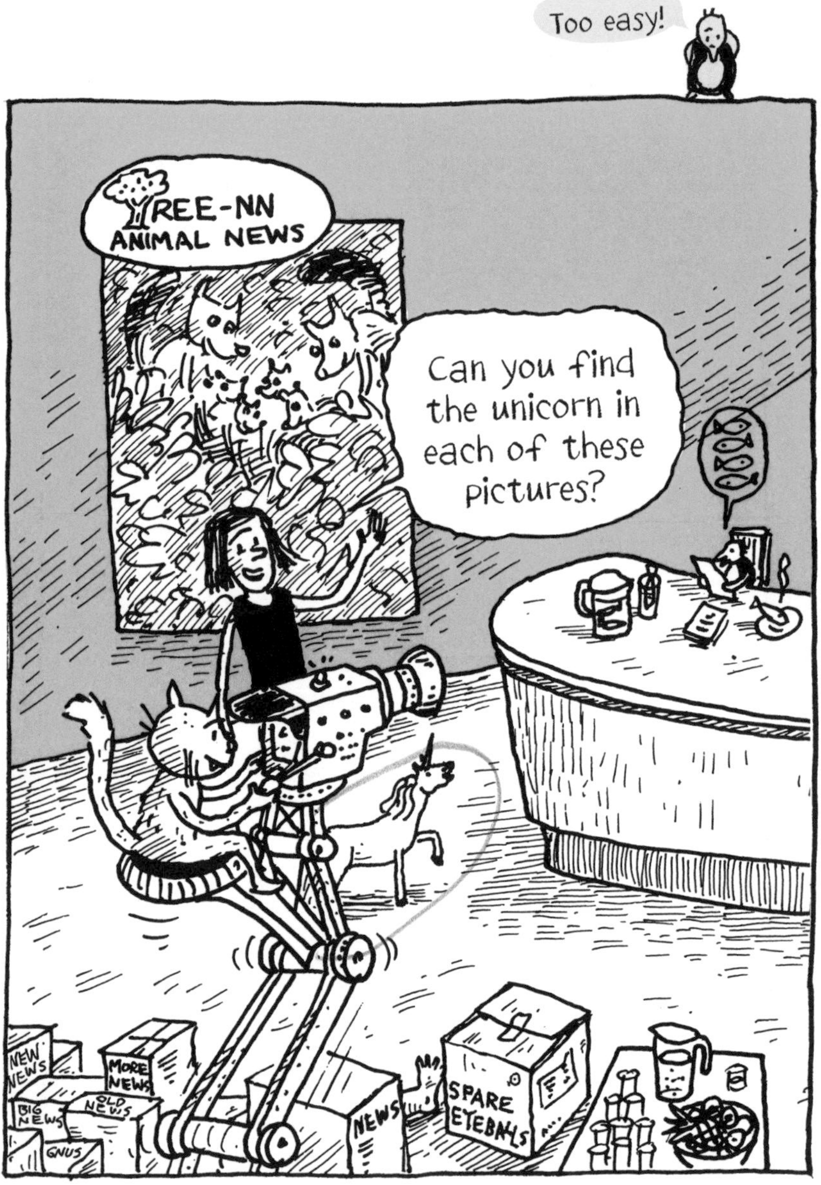
Too easy!
TREE-NN ANIMAL NEWS
Can you find the unicorn in each of these pictures?
NEW NEWS
MORE NEWS
BIG NEWS
OLD NEWS
GNUS
NEWS
SPARE EYEBALLS

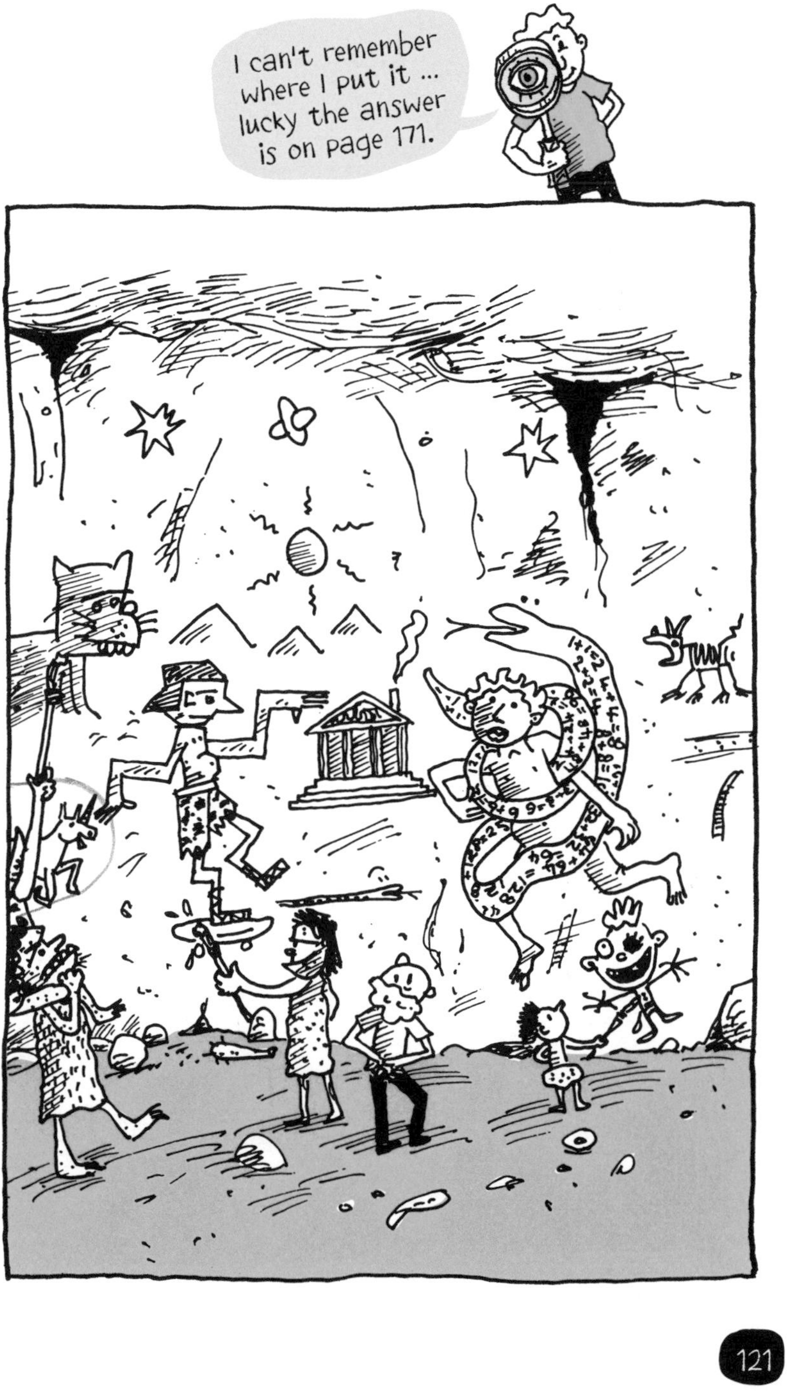
I can't remember where I put it ... lucky the answer is on page 171.

THE REALLY HUNGRY CATERPILLAR'S STORY

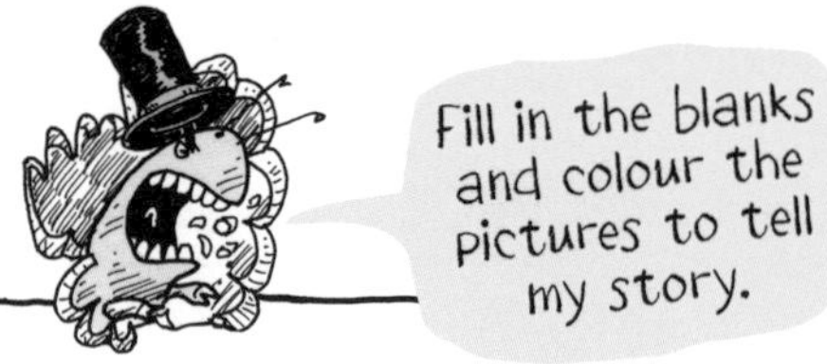
Fill in the blanks and colour the pictures to tell my story.

The really hungry caterpillar

ate one _ _ _ _ _ _ _

fried- _ _ _

_ _ _

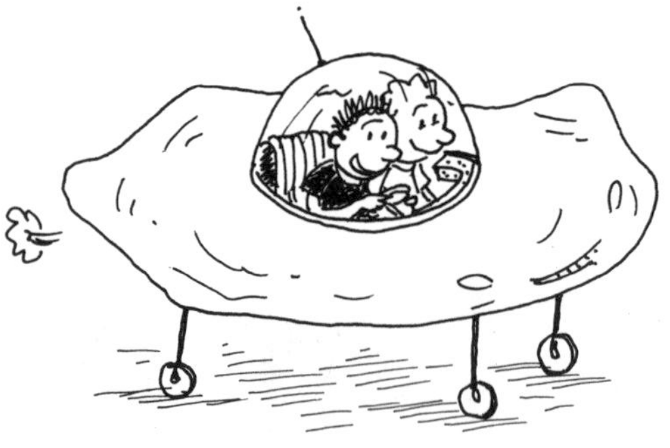

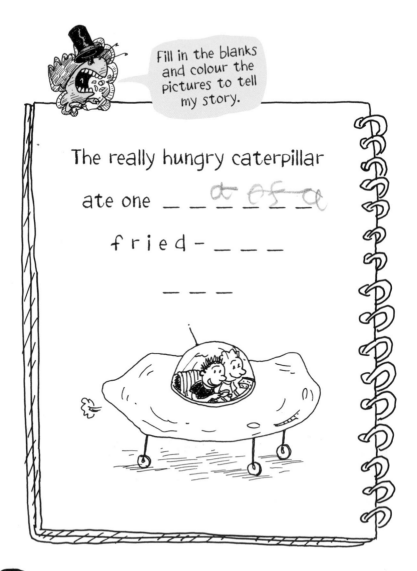

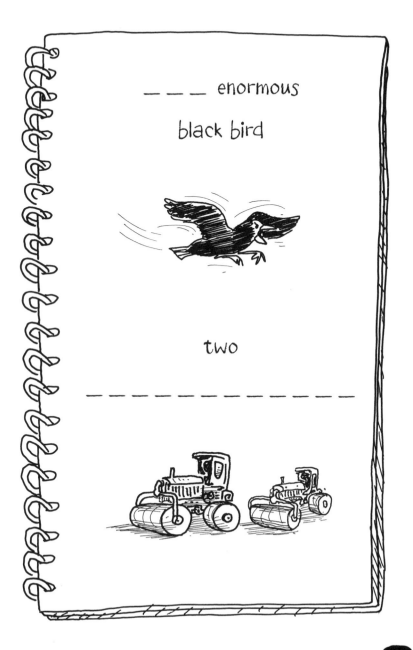

_ _ _ enormous

black bird

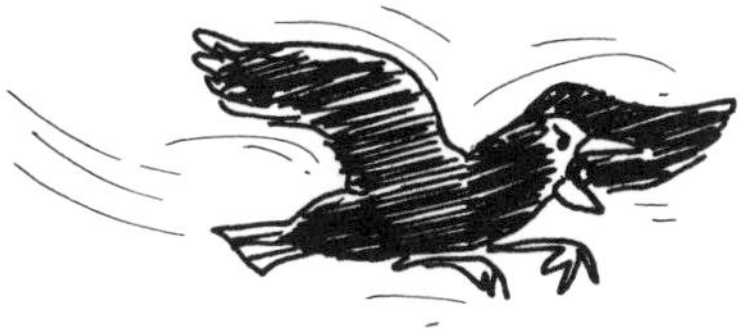

two

_ _ _ _ _ _ _ _ _ _ _ _ _ _

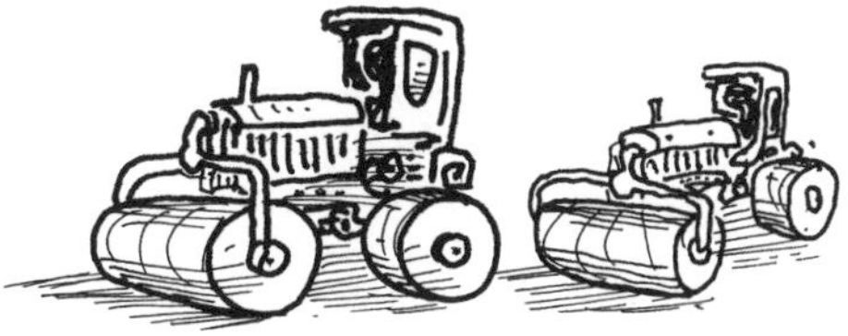

three rhinoceroses

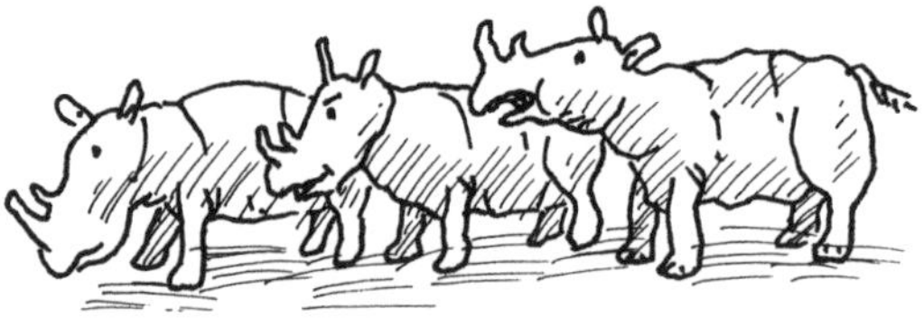

four wacky waving

inflatable _ _ _ -

flailing stick men

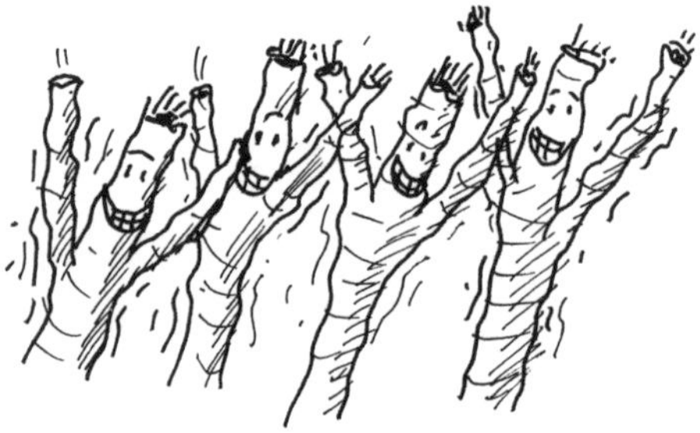

five giant mutant

spiders

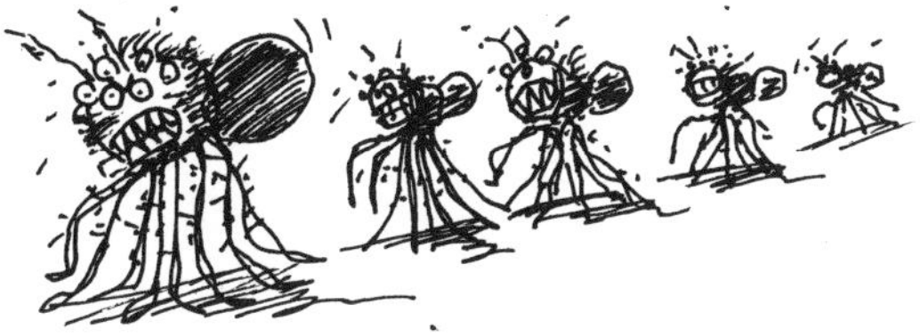

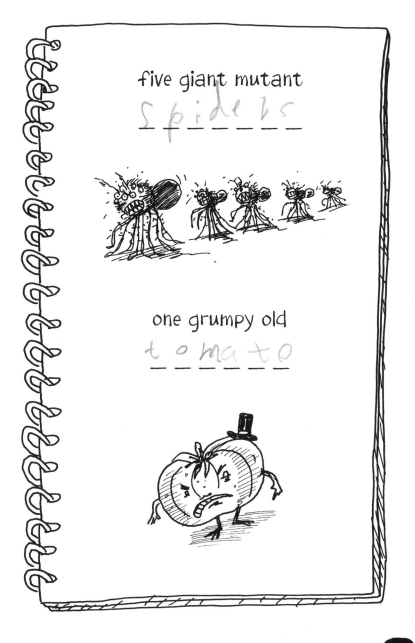

one grumpy old

tomato

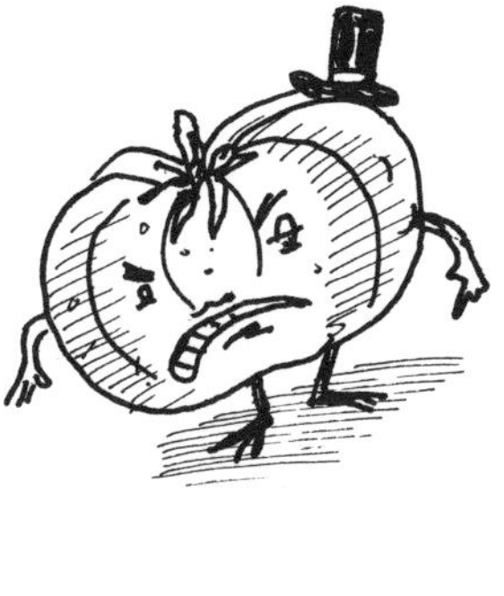

one wall of

asporiges

spears

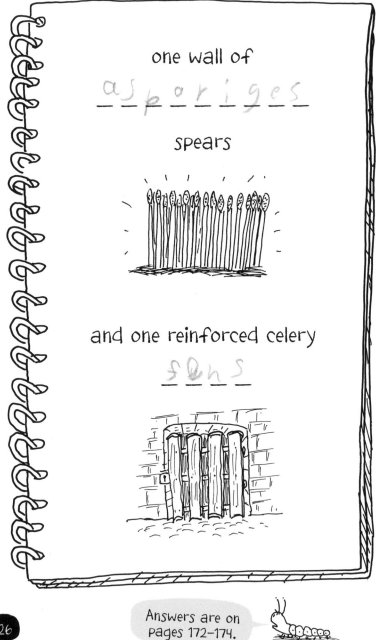

and one reinforced celery

fehs

Answers are on
pages 172–174.

WHAT FAIRYTALE IS THAT?

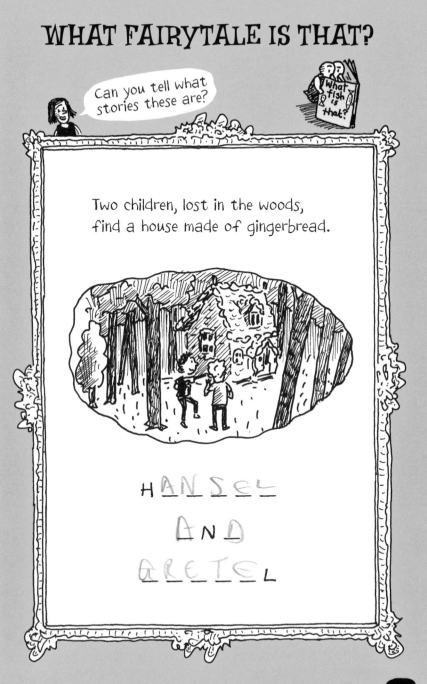

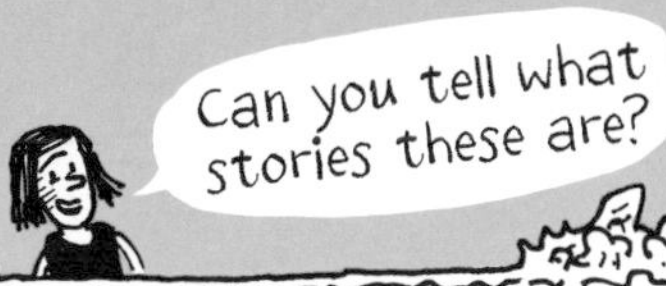
Can you tell what stories these are?

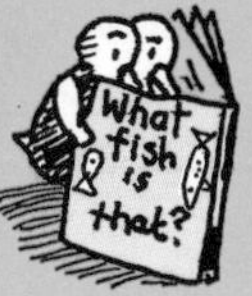
What fish is that?

Two children, lost in the woods, find a house made of gingerbread.

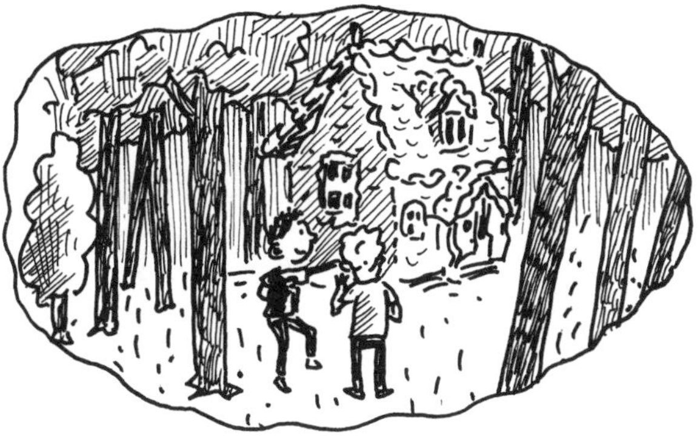

HANSEL

AND

GRETEL

While walking through the woods to Grandmother's house, a young child encounters a wolf.

L I t t L c
 R E d
 r i d i n G
 H o o d

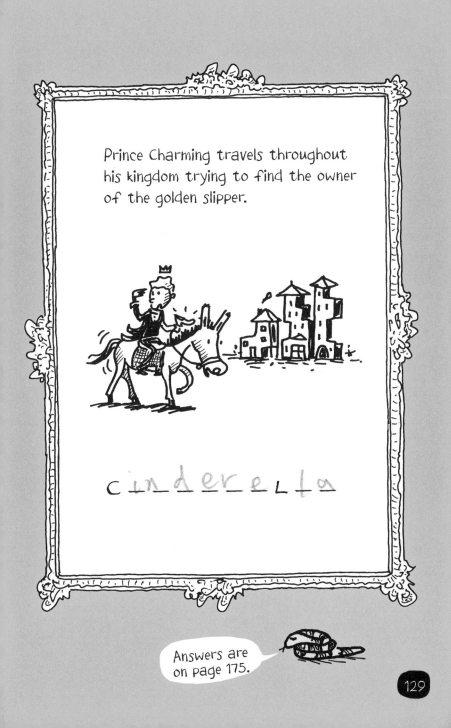

Prince Charming travels throughout his kingdom trying to find the owner of the golden slipper.

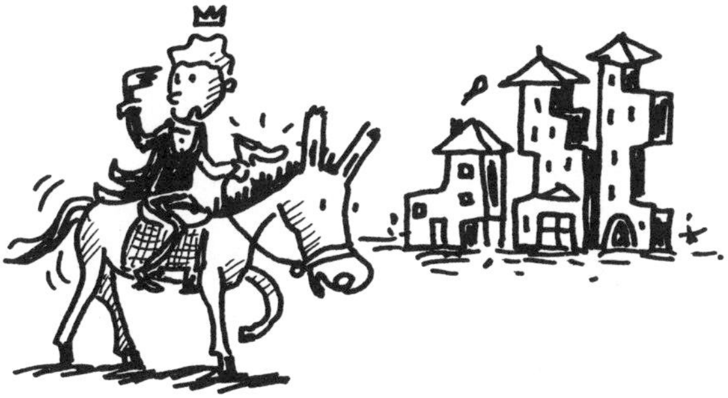

cinderella

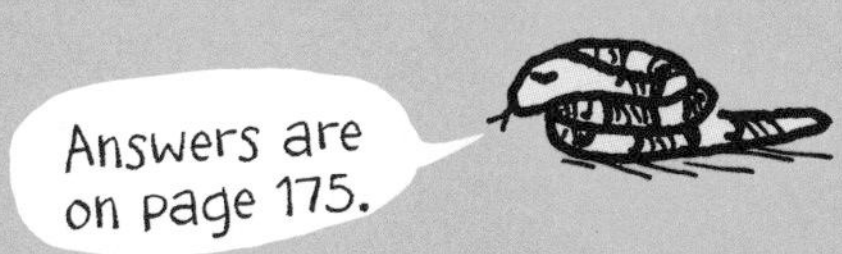
Answers are on page 175.

WHO REALLY SAID WHAT?!

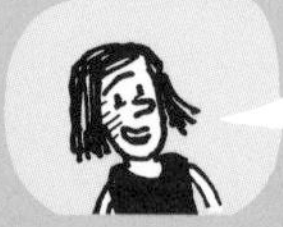

These quotes are all mixed up. Draw a line from the speech bubble to the character who REALLY said it.

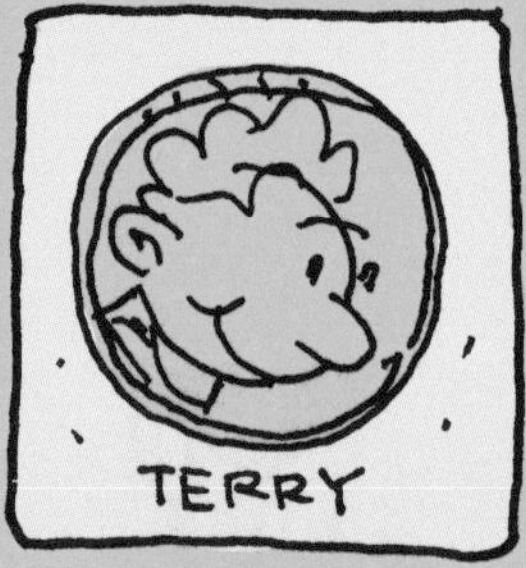
TERRY

That's crazy! SO crazy it just might work!

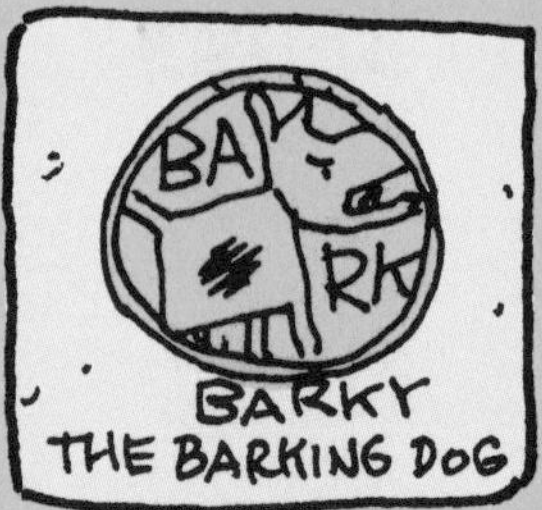
BA
RK
BARKY THE BARKING DOG

The sharks are sick! They ate my underpants!

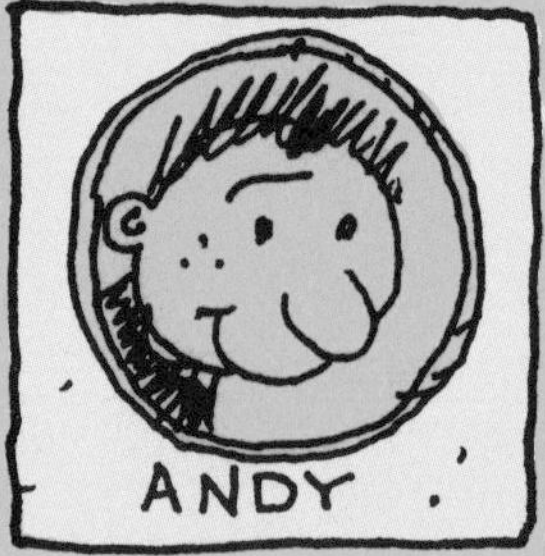
ANDY

BARK! BARK! BARK! BARK! BARK! BARK!

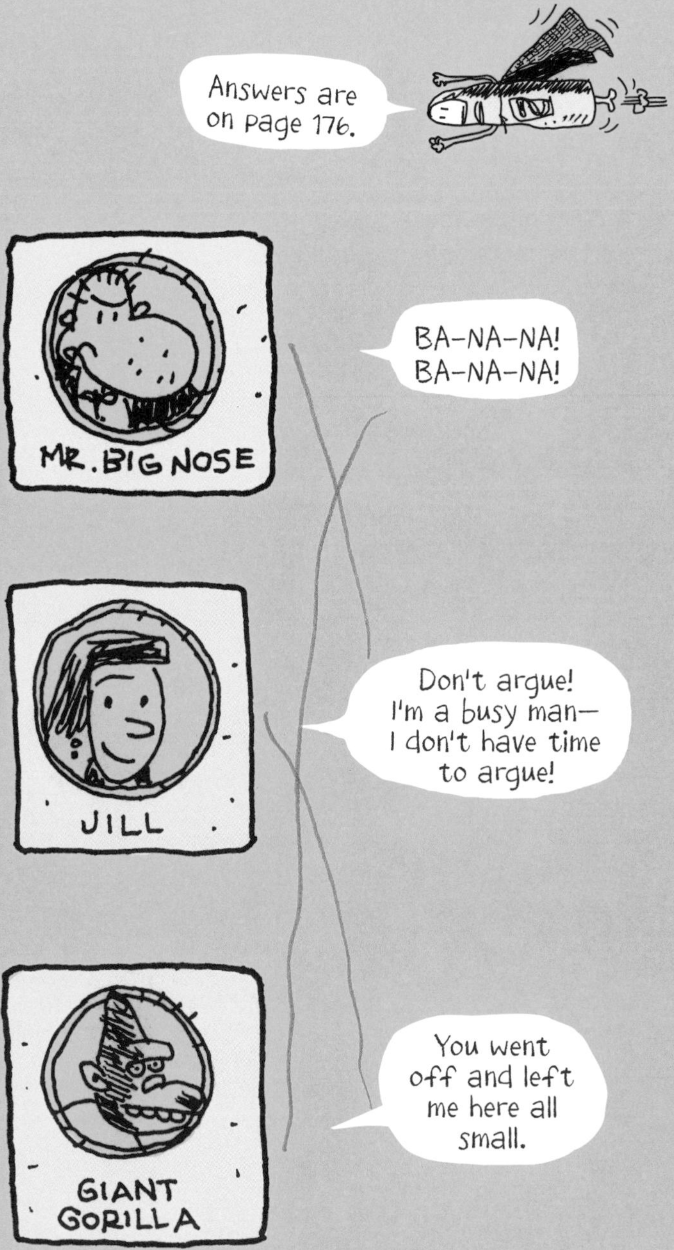
Answers are on page 176.
MR. BIG NOSE
BA-NA-NA! BA-NA-NA!
JILL
Don't argue! I'm a busy man— I don't have time to argue!
GIANT GORILLA
You went off and left me here all small.

CANNON-BLASTING TIME

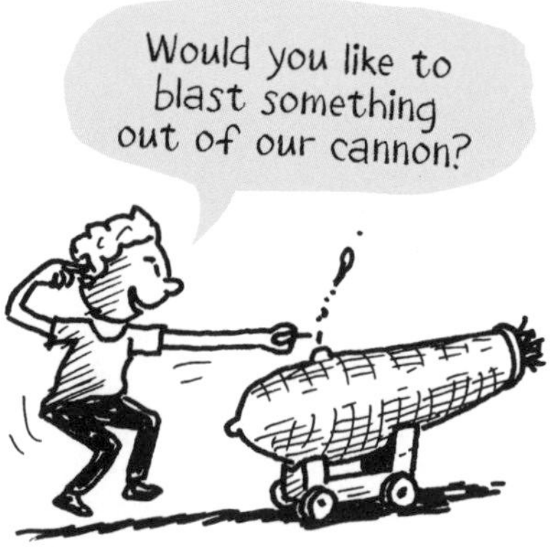
Would you like to blast something out of our cannon?

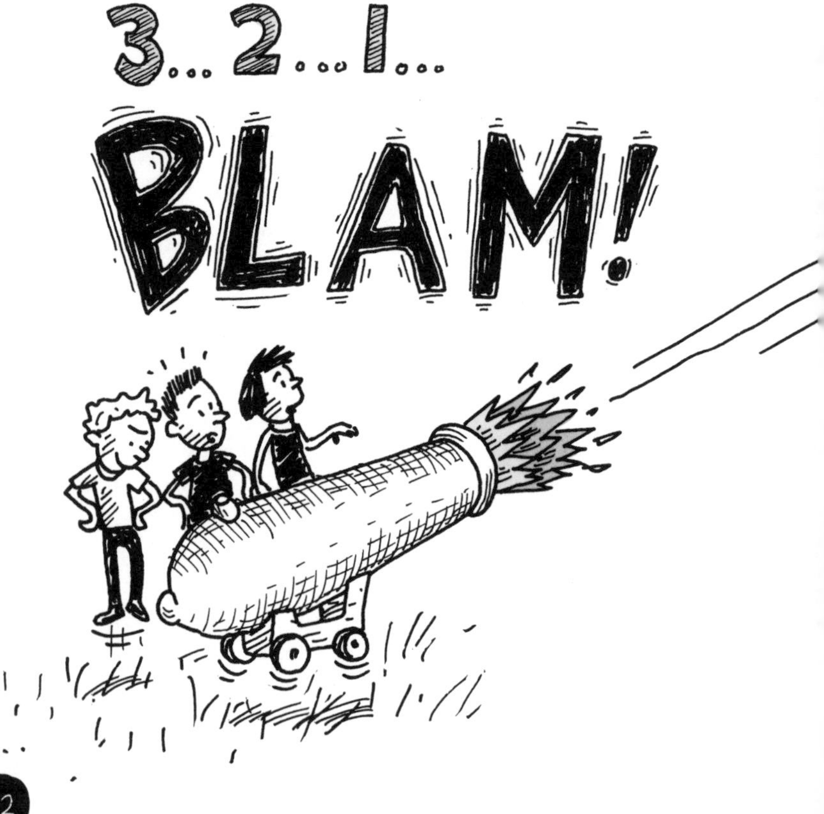
3... 2... 1...
BLAM!

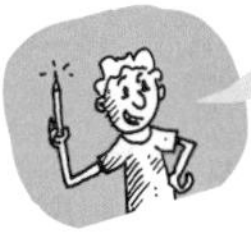

Draw what (or who) it is flying through the air.

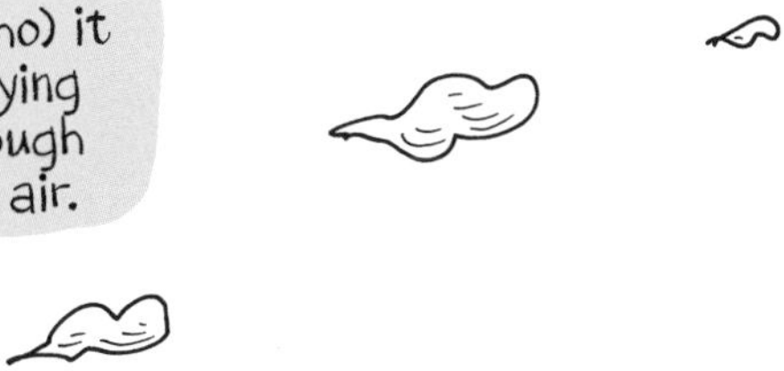

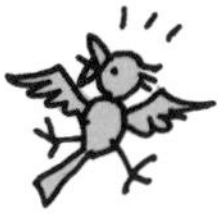

Or, maybe, your teacher ...

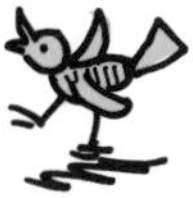

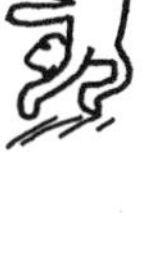

You could draw your little brother ...

DINNER TIME

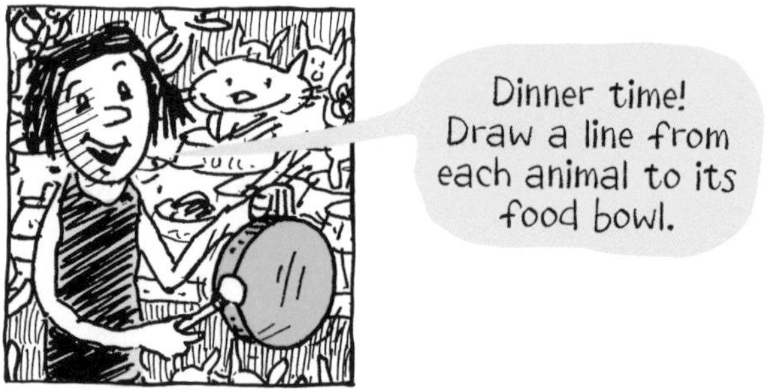
Dinner time! Draw a line from each animal to its food bowl.

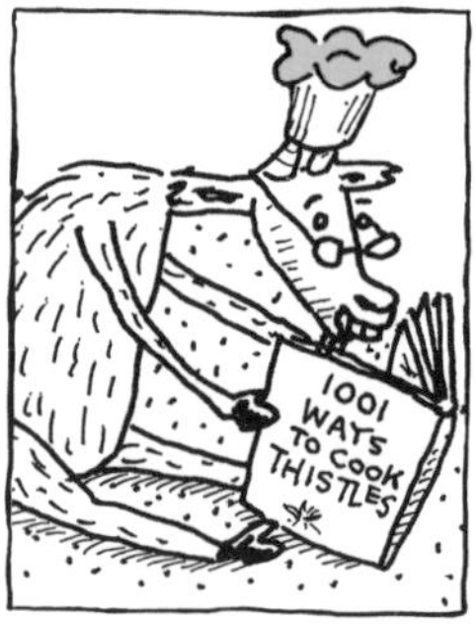
1001 WAYS TO COOK THISTLES

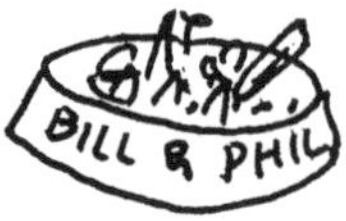
BILL & PHIL

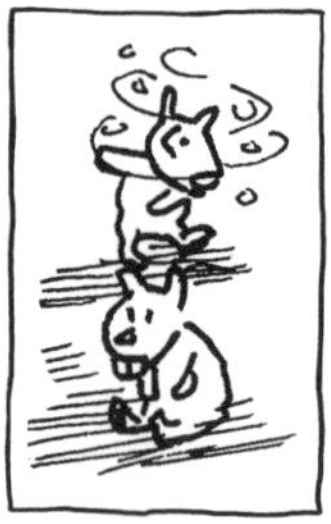

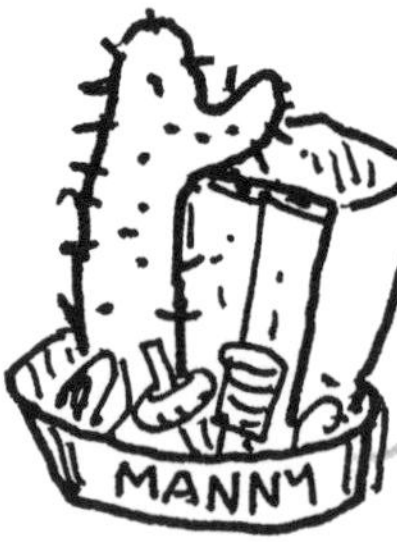
MANNY

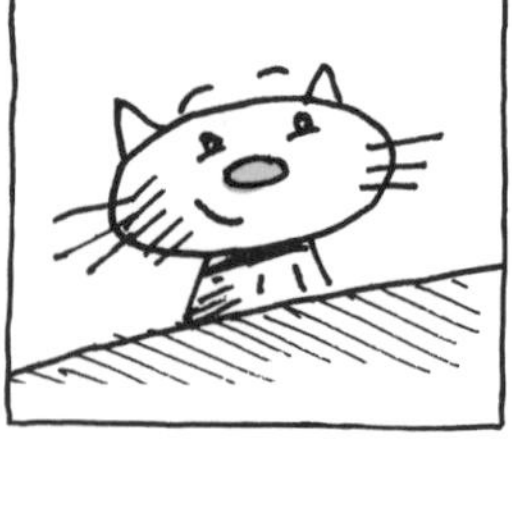

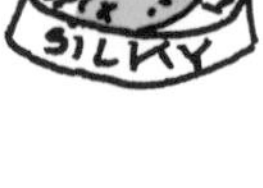
SILKY

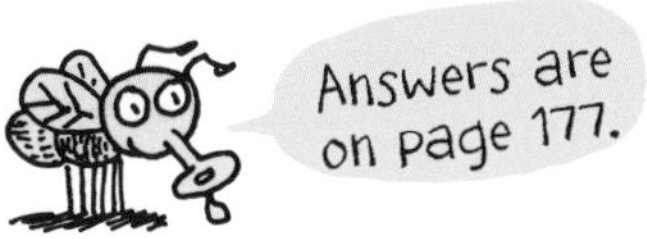
Answers are on page 177.

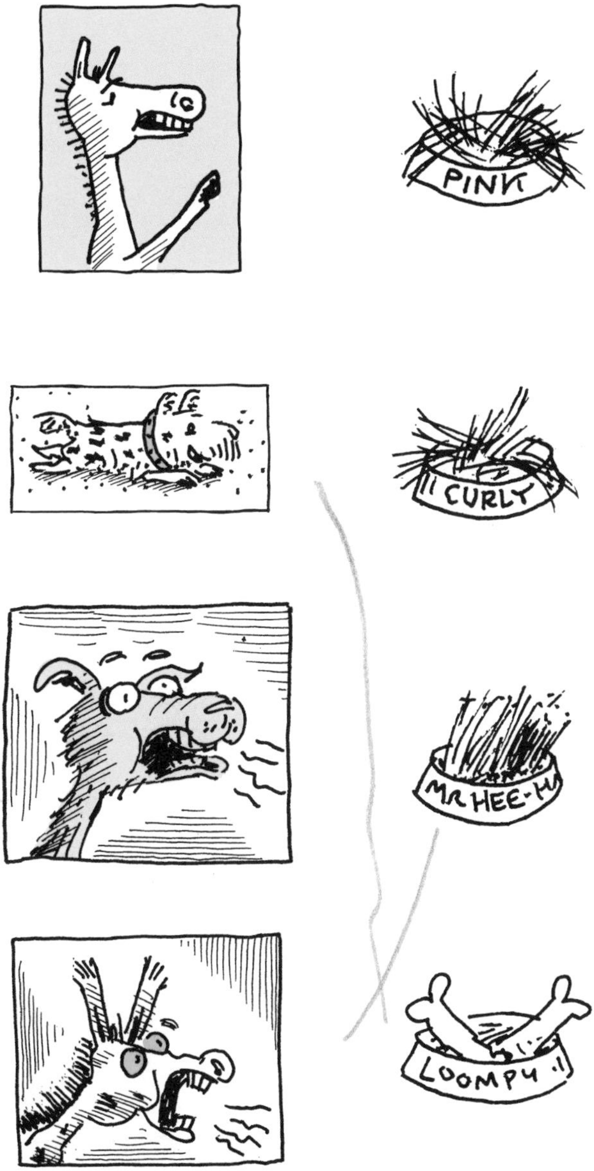
PINK
CURLY
MR HEE-HA
LOOMPY

TRAM-RIDE TIME

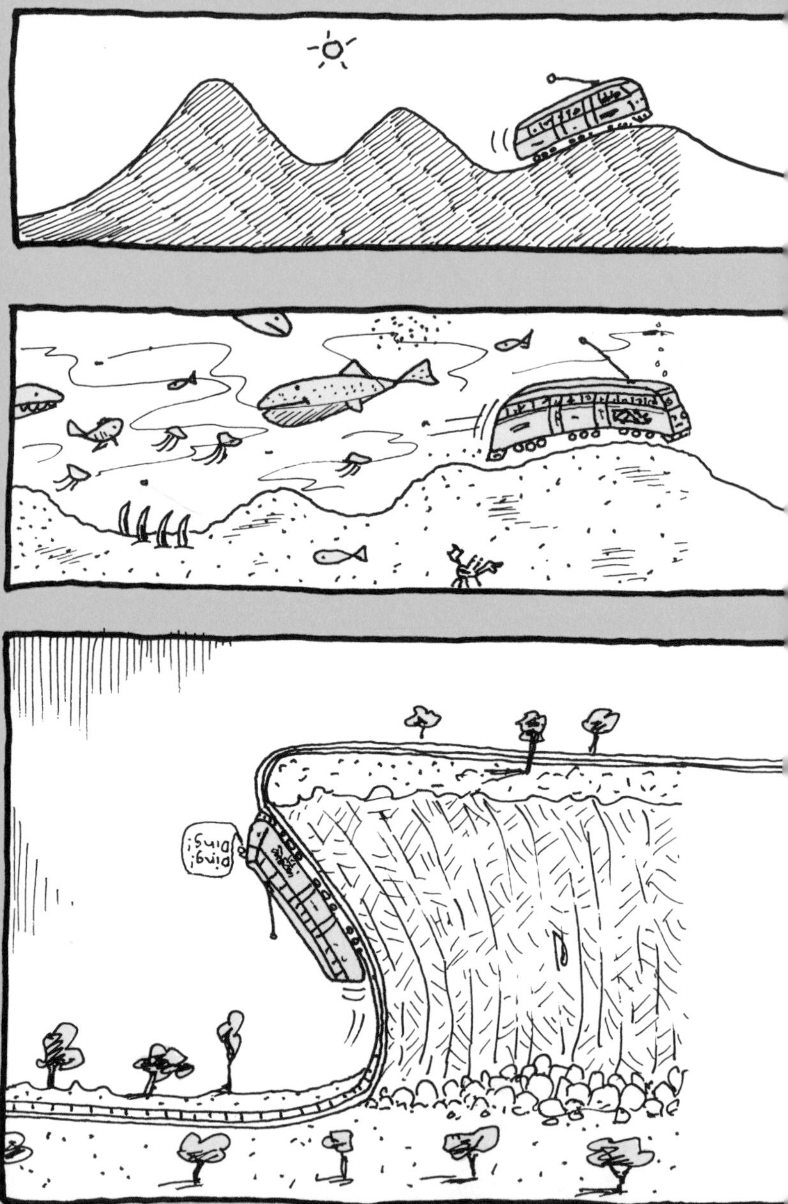

Ding! Ding!

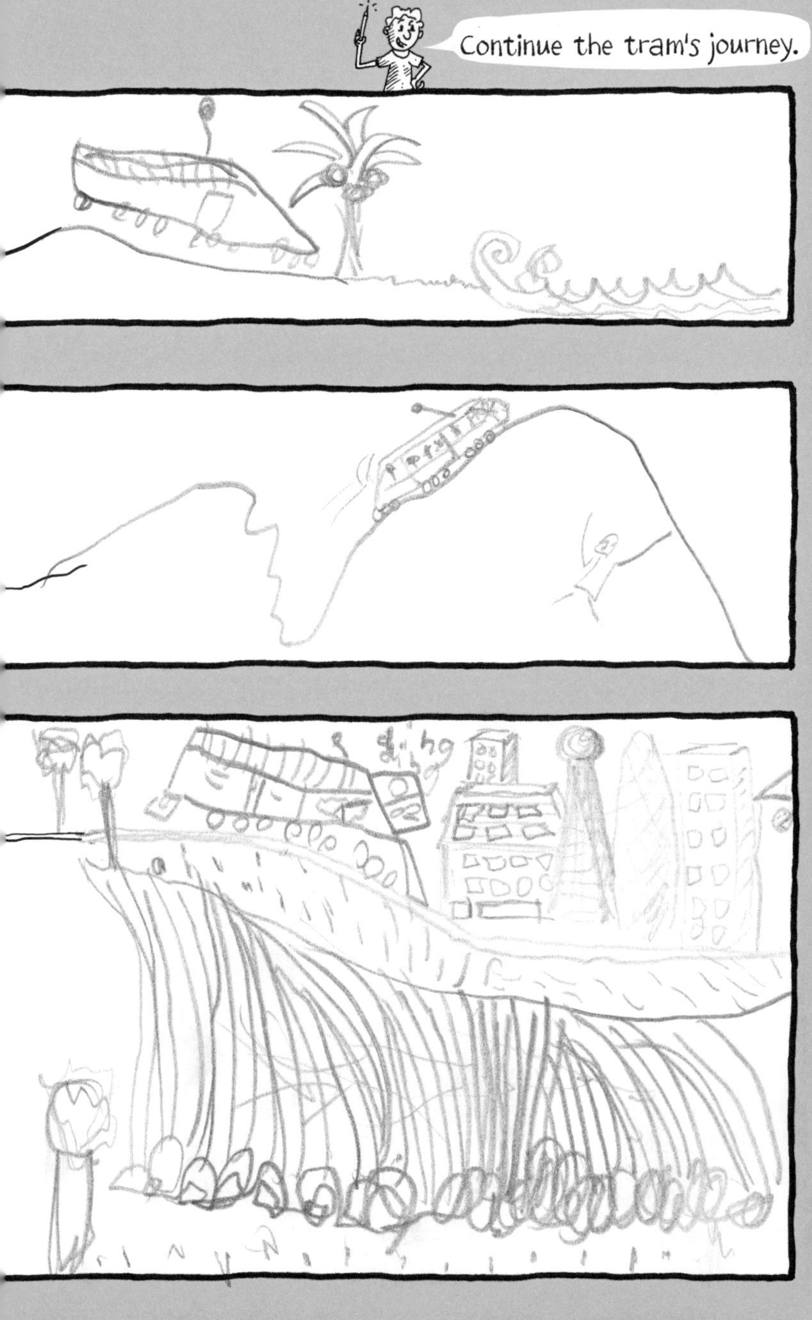
Continue the tram's journey.

FIND THE ODD ONE OUT

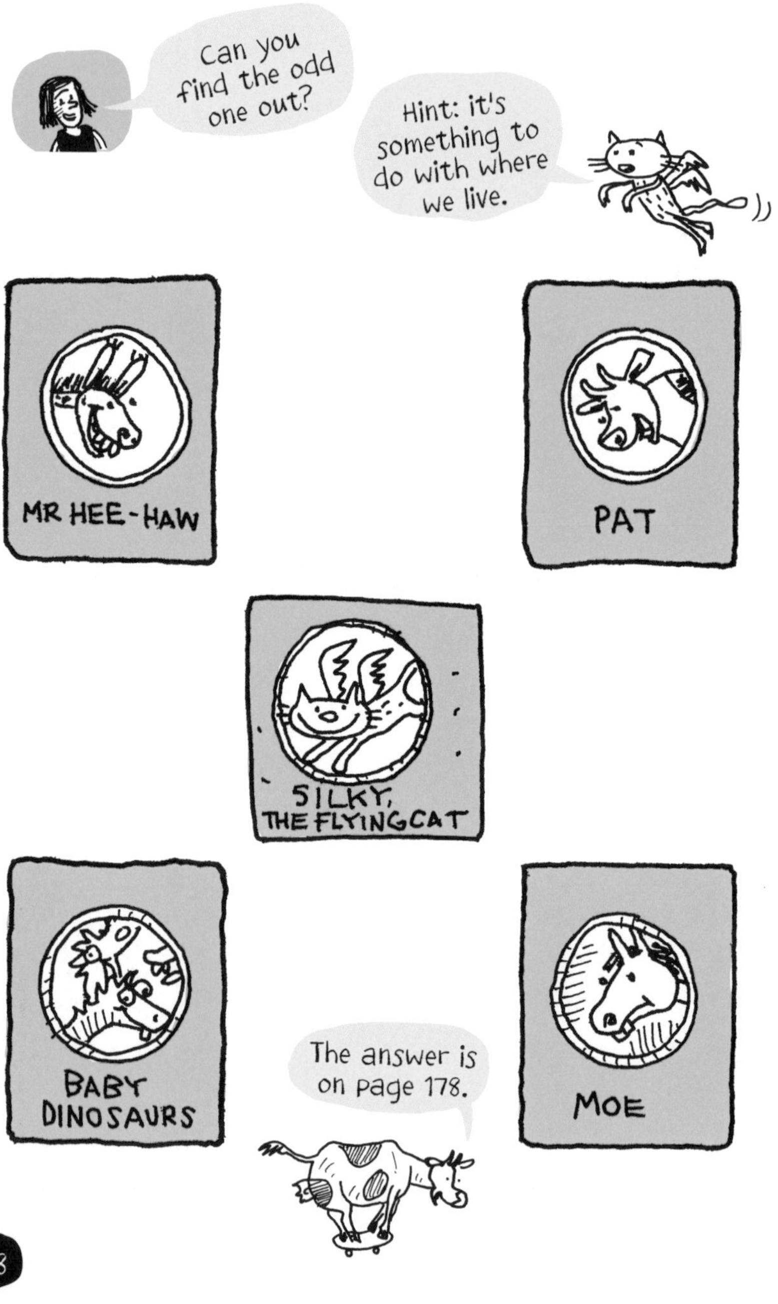
Can you find the odd one out?
Hint: it's something to do with where we live.
MR HEE-HAW
PAT
SILKY, THE FLYINGCAT
BABY DINOSAURS
MOE
The answer is on page 178.

TREE-COLOURING TIME

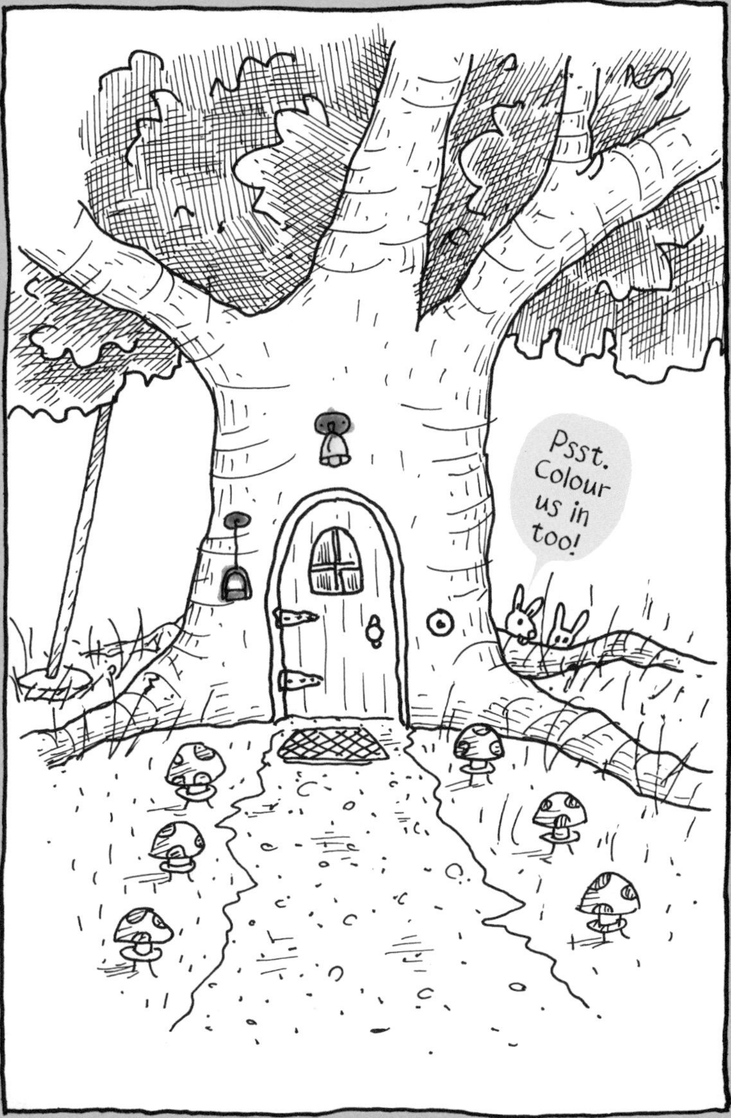
Psst. Colour us in too!

TREEHOUSE TRUE OR FALSE?

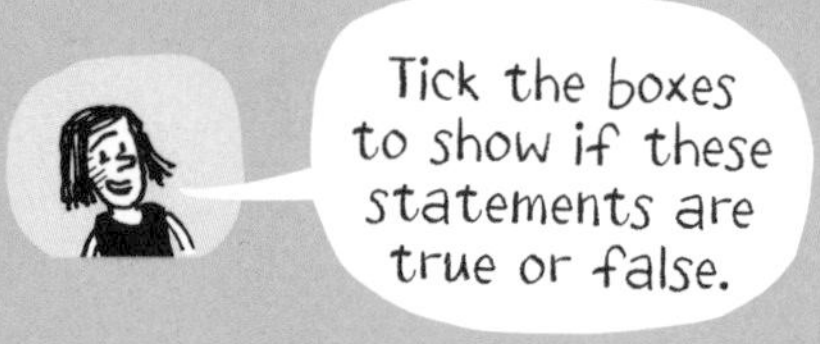
Tick the boxes to show if these statements are true or false.

T F

1. Silky is my favourite pet.
2. Mr Big Nose has a very bad temper.
3. Ninja Snails move very quickly.
4. Andy and Terry live in a 13-storey caravan.
5. I live in a house full of animals.
6. Andy and Terry love vegetables.
7. Bill the postman is a policeman.
8. Terry painted Silky yellow.
9. The Trunkinator is a boxing elephant.
10. Andy and Terry once worked in the monkey house at the zoo.
11. ATM stands for Automatic Tea Machine.
12. Prince Potato really likes Andy and Terry and is happy to spend time with them.
13. The treehouse has a see-through swimming pool.

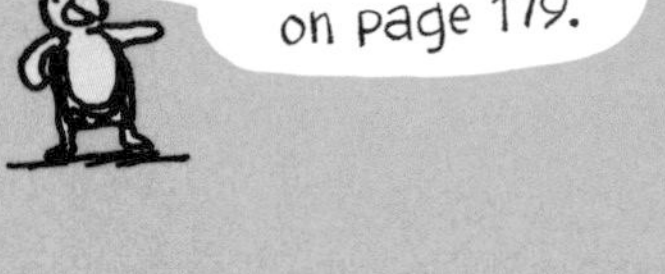
Answers are on page 179.

FIND THE ODD ONE OUT

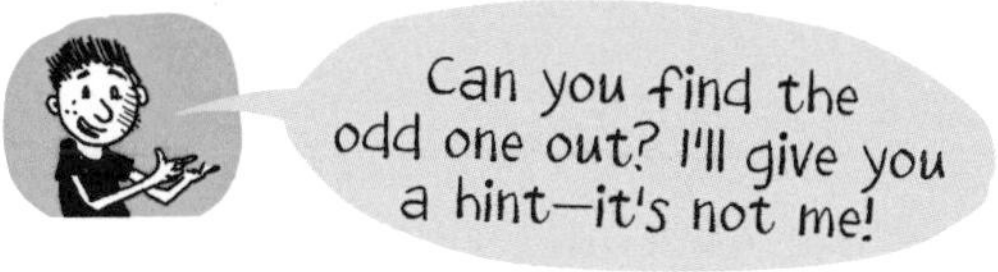
Can you find the odd one out? I'll give you a hint—it's not me!

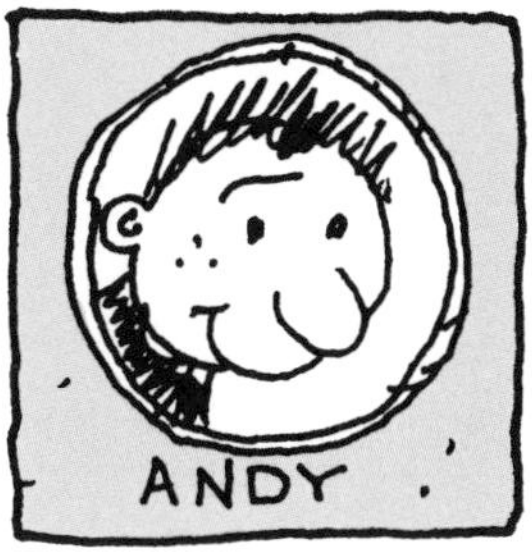
ANDY

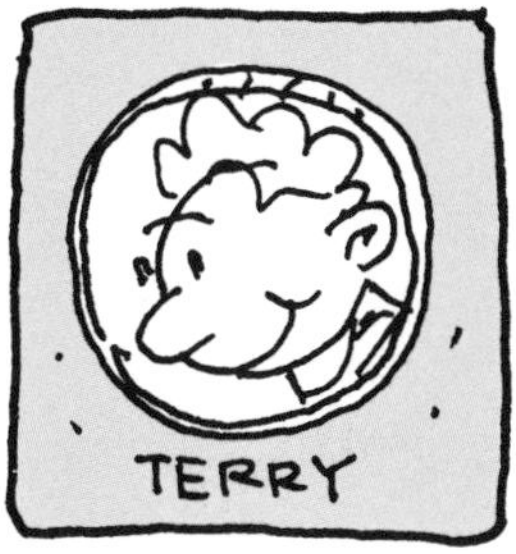
TERRY

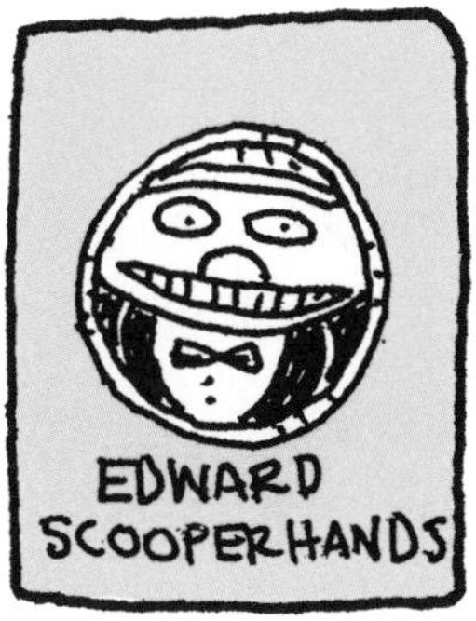
EDWARD SCOOPERHANDS

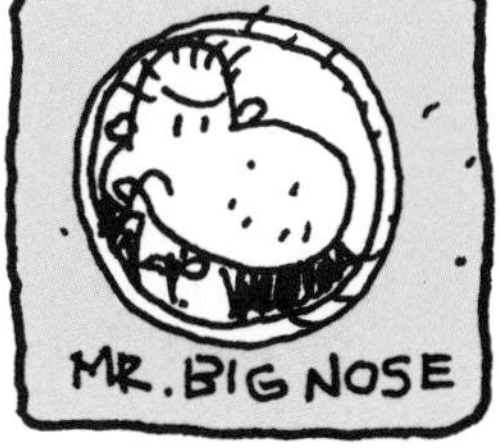
MR. BIG NOSE

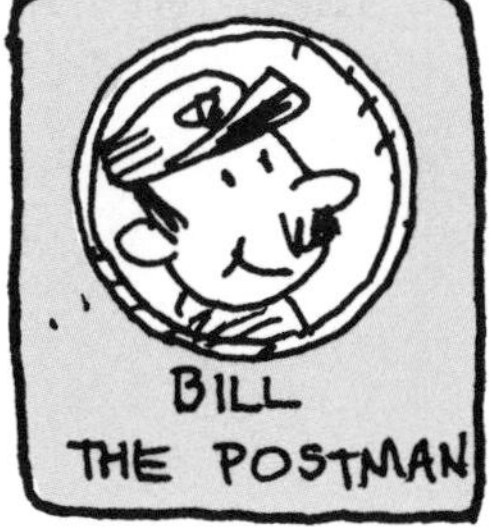
BILL THE POSTMAN

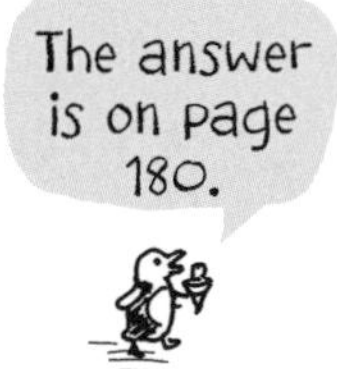
The answer is on page 180.

TREEHOUSE CROSSWORD

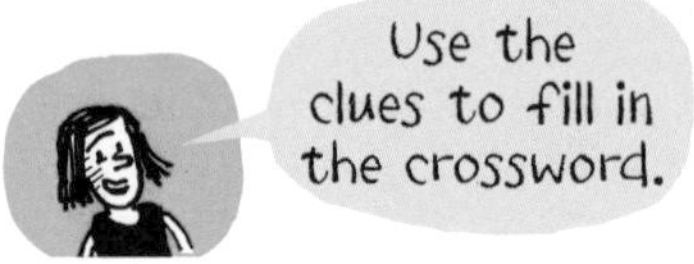
Use the clues to fill in the crossword.

ACROSS

1. He writes the words
3. He draws the pictures
7. Very wise animals that live in the treehouse
9. Short for Automatic Tattoo Machine
10. What Terry is training his snails to be
14. Andy and Terry have a Flying Fried-Egg — — —
15. He's a postman

DOWN

1. They live in the ant farm
2. Andy and Terry have a Maze of — — — —
4. Andy and Terry have a Rocking Horse — — — — — — — — —
5. The part of the Flying Fried-Egg Car that Andy and Terry sit in
6. Terry's second favourite TV show is Buzzy the Buzzing — — —
8. What Terry made a time travel machine in
11. Andy and Terry's neighbour and friend
12. Jill's pet cat
13. What Terry and Andy live in

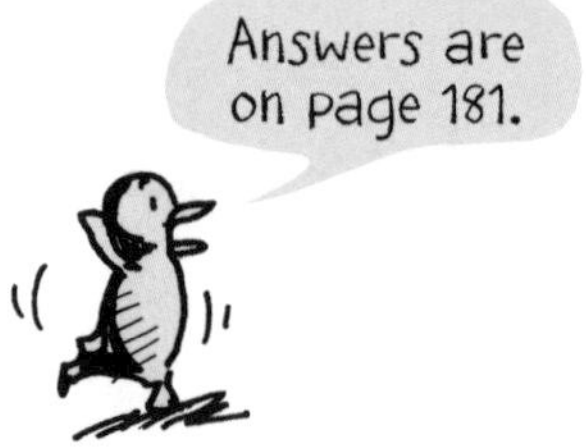
Answers are on page 181.

CROSSWORD! CLUES! POOP!-POOP!

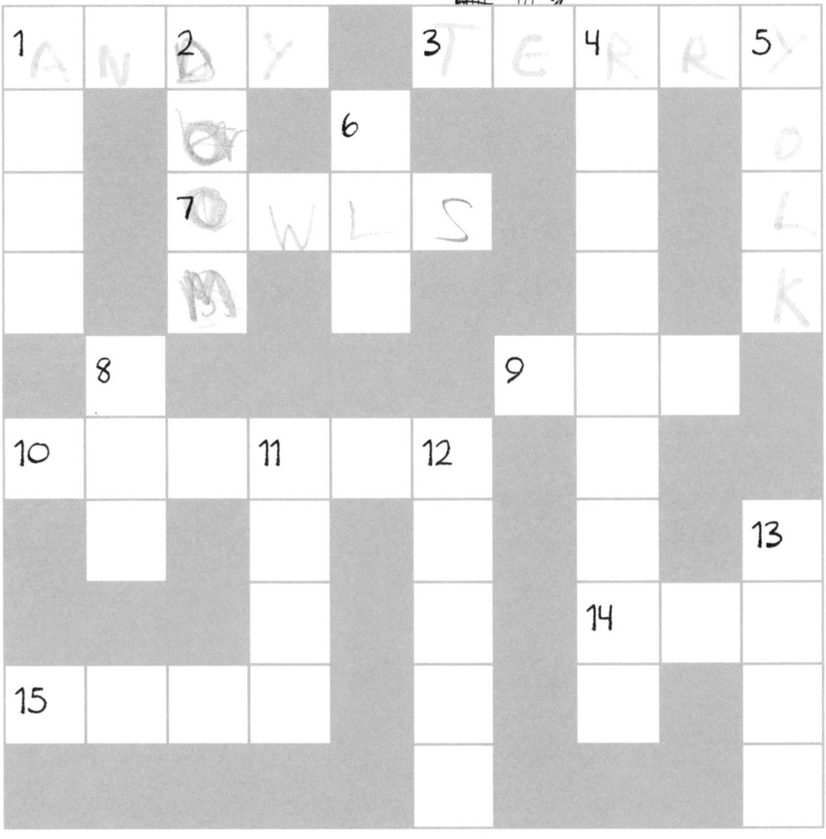

1 A	N	B Y	Y		3 T	E	4 R	R	5 Y
1			B					R		O
			7 O	W	L	S				L
			M							K
	8					9				
10			11		12					
									13	
							14			
15										

143

DRAW ANDY IN DANGER

I love drawing pictures of Andy in terrible danger. Help me finish these ones by drawing over the lines in the pictures of the dangerous animals.

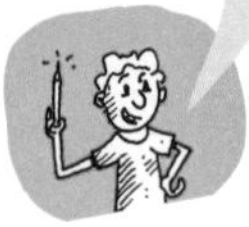

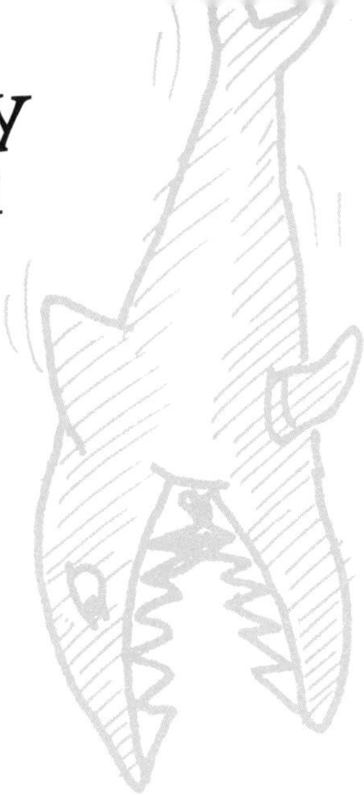

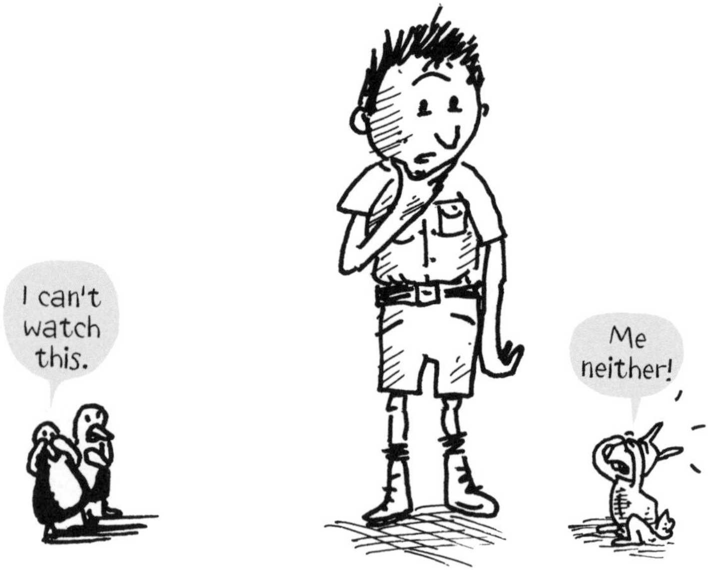
I can't watch this.
Me neither!

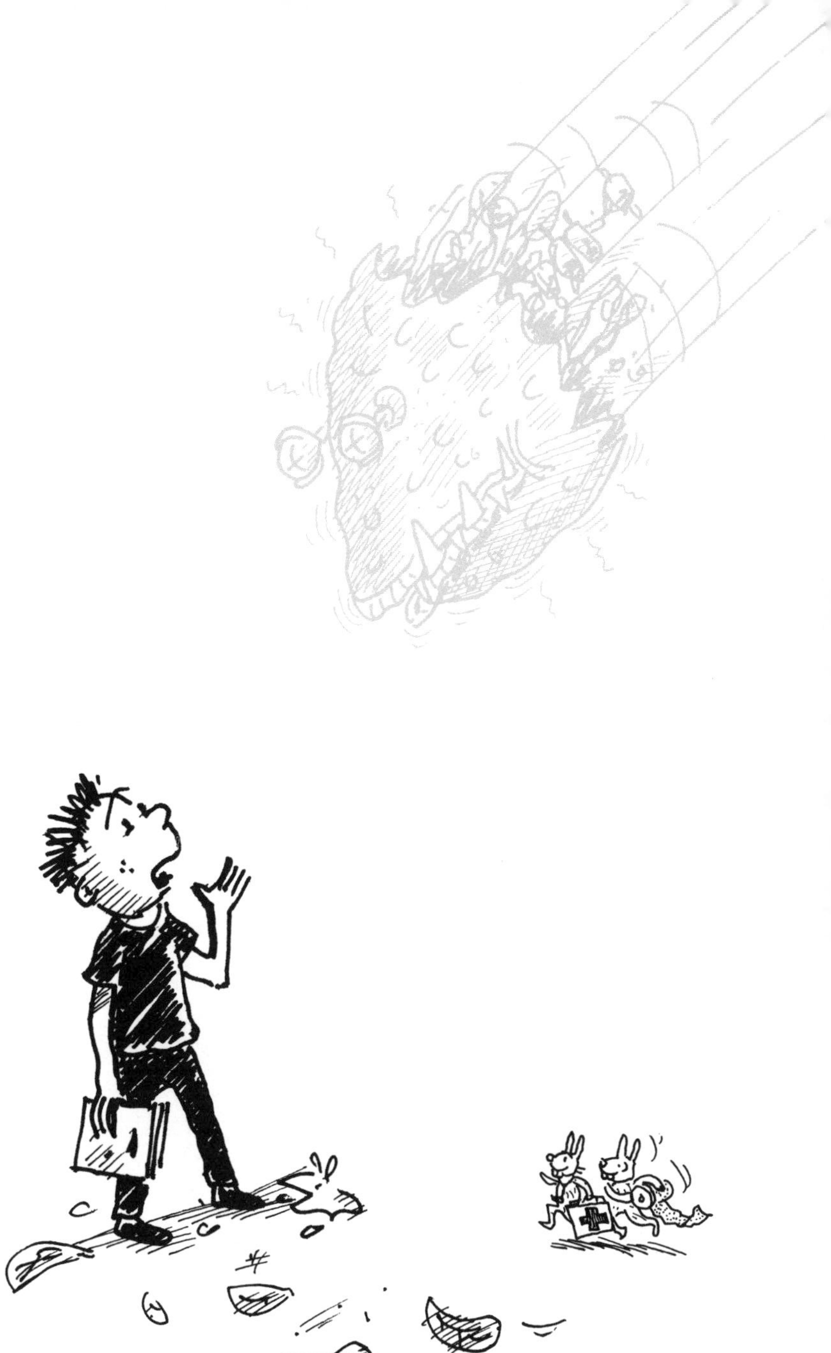

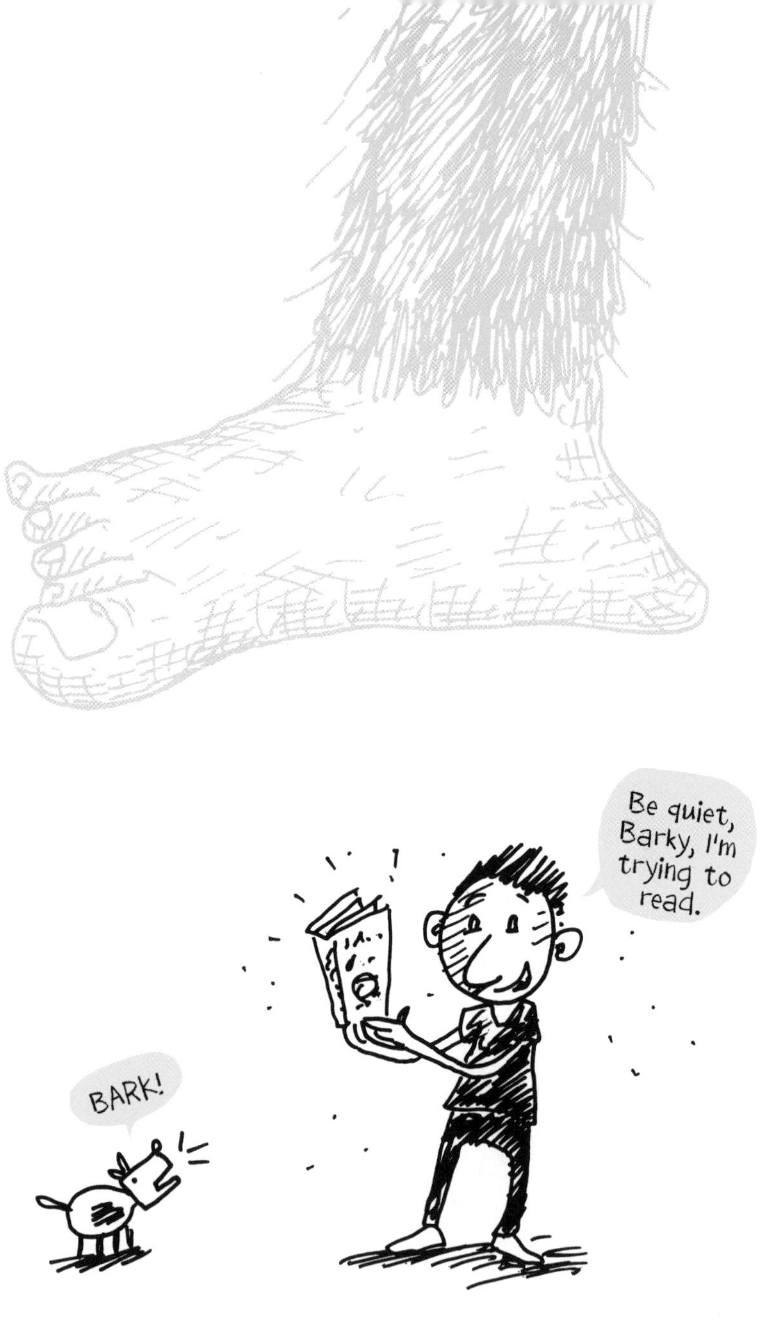
Be quiet, Barky, I'm trying to read.
BARK!

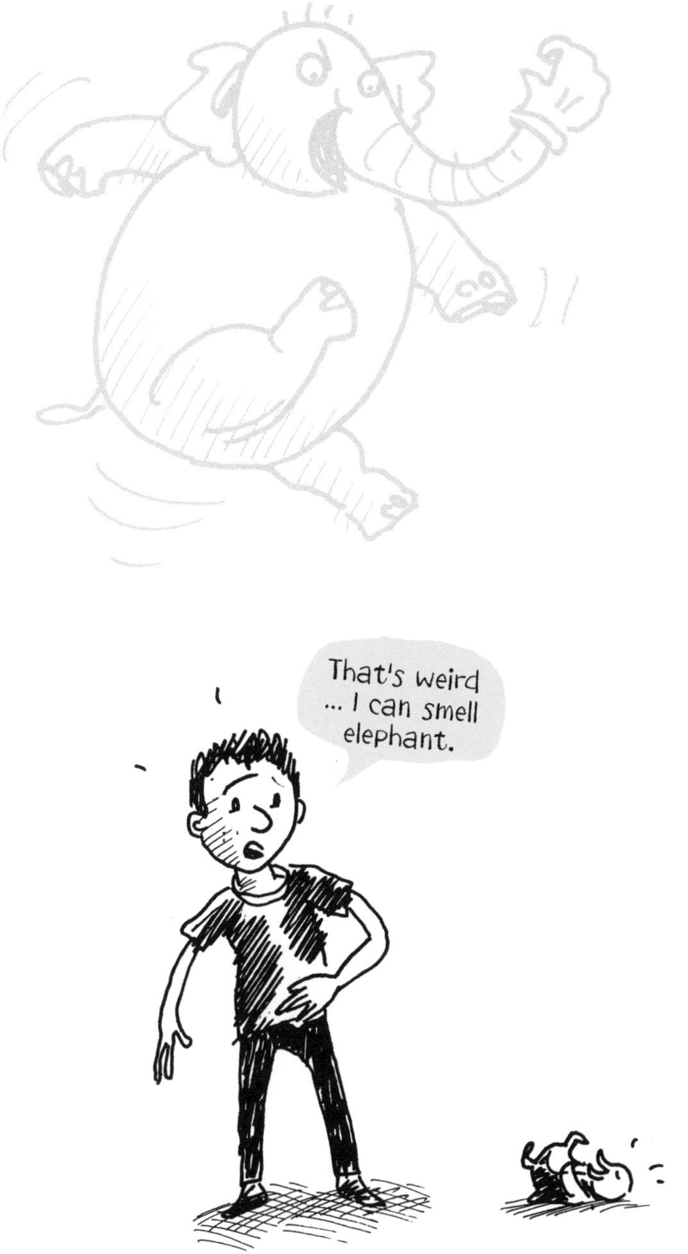
That's weird ... I can smell elephant.

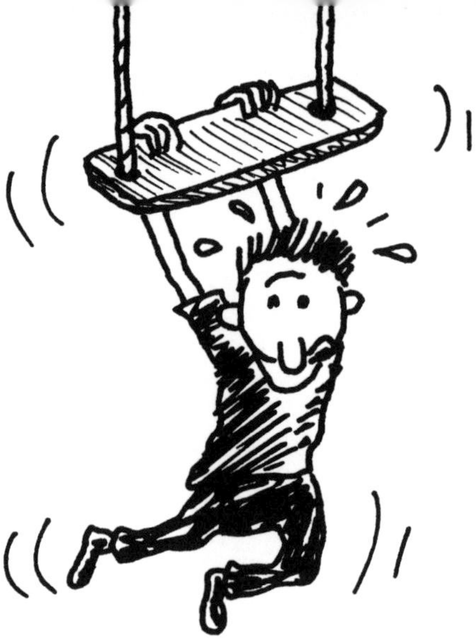

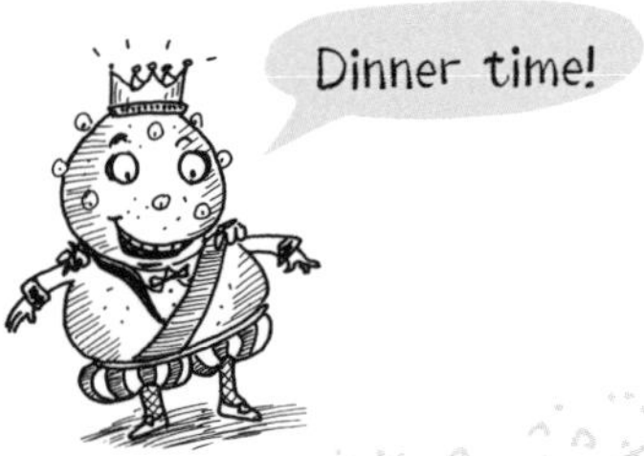
Dinner time!

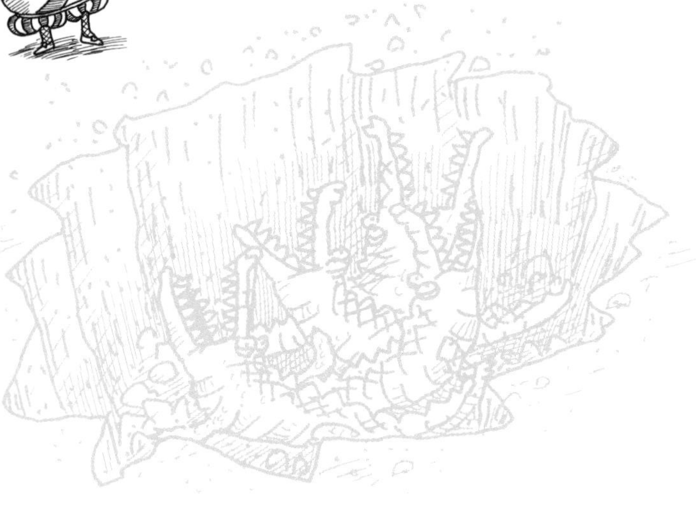

CATAPULT FUN

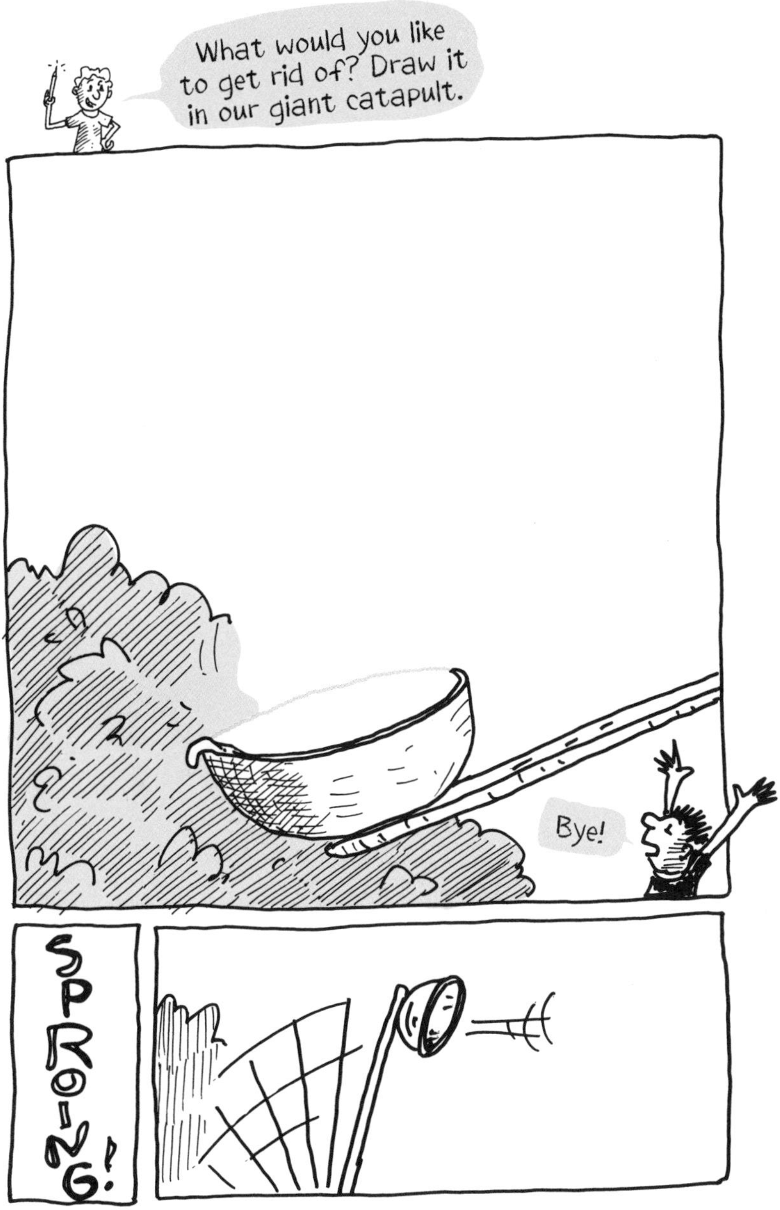
What would you like to get rid of? Draw it in our giant catapult.
Bye!
SPROING!

ANTI-GRAVITY TIME

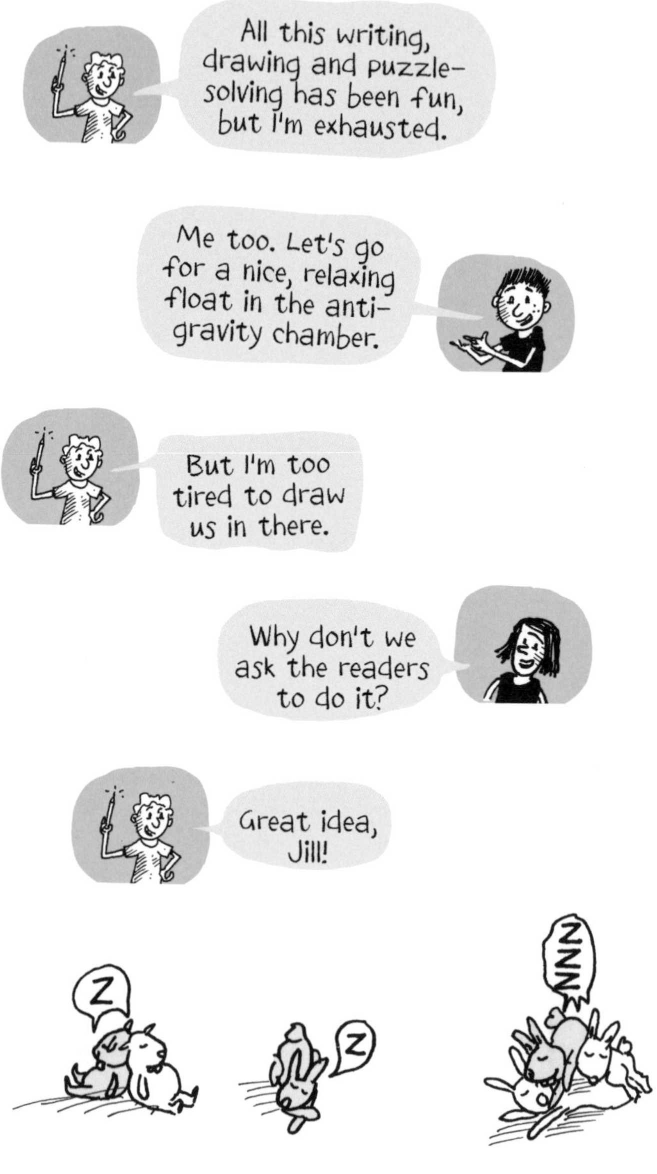
All this writing, drawing and puzzle-solving has been fun, but I'm exhausted.
Me too. Let's go for a nice, relaxing float in the anti-gravity chamber.
But I'm too tired to draw us in there.
Why don't we ask the readers to do it?
Great idea, Jill!
Z
Z
ZZZ

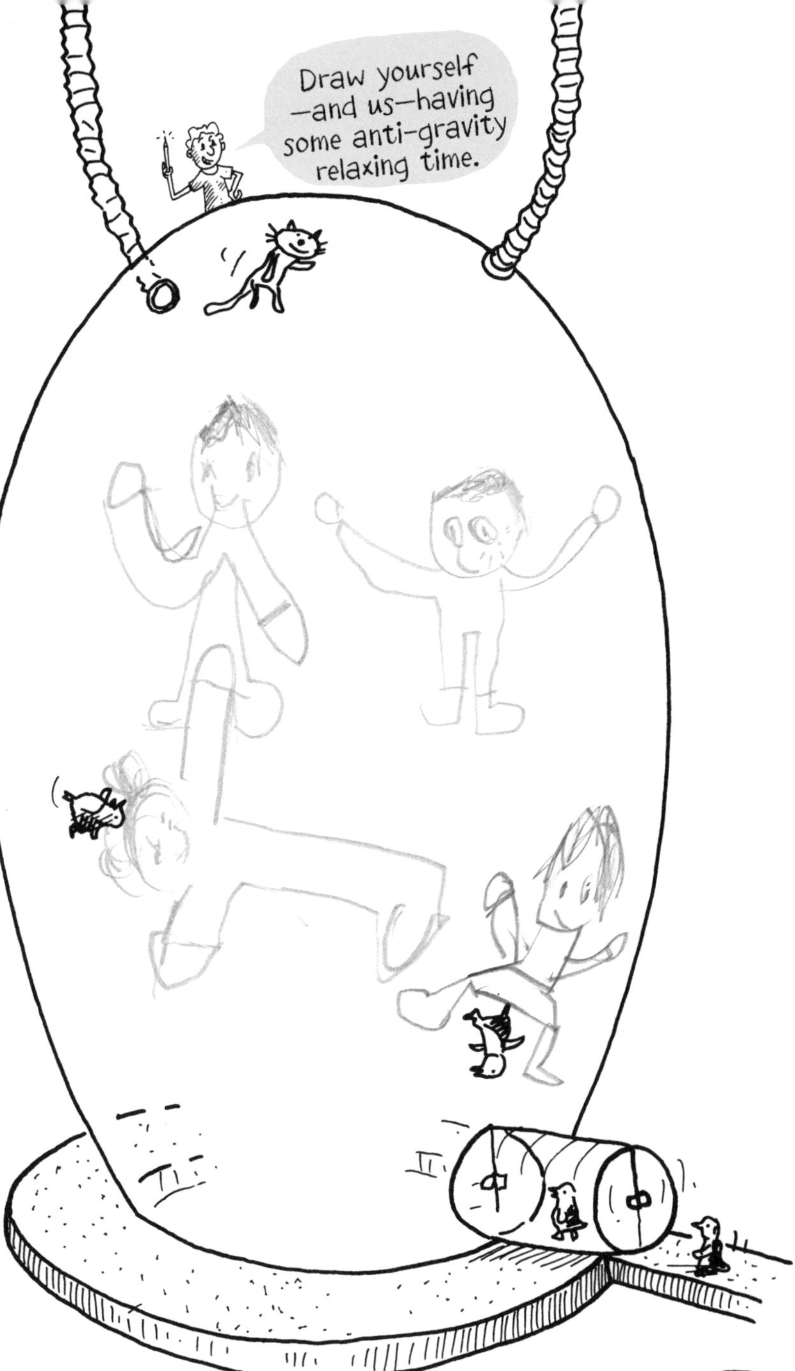
Draw yourself
—and us—having
some anti-gravity
relaxing time.

ANSWER TIME

SPOT THE DIFFERENCE (PAGES 32-33)

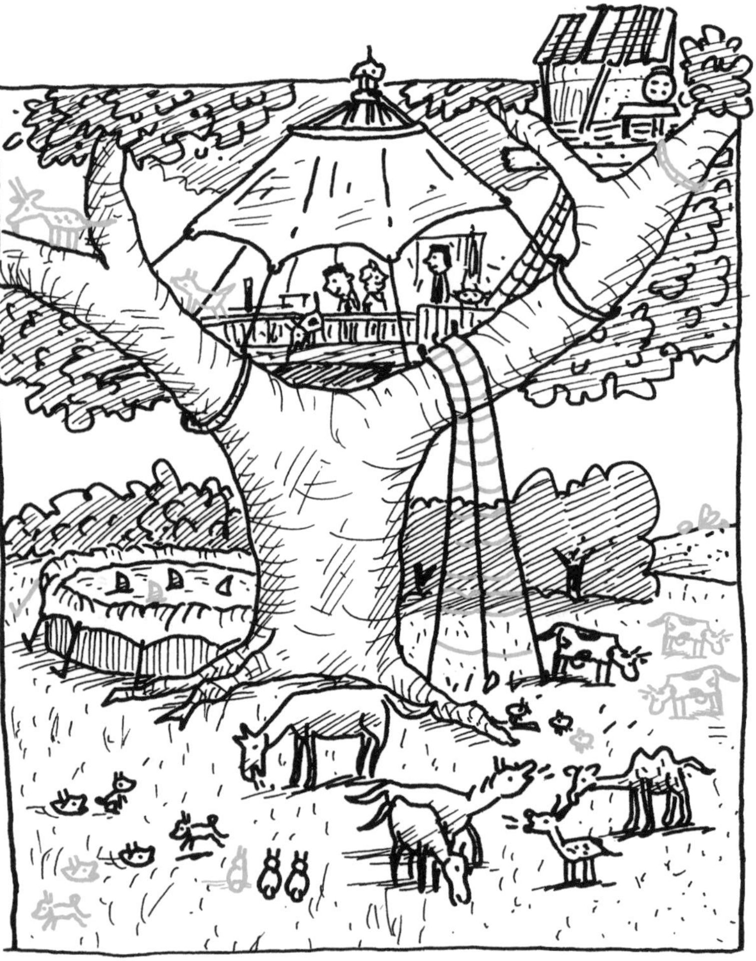

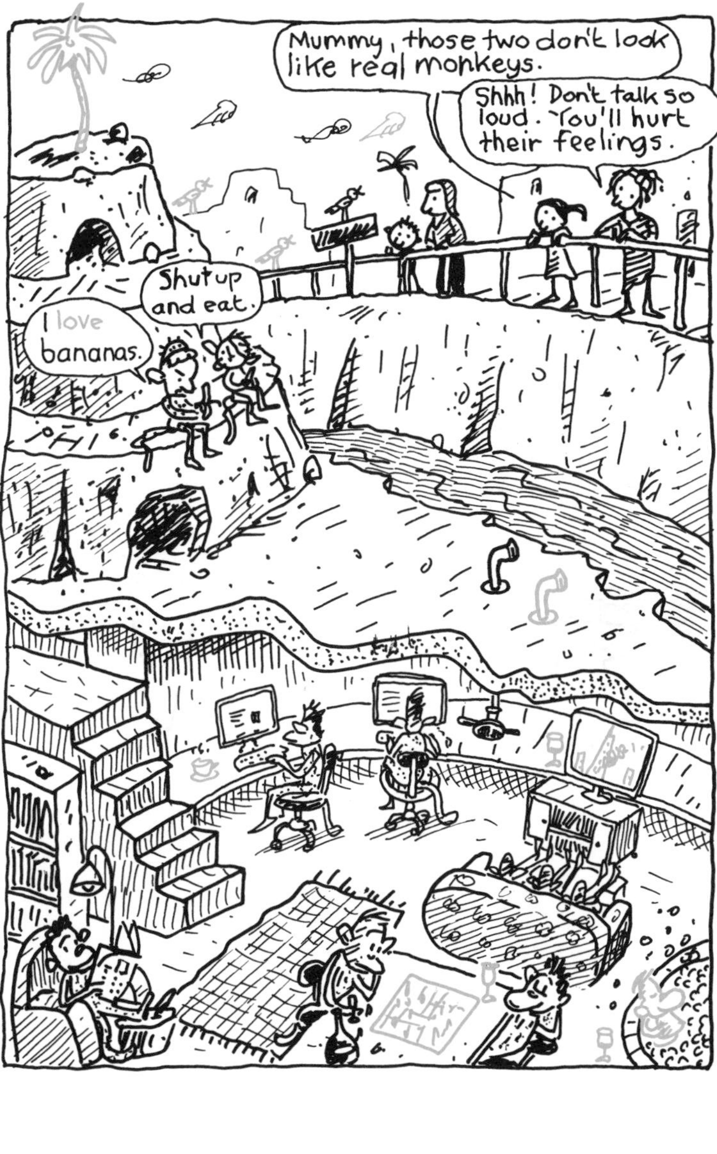
Mummy, those two don't look like real monkeys.
Shhh! Don't talk so loud. You'll hurt their feelings.
Shut up and eat.
I love bananas.

ESCAPE THE MAZE OF DOOM (PAGE 46)

YOU ARE HERE
YOU WERE HERE

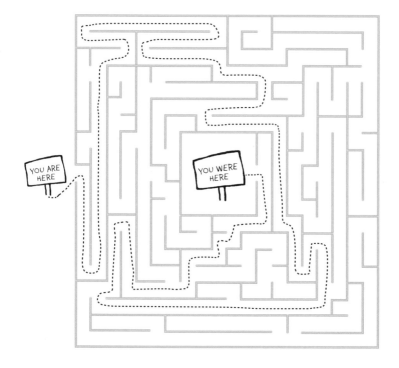

13-STOREY TREEHOUSE WORD SEARCH (PAGE 48)

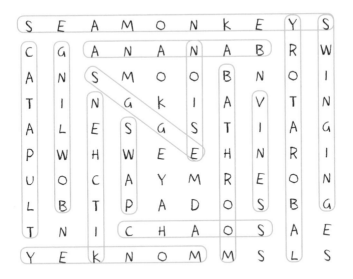

S	E	A	M	O	N	K	E	Y	S
C	G	A	N	A	N	A	B	R	W
A	N	S	M	O	O	B	N	O	I
T	I	N	G	K	I	A	V	T	N
A	L	E	S	G	S	T	I	A	G
P	W	H	W	E	E	H	N	R	I
U	O	C	A	Y	M	R	E	O	N
L	B	T	P	A	D	O	S	B	G
T	N	I	C	H	A	O	S	A	E
Y	E	K	N	O	M	M	S	L	S

Solution: MONKEY MADNESS

26-STOREY TREEHOUSE WORD SEARCH (PAGE 54)

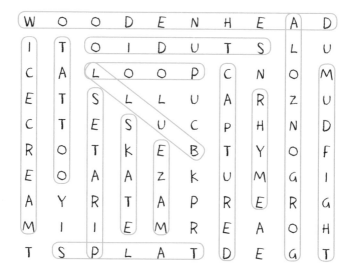

W	O	O	D	E	N	H	E	A	D
I	T	O	I	D	U	T	S	L	U
C	A	L	O	O	P	C	N	O	M
E	T	S	L	L	U	A	R	Z	U
C	T	E	S	U	C	P	H	N	D
R	O	T	K	E	B	T	Y	O	F
E	O	A	A	Z	K	U	M	G	I
A	Y	R	T	A	P	R	E	R	G
M	I	I	E	M	R	E	A	O	H
T	S	P	L	A	T	D	E	G	T

Solution: UNLUCKY PIRATE

Eeeee-yaahhhhhhhhh!

39-STOREY TREEHOUSE WORD SEARCH (PAGE 61)

T	R	A	M	P	O	L	I	N	E
W	E	T	A	L	O	C	O	H	C
A	V	T	O	O	R	T	E	E	B
T	O	S	P	O	O	N	C	I	L
E	L	M	S	L	A	P	A	Y	R
R	C	O	S	L	A	P	N	K	O
F	A	O	S	L	A	P	D	L	C
A	N	N	T	E	R	R	Y	I	K
L	O	D	I	P	U	T	S	S	E
L	U	N	I	N	V	E	N	T	T

Solution: SLAP! SLAP! SLAP!

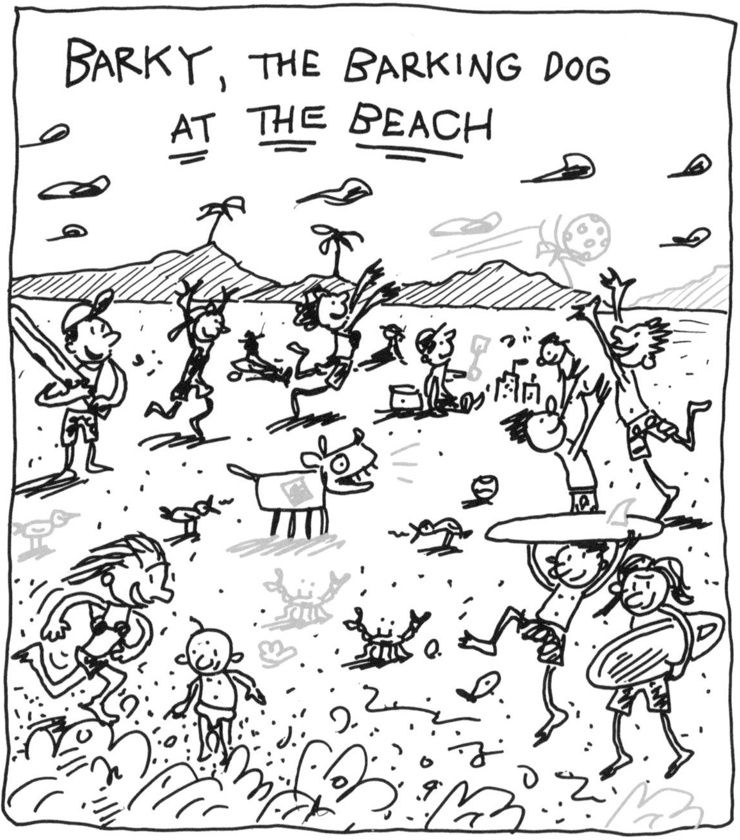
BARKY, THE BARKING DOG
AT THE BEACH

1. What is the name of the sea monster Terry fell in love with?

   Mermaidia

2. What is the worst job Andy and Terry ever had?

   Filling in for the monkeys at the zoo

3. What is Terry's favourite TV show?

   The Barky The Barking Dog Show

4. What colour did Terry paint Silky?

   Yellow

5. What is the name of Andy and Terry's publisher?

   Mr Big Nose

6. What is the name of the pirate who captured Andy, Terry and me?

   Captain Woodenhead

7. How many flavours of ice-cream are there in Edward Scooperhands' ice-cream parlour?

   78

SPOT THE DIFFERENCE (PAGES 74-75)

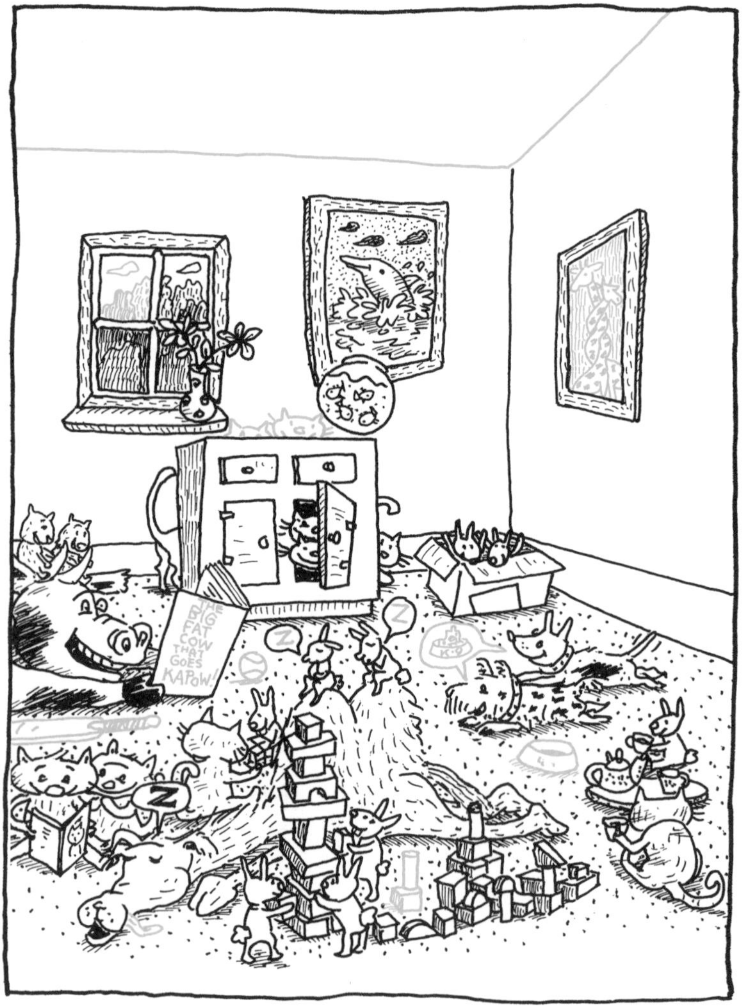
THE BIG FAT COW THAT GOES KAPOW!
Z
Z
Z

52-STOREY TREEHOUSE WORD SEARCH (PAGE 76)

D	E	T	E	C	T	I	V	E	S
E	P	E	C	N	I	R	P	Y	E
G	O	N	B	I	G	D	A	L	R
G	T	S	O	T	V	I	P	F	E
P	A	N	N	S	E	S	A	R	M
L	T	A	I	Y	E	G	T	E	E
A	O	I	N	D	G	U	T	T	M
N	E	L	J	N	T	I	Y	T	B
T	A	S	A	A	B	S	L	U	E
E	T	E	R	R	Y	E	S	B	R

Solution: EAT VEGETABLES

VEGETABLE PATTY SAYS:
EAT YOUR VEGETABLES!

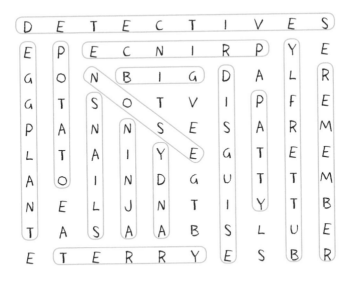

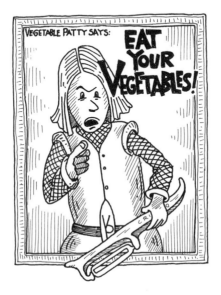

SPOT THE DIFFERENCE (PAGES 86-87)

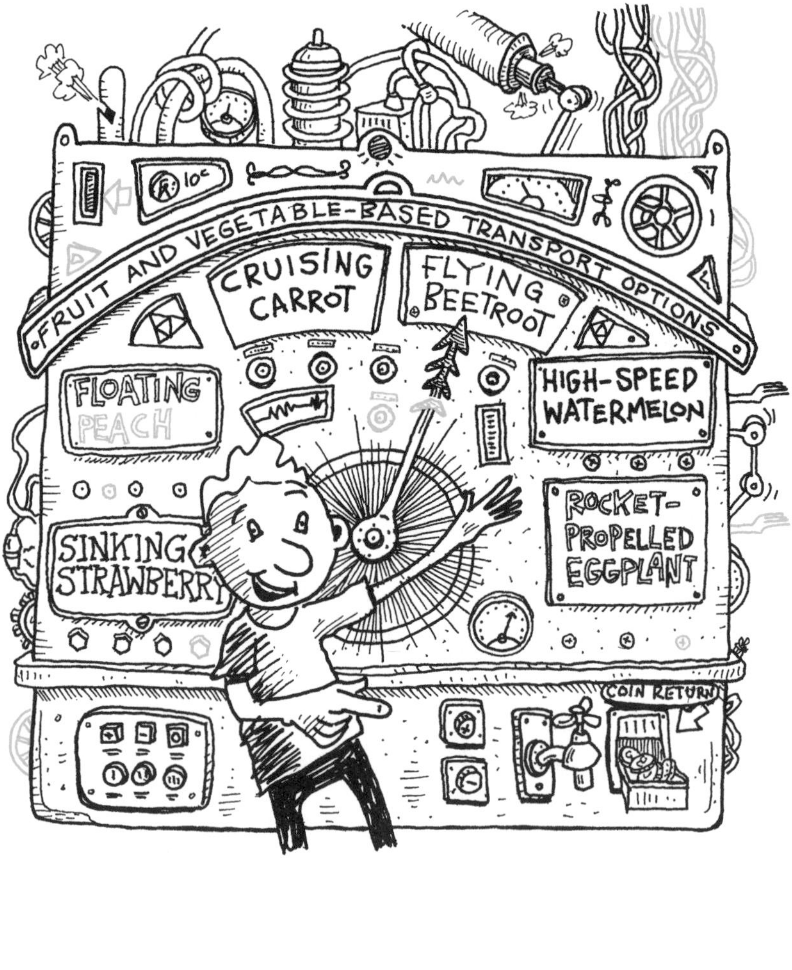

FRUIT AND VEGETABLE-BASED TRANSPORT OPTIONS
CRUISING CARROT
FLYING BEETROOT
FLOATING PEACH
HIGH-SPEED WATERMELON
SINKING STRAWBERRY
ROCKET-PROPELLED EGGPLANT
COIN RETURN

ANIMAL SCRAMBLES (PAGES 90-91)

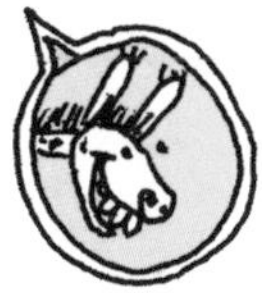

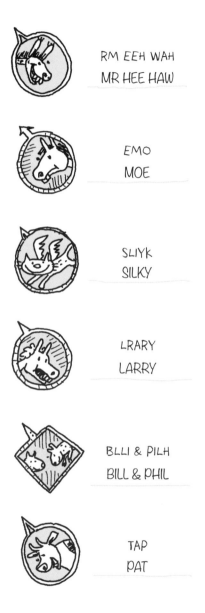

RM EEH WAH

MR HEE HAW

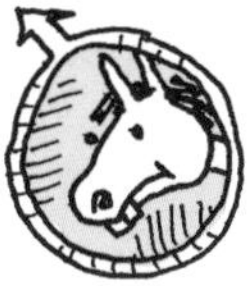

EMO

MOE

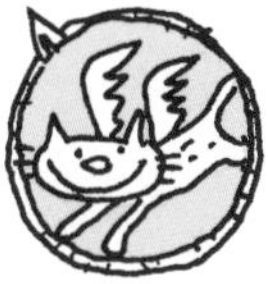

SLIYK

SILKY

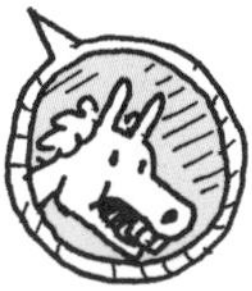

LRARY

LARRY

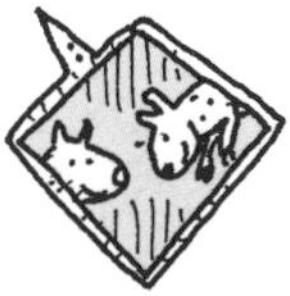

BLLI & PILH

BILL & PHIL

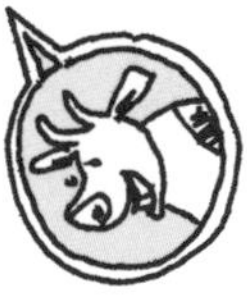

TAP

PAT

65-STOREY TREEHOUSE WORD SEARCH (PAGE 93)

B	G	S	B	T	P	Y	G	E	L
U	N	U	A	S	B	I	N	P	E
B	I	P	R	N	E	R	I	F	V
B	N	E	C	O	T	L	O	P	A
L	O	R	P	S	O	S	F	O	R
E	L	B	L	P	E	R	M	I	T
W	C	W	T	R	E	E	N	N	E
R	O	T	C	E	P	S	N	I	M
A	S	P	S	S	P	M	A	R	I
P	O	N	D	S	C	U	M	P	T

Solution: POOP-POOP

CHICKEN!
CHUTNEY!
POOP-POOP!

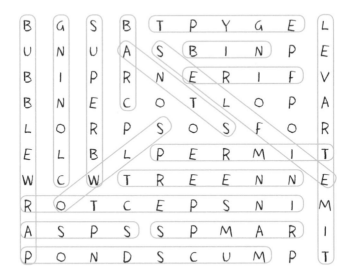

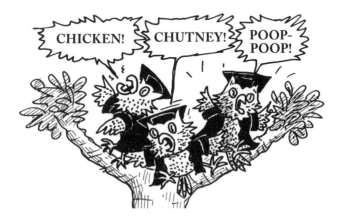

FIND THE ODD ONE OUT (PAGE 94)

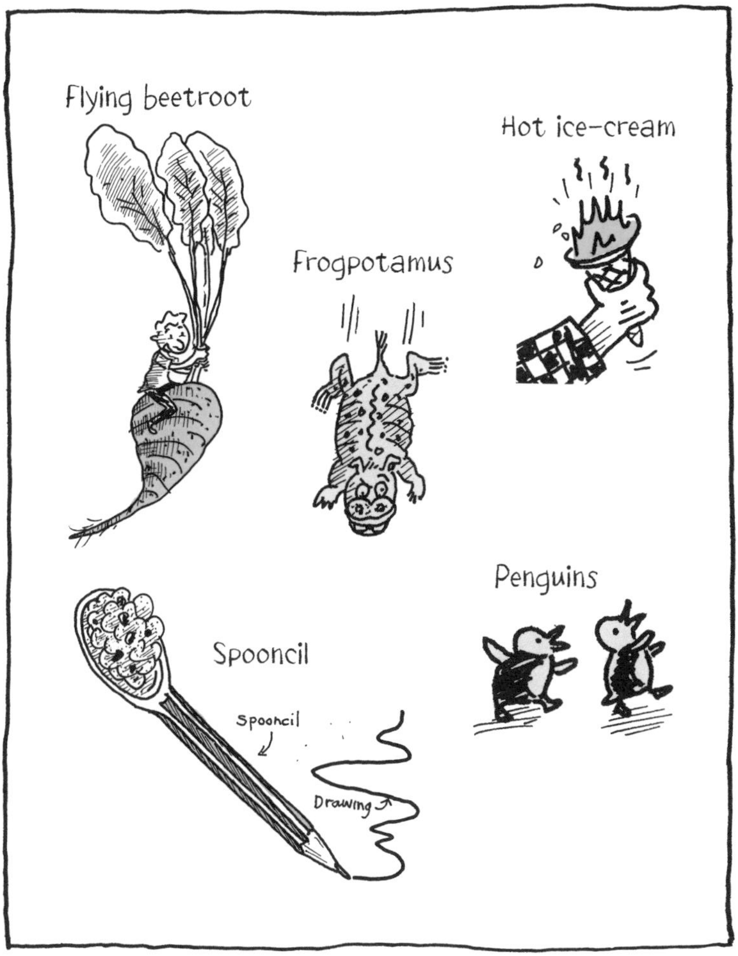
Flying beetroot
Hot ice-cream
Frogpotamus
Penguins
Spooncil
Spooncil
Drawing

Answer: Spooncil.

It's the only one Professor Stupido didn't un-invent.

TREEHOUSE CODE TIME (PAGE 115)

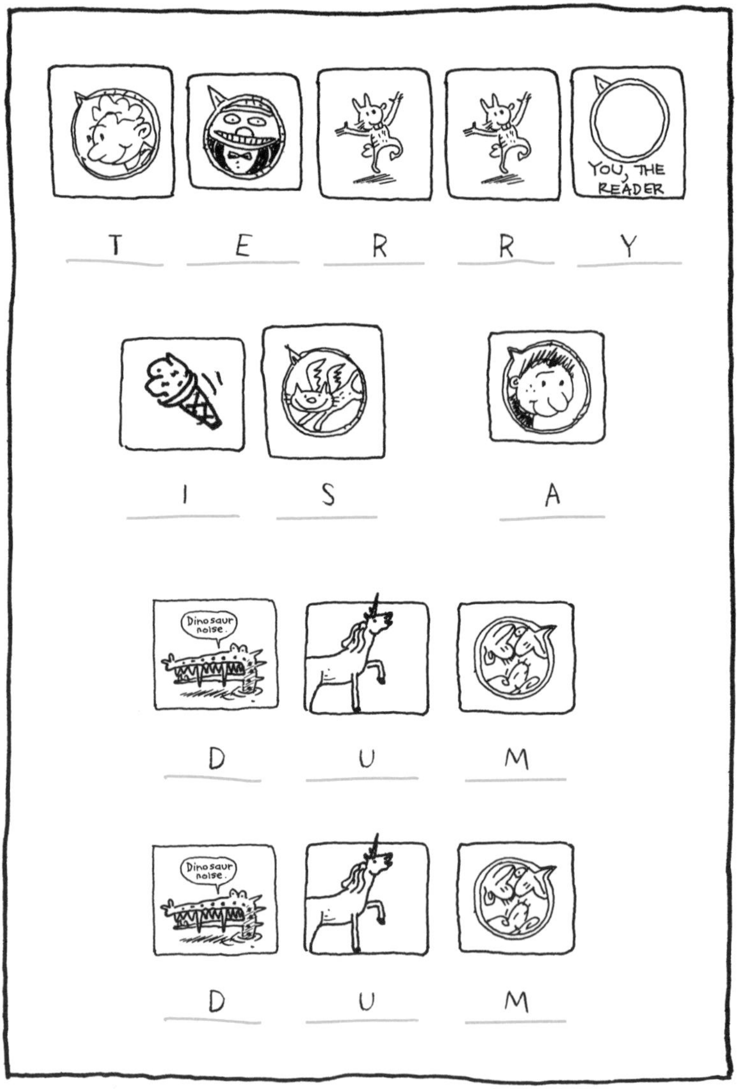
YOU, THE READER
T E R R Y
I S A
Dinosaur noise.
D U M
Dinosaur noise.
D U M

TREEHOUSE CODE TIME (PAGE 116)

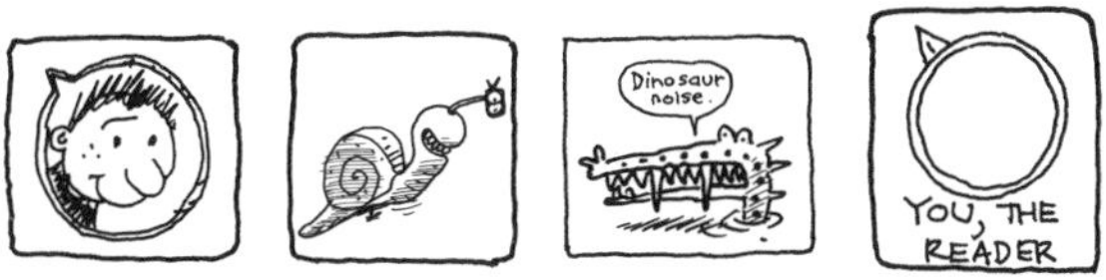
Dinosaur noise.
YOU, THE READER

A N D Y

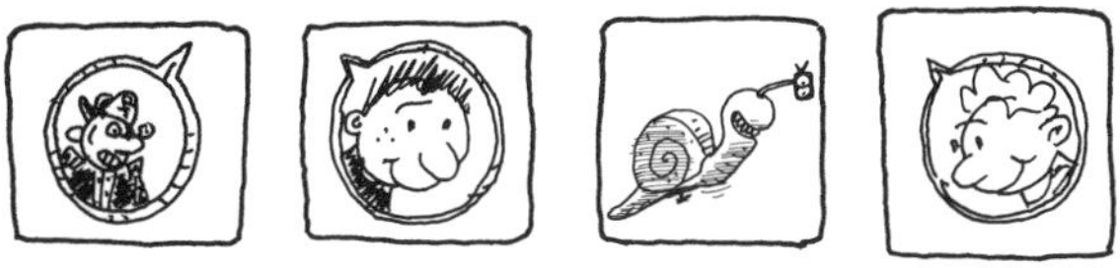

C A N' T

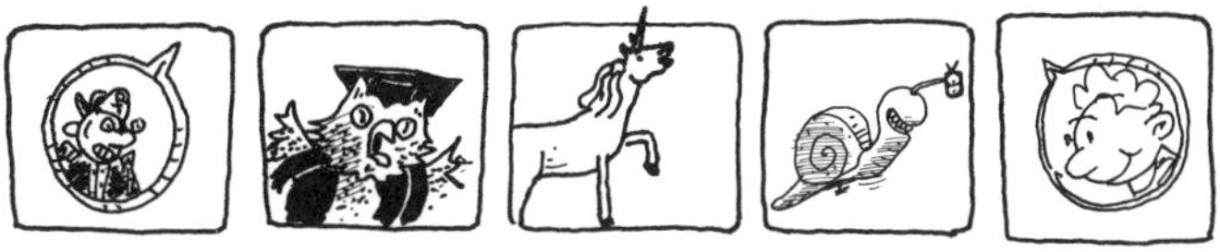

C O U N T

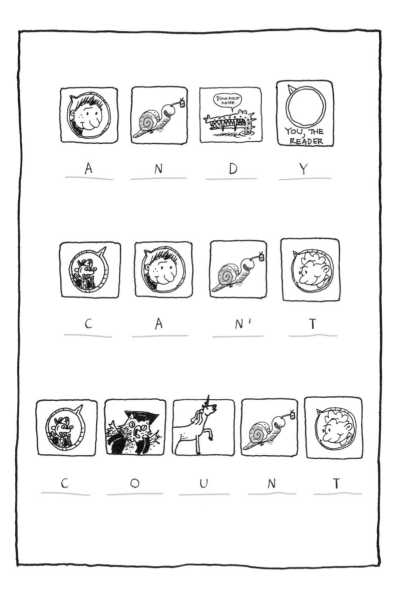

TREEHOUSE CODE TIME (PAGE 117)

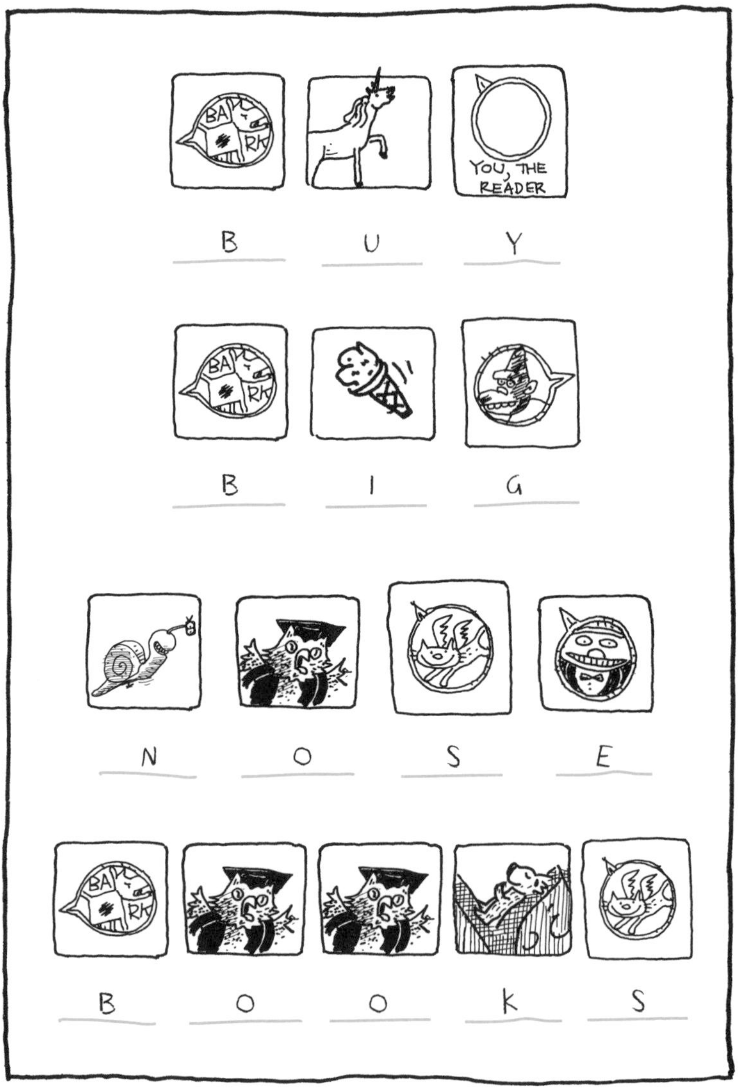

BA
RK
YOU, THE READER
B U Y
B I G
N O S E
B O O K S

TREEHOUSE CODE TIME (PAGE 118)

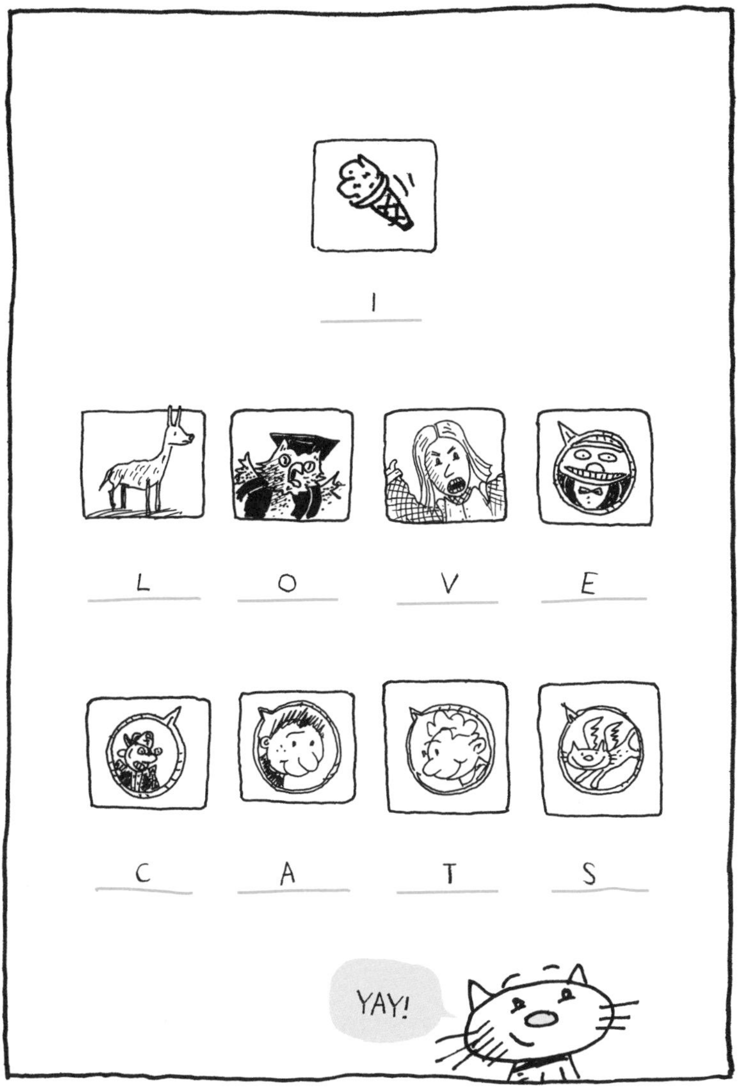
I
L O V E
C A T S
YAY!

TREEHOUSE CODE TIME (PAGE 119)

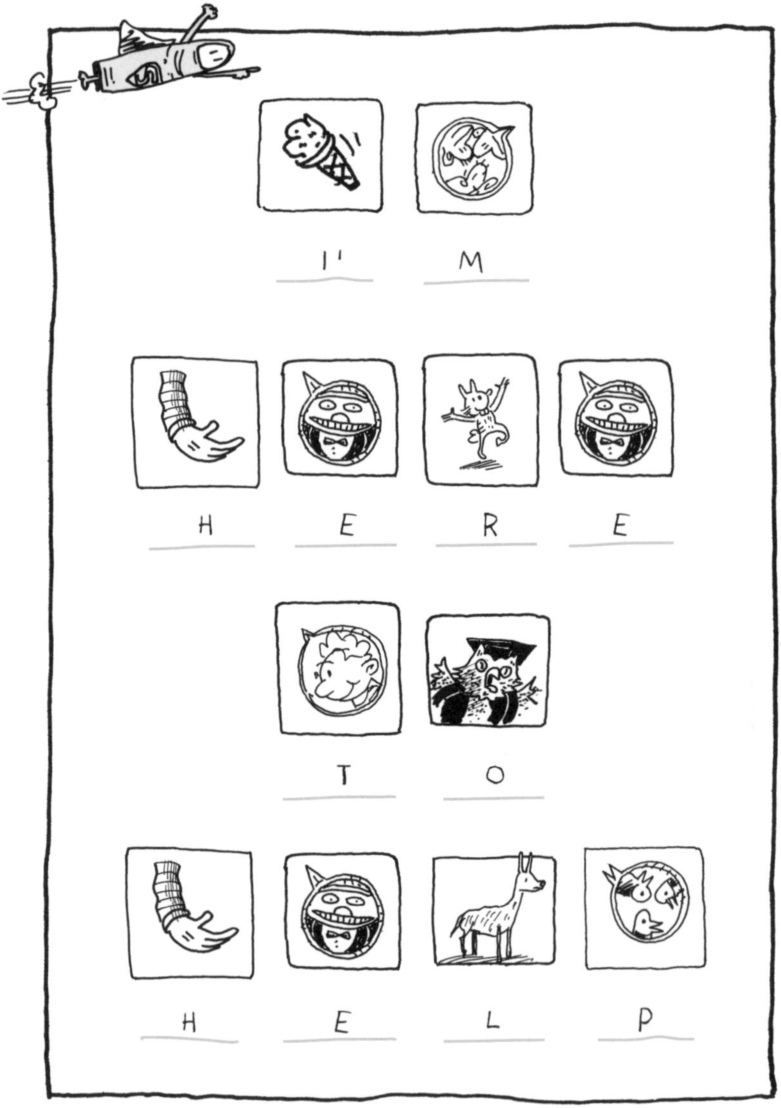
I' M
H E R E
T O
H E L P

FIND-THE-UNICORN FUN (PAGES 120-121)

REE-NN ANIMAL NEWS
Can you find the unicorn in each of these pictures?
NEW NEWS
MORE NEWS
BIG NEWS
OLD NEWS
GNUS
NEWS
SPARE EYEBALLS

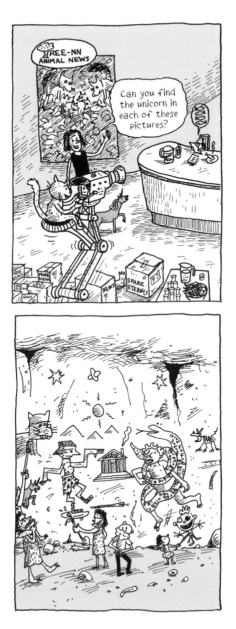

THE REALLY HUNGRY CATERPILLAR'S STORY (PAGES 122-126)

PAGE 122

The really hungry caterpillar

ate one F L Y I N G

f r i e d - E G G

C A R

PAGE 123

O N E enormous

black bird

PAGE 123

two

S T E A M R O L L E R S

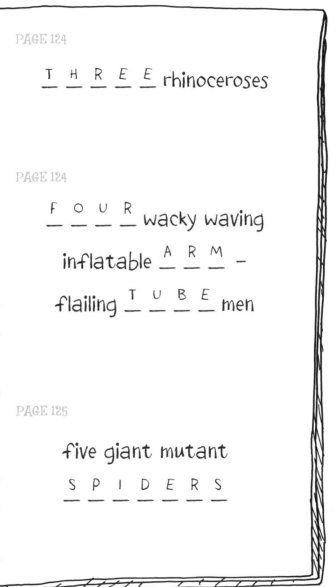

PAGE 124

T H R E E rhinoceroses

PAGE 124

F O U R wacky waving inflatable A R M - flailing T U B E men

PAGE 125

five giant mutant S P I D E R S

PAGE 125

one grumpy old

T O M A T O
_ _ _ _ _ _

PAGE 126

one wall of

A S P A R A G U S
_ _ _ _ _ _ _ _ _

spears

PAGE 126

and one reinforced celery

D O O R
_ _ _ _

WHAT FAIRYTALE IS THAT? (PAGES 127-129)

PAGE 127

HANSEL
AND
GRETEL

PAGE 128

LITTLE
RED
RIDING
HOOD

PAGE 129

CINDERELLA

WHO REALLY SAID WHAT?! (PAGES 130-131)

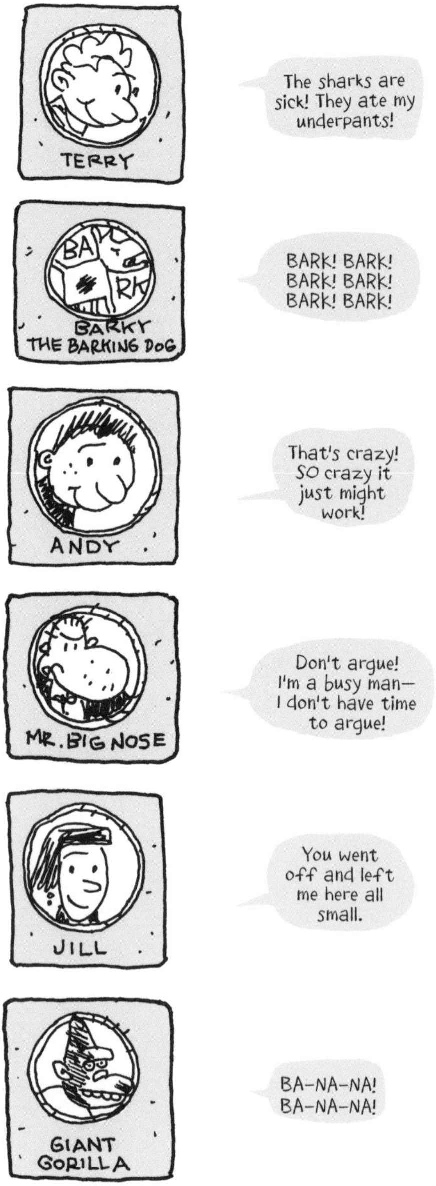
TERRY
The sharks are sick! They ate my underpants!
BARKY THE BARKING DOG
BARK! BARK! BARK! BARK! BARK! BARK!
ANDY
That's crazy! SO crazy it just might work!
MR. BIG NOSE
Don't argue! I'm a busy man— I don't have time to argue!
JILL
You went off and left me here all small.
GIANT GORILLA
BA-NA-NA! BA-NA-NA!

DINNER TIME (PAGE 134-135)

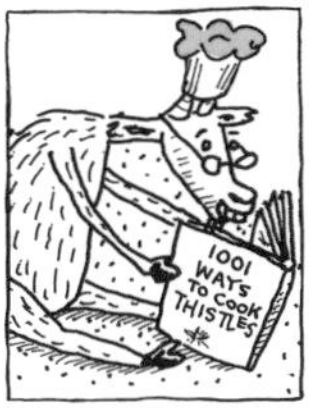
1001 WAYS TO COOK THISTLES

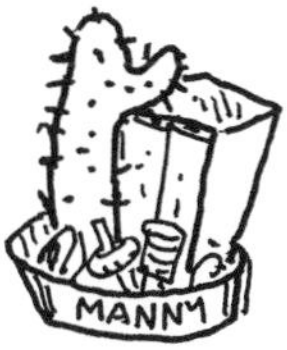
MANNY

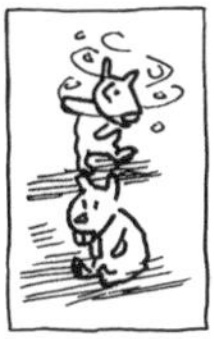

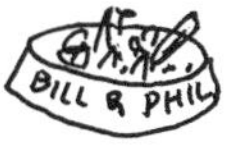
BILL & PHIL

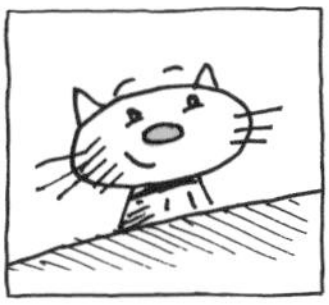

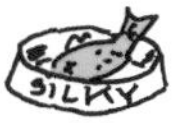
SILKY

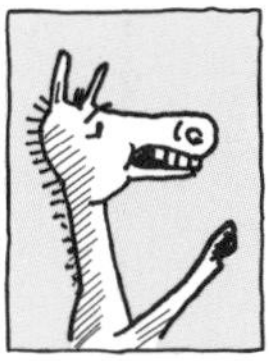

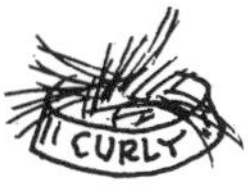
CURLY

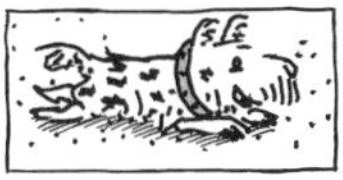

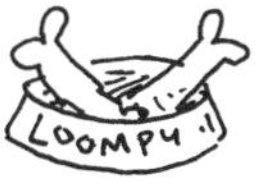
LOOMPY

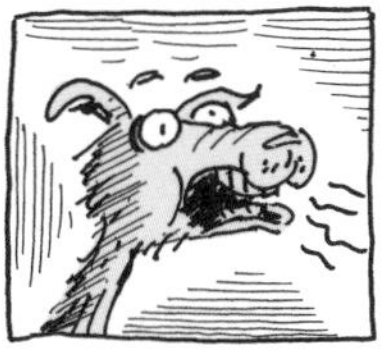

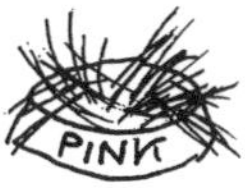
PINK

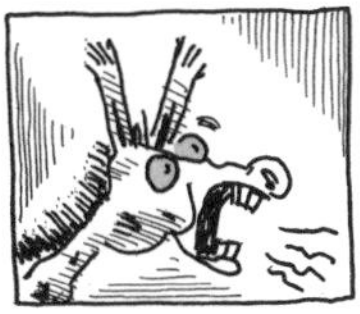

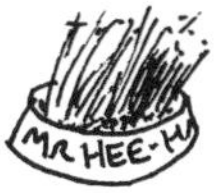
MR HEE-H

FIND THE ODD ONE OUT (PAGE 138)

Answer: The baby dinosaurs are the odd ones out. They live in the treehouse, but all the other animals live at Jill's house.

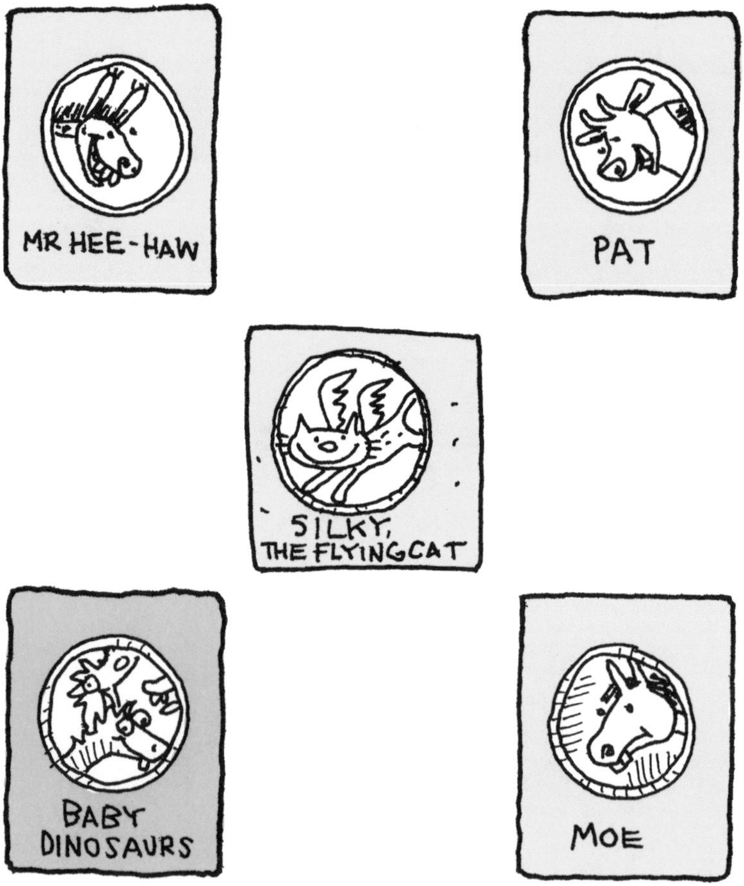
MR HEE-HAW
PAT
SILKY, THE FLYING CAT
BABY DINOSAURS
MOE

TREEHOUSE TRUE OR FALSE? (PAGE 140)

T   F

☑ ☐   1. Silky is my favourite pet.

☑ ☐   2. Mr Big Nose has a very bad temper.

☐ ☑   3. Ninja Snails move very quickly.

☐ ☑   4. Andy and Terry live in a 13-storey caravan.

☑ ☐   5. I live in a house full of animals.

☐ ☑   6. Andy and Terry love vegetables.

☐ ☑   7. Bill the postman is a policeman.

☑ ☐   8. Terry painted Silky yellow.

☑ ☐   9. The Trunkinator is a boxing elephant.

☑ ☐   10. Andy and Terry once worked in the monkey house at the zoo.

☐ ☑   11. ATM stands for Automatic Tea Machine.

☐ ☑   12. Prince Potato really likes Andy and Terry and is happy to spend time with them.

☑ ☐   13. The treehouse has a see-through swimming pool.

FIND THE ODD ONE OUT (PAGE 141)

Answer: Edward Scooperhands is the odd one out. He is a robot, but all the others are human beings.

ANDY

TERRY

EDWARD
SCOOPERHANDS

MR. BIG NOSE

BILL
THE POSTMAN

TREEHOUSE CROSSWORD (PAGE 142-143)

A	N	D	Y		T	E	R	R	Y
N		O		F			A		O
T		O	W	L	S		C		L
S		M		Y			E		K
	B					A	T	M	
N	I	N	J	A	S		R		
	N		I		I		A		T
			L		L		C	A	R
B	I	L	L		K		K		E
					Y				E

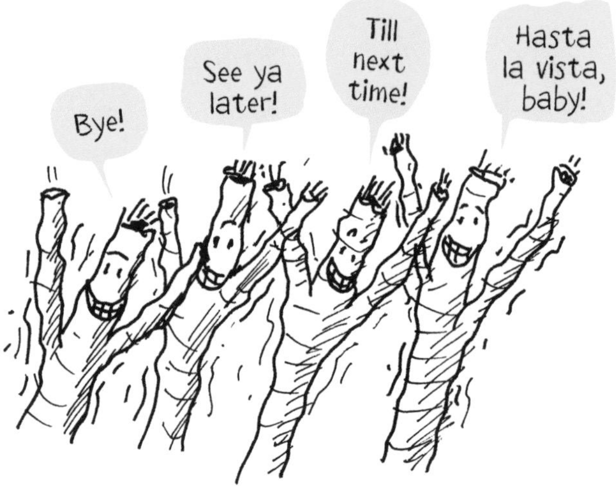
Bye!
See ya later!
Till next time!
Hasta la vista, baby!

Have you read

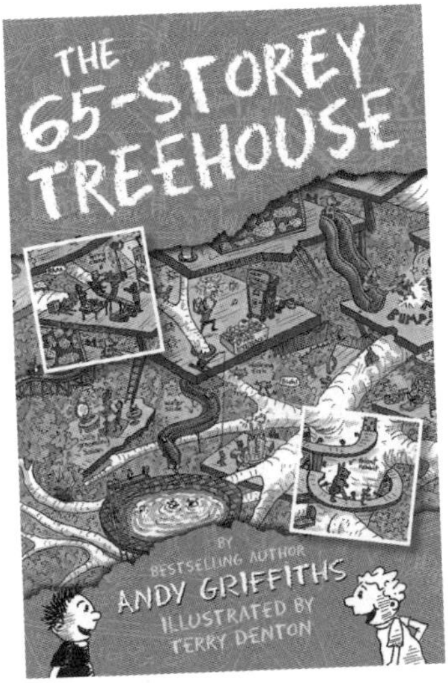
THE 65-STOREY TREEHOUSE
BY
BESTSELLING AUTHOR
ANDY GRIFFITHS
ILLUSTRATED BY
TERRY DENTON

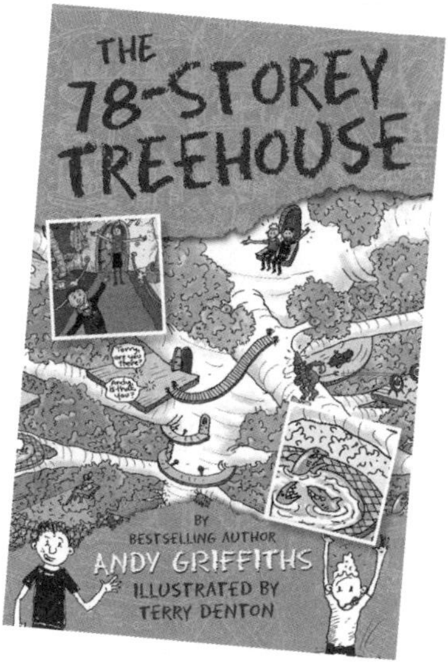
THE 78-STOREY TREEHOUSE
BY
BESTSELLING AUTHOR
ANDY GRIFFITHS
ILLUSTRATED BY
TERRY DENTON

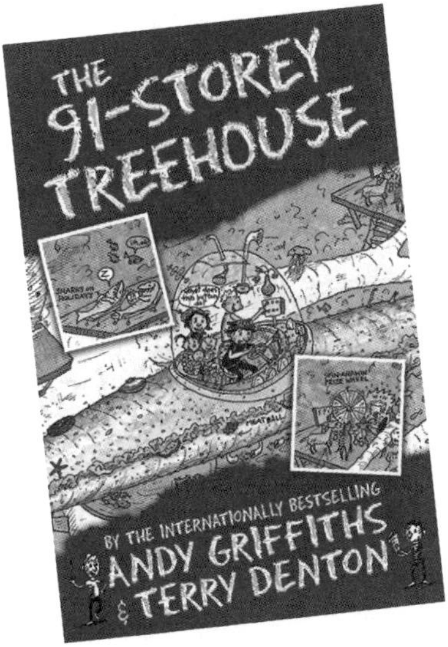
THE 91-STOREY TREEHOUSE
BY THE INTERNATIONALLY BESTSELLING
ANDY GRIFFITHS
& TERRY DENTON

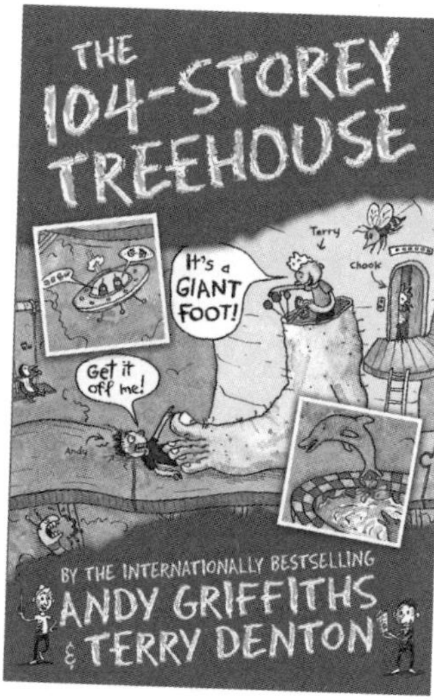
THE 104-STOREY TREEHOUSE
Terry
Chook
It's a GIANT FOOT!
Get it off me!
Andy
BY THE INTERNATIONALLY BESTSELLING
ANDY GRIFFITHS
& TERRY DENTON

THE 117-STOREY TREEHOUSE

Join Andy and Terry in their newly expanded
117-storey treehouse featuring 13 brand-new,
surprising, crazy and fun-packed storeys!